MAKE ROOM FOR LOVE

DARCY LIAO

CONTENT WARNINGS

Content warnings are available on the author's website at darcyliao.com/content-warnings.

1

THERE WAS nothing like being crammed together with hundreds of gorgeous, strobe-lit people on a dance floor to make you feel alone. Mira exhaled as the doors of the club closed behind her, muffling the pounding music. She needed a break.

This was supposed to be a fresh start—her first time reemerging from her friends' apartment since the breakup, aside from unavoidable trips to campus and the corner bodega. She'd let Vivian and Frankie drag her out to Volume, their favorite queer club. They'd helped her move her paltry possessions out of Dylan's condo, and they were letting her crash on their couch, so Mira couldn't really say no.

It had been good to let the music drown out her thoughts, to dance in a crowd where she was far from being the only brown trans girl, to forget about the rest of her life. But then, among all the effortlessly beautiful people getting very close to each other, all the fishnets and leather and glitter, reality had set in again.

Her long nightmare with Dylan was over. But now she

was single for the first time in years, with nowhere to live and no idea of what to do with herself. Thank god she was finally free of him. But what was she supposed to do, when she still didn't *feel* free?

Mira walked a block away from Volume, enough for the bass to stop rattling her skull. She wasn't a smoker, but she almost wished she were, like most of the people scattered on the sidewalk. It would give her something to do other than feel sorry for herself.

Maybe it was time to go back to Vivian's apartment. She could let herself in with the spare key and fall asleep on the couch alone. She reached for her phone to text Vivian.

"Mira!"

Mira's chest clenched. That was a voice she never wanted to hear again.

She immediately spotted him. Dylan was half a block away on the sidewalk, heading toward her with two men she didn't recognize, all looking like Brooklyn literary dirtbags about to hit up the bars. Dylan had more stubble than usual. Malice gleamed in his eyes.

"You've been ignoring my texts," he shouted. A few people near him turned around. Mira's face flushed in shame. "I'm sorry, okay? You never even let me apologize."

He didn't sound sorry. He always berated her in this tone of voice, but now he was bold enough to do it in public, which chilled her. The nerve he had to talk to her like this after he'd cheated on her was unbelievable. But icy fear gripped her, and she couldn't move or speak. She may as well have been back in his condo, silent as the walls closed in on her.

"Hey, Mira, I'm talking to you," Dylan said. "You really think you can just keep ignoring me?"

They were getting closer. Dylan's friend was looking

her up and down without even bothering to hide it. She shouldn't have worn this tiny dress. Arriving with Vivian and Frankie was one thing, but now it was dark and chilly, and the sidewalk no longer seemed very populated. No one was coming to her aid. She was outnumbered and alone.

She looked around, panic rising. There was no escape. She couldn't get back into the club without getting past Dylan. In the other direction were dark streets and empty warehouses, and she couldn't run in these heels—

"Hey!" someone called.

Mira nearly jumped. A tall woman was approaching from across the street, making eye contact with Mira. "Haven't seen you in a while," the woman said, her voice cutting through the club music and street noise, her strides deliberate and long.

Mira gaped in confusion. This woman was curvy and even taller than Mira, with light golden skin and East Asian features. Her long, thick hair streamed behind her. She wore a black leather jacket and work pants with a rip in one knee.

Was she talking to Mira? The woman was stunning. Mira couldn't possibly have forgotten meeting a woman who looked like this.

She glanced around. Dylan and his friends were also a few feet away now. Too close. Who was this long-haired butch talking to?

Then Mira caught on. "Oh!" Relief rushed through her, so pure she could weep. Dylan trying to humiliate her was somehow less surprising than having a stranger stand up for her. "Um, I also... I haven't seen you..."

The mystery woman stepped close. "Want to talk?"

Her commanding aura radiated from her like heat. She was in charge now. Mira nodded.

The woman took Mira by the arm. Her hand was big and shockingly warm against Mira's bare skin, and she gently but firmly guided Mira to turn away from Dylan and his friends. Mira had no time or wits to think twice. She simply went where her rescuer was taking her.

"Is he bothering you?" The woman's voice was a low, soothing rumble.

Maybe Mira ought to explain that this was her ex-boyfriend, that he was mostly harmless, that she was sorry for wasting this woman's time. She probably had more important things to do.

Instead, Mira said, "Yeah."

"Hey," Dylan shouted. "I'm talking to you." Mira instinctively started turning around, but the woman guiding her didn't stop or hesitate, and Mira thought better of it. "Mira!" Dylan called, and she winced. His footsteps were too close. She moved closer to the woman, closer to her solidity and warmth.

The woman let go of Mira's arm and turned around. Mira turned, too, her skin still tingling from the woman's touch. Dylan was right in front of them, and the other men stood just a step back. The harsh streetlights distorted their faces. Mira edged behind the woman, who was as thick and sturdy as a wall.

"Leave her alone," the woman said, just loudly enough that the passersby couldn't ignore her. Someone stopped on the sidewalk a few feet away.

"That's my girlfriend," Dylan said. This woman was nearly as tall as he was, and he was clearly trying to puff himself up despite being built like a twig. "We were having a conversation." He looked at Mira, and Mira flinched.

"Doesn't seem like she wants to talk," the woman said.

Unlike Dylan, she didn't need to yell to make her presence felt.

"Who the fuck are you?"

The woman's stance shifted subtly. She wasn't flinching. She was steeling herself. "Leave her alone."

They faced each other down. The air thickened with tension. Dylan's friends hovered behind him, casting long shadows.

Mira's heart pounded. Was this stranger actually intending to physically defend her? Dylan had never been in a fight more serious than sniping at other literary figures online, but he had backup, and maybe he and his friends were stupid enough to try something. What if—*oh, god*—what if this woman got hurt for Mira's sake?

Then Dylan deflated, apparently realizing that he'd picked the wrong person to fuck with. "All right."

He shrugged, clearly trying to seem less embarrassed than he was. After one last hostile glare at Mira, he turned and walked away. One of his friends followed. The other one, the one who had been ogling Mira, stared in confusion for a second before scurrying off.

As their backs receded, Mira's terror drained. Exhaustion came flooding in. She wanted to go home.

But she didn't have a home. She only had the couch in Vivian's living room.

The woman turned around. Mira had been standing far too close, and she scrambled to step back. The woman's well-worn leather jacket and black hair gleamed in the streetlights. There was a carabiner of keys clipped to one of her belt loops. Confronted with this butch who knew exactly how she wanted to move through the world, Mira felt insubstantial, like a leaf swept up by the wind.

"You okay?" the woman asked.

Mira was still stiff with fear. That had been ugly, and it could have been even worse. "Um, yeah, I'm okay." Her own words were distant, as though they weren't coming from her. "Thank you," she remembered to add.

The woman shrugged. She didn't smile. "You need anything?"

Although she had softened from earlier, the woman's gaze was still intense. She had dark, serious eyes and strong features that were striking without a trace of makeup. Being on the receiving end of her attention, and having to look up to make eye contact, made goosebumps prickle all over Mira's skin. "I think I'm okay," she said automatically. This woman had already done too much, and Mira didn't want to be further indebted to her. "Um, are *you* okay?"

"I'm fine." She seemed surprised, maybe irritated, that Mira had asked. "Are you here by yourself?"

"No, I'm, uh, I'm with my friends. They're inside."

"You going back in?"

Mira shook her head. She needed to go home—to Vivian's living room—and get under the blankets and cry. She was supposed to be enjoying her freedom from Dylan. Instead, she had crumpled at the sight of him and hid behind this stranger, who had probably never been scared of an awful man even once in her life.

"You need someone to walk you to the subway?" The woman asked.

Mira didn't want to say yes. But Dylan and his friends had gone in that direction, and she didn't want to run into them, not alone. And she couldn't ask Vivian and Frankie. They deserved to have a good time without Mira's drama, and she couldn't face going back into the club to find them. She grimaced. "Well, I don't want to make you go out of your way."

The woman shrugged again. "I'm heading out, too. You want to go?"

"I— Yeah."

"Are you cold?"

Mira *was* cold. She had been hugging herself all this time, she realized. Even more than that, she hated being so exposed in this tight dress now that Dylan and his cronies had seen her. She could still feel their gazes clinging to her body.

"A little," she said.

The woman took off her leather jacket and held it out, offering it to Mira. She was wearing a white T-shirt, tight around her wide shoulders and her generous breasts. Her biceps and forearms were thick and tanned. This woman's work pants were torn and faded from actual work, most likely. And she probably could have snapped Dylan in half.

She was still holding out her jacket. Mira had been staring. She flushed. She wasn't into women; it wasn't like that. But this woman was tough and brave, everything Mira wasn't and wished she were, and it was hard to tear her eyes away.

She could refuse, but this woman was clearly not interested in a back-and-forth of social niceties. She was being kind to Mira. It would be easiest to go along with it.

"Thank you," she said, and took the jacket.

It was surprisingly heavy. Mira put it on, trying to ignore her stomach fluttering at the novelty of wearing a stranger's clothes. The jacket was an oversized cocoon on her, reaching the hem of her dress, and it was warm from the other woman's body heat.

A sense of calm suffused her. For now, she was safe.

"Thank you so much," Mira said. "Um, won't you get cold?"

"Looks like you need it more than I do."

All right, then. "Well, I'm ready to go."

THEY STARTED WALKING. The woman had long legs, and Mira had to work to keep up in her heels. "Um, thanks again for helping me. I'm Mira, by the way."

"Isabel."

"Nice to meet you." Isabel probably didn't feel the same way. She'd had her night cut short by a straight girl's boyfriend drama. "I didn't know he would be there," Mira continued, grasping for something to say.

"You don't have to apologize for him." Isabel didn't sound like she was trying to be reassuring. She was simply stating a fact.

And she was right. "I guess not."

As they walked away from the clubs and bars, the music and laughter faded behind them. On this quiet residential street, the early autumn leaves rustled on the ground with every footstep. Isabel's keys jingled on her carabiner.

Isabel didn't seem bothered by the cold. She didn't seem bothered by *anything*. She was one of those self-possessed people Mira had seen at the club who knew exactly what they wanted and how to get it. Mira couldn't stop sneaking glances as Isabel looked straight ahead.

She'd gotten used to the silence when Isabel said, suddenly, "Do you live with him? Is that where you're going?"

"What? Oh, no. No." As much of a mess as her life was, it could be worse. "I broke up with him a few weeks ago, and I'm crashing on my friends' couch right now." Dylan had called her his girlfriend just now. The word made her stomach churn. How had she *actually* been his girlfriend for so long? "And I haven't seen him since the breakup. I guess it still hasn't gotten through to him that someone could leave him without his approval."

Isabel snorted. "Sounds like it was about time."

Mira smiled. It made no difference what a stranger she would never see again thought of her decision, but a weight eased within her all the same. At times in the last three weeks, she'd wondered whether Dylan had truly been bad enough to justify throwing away everything: a nice condo, a measure of safety, a promise of a future where she'd belong to him forever.

All of that had been based on wishful thinking and lies. He'd been cheating on her for months. Even so, when Dylan had been shouting at her tonight, she'd felt a flicker of doubt. Was she being unreasonable?

But now, walking alongside this stranger who had seen the worst of him, the *real* him, it was hard to remember why she'd ever second-guessed herself.

They walked for another block in silence. Then Isabel said, "You said you're staying with your friends?"

"That's right."

"Do you have a place to go after that?"

Isabel had a funny idea of small talk. "Um, not yet. I'm looking at apartments now, but nothing has worked out." That was one of the things Mira was trying to take her mind off—trawling Craigslist, sending emails about the few places she could afford, and being ignored or rejected every time. There were two weeks left in September, and she couldn't possibly impose on Vivian and Frankie beyond that.

Isabel remained silent for a few long seconds. Then she said, "I have a spare room in my apartment in Astoria. Just until my lease runs out. You can take a look if you want."

"Oh, that's— How much is it?" Mira couldn't get her

hopes up. She wasn't going to be able to afford it on her grad student stipend.

"Let's say eight hundred a month."

"In a two-bedroom apartment?"

Isabel nodded.

That was suspiciously low. Mira had trusted Isabel out of instinct, but maybe she shouldn't have. As if sensing her doubts, Isabel continued, "There's nothing wrong with the room. It's just small. I wouldn't offer otherwise."

It was probably better than the windowless bedroom Mira had lived in before Dylan's condo. "How small is it?"

"You could fit a full bed with a little space to walk around."

That wasn't so bad, especially if Mira got a twin bed. She wouldn't be sharing it with anyone anytime soon. "Who's living there now?"

"No one in the last few months. Before that..." For the first time tonight, Isabel seemed hesitant. "I lived with someone, and it was her painting studio."

So they were in the same situation. Mira felt a strangely intense pang of sympathy. Isabel said stiffly, "I can't afford the rent on my own anymore, but I don't want to charge anyone more than I have to. I haven't been looking for someone until now, but I figured... I'm moving out at the end of the year. You can have the room until then."

"Thanks. Um, that sounds like it could work." There was no reason to not see the place, at least. "It's not easy to find housing as a broke trans girl in this city," Mira added, trying to keep her tone casual as she voiced the miserable, infuriating truth. She needed to be sure Isabel knew she was trans. It wasn't fair that she had to protect herself this way, but no part of this was fair.

"I'm sorry for that." If Isabel had any kind of problem with Mira, her stony demeanor didn't show it.

Mira relaxed slightly. Maybe this would work out. They clearly weren't going to be friends, which was fine. They'd live together for a few months, Mira would get back on her feet, and they would go their separate ways.

They exchanged numbers next to the subway entrance. Isabel was headed in the other direction. "Thanks again for everything," Mira said.

Isabel nodded. A single stud earring in her right ear glinted in the light. "Take care."

Mira smiled. "Have a good night." She turned to go down the stairs.

"Can I have my jacket back?"

Mira turned around, embarrassed. There was the barest trace of a smile on Isabel's face. Mira's stomach did a flip.

"Sorry," she said, blushing. She took off the jacket and gave it back to Isabel.

Isabel slipped it back on her impressively muscular shoulders in one easy motion. For her size and obvious strength, her body was so graceful. "Get home safe," she said, and turned to cross the street.

She walked away, her hair a dark waterfall down her back, her work pants tight over her thick curves. Mira lingered by the subway entrance and watched her. What was it like to move through the world knowing it was your right to take up space? What had Isabel's girlfriend been like? Had they broken each other's hearts?

A gust of wind chilled her. She wasn't wearing Isabel's jacket anymore. She turned and went down the stairs.

2

THIS WAS A BAD IDEA. There was still time to back out. A shitty thing to do, since Mira needed a place to live, but Isabel hadn't promised her anything.

She hadn't opened the door to the spare room since Reina moved out. Aside from a few smears of paint on the wood floor, it was stripped bare. No half-finished painting on the easel, no canvases and supplies haphazardly stacked on shelves. Just Mira standing in the middle of the room.

Mira was pretty, if you liked mousy, shy girls. Tall, willowy, slightly hunched over like she was trying to be unnoticeable. Brown skin, big dark eyes, thick long lashes. Big hair in loose curls falling over her shoulders. She looked more comfortable in her sweater and wool skirt than in that clingy dress from last weekend. Not that Isabel had been looking.

At least, she'd tried not to look. She'd only wanted to keep this girl safe.

Mira slowly turned around, blinking. There was nothing to see. She was just thinking, like Isabel was. Maybe picturing all her things in the room.

Isabel didn't want her here. It had been one thing to offer up her spare room when this scared girl had needed help. Isabel needed a roommate, and Mira needed a room. But seeing Mira here made it real: Isabel would be living with a stranger, in this apartment full of the worst memories of her life.

If Isabel wanted to back out, she'd have to say so now. Then she'd start working overtime again, and her bad knee would only get worse. But it would only be for a few months, and then she'd find a place she could afford on her own. She would survive.

"It's a nice room," Mira said.

Isabel shrugged. There was no need for Mira to be polite. "It's not much. Let's talk in the living room."

Isabel had dusted all the furniture that morning, sneezing the whole time. The plants on the windowsill were half-dead, but there was nothing she could do about that now.

Mira walked by, and the faint scent of coconut shampoo trailed after her. It took a second for Isabel to place it: Her leather jacket had smelled like that, too, after Mira had returned it.

Mira sat on the edge of the couch, radiating anxiety. Isabel was going to have to get used to seeing that. She had collapsed on that couch when she'd gotten the phone call with the worst news of her life. Then she'd sat on that couch when Reina confessed that she was leaving, that she had been applying to artist residencies in secret, that she couldn't take it anymore. That it wasn't Isabel's fault for being so shattered by grief. But whose fault was it, then?

Isabel didn't miss her ex much these days. But she'd had a life once as a caring, supportive partner, as the second of three inseparable sisters. All that was gone now, and Isabel was left to rattle around the apartment alone.

Isabel blinked. The ghosts in her memories vanished. There was a real person sitting in front of her.

If Mira was already here, there was no harm in asking some questions. Isabel sat on the other side of the couch. Her knee throbbed, and she winced. "Let's talk about what we're looking for. I mentioned the important things. No loud noise after nine p.m. since I get up for work early. And I want the apartment to stay as clean as it is right now. I don't cook much, so the kitchen's mostly yours."

"That's all fine with me." Mira was fidgeting with the hem of her skirt. Her nails were a pale pink. "Um, I'm a grad student, and I usually work until pretty late. I work mostly out of my office on campus, so you won't have to deal with me being around except in the evenings. I cook a few times a week. And I might occasionally have a friend over." She took a deep breath. "As for what I'm looking for, I guess I just want a quiet place to live, now that I'm by myself. I don't need much else."

Guilt gnawed at Isabel. She couldn't just tell Mira to go away. The ex-boyfriend had been a real piece of work, and Mira had been afraid.

People had to look out for each other. If she didn't want Mira to be in danger, she had to give Mira a place to live. And this shy mouse of a grad student wasn't going to cause Isabel any problems. Even if she did, they'd both be out of here in a few months.

"Out of curiosity, what do you do for work that makes you wake up so early?" Mira asked.

"I'm a union electrician." Isabel forced herself to smile. If they were going to be roommates, she'd have to get used to small talk.

"Oh, wow!" Mira hesitated. Isabel wasn't surprised. A lot of people, including most of Reina's artist friends, had no idea how to make conversation with a construction worker. "I read about the strike at the power plant that ended last month," Mira continued. "I'm sorry it didn't go the way you all wanted."

"Oh, uh, thanks." Isabel had walked the picket lines for months, all through the sweltering summer, when she wasn't working at her own job. The contract negotiations had still fallen through. She hadn't expected Mira, of all people, to know that. "Is that related to what you study, or something?"

Mira smiled. She had a cute smile, the corners of her eyes crinkling. It was surprising to see her with an expression that wasn't scared or anxious. "No, I'm a classicist. But the grad students at my university are organizing a union. We try to stay informed on the labor movement more broadly."

Huh. "How's that going? Are they trying to union-bust you?"

Mira let out a loud, ringing laugh that was surprisingly endearing. "Oh, yes. Absolutely. We do most of the teaching at the university and a lot of the research grunt work, and the university insists we're not workers, we're just students, and we should be grateful for the so-called training we get. The undergrads pay sixty thousand dollars a year to attend, and the university has a multi-billion-dollar endowment, but they won't pay a living wage to those of us who are actually teaching the classes."

That sounded about right. Mira sighed. "Sorry. I didn't mean to go on about it. It's just that after five years of grad school, starting my sixth, I'm sick of it."

Isabel gave her a smile. A real one, this time. "You don't have to convince me. I'm not on your bosses' side."

Mira's posture loosened up. Isabel was relieved, too. There was no point to Mira feeling like she was being interrogated. "They're trying to squeeze more work out of us, and it's bad for the undergrads, too. I can't teach Latin to forty students and do a thorough job of grading all their papers every week. And it makes me *furious* when the administration tells us that we're trying to shirk our duties, or that we're going to compromise the undergrads' education if we unionize. The university couldn't function if we all stopped teaching—if we stopped leading recitations and grading homework and exams and having office hours. They *know* that"—Mira made a gesture for emphasis, making her curls bounce—"which is why they're afraid of us."

Mira's eyes were bright. She'd turned into a different person. But she wasn't—that fiery core had been there all along. Why had this woman been with a boyfriend like *that*? Isabel would never know. "Well, I respect that. And if you ever go on strike and we're working on your campus, we're not going to cross the picket line."

"Thank you." Mira looked down for a moment, her self-consciousness returning. "We have a long way to go. We're going to start asking people to sign union cards soon, to show they want the union to represent them. And once we get enough people to sign cards, we'll have an election to force the university to recognize us and bargain with us." She took a breath. "I think we can win. But it'll be a lot of work, on top of all the teaching and other work we have to do. And, of course, our own research. The supposed reason why I'm in grad school in the first place."

Mira paused and looked at Isabel, as though gauging

Isabel's reaction, with those big, brown eyes. Desire pierced Isabel like a lightning bolt.

Mira wasn't just pretty. When she was animated, she was beautiful. In this dreary apartment, everything about her stood in sharp relief: the striking planes of her face, the rich plum lipstick playing up the curve of her mouth, the way her nearly black curls turned red and gold where they caught the afternoon light.

And the conviction in her voice, and the fire in her eyes. Mira wasn't as timid as she'd seemed, and it was driving Isabel wild.

Apparently Isabel's interest in women was reawakening after the months she'd spent alone. It wasn't personal, and it didn't mean anything. She hadn't so much as flirted with anyone since Reina left. Of course the first attractive woman to cross her path would light her up like this.

Never mind that she'd seen plenty of beautiful women at the club, all dressed to impress. None of them had set Isabel on fire like this grad student in a cute little sweater talking about labor organizing in Isabel's living room.

It didn't matter. She was here to find a roommate, not a replacement for her ex. "Well, uh, good luck." She winced. Was that really the best she could come up with? "So you said you study Classics? Like, Ancient Rome?" Mira nodded. "What's your research about?"

"Oh, well, I study Greek and Latin poetry. Um, my dissertation is about Latin lyric poetry—you know, Horace and Catullus—and its relationship to the earlier Greek models. I don't know if you're familiar..." Mira trailed off. Isabel shook her head, eager to hear more.

"Oh." Mira looked at her lap. A ringlet of dark hair fell over her face. "Well, never mind. I don't want to bore you."

That stung a little. Not for any real reason. Maybe

Isabel wouldn't understand, anyway. But she was good with languages. She spoke better Cantonese than either of her sisters ever had, and her Spanish was decent, too.

She'd gotten too comfortable with Mira. Was she really this starved for conversation? Mira didn't have to talk to her, and she didn't have to talk to Mira. They didn't have to be friends. "Well, let me know if you want to take the room," she said, more stiffly than she'd intended.

"Right," Mira said. Isabel stood, and Mira scrambled to stand, too. "Um, actually, I've decided that I do want the room. If that's okay."

"Sure." There was no backing out now. She had a roommate. Just for a few months, and then she could go back to being alone.

Mira was queasy from the drive as she rang the doorbell to her new building—three stories tall, like its neighbors on the block, with a humble laundromat on the first floor. Isabel opened the door, wearing a gray sweatshirt, jeans, and slippers.

Seeing Isabel in her soft-looking house clothes was disarming. Although Isabel herself didn't look soft, and she didn't smile.

"Hi," Mira said. Would Isabel ever become less intimidating? "This is my friend Frankie. Frankie, this is Isabel, my, uh, roommate."

"Nice to meet you!" Frankie said. Isabel gave her a nod, and they sized each other up in the way that butches did, at least in Mira's limited experience. Although the two of them couldn't have been more different. They were both Chinese—so Mira surmised, from the paperwork that had read *Isabel Wong*. But Frankie was grinning, short-haired, and half a foot shorter.

"Here are your keys," Isabel said, handing them to Mira. "You got anything else in the car?"

Between the three of them—mostly Isabel and Frankie—they made quick work of carrying Mira's clothes, books, plastic dresser, new twin-size mattress, and pile of used bed-frame parts up two flights of stairs and into Mira's new room. "Let me know if you need anything," Isabel said.

Without waiting for a response, she went back to her own room and shut the door. Her room shared a wall with Mira's, but it may as well have been a continent away.

Mira and Frankie exchanged a look. "You weren't kidding about her being the strong, silent type," Frankie said quietly.

Mira smiled, then stopped smiling as she surveyed the room. She had a suitcase of clothes, two boxes of books, and an unassembled bed. There was nothing like seeing your worldly possessions all in one place to make you question your entire life.

In her two-plus years of living with Dylan, his apartment had never become hers. All the expensive furniture had been his. She had been just another nice thing that he owned.

"You look like you're thinking too much," Frankie said. "You want me to tell you what we're growing on the farm this month?"

"Yes, please," Mira said. She learned all about the end of the growing season at Frankie's rooftop farm as they puzzled over putting the used bed frame together—without instructions, it took the better part of an hour. Finally, they unrolled the foam mattress from the box and made the bed.

It was sinking in: This was Mira's new home. She had

the uncomfortable sense of regressing to an earlier stage of life. Frankie and Vivian lived like grown adults; Mira was single, starting over, and sleeping in a twin bed for the first time since college. Adrift and lost.

She hung up a few dresses and blouses in the tiny closet and put her other clothes in the flimsy plastic drawers, gratefully letting Frankie do most of the talking. Once she was done, she sat on her new bed, suddenly exhausted.

"You okay?" Frankie said. "Need a break?"

"Yeah. I think I can take care of the rest myself."

Frankie sat down and put an arm around her. "You sure?"

Mira leaned against her friend. "Yeah, I'm sure. Thanks a lot, Frankie. I really appreciate it."

Frankie squeezed her. "You know you can call me and Vivian any time, okay? We're here for you. And we're so proud of you."

Frankie and Vivian were basically her lesbian moms. Vivian was the first trans woman Mira had met in New York City, back when Mira had turned up, painfully shy, at a support group for Asian trans women that Vivian was running at the time. She and Frankie lived together in their apartment full of plants, watching over Mira, letting her cry on their shoulders. They'd taken care of her after her surgeries. They'd hated Dylan from the beginning.

Mira had mixed feelings. She loved Vivian and Frankie, and she would trust them with her life. But she was twenty-seven years old, and maybe she shouldn't need her friends to hover over her all the time.

Mira's parents in Chicago loved her too, in their own way. They were eighty percent there in understanding her, which wasn't terrible. But the matter of why she'd had to run from Dylan—and why she'd stayed for so long—was firmly in the other twenty percent. They couldn't understand all the compromises she'd been forced to make, and she didn't want to face their pity.

"Thanks," she said to Frankie. She needed to be alone for a while.

They hugged each other goodbye at the door. "Those plants are in bad shape," Frankie said, looking at the windowsill. "Text me some close-up photos. I bet we can bring them back to life. And keep us updated, okay?"

With Frankie gone, Mira returned to her room. The boxes of books took up too much of what little space she had, and they were too tall to fit under the bed. She struggled as she pushed one of them against the wall. How could a few dozen books be so heavy?

She'd been stubborn in bringing them with her. But her books had been among the few things in Dylan's apartment that had truly been hers. They'd reminded her that she was a person with her own intellectual ambitions, not just Dylan's girlfriend. Even if Dylan hadn't wanted to make space on his own shelves, and they'd gone under the bed.

Now she was alone in her own room with her own books. She was finally free, and she'd never let herself be trapped again. But whatever comfort she took in that was drowned out by her fear. This was her home now, a cramped room in a near-stranger's apartment in an unknown neighborhood. *What now?*

She sighed. *One thing at a time*, Vivian had told her. There had been a half-empty bookshelf in the living room. It wasn't nearly big enough, but maybe Isabel would let her put a few books there.

Mira returned to the living room. It was spacious and full of sunlight, with a comfortable couch that Mira had sat on, a similarly well-worn armchair, and a coffee table made of what looked like real wood instead of particleboard. At the other end of the apartment was a tidy kitchen, separated from the living room only by a small dining table.

The apartment wasn't slick and curated like Dylan's, but it didn't look lived-in, either. The blanket and throw pillows on the couch seemed undisturbed since Mira's first visit. There was something chilly about the apartment, even if it wasn't nearly as forbidding as Isabel herself.

Maybe Mira would get used to having dinner at the table and curling up on the couch with a book, and the apartment would eventually feel cozy and warm—but would she have time to get used to it? She would be leaving in a few months. And she couldn't imagine Isabel doing any of those mundane, domestic things herself.

Mira went to the bookshelf. There were a few dozen hard sci-fi paperbacks she didn't recognize, alongside the classics by Le Guin and Butler. A framed photo sat on the top shelf. She picked it up.

In the middle of the photo was a woman in a wedding dress, looking so much like Isabel that Mira thought it was her for a moment. But Isabel was in the photo too, wearing a dark suit and a pink tie with her long hair loose, and another younger woman with the same family resemblance wearing a dress in the same shade of pink. They all had their arms around each other in a line, radiantly happy.

Mira couldn't look away. Isabel was grinning, and so full of joy she was almost unrecognizable. She looked a decade younger.

There were soft footsteps behind her. Mira turned. Isabel was going back into her room; she must have seen Mira looking at the photo. All Mira saw was a blur of dark hair before Isabel shut the door.

3

"I DON'T KNOW if you all saw the bad news in the group chat," Mira said. "In case any of you missed it, our speaker from the teachers' union canceled at the last minute, too. So, um, we don't have any external speakers booked right now."

Someone on the video call booed. He was clearly booing the speaker, not Mira, but she was still struck by guilt. "Sorry, everyone. I know this puts us in a bad spot."

The kickoff rally for the union had to go well. Over a third of the graduate student body had RSVP'd, and local news would be there. This was their chance to win over hundreds of their fellow grad students at once, and Mira was in danger of screwing it up.

"It's not your fault," Shreya, the vice president, said. Other people nodded in their rectangles on Mira's laptop screen.

Mira rubbed her tired eyes. It had been a long day, and it wasn't over. Her work usually followed her home. After this meeting, she had plenty of papers to grade, sitting in tall piles on the dining table next to her.

"Maybe one of us could give another speech after Shreya talks," someone else said.

"I don't know if that's the best idea," Mira said. "We want everyone at the rally to understand that we grad students are part of the broader labor movement. I think that's important for getting people on board, to recognize that we're not just students, we're workers, and we deserve rights and protections like other workers do. So we need speakers who do other types of work."

Shreya said, "Mira's right. So what are we going to do?"

Mira grimaced. "I'm not sure. Um, I guess I'll ask our speakers who canceled if they know anyone who'd be willing to step in. And maybe we could all reach out to whatever contacts we have?"

Her despair was mounting, and it wasn't only about the rally speakers. When she'd been with Dylan, her life had increasingly revolved around him until she'd had nothing left for herself. She'd stopped attending union meetings, stopped seeing her friends, stopped being able to imagine any other life.

If the grad students had unionized years ago, things might have been different. She wouldn't have been broke when Dylan had asked her to move in. She would have had options. In a different, better world, there was a Mira who wasn't hurt and struggling to claw her way out of a hole.

She had to take her life back. She had to prove that she was still committed to the union. But both the speakers she'd booked had canceled three days before the rally. Maybe it wasn't her fault—but she needed to accomplish *something*, and now even this simple task was slipping out of her grasp.

They compiled a list of people to contact. At some point, Isabel came home later than usual in her grimy work clothes. She went to the bathroom to shower, returned to her room in a bathrobe, and shut the door loudly enough to startle Mira. It was the third time Mira had seen her in two weeks.

The chances of finding last-minute speakers were not good. Mira let out a long sigh after she disconnected. She still hadn't eaten dinner, and her students' papers loomed.

Her phone buzzed. It was a reply from her father. *I have plenty of contacts in the teachers' union in Chicago, but not in New York, I'm afraid. Your mother is reporting on fisherpeople in Alaska with spotty cell service for the next month.* Followed by an article about the farmers' protests in India. *Thoughts??*

Mira smiled for a moment. It had been worth a try. She stood up, stretched, and yawned.

Isabel opened her bedroom door. "Mira."

Mira jumped. "Yeah?"

Isabel was scowling. Her hair was wet from her shower, and her shoulders, bare in a white tank top, were impressively muscled. She was as well-sculpted and cold as a statue. "Can you stop taking your calls in the living room?"

Mira froze. She'd done something wrong. "Sorry." The word came automatically. "I'm sorry. I didn't mean to bother you."

"It's louder than you think. If you really need to do it, do it in your room and keep it down." Isabel glared at Mira's papers on the table. "And it'd be great if you could stop leaving your hair clips and clothes and papers all over the place."

"I'm really sorry." Mira was forgetful when stressed, and she knew it was a bad habit—taking up too much space —but this had been the worst, most stressful month of her life. "I didn't mean to. I'll try not to anymore."

Isabel gave her a hard look, then turned away. The conversation was over. She started closing the door.

Maybe this was Mira's fault as always. But after the day she'd had, this particular indignity made her snap. Isabel clearly never wanted a roommate, but she didn't have to remind Mira of it like this. "I didn't know it would bother you so much." Isabel turned back around, and Mira knew she ought to shut up, but she couldn't stop herself. "If you wanted a completely silent apartment all to yourself, as though I don't live here, you could have told me."

Surprise flickered over Isabel's face. Then she shut the door.

Mira's nausea rose. Why had she tried to argue back? Isabel hadn't even responded, as though Mira were too unimportant to bother with. Maybe she was.

Just because Isabel had once done something decent for her didn't mean she'd be nice or understanding. Mira sat down and put her face in her hands. Shame on her for expecting too much.

She didn't have time to dwell on this. She had to live here, whether she liked it or not, and she had too much work to do.

MAYBE ISABEL HAD FUCKED UP. After she'd gone off at Mira last night, the doubt had plagued her all day like a hangover. It had started when she'd gotten up in the morning and found Mira's papers in one tidy pile on the table.

Mira hadn't needed to do that. It wasn't as though Isabel had been eating dinner, or doing much of anything besides stewing in her room.

Back at home, holed up in her room again as Mira

worked in the living room, the guilt was stronger than ever. Mira was right. What the hell had she been thinking? She was a grown woman losing it at her roommate for making sounds and leaving her things out in the apartment they both lived in.

Isabel sat on the edge of her bed and groaned. She needed to apologize.

Yesterday had been awful. Her new apprentice was still in the habit of asking the men around her for a second opinion, and she'd used up most of her patience at work. Then she'd found out through her mother that Grace had set a wedding date. She and her little sister hadn't talked in months, and apparently Grace was still angry.

She'd wanted to wallow in shame alone. Instead, she'd come home to Mira talking on a call—at a normal volume, but it had grated—and when she'd retreated to the bathroom to shower, she'd found Mira's hair clip left next to the sink. A reminder that the apartment wasn't private anymore. If she showed any weakness, Mira would see.

None of that was an excuse. She was an adult. She had to apologize.

She rubbed her face and exhaled. Everything had been easier when she was working seventy hours a week, racking up the overtime pay, collapsing in her bed night after night and falling into a dreamless sleep. It was torture to have so much free time, hours and hours to kill every day. The forty-hour work week had been hard-won, and Isabel wasn't putting it to good use.

The sound of Mira typing on her laptop filtered through the door. What was Isabel going to say to her? It was an awful, too-familiar feeling: being in close quarters with someone she'd let down, shame and regret filling up every room.

After turning her apology over and over in her mind, Isabel got up and opened the door.

Mira's head jerked up. For a moment, she looked like she had after her ex had threatened her outside the club. She had looked like that last night, too. Afraid.

Yeah, Isabel had fucked up. Of course the ex would have been an asshole to Mira while she lived with him, and of course Isabel had just done the same thing. For the first time, Isabel noticed dark circles under Mira's eyes under her fading concealer.

"Sorry," Isabel said, the words she'd prepared getting scrambled in her head. She ran a hand through her hair. "You were right. I, uh— It's not okay for me to talk to you like that. I won't do it again."

"It's okay."

"No, it's not." Mira seemed taken aback. Isabel sighed. "Hey, if there's anything I can do for you, just, uh, let me know." She had to try to make it up to Mira, even if their lives had nothing to do with each other.

"Um..." Mira paused like she was actually considering the offer. "That's okay. Thank you."

There was no reason to beat around the bush. "You sure?"

Mira grimaced. "Well, you're under no obligation. Sorry if this is..."

"You can say it."

Mira now looked even more stressed, if anything. "Okay, I just thought I'd ask. My union is having an important rally in two days, but all our speakers canceled. Do you know anyone from your union who might be able to give a ten-minute speech? I know it's a lot to ask."

Isabel exhaled. What a relief: something doable. Her old friend Anthony was working as a staff organizer for the electricians' union, although he was busy these days with his newborn daughter. Then there was Steve, the journeyman who'd taught her all about labor solidarity back when she was an apprentice, though he'd retired and probably wouldn't come all the way from Jersey. Still, it was worth a try. "Sure, I know some guys I could ask."

Mira's face brightened. "Really? Thank you so much. I appreciate it."

"I'll try, but no guarantees. Also, uh, about what I said earlier. You don't have to worry about it. Talk wherever you want and leave things where you want. It's your apartment."

Mira frowned. "If it bothers you..."

"It's fine."

"Well, if something does bother you, I'd like to know."

Isabel shrugged. "Maybe use headphones when you're on a call in the living room. Don't worry about everything else I said."

"I can do that. Sorry." Mira still looked skeptical. "Are you sure? Because I don't want to do anything to bother you again."

She didn't want Isabel to snap at her again. Trying to make Mira feel better with an unrelated favor wasn't going to be enough, and Isabel should have realized that. "Sorry. I... To be honest, I'm not used to having anyone else around. I've been living alone for half a year."

"I can understand that." Mira's smile was strained.

Isabel winced. Admitting all this was like pulling teeth. "I'm not making excuses. I'm saying, I might be bothered in the future. Just by not being alone in the apartment anymore. And that's not your problem, and I'll deal with it myself. Or, uh, I'll talk to you about it without blowing up at you."

"Okay. Thank you for saying that." Mira hesitated. "Are we okay now?"

"That's up to you."

Mira gave her another smile, sweet and warm. And pretty, too, but Isabel had no business thinking that. "Okay," Mira said. "I think so. We're okay."

That could have been a lot worse. "Uh, I'll talk to those guys I mentioned. Have a good night." Time for Isabel to quit while she was ahead. She went back into her room.

Her friend Anthony was busy. So was Steve, though it had been good to hear about his grandkids and the old cars he was fixing up. So were the few other people she had asked as a long shot.

At least she'd tried. Hopefully Mira would appreciate that.

She found Mira at the table surrounded by piles of papers again. She was wearing reading glasses, chunky frames perched on her elegant nose. Isabel nearly stopped short. She hadn't known Mira wore those.

Now was not the fucking time. She broke the news to Mira. "Oh," Mira said. "Well, thanks anyway. I appreciate you asking."

"Did you find anyone else?"

"Sort of."

"Yeah?"

Mira clearly hadn't expected Isabel to keep asking questions. "Well, a grad student organizer from NYU agreed to give a speech, which is at least something. I'm not sure anyone else would agree to fill in, at this point, since it's tomorrow. I guess we'll just have to go with what we have."

Mira's disappointment made Isabel ache. She didn't

want to let Mira down, not after getting her hopes up. "How important is it to find someone else?"

Mira still seemed suspicious of Isabel's interest, but she started to explain. "I want everyone to understand that it's not just about us," she continued, "and not even just about grad students everywhere, but about every working person. And that we, as grad students, are going to show up for the dining hall workers and the adjuncts because we're all in this together. But...I don't know. Maybe that was too ambitious and it doesn't matter."

Mira was so sincere. So hopeful. It had been a long time since Isabel was hopeful about anything. "I'll do it," she blurted out.

"What do you mean?"

That had been stupid. Isabel had never given a speech in her life. "I figured... I've been an electrician for a decade. And I salted a shop a few years ago, so I know what it's like to be organizing people. Never mind. You probably want someone else."

"No, I didn't mean... Sorry. I mean, that's kind of you to offer, but you don't have to."

Isabel shrugged. "I can. If you want a regular person." Mira was frowning. Probably trying to figure out whether she'd really be stuck with Isabel for something that mattered this much to her. "Hopefully you find someone else. I just figured... As a last resort."

"Well, of course we want a regular person. I think people would love to hear from you. What you said about being a salt sounds fascinating. So you got hired at a non-union shop, and then you convinced your coworkers to unionize?"

"Pretty much." What Isabel remembered about it

wasn't their victory. It was that she never got to tell her older sister about it.

Isabel had locked up her memories from that unspeakably awful year. She could pick out a few of them for this speech. But maybe she shouldn't have offered in the first place.

"Wow. Are you really okay with it?" Mira might have sensed her discomfort. But Isabel wasn't going to explain.

There was no backing out now. She couldn't let Mira down. "Yeah."

Mira's frown turned into a hesitant smile, which became less hesitant as she realized Isabel was serious. "Thank you so much." Once again, that smile was radiant. Something dangerous stirred in Isabel's chest. "You don't know how much this helps. Are you going to have enough time to prepare? I know it's on short notice."

Time was something Isabel had far too much of, these days. "Yeah, that's not a problem."

4

"Finally, I want to say that when I started as an apprentice, I only thought of being an electrician as a job that would pay me good money. I didn't know anything about the history of our union, or how easily the wages, benefits, and rights we've won could be taken from us."

All around Mira, the audience was silent and rapt. Isabel went on. "What it took was a journeyman I had as an apprentice who taught me all this. He encouraged me to go to union meetings and pay attention to our labor history classes in night school. He told me to never forget what working people who came before us have sacrificed to make our lives possible."

Someone cheered. Isabel looked up from her old-school notecards and smiled. She made eye contact with Mira, giving her a quiet thrill. "He never let me get away with talking about the union like it's a third party. I am the union, and I'm responsible for the union and for my sisters and brothers, and they're responsible for me. And I hope that you all know that you are your union, and you're going to keep fighting for yourselves and for each other. And if you keep doing that, you're going to win."

The hall erupted in applause. Mira was dazed as she clapped. It wasn't easy to fire up a room full of cynical grad students. The truth was that she'd had tempered expectations for Isabel's speech, and Isabel had far surpassed them.

Standing at the podium, wearing the sweatshirt and jeans she'd worn to work, Isabel had been mesmerizing. As a rule, Mira distrusted anything resembling an inspirational speech. But in those ten minutes, she'd been as captivated by Isabel as she'd been on the night they'd met.

No amount of seeing Isabel at home could shake Mira's sense that Isabel was extraordinary, larger than life, a mystery she couldn't solve. Isabel had stood up to Dylan so fearlessly that Mira's heart still raced at the memory. She had zero interest in small talk, but her speech had been astonishing. She'd been callous to Mira, and it had hurt— and then she'd apologized so stiffly that Mira knew it had to be sincere.

Isabel returned to her seat, barely acknowledging the applause, which was very much like her, too.

Shreya took over. To the buzzing crowd, she reiterated their goal: Once enough grad students signed union cards, they could hold an election. If they won, the university would be forced to recognize the union, and the union would negotiate for a better, fairer contract for everyone. She explained how to sign a card by filling out a form online. Both of Mira's neighbors took out their phones.

Mira found Isabel afterward in the crowd, with her backpack and hard hat, looking out of place but nodding at people who were thanking her. "That was wonderful," Mira said, still high on her excitement. "Thank you so much, Isabel. We're all so grateful."

Isabel gave her the brightest smile Mira had ever seen from her. She glanced at the floor. If Mira didn't know better, she would have said that Isabel looked shy. "No problem," Isabel said. "I'm glad it went fine."

"Everyone loved it." They started walking. "What you said at the end was amazing. I can't believe you put that together in one day."

Isabel shrugged in the way she did whenever Mira thanked her. "Just doing what I can."

She held the door for Mira as they exited the building. It was time to take the train home. They'd never spent so much time together before, and Mira was resigning herself to a ride in silence when Isabel said, "I didn't realize it was so bad. That they make you do lab work without the right protective equipment."

Mira's friend in chemical engineering had given a speech about it. "It's awful, isn't it? We helped him pressure his advisor, but it doesn't stop other people's advisors from trying the same thing. At least the humanities departments aren't literally toxic."

Isabel snorted. After a few seconds, she asked, "Do you like grad school?"

The question was so simple that Mira struggled to answer. "I do, actually. I feel fortunate to be able to study what I love for seven or eight years of my life. And to have health insurance for that long, even if it's not very good." Insurance had covered only part of what she'd needed for her surgeries, and only the ones they'd deemed necessary. Dylan had covered the rest. Mira tried to quell her ever-present guilt about being insufficiently grateful, both to him and to the university. "I'd like it more if we won a fair contract and I wasn't so overwhelmed by my teaching, that's for sure."

Isabel nodded. "So you don't like teaching? I wouldn't like it either."

That wasn't what Mira had meant. "I do like it. I care a lot about my students. I wish I weren't so overworked so I could be a better teacher to them."

Apparently Isabel's opinion mattered to her, whether she liked it or not. But the wider world didn't understand her discipline, and plenty of people in her department—mostly hotshot men—didn't see the point of caring about the undergrads, and she was always trying to stake out her own ground.

Isabel said nothing. Maybe she didn't care. Nevertheless, Mira continued, "It matters to me because Classics as a field can be so elitist, and I don't want my students who didn't take years of Greek and Latin in private school to think that it's too late for them. One of my students nominated me for a teaching award last year, and she said that she wouldn't even have considered being a Classics major if it weren't for my class. That's what keeps me going, sometimes, when I think about giving up on grad school." Which she contemplated a few times a year. More often when she had a thesis chapter due.

Isabel was silent for a moment. Then she said, "Sounds like you're a good teacher."

Mira flushed. "You don't have to say that. You haven't seen me teach." She wasn't in the habit of mentioning her accomplishments like this.

"Did you win?" Isabel said.

Mira replayed their conversation. "The award?" She flushed more deeply. "Um, yeah, I did."

"Sounds like you're a good teacher."

Mira smiled. Truthfully, she was proud of her award. And there was no need to go on the defensive. Isabel wasn't in her academic bubble, which was refreshing, given that Mira spent most of her time around people who either dictated her job prospects or saw her as competition. "I think that's what makes grad school worth it for me, ultimately. Seeing my students realize that they have a future as a classicist, or a philosopher or an historian or whatever they want to be."

Isabel nodded. The setting sun illuminated the angles of her face and the tendrils of hair that had come loose from her braid. And that little silver stud earring. Mira almost tripped on the sidewalk, distracted.

"I only said I wouldn't like teaching because I was a bad student," Isabel said. "I dropped out of college after my junior year."

"Really?" They were at the subway entrance. Mira went down the stairs first.

"I tried out a few engineering majors," Isabel said behind her. "I did an internship, and I didn't know it was just sitting at a computer tinkering with CAD drawings all day. I asked my boss when we got to do the actual work, and he got offended and told me I could be a construction worker if I wanted to be on the job site so badly."

Mira laughed. It was thrilling to walk with Isabel and listen to her talk, as though her conviction could rub off onto Mira that way. "And so you did?"

"I applied for the union apprenticeship, and I got a call the summer before my senior year, so I dropped out."

Mira was hit by a pang of...something. Maybe admiration or envy. She mulled it over as she went through the turnstile. What was it like to be so decisive, to simply do what you thought was right? Whatever it was that Isabel had, Mira didn't have it.

She did the math. Isabel had been an electrician for a

decade, which meant she was around thirty-one. Maybe Mira would have her life together at that age. "Seems like you made the right choice," she said.

"I love what I do." Pride radiated from Isabel's words, as obvious as the union stickers on her hard hat. "Can't imagine doing anything else."

The approaching train was deafening, interrupting the longest conversation they'd had so far. Mira longed to know even more. But she knew so little about Isabel that she couldn't get a foothold on what to say.

On the train, it was, surprisingly, Isabel who spoke first. "Shreya said you're going out and asking people to sign union cards. How's that going?"

"I think it's going well. We have a few hundred so far."

"I mean for you."

"Oh, um, I haven't really talked to anyone yet. Just a few people in my office." All of whom were going to sign cards anyway.

"Why not?"

Mira looked at her lap. There was no good reason. She could try to deflect, and Isabel would leave her alone, but Isabel's own forthrightness discouraged her from that approach. "I don't know. I guess I'm just scared." She was so tired of settling for what she'd been given in life. But asking for more was easier said than done.

Mira's strengths when it came to union organizing were more along the lines of emailing to reserve the campus event space. Maybe following up politely if she didn't get a response. Not going out and talking to people who might be hostile to her.

"Scared of what?" Isabel asked.

Mira didn't have a good answer to that, either. "I'm nervous about talking to strangers. I guess I'm afraid I won't be able to be persuasive or respond to what people say, and it'll make the union look bad."

"Have you had any training?"

"Yeah, I attended a training. But I still don't feel prepared."

"It takes practice, like anything else," Isabel said, as though it were inconsequential to fail and humiliate oneself. "I told you about the time I was a union salt. My first few times talking to my new coworkers, I came off as way too aggressive, and I turned some people off. But we still won the election."

"I don't think I'll have that problem. Being too aggressive, I mean."

The corner of Isabel's mouth quirked upward. "You know what I'm saying. I can give you more practice, if you want."

Isabel was taking this seriously. She was taking *Mira* seriously, maybe more seriously than Mira took herself.

The idea of having a charged back-and-forth with Isabel, even if they were only role-playing, made her stomach drop. It would be good for her. But she was intimidated enough by Isabel during this ordinary conversation. Having to stammer her talking points or argue back while Isabel evaluated her, those dark, intense eyes meeting her own...

"That would be really kind of you," Mira said faintly. "I might take you up on it. Thank you." Time to change the subject. "It must have felt amazing to win that election in that shop you were salting, after all that hard work."

Isabel frowned and looked down. Had Mira said something wrong?

"Yeah," Isabel said, suddenly subdued. "I don't talk

about it much. My sister died two months before the election."

"Oh my goodness, I'm so sorry." It was clear that Isabel was trying to close the topic, not open it. Mira couldn't have known, but she wanted to kick herself. "I didn't mean to make you talk about it." When Isabel had told those stories in her speech, she must have been thinking of her sister the whole time.

Isabel was silent as the train rumbled on. Finally, she said, "I'll help you with whatever you need." She was now as hard and remote as ever. Mira wouldn't be hearing more about Isabel's sister. "I can help you practice. Just let me know."

5

"Can we do this without video today?" Isabel said. "I need to make dinner."

"Sure." Cat's new pink, shaggy haircut disappeared on Isabel's phone screen.

Isabel set her phone aside and put on her apron. "Tell me more about this big DJ set you're doing this weekend."

"Oh, it's one of those all-day parties at Volume, and I'm going on at eight a.m."

"Congratulations. People really stay out until eight a.m.? I feel old." Isabel took a package of instant ramen—chicken flavor today—out of the pantry.

"You *are* old. You don't think it's romantic to dance while the sun comes up?"

"I see the sunrise when I'm working in the winter all the time. I'm—"

"Okay, okay, we get it," Cat said. Isabel didn't need her to be on video to know she was rolling her eyes. "You have a job where you work regular hours and have health insurance. You don't have to rub it in."

"Hey, you know I'm proud of you. I know it's a big deal. Can I come in the morning instead of being there all night?"

"Yes, they do let old people in. You'll get a senior discount. Seriously, though, it'd be great to see you. I'm playing some of my own stuff, too."

The joke was hitting too close to home. Soon, Isabel would be older than Alexa ever got to be. "That's great," she said, distracted. "Yeah, I'll be there this time. Send me the ticket link."

"I will. No pressure. I mean, if you need to rescue another damsel in distress, I'd understand."

Isabel bristled more than she should have. "It's not like that."

"Not like what?"

Isabel checked the pot on the stove. The water was boiling. She dropped in the ramen and dumped in the contents of the flavor packet. "It's not like that," she said again.

"Okay. How is she, by the way? Mira, right?"

"How's my roommate? I don't know. I don't see her much." She was giving Mira some union organizing practice tomorrow. But that would take an hour at most, and she'd do it for anyone.

"Well, that's good, right? You didn't want a roommate in the first place."

Isabel cracked an egg into the ramen broth, and then another. The egg whites turned opaque as they swirled.

A few weeks ago, she would have said yes to Cat's question easily. But she was getting used to Mira being around. Mira had a smile for her whenever they saw each other, and sometimes Isabel was even moved to smile back. Mira cooked and worked on her laptop and occasionally took her calls, and she was doing something with the plants that made them less dead. She still left her books and hair clips scattered everywhere, which irritated Isabel less these days than it ought to.

If all those signs of life disappeared... The apartment might feel lonely. Maybe she had been lonely all along before Mira arrived.

Isabel pushed the idea aside. She was fine on her own. "I guess. It's only for a few months." A few months until she had to pack up everything she owned and leave the apartment she'd lived in for half of her adult life.

"Where's Mira going to go?"

"Not my problem." Isabel stirred the eggs and noodles with a pair of chopsticks. "How's Grace?"

"She's busy with wedding planning, obviously. Have you talked to her since the last time you asked me?"

"No." Isabel stirred her ramen vehemently.

"Okay. So you're still making me the go-between for the two of you. She's fine, but kind of stressed."

Isabel was stressing out Grace, and she was stressing out Cat, too, but there was nothing she could say to fix it. "Is her fiancé not helping her with the wedding planning?"

"Kevin is helping her plenty." Cat sighed. "Isabel, I think you need to—"

Isabel winced. "Okay, okay, you're right. Don't tell Grace I asked that. I'm glad Kevin is... I'm glad things are going well for them." Alexa's death had torn them all apart. Even talking to Cat, Alexa's widower's sister, was getting harder. Every subject was full of landmines.

"Okay, you don't need to apologize to *me*," Cat said. A long silence followed. "What are you doing these days, now that you're not working all the time?"

"Not much. Going to physical therapy. Walking around. Watching TV. Reading." None of these things helped her relax. They gave her too much time to think and made her restless. She had the constant sense that she was supposed to be doing something else.

"You're not going out anywhere or spending time with anyone?"

"I'm going out. How else would I hear your sets?"

"I mean other than that." Cat paused. "I know you don't want to hear this. But I'm worried about you."

"I'm fine."

Cat sighed again, dragging it out audibly. "How's work going?"

"Work is good. I'm still working at that MTA facility. The new apprentices are here." This was safer territory. She told Cat about the apprentice who was testing her patience. And she heard all about Cat's day job as a spa receptionist, and the new people in her life: cute mechanic from the bike shop, hot tattoo artist who was bad at texting back.

When they said goodbye, the air between them was more or less cleared. Isabel carried her ramen to the table. There was an abandoned mug with three tea bags in it next to the pile of student papers that now lived on the table permanently. Mira had marked up some of them in her elegant cursive with a purple pen. Isabel smiled, then caught herself.

She might go out of her way to help Mira find a new place. But after that...

She hadn't been lying to Cat. Mira wasn't awful to talk to. And of course Isabel supported the grad students as a matter of principle. But whatever Mira did after that wasn't Isabel's problem, even if she occasionally had a hard time remembering it.

. . .

W<small>HEN</small> I<small>SABEL OPENED THE DOOR</small>, the apartment smelled good. Mira was cooking something full of aromatics and spices. She was standing at the stove, and she greeted Isabel, looking flustered. "Sorry, this is taking longer than I expected."

"That's fine. I need to shower and eat." It was true, but Isabel lingered by the kitchen. She'd gone straight from work to taking her aunt to the doctor, and she was tired and starving. Coming in from the cold and finding Mira making dinner was stirring something up inside her.

She looked away. No point in dwelling on some domestic fantasy. She was just hungry, was all. She needed to get some food in her.

"Actually," Mira said, "I was wondering if you wanted to have dinner together, so I can thank you for helping me."

Isabel opened her mouth to say no. But there was a bright-looking stew on the stove, and the rice cooker on the counter was full of warm rice. She didn't have the willpower to refuse.

She'd have to do something for Mira later to make it up to her. "Uh, thanks. I appreciate it. Can I help?"

Mira dipped a spoon into her pot of stew. "That's okay." She blew on her spoonful, tasted it, and smiled. "Almost done."

Isabel's heart beat faster. Seeing Mira in her kitchen, licking the spoon and giving her that smile...after months and months of returning to a dark, empty apartment, it was too much. She nodded and hurried to her room. She needed to clear her head.

When Isabel came back out, showered and dressed, Mira set two big, wide bowls on the table. Rice topped with a scoop of fiery-red vegetable stew, cabbage flecked with coconut and mustard seeds, a generous dollop of yogurt. An open store-bought jar of mango pickle sat in the middle of the table.

They sat down. Isabel couldn't remember the last time she'd had a home-cooked meal other than instant ramen, fried rice, or boxed mac and cheese, and some of those were stretching the definition. She took a bite. It was delicious— bright and sunny from tamarind and mango pickle, perfect for the gray October evening. She had a few more big bites, then remembered her manners. "It's good. Thanks. I like the cabbage."

Mira smiled. Yearning tugged at Isabel. She wanted to keep seeing that smile lighting up Mira's face.

There wasn't anything wrong with that. Mira was going through a tough time, and it was good to see her happy about something, even something as small as Isabel complimenting her cooking. Mira always seemed surprised by the simplest things, like she didn't expect much out of other people.

"I'm glad you like it," Mira said. She scooped out more mango pickle from the jar. "It's such a relief to be cooking for myself again and making whatever I want to eat. And in such a nice kitchen, too. I didn't even know how much I missed it."

"You used to cook for your ex?" The idea of it rankled Isabel.

Mira's smile turned sardonic. "He wanted to eat what his mom used to make for him, but he wasn't willing to make it himself. Let's just say that."

Isabel snorted. It was still a mystery why this smart, funny, beautiful woman had ever dated someone like that. Then again, her own little sister... But now wasn't the time to think about Grace and her lackluster fiancé. "If he didn't like this," Isabel said, gesturing to her food, "that's his problem."

"That's sweet of you," Mira said. Isabel's face turned hot. People called her plenty of things. *Sweet* wasn't one of them. "I had rice and sambar for dinner a lot when I was growing up, so this is comfort food for me. I know other South Asian kids complained about not having pizza or hamburgers, or what have you, but I never felt that way."

"Where's your family from?" On second thought, maybe Isabel shouldn't have asked. Mira was probably sick of being asked where she was from, and what she was, and things of that ilk. Or maybe she didn't want to talk about her family. It was just a little too easy to talk to Mira, and sometimes things slipped out of Isabel's mouth. "If you want to say."

"I don't mind you asking." There was a mild emphasis on *you*. "My dad is Indian and originally from Chennai, and my mom is white and Jewish and grew up here, in New York, although she and my dad settled in Chicago. This was in the eighties, when it was a lot harder to get good Indian food, especially South Indian, so my dad had to figure out how to cook. My mom told him she'd only marry him if they only had one child and she didn't have to do any of the cooking."

Maybe that was what Mira wanted in a relationship, too. Someone who would support her while she lived her own life, someone she could rely on for the everyday things. She deserved it after what that man had put her through. "You learned how to cook from your dad?"

"A little. I mostly learned from food blogs and YouTube videos." Mira paused. "We get along, more or less. It's just that my dad is the most pedantic person I've ever known.

Which, given that I've spent five years in grad school, is saying something."

Isabel smiled. "I've done that too. I'm too proud to ask my mom to teach me to cook, after I refused when I was a teenager." She sighed. "Although I should. She's getting older. She's not going to be here forever."

It always came back to the wound at the center of her family, the one that would never heal. The silence settled over them. She'd gotten too comfortable with Mira, and it left an opening for Mira to pity her. She'd told Mira about losing Alexa just to get it over with. Maybe that had been a mistake.

Mira nodded. Maybe she was pitying Isabel, or maybe not. Thankfully, she didn't say anything trite for the sake of it, like a lot of other people would have done.

They finished eating in a comfortable enough silence. It was time for Isabel to wash the dishes. She reached for Mira's bowl, and her fingers closed over Mira's.

Isabel jerked away as though she'd been shocked. Mira's hand was warm, and it had been months since Isabel had touched another person and felt the heat of their body. No, that wasn't true. She'd grabbed Mira's arm outside of Volume that night, and feeling her bare skin had been like touching a live wire. Mira had tensed up at first, and that tension had gradually given way...

She reached out again and yanked the bowl out of Mira's hands. "I'll wash up. You cooked."

Mira looked startled. "Well, I wanted to thank you for helping."

"I'll do it." Isabel grabbed her own bowl and carried both to the sink, putting Mira firmly out of sight.

She had a role to play. She was helping Mira with her

union organizing, and that was that. Once she was done with the dishes, they sat back down at the table.

Now Isabel was on firmer footing. This was like training apprentices at work. Never mind that no apprentice had ever knocked her so off-balance. "I'm a grad student and a worker, and you see me in the..."

"Computer science building."

"That's where you're going?"

Mira grimaced. "I was late in signing up, and this was the only slot left. Normally I'd be in my own department."

"Okay, in the computer science building. And I look tired from working all the time."

Mira laughed. Then she sobered up and looked at her lap. A ringlet that had come loose from her hair clip fell into her face. Isabel itched to tuck it behind her ear.

"Well... I guess I would approach you," Mira said. "And I would introduce myself—"

"Say it to me like it's real."

Mira looked up and blinked, her long lashes fluttering. She had such gorgeous deep brown eyes. "Hi, I'm Mira Levin, and I'm with the Graduate Workers' Union. Do you, um— Do you have some time to talk with me about your experiences as a graduate worker?"

"Sure. Make it quick."

Mira dropped her gaze before making eye contact again. She was startlingly sexy when trying to project confidence. "I'm interested in hearing about the problems you're facing as a grad worker right now, whether it's in teaching, or your research, or housing, or something else."

The low-burning fire in Mira, flickering under all her self-doubt, was intriguing. Isabel wanted to see more. She settled back in her chair and eyed Mira skeptically. Anxiety flashed across Mira's face, but she held Isabel's gaze. She looked like the shy, determined academic she was, in her prim cardigan with a single button undone.

"I can't afford to live less than an hour away from campus on my stipend," Isabel said. "And my advisor harasses me and my coworkers. And the university won't help me with my student visa."

"Wow, you really paid attention during the rally."

Isabel raised an eyebrow. "Is that what you'd say to me?"

She hadn't been fully honest with herself. She wasn't just helping Mira because she believed in lifting up all working people. She did believe in that, of course. But, more than that, she hated the thought of Mira running out of money and having no one to turn to for help.

She wanted to protect Mira. The instinct that had kicked in that night at the club had never gone away.

And the truth was, she'd been looking at Mira's mouth, at the one undone button of her cardigan under her collarbones. Knowing that if they were in any other situation at all—if they weren't roommates, if Isabel weren't a mess—Isabel would be imagining undoing the rest of those buttons, one by one, all the way down.

She forced herself to look at Mira's eyes. Those dark eyes that were so easy to get lost in. Isabel was in trouble.

"No." Mira smiled and glanced down. Then her serious demeanor returned. Isabel was in deep, deep trouble. Or she would be, if she didn't control herself. "First of all, I'm sorry to hear that," Mira said, to the downtrodden grad student Isabel was role-playing. "That's terrible and unfair to you. You shouldn't have to deal with that by yourself. Have you been able to get any help or support for any of these issues?"

Mira's sympathy was so convincing that Isabel was caught off-guard. She was mesmerized, tempted to open up about her nonexistent advisor. "No," she said curtly, pushing her emotions down. "I can't just ask the grad student office if they'll pay me more."

"Well, no, I suppose you can't." Mira's spine straightened. "But all of us can, if we do it together."

Isabel needed to get a grip. Mira had an election to win, and if all her coworkers were as determined as she was, they were going to pull it off. She gave Mira a look of suspicion and took in the way Mira stiffened, first from nervousness, then from resolve. Isabel asked, "Why should I believe you?"

AFTER AN HOUR OF PRACTICE, Mira had loosened up. She still tended to look at Isabel like she was being graded on a test. But it was a start, and Mira would be learning by doing the real thing soon enough.

"You did good," Isabel said. A playful tension had built up in their back-and-forth exchanges, and Isabel had tried to not get distracted. Though maybe she hadn't tried her best.

Mira beamed. "Thank you. I'm really grateful."

"You'll get better as you do it more. But you're better at listening to people than I ever was." At that, Mira scoffed and looked down. "I mean it. You're..." What was the right word? Mira was sincere and kind and determined, and Isabel ached to protect her and see her grow. None of that would come out right if Isabel said it. "You're sympathetic."

"Is that your way of telling me I'm too soft?"

Mira's tone was teasing, but there was real insecurity under those words. Isabel's anger flared at whoever had planted the idea in Mira's head. "No, it's a good thing. I'm not bullshitting you. I want you to win."

"I know. Thanks again for all your help. You don't know how much I appreciate it."

That was Mira again, so thankful for the simplest things. "Hey, you know..." Isabel wasn't the world's most inspirational journeywoman, but the occasional pep talk was good for people, especially for the younger women she worked with. And that speech she'd given hadn't been too bad. "Just remember you have a right to be talking to people and asking these questions and building these relationships. These are your coworkers, even if you don't know them yet. If people give you shit for it at first, so be it."

"I guess so." Mira seemed unconvinced.

Isabel pressed on. "It's harder for women to be out there doing these things. But the labor movement wouldn't be what it is without us. Especially us queer women."

"Thanks." Mira hesitated. "I don't generally call myself queer, since I only date men, even though I know other people use the word that way. But I take your point."

A full-body shudder of embarrassment went through Isabel. She'd assumed all this time that Mira was bi. They'd met outside of Volume—but of course straight trans women went there.

There had never been any reason to assume that Mira liked women. Isabel was such an idiot. It served her right for spouting unsolicited inspirational talk.

That wasn't the real problem. The real problem was that there was no reason to take this so personally. Unless her mistake had just been wishful thinking, which was far worse. All her tender thoughts and feelings about Mira, ones she hadn't wanted to think about too carefully, were even more humiliating in this light.

Almost nothing fazed her this badly, but right now, Isabel wanted to crawl into a hole. "Sorry."

"It's okay." Mira didn't seem bothered. "Anyway, thank you again. I hope I can make you proud."

Isabel forced a smile. "Don't worry about me. Do it for you."

6

THE COMPUTER SCIENCE grad lounge was more populated than Mira had hoped. One person was wearing pajama pants and typing on his laptop. Another person was engaged in the instantly recognizable activity of grading student midterms. Two people were talking rather loudly over coffee.

Mira took a deep breath, which did nothing to settle her nerves. She shouldn't have procrastinated on signing up for a slot. Next time she'd pick more familiar territory, but she had to get through this first.

If she didn't try her best, nobody would know. But that wasn't the point. She had a goal to accomplish. Like Isabel had said, she *was* the union, and she couldn't wait for someone else to do it.

Who was the most promising person to talk to? Maybe the woman grading the tall stack of exams. She seemed likely to support contractually limiting everyone's teaching workload.

Mira took another breath and approached the woman. "Hi."

No response. Mira noticed the earbuds. "Hi," she said again, more loudly. The guy wearing pajama pants glared at her.

The woman took an earbud out. "Hi," she said, not seeming pleased to be interrupted.

"Hi," Mira repeated once more, feeling ridiculous. "Um, my name's Mira Levin, and I'm with the Graduate Workers' Union—"

"I'm an international student." The woman started to put her earbud back in.

"International students can be union members, too," Mira said hastily. She sat down in the facing seat. Should she have asked to sit down first? "You can sign a union card and vote in the election, just like anyone else. In fact, we're especially interested in listening to the concerns of international students. We have a working group for that." Mira recalled the advice she'd gotten during training, to always end with a question. "So, uh, have you had any issues with the administration when it comes to your student visa?"

The woman put her earbud on the table, which was a good sign. "With my visa, not really. But I couldn't get into the grad student housing, and I had trouble finding an apartment without a US credit history."

Mira could commiserate all too well. "Oh, that's so frustrating." Would it be a good idea to bring up her own issues? What would Isabel do? Mira had no idea. "Um, I didn't get into the grad housing either and had to live in an illegal sublet for a while. Anyway, we're going to demand that the administration increase our stipends so we can actually afford to live in New York City—"

"Okay, can I look into this later?" the woman said. Had Mira said the wrong thing? "I need to work."

Mira could point out that it took less than a minute to sign a union card online. But maybe it was a bad idea to push her luck. "Okay," she said, as the woman put her earbud back in. "Well, thank you for your time."

The conversation was over. Mira stood up, painfully aware of being an interloper.

She approached the two men talking. Best to get it over with. "Excuse me. I'm Mira, and I'm—"

"We're busy," one of them said.

"I already signed a union card," the other said.

"Oh." Maybe Mira ought to talk to the first man, but she had no way to push past his dismissal. "Okay, sorry to bother you. And, um, thanks," she added for the second man.

He spared her a glance. "Good luck." The two resumed their conversation.

This was painful. Mira wanted to bolt and hide in her office or go home. She wasn't cut out for this.

She approached the man in pajama pants. "Hi, I'm—"

"I heard you," he said. "You're the third person who's tried to talk to me about the union this week. You want to know what the biggest problem I have is as a grad student? It's that you people keep bothering me when I'm trying to get work done. What the hell do I have to do to make you leave me alone?"

Mira's face burned. The man's voice was loud, and people turned to look. What had she done wrong? Mira wanted to say something, anything, but no words came. She was rooted to the spot.

"Some of us have real work to do," the man continued. "Maybe you should try it sometime." He turned back to his laptop.

Other people were still staring at her. She was a spectacle. "Sorry," she managed to say. She ran out of the room, nearly tripping on a chair.

Tears welled up in her eyes. What was wrong with her? The computer science building was all futuristic glass surfaces and open spaces, and Mira ran down the hallway, desperate for privacy. She found a restroom and locked herself in a stall. Nobody else was in here, as far as she could tell, but she still tried to hold back her sobs.

Hot shame bubbled in her chest. She needed to quit the union, or drop out of grad school. Anything to hide from aggressive men shouting at her while she cowered in silence.

Maybe the problem was that she was pathetic. Maybe if she ran away and cried merely because a stranger was rude to her, then she had deserved it. Tears rolled down her face as she drowned in shame.

Isabel wouldn't have reacted like that. She would have just brushed it off. The story she'd told in her speech had been harrowing. When her boss had found out she was trying to unionize his workers right under his nose, he'd screamed at her and tried to fire her, and she had stood her ground and calmly reminded him that retaliation was illegal and he'd be sued for all he was worth. A grad student being rude to her would be nothing to her.

If anyone was upset with Mira for starting a conversation, that was their problem, Isabel had said. But it felt like Mira's problem. And Mira did have a problem. She was oversensitive—that was what Dylan had called her. Always overreacting to things. And she was proving him right.

She had been in the bathroom for a while. She reluctantly took out her phone to check the time.

Isabel had texted her half an hour ago. *Good luck today. You'll do great.*

A new wave of shame washed over Mira, and she started crying again. They never texted each other unless Mira locked herself out of the apartment or they were out of toilet paper. Isabel had gone out of her way during work to encourage her, and she had failed and let Isabel down.

It was worse than letting down the union. This was personal. Isabel had believed in her—she'd believed that Mira was capable of a fraction of what Isabel herself was capable of, and it turned out that Mira was not.

Some of us have real work to do. That had stung. Mira had work to do, too. She could have spent the afternoon catching up on grading, or preparing for class, or reading articles from the ever-increasing pile of journals that demanded her attention. But she felt too stupid and small to do any of those things now.

She would have to go home. She didn't want to run into Isabel, but with any luck, she wouldn't. She could go straight to her tiny room and cry in her bed. At least she wasn't trapped in Dylan's apartment anymore.

That was something to be grateful for. Enough that Mira gathered up her strength, dabbed her face with toilet paper, and left the stall so she could head home.

you make every day feel
more magical than the last.
I dont know what I did so
right in life to deserve
somebody as incredible, soft,
kind, beautiful, loving, thoughtful,
funny, etc... as you. but I'd
do it a million times over.
my life has never known so
much joy! I'm so in love with
you it fills every part of me
with gratitude. ♡ Cal

7

"Oh, hi," Mira said, coming through the door earlier than usual. She didn't seem happy about finding Isabel on the couch.

Isabel put down the mail she'd been sorting through. Mira's eyes were puffy, her makeup smudged. She looked bowed down by the overstuffed messenger bag she carried to work.

Isabel's anxiety spiked. If anything bad had happened to Mira, she wanted to know. She resisted the urge to rush to Mira, to ease that heavy bag off her shoulders. "You okay? How'd it go?"

Mira grimaced. "Not good."

"What happened?" Isabel said, too quickly. "Never mind. You don't have to tell me."

"Nothing too bad." Mira's voice was strained. "I didn't do a very good job. I only talked to two people. One of them was a little rude to me and I overreacted." Her face wobbled like she was about to cry.

Shit. Isabel wasn't good at this. She wanted to hunt down whoever had done this to Mira, but that wasn't going to help. At work, when younger women came to her crying, Isabel could usually help—backing them up when they reported whoever had wronged them, or getting into confrontations herself. But that wasn't an option now.

And part of her wanted to take Mira into her arms, to hold her tight, to protect her from every awful thing in the world. It wasn't a small part of her. It was overwhelming. But that was even less of an option.

Alexa had always been better at this. Comforting people, soothing their tears. What would she have done? "Do you want some tea?" Isabel said, desperate.

Mira blinked. "Sure. Thanks."

Isabel stood and nodded toward the dining table. "Sit down."

At least now she had something to do. Mira always made tea by dunking two or three black tea bags at a time in boiling water, and Isabel could do better than that. She filled the electric kettle with water, turned it on, and rummaged through the pantry until she found the good looseleaf black tea. After a moment's thought, she took the glass teapot from the highest shelf in the cupboard and tipped a mountain of tea leaves into the strainer. If Mira liked her tea strong, so be it.

She exhaled. The water started boiling, and the kettle shut off. She poured hot water into the teapot and carried it out, along with two mugs, and set it on a dish towel on the dining table.

She sat across from Mira with the teapot between them. The tea leaves unfurled in the water, turning it amber. Isabel had once given Alexa a teapot like this for her birthday—it was the kind of fancy, impractical thing her sister had liked. Then Isabel had grudgingly enjoyed using it on her visits so much that Alexa had given her the same teapot to tease her. Isabel hadn't used it in a very long time.

Mira sighed, interrupting Isabel's thoughts, which was for the best. She pushed a pile of her students' papers aside. "I know union organizing requires a thick skin. I just need to get better at it. It shouldn't matter so much what people say to me."

"You don't have to make excuses for people who are rude to you." It was an attempt at being comforting. But to Isabel's own ears, she just sounded brusque.

"I guess not." Mira sniffled, clearly unconvinced.

Mira was so crushed, and Isabel's heart was breaking, too. She was at a loss as to what to say. "Uh, be right back." She took the box of tissues from her bedroom and put it in front of Mira.

"Thank you." Mira's voice trembled. She took a tissue and blew her nose.

Isabel sat back down. "What happened?"

Mira eyed her nervously. Maybe Isabel was being overbearing. Mira hadn't said she wanted to talk. They were on decent terms as roommates, so Isabel hoped, but it didn't mean Mira trusted her.

But Isabel was the only person around. Sometimes you had to step up simply because you were there, no matter how inadequate and unprepared you were.

Mira recounted what had happened. "I'm so embarrassed." She dabbed at her face. "It wasn't a big deal. I'm just really oversensitive. Sorry for making you listen to all this."

Isabel tamped down the increasingly strong, futile urge to hold Mira and wipe her tears away. She had to say something. Never mind how bad she was at inspirational talk.

"Hey, don't apologize. You didn't do anything wrong. It's not okay for anyone to talk to you like that, all right?"

Mira said nothing. Isabel was in way over her head. "Uh, the tea's ready." She returned to the kitchen for milk and sugar. Mira liked plenty of both.

She poured tea for them. It was going to be too strong for Isabel, but that was fine. She pushed one steaming mug toward Mira, who poured in several glugs of milk, added a heaping spoonful of sugar, and took a drink. Her nails were plum today.

If Isabel couldn't close the distance between them, then this was all she could do. Make Mira a little warmer.

"Thank you," Mira said. "Oh, this tea is good. Anyway..." She sighed, her eyes downcast. "What you said. Maybe it's not okay, but he said it anyway, and there's nothing I can do about it. I just have to get over it."

"No, you don't." At that, Mira looked taken aback. "You don't, okay? You can be pissed off. I wouldn't let anyone talk like that to me."

Mira frowned. "That's the whole point. Of course you wouldn't. You would have done something other than apologize and run away, which is what I did, because I'm not like you." She sniffled. "You've dealt with so much worse and you've always been able to overcome it. I feel like such a coward."

Isabel's heart sank as she saw what Mira saw. She'd spent her whole life acting like nothing could get to her. She had been out and uncompromisingly butch since she was thirteen, and she was a construction worker. It was simply the price of living her life.

It was what the men she worked with saw, and the women, too. If Isabel ever shared any of her struggles with other women at work, it was calculated to encourage them, not demoralize them. Sometimes she forgot that she was acting at all.

And Mira had believed it. How could she not have? Isabel had kept up the act for her, like she did with everyone else. The only person who had known better was Alexa, and she was gone.

Isabel was exhausted. She had been propping herself up for so long.

She took a sip of tea. It was too bitter, almost undrinkable, which was what she needed. This wasn't about her. It was about Mira.

"You're not a coward," Isabel said. She was dead serious —she owed that to Mira—and she hoped Mira could see that. They'd never talked about the night they met, but it had been obvious how much it had cost Mira to leave her ex.

"I am." Mira sounded wretched. "I just want to give up. We're not going to get a contract until next year at the earliest, and hopefully that'll be my last year. Maybe second-to-last, at the rate my dissertation is going." Her gaze was still lowered. "I just want to keep my head down and let things happen. If we lose, so be it. I don't think that what I do in the union matters. They'll succeed or fail without me. Maybe that's not true for other people in it. It couldn't be true for you. But it's true for me."

Mira's demeanor could change in an instant. She was radiant when she let the fire inside her show, but now her flame had been snuffed out. Isabel's anger surged. Not at Mira, but at whatever had made her feel this way. "What the hell do you think I have that you don't?"

That startled Mira. "Everything," she said, as though it were obvious. "All the stories you told in your speech—I could never do any of that. And you stood up to Dylan when I couldn't even say anything because I was so afraid. And I was with him for two years in the first place because I was too scared to leave him. I just couldn't do it."

"You still broke up with him."

Mira gave her a defiant look, as though she couldn't believe Isabel was so dense. "He cheated on me. That was the clearest possible reason he could have given me. And I still..." Mira was crying now, speaking through sobs. "He kept texting me afterward. He was surprised I didn't run back to him. And I know why. Because I let him trample all over me the whole time we were together. And he wasn't totally wrong, because even after all that, I still second-guessed myself and thought about going back." Mira took a shuddering breath. "So pathetic."

"So you made a hard choice," Isabel said. Mira stared at her blankly. Isabel exhaled and rubbed her face. "It's not easy for me, either. I don't just pick myself back up every time someone says something to me or tries something. I told you all about the time the owner of the shop I was salting was cornering me in his office and screaming in my face, calling me..." Isabel shook her head. Mira didn't need to hear it.

Mira nodded. Isabel sighed again. "I had a brave face on while he screamed at me. But I cried in the porta-potty afterward. I couldn't let him or the other guys see." Admitting it made her gut twist like she was in free fall. "Some things just wear you down, and it never gets easier. The point is, you're not a coward just because you're scared."

Mira needed to hear something to keep her going, just this once. Isabel wasn't going to get into the habit of pouring her heart out.

"I guess so." Mira looked at her tea for a few seconds, her shoulders hunched, emotions flickering across her face that Isabel couldn't fully see. "Crying in a porta-potty sounds awful. Makes me feel grateful to be crying in a regular bathroom."

"Hey," Isabel said, "you don't have to compare yourself —" Mira looked back up, smiling faintly.

Isabel relaxed. They eased into a more comfortable silence. Then something occurred to her. "What you said earlier about being oversensitive. Did someone say that to you? Like your ex?"

Mira stiffened, and she nodded. She folded into herself, her light growing dim again.

Isabel didn't pick fights. She'd been in one real fight—not by choice—and had broken up a few others, and that had been enough. But part of her wished she'd really done something to make Dylan regret what he'd done to Mira.

"Fuck him," Isabel said. Mira gave her another small smile.

Isabel poured more tea for Mira, who added milk and sugar until it turned a light tan color, and they drank their tea together.

Mira deserved so much. She deserved to be free from her awful ex, and from the hold he still had over her. She deserved to be paid fairly and to not be overworked. She deserved a warm, safe apartment to come home to, and sweet milky tea whenever she wanted it, and every other small comfort and joy.

She deserved someone who would take care of her and treat her right. Someday she'd find the right man. Probably long after she moved out of Isabel's apartment. That was none of Isabel's business.

Mira broke the silence. "I just wish I had better news after you helped me."

"You're not doing this for me."

"I know. I'm doing it for myself, and all my coworkers." Mira hesitated. "I kept thinking, what would Isabel say? But I guess that's not... I don't have to do that."

"Don't. Look, they're your coworkers, and you know how to talk to them. You're smart. You can figure it out." Mira scoffed. Isabel went on. "Don't think about me. Forget everything I've told you, if that's what you need to do."

"I'm not going to do that. It was helpful."

Isabel shrugged. "You're a good listener. And you care about people when you talk to them. You're better at that than I ever was. I'm serious. Just keep doing that."

Mira groaned. "I don't know if I want to try again. And I know what you're going to say. If everyone thought this way, we'd never get anything done."

"You're saying it, not me." They shared a smile. "It's not enough to just win your election. You're always going to have to get together with your coworkers and fight to keep your rights. If you stop, your bosses are going to take back everything you've won."

"I know."

"You might as well make a habit of it now."

Mira's brows lifted slightly. "You're pretty persuasive."

"But don't listen to me," Isabel added. How had she gotten so swept up in this? "It's your life."

8

"BUT THE QUEEN, for a long time wounded by heavy trouble, feeds the wound by her veins and seizes... Is that right?"

"Almost," Mira said. This was Lauren's second ever Latin class, and she always needed a bit of reassurance during office hours. "You're doing great. Take a look at the verb ending again."

"Oh, it's passive. Right?" She looked at Mira, who nodded. "She's seized by a secret flame."

"That's right." It was a relief to slip into her teacher role, leaving her own problems behind for the time being. "Nice job translating those ablatives. Does anyone know what kind of ablative *venis* is?"

"Instrumental ablative," said Colin, to Lauren's right.

"Great, instrumental ablative. Dido feeds the wound with her veins. What does that mean? Lauren, do you know?"

"She's letting her love for Aeneas suck the blood out of her?" Lauren ventured.

"Perfect," Mira said. Lauren beamed.

A few more undergrads had come in, some of whom Mira didn't recognize. Word had gotten around, apparently, that she was the most helpful of the TAs for Latin Poetry, and students who weren't in her section were showing up. Mira didn't mind helping them, exactly, but she had her work cut out for her.

In fits and starts, the two dozen undergrads who drifted in and out of her office worked out Queen Dido's admiration of Aeneas, her reawakened desire, her rapidly weakening resolve to never marry again. The official end of office hours came and went. Mira stayed an extra ten minutes and then shooed most of the students out, feeling slightly guilty like she did every time.

Lauren was still working in a corner, mumbling as she traced the words on the page. "Lauren, I have to leave, unfortunately," Mira said. Lauren's head jerked up, and she scrambled to collect her things. "You don't have to rush," Mira added. "Great job today."

"Oh, thanks! Um..." Lauren looked sheepish. "I meant to talk to you sometime about whether I should be a Classics major. I'm a sophomore, so I kind of have to decide soon. Like, really soon. But I know you have to go."

Mira grabbed her messenger bag. "Do you have some time now?" Lauren nodded. "You can walk with me while I get lunch."

Lauren's face lit up. Mira was long used to it, but occasionally she was acutely reminded that her undergrads looked up to her as an authority figure. "That would be great," Lauren said. "I have to submit the form by Friday, and I'm having trouble deciding. Are you sure it's okay?"

"Of course." It would be better than dwelling on her own anxieties. Mira was good at being a reassuring TA, if nothing else. "I'd be happy to talk."

They headed toward the food trucks. Lauren explained her situation. Her parents wanted her to major in pre-med, and she was dutifully taking her science classes. But she'd taken Greek and Roman Mythology to fulfill a requirement, and it had lit a fire in her. She'd gotten a glimpse into an ancient world, full of people who were alien yet familiar in their passions and fears and hopes, and she wanted more.

She had been intent on reading Virgil and Ovid in the original, and she'd worked harder in her Intro Latin class than she ever had in her life. Now she was taking Latin Poetry, Intro Ancient Greek, and two science classes, which was unsustainable. It was time to choose.

"Did you have to decide between Classics and something more 'practical'?" Lauren made air quotes.

Mira pursed her lips. So much for avoiding the subject of her own life. Still, she would do what she could for Lauren. "Not exactly. My parents didn't mind me becoming an academic, so I didn't have to worry about that." They would have objected far more to Mira becoming an investment banker. "And I was dreadful at math, so most of the practical majors were out of the question anyway." Lauren laughed politely. "But I thought I could be equally happy in philosophy or literature or history. And then I took my first Latin class as a freshman, like you, and that's when I knew."

"Oh, that's good. Sometimes I worry that I started too late."

"You didn't. You're doing great, okay?" Lauren was clearly hanging on her every word. "Learning to read poetry is a big step up from the intro class. It's been wonderful to see your progress."

They lined up at the food trucks, which didn't serve up anything fancy. Just hot meals for broke grad students who showed up reliably at lunchtime. "We can keep talking, if you want to stick around for lunch," Mira said.

Lauren looked delighted, like she was being let in on something. "Oh, sure! I'd love to."

Mira had had TAs and professors in college that she'd admired, brilliant women who didn't let Mira get away with anything less than her best work. Mira wouldn't be herself without them. When she'd imagined her own future, she hadn't only seen herself as an academic, but as a woman, too —finding her own path in academia, as murky and frightening as that vision was.

The thought of an undergrad seeing *her* that way, as not only authoritative but aspirational, was vertigo-inducing. Mira hoped she was worthy of it.

She ordered the tofu and eggplant with a side of stir-fried cabbage, and Lauren ordered the exact same thing. They took their food to the benches nearby. "What do you think I should do?" Lauren said.

Mira was in no position to give advice to anyone. What was she doing with her Classics degree? She was scraping by on her grad school stipend and living in a tiny room, and last week she'd humiliated herself on campus and cried her eyes out in front of her roommate. And Isabel hadn't humiliated her a second time; she'd been as blunt and as kind to Mira as on the night they'd met, and she'd helped Mira put herself back together. Mira hadn't stopped thinking about it since. She could barely make sense of her own life anymore.

Maybe becoming a doctor was the safer move. "You could get a minor in Classics instead," she said weakly. "It would be easier to keep up with your pre-med classes."

"I know. But the thing is, I don't know if I want to do pre-med at all. I don't want to take the required classes. I don't think I actually want to be a doctor." Lauren paused ominously. "Do you think I have any chance of getting into grad school if I keep working hard?"

"Oh, absolutely," Mira said. That much wasn't in doubt. "I think if you continue at this rate, and start developing your own research interests and write a strong senior thesis, a lot of grad programs would be fortunate to have you. The real question is whether you actually want to go to grad school. And that's a decision you shouldn't take lightly."

It became clear that Lauren had no idea what grad school was like. Mira tried to explain that after six or seven or ten grueling years of a Ph.D. program, a tenure-track academic job was by no means guaranteed; that most universities didn't pay their grad students nearly enough; that the teaching burden could be nearly unbearable; that one's professional life and future prospects were dictated almost entirely by one's advisor, who could be negligent or abusive. Lauren looked at her wide-eyed.

"I don't mean to scare you off," Mira said, even though she had meant exactly that. "I'm fortunate to be able to study what I love and to teach all of you. Just think about it carefully."

"Is that why you're all unionizing?"

"For those and many other reasons, yes." Mira smiled. "Try to pick a place where the grad students are unionized, if you can. Hopefully, by the time you apply, that'll be everywhere."

Guilt crept up on her. If she didn't do her part, she had no right to be saying this to Lauren. And she was angry— angry that she couldn't wholeheartedly tell one of her brightest students to pursue a life studying what she wanted, and instead had to warn her away.

Mira hadn't had an easy time in grad school; even so, she'd been lucky in so many ways. But luck shouldn't enter into it at all. She had to make a better future for her students.

And maybe she owed something to the twenty-year-old Mira who'd been on the cusp of taking so many big risks, and who had deserved a better future than moving in with Dylan out of desperation. Maybe her present self deserved a better future, too.

They talked more about Lauren's aspirations, what classes she wanted to take, how she might win over her parents. Mira explained her own research on the lyric poets. Lauren asked, "Can I study that in grad school too?"

Back in her office, Mira pulled up the spreadsheet for canvassing grad students about the union. The slot for the Classics building was open this time, thank goodness.

She could do this. Her despair from Friday had receded, and now she could take a longer view.

Isabel had told her that she needed to find her own way of doing things. Mira knew how to talk to people. She'd spent all morning doing it: listening to her students, building trust with them where she could, not worrying too much if they didn't pay attention. She'd been doing this for years. And one bad day didn't count for much—she still had most of her working life in front of her. Mira signed up.

9

Isabel woke up, before her alarm, to a strip of light under her bedroom door. Waking up early was normal these days, now that she wasn't exhausted every night. The light being on in the living room was not.

She got out of bed, stretched, and opened the door. Mira was sitting at the dining table, slightly slumped to the side. Her eyes were closed, long lashes resting on her cheeks, and her chunky glasses sat crooked on her face. Isabel's concern flared for a moment. But there'd been no need—Mira had dozed off while working.

She looked like a wilted flower. Isabel was struck by a pang of tenderness so intense it hurt. She wanted to carry Mira to that narrow bed of hers and let her sleep.

Mira stirred. She opened her eyes, saw Isabel, and yelped. Isabel winced. She should have just woken up Mira right away.

"Sorry," Mira said, for some reason. Her voice was blurry from sleep. She took her glasses off and rubbed her eyes. "Did I wake you up? What time is it?"

"It's four," Isabel said, self-conscious. "I usually get up around now."

"Huh? Oh, it's late."

Isabel nodded, feeling ungainly in her own living room. Early mornings were *her* time—the city outside was as quiet as it ever was, and she could go about her routine in peace. She was used to Mira's presence, and used to keeping her emotions on a tight leash. But having to share her sacrosanct morning hours with Mira was throwing her off. That, and the guilt from watching Mira sleep for a second too long.

Mira yawned, stretched her arms, and grimaced. Her movements were stiff, probably from being hunched over for hours. "I remember looking at the clock at three. So it's only been an hour."

Isabel walked to the drip coffee maker and got it started. It was something to do other than staring uselessly at the beautiful, rumpled girl in her living room. Her coffee maker had plenty of bells and whistles and had cost a fortune. Isabel had bought it when she turned out as a journey-woman, and she was going to depend on that thing for the rest of her working life. "Did you have to work late or some-thing?" she asked, with her back to Mira.

"Well, I was going to finish these earlier today, but—what did I—oh, yeah. I spent the afternoon in the grad student lounge, talking to people about the union. I got two more people to sign cards."

"Hey, that's great." Isabel had some time before she had to get going, and her coffee wouldn't be ready for a few minutes. Did Mira want to talk? After their conversation last week, Isabel had no idea where they stood. She wasn't used to second-guessing herself like this.

She sat down at the table across from Mira before she could talk herself out of it. "How'd it go?"

It had gone well. Not only had Mira persuaded two people to sign cards, but one of them had asked Mira about attending the weekly meetings. She'd met a first-year who was still on the fence, but they'd had a good conversation. Nobody had been rude to her. They were four hundred cards away from their goal. Mira was talkative this early in the morning—or, for her, late at night—and clearly proud of what she'd done.

"Two fewer cards left to go now," Isabel said.

"I don't think I could have done it if it weren't for what you said to me last week."

Isabel glowed with warmth. She'd managed to be help-ful. She shrugged. "You're the one doing the work."

"Well, what you said about finding my own way to do things—I think I needed to hear that." Mira smiled. "Do you mind if I ask you a favor?"

"Any time."

"Could I have some of the coffee you're making?"

Isabel couldn't help smiling back. "Sure. Are you sure you want it?" The fantasy of carrying Mira to bed and tucking her in returned in full force. Mira's blouse was wrinkled, and it couldn't have been comfortable to doze off in. She deserved some real rest.

Mira halfheartedly picked up a paper and set it down. "I have five more of these. It'll take me at least another hour at this rate."

"Then sleep for a few hours and do it when you wake up."

"I guess you're right. It wouldn't be a fun day if I had to teach without any real sleep." Mira looked glumly at the papers again. "Sometimes I feel like I'm always either working or avoiding work, and I never get a break. And the more I feel that way, the more burned out I get and the slower I work. It's setting in much earlier than usual this semester. Probably because my whole life fell apart, and I had to move and start over." She sighed. "Anyway, I'm sure it's different for you."

"Well, I can't dig trenches and run conduit at home." But Isabel knew what it was like to overwork herself to the brink of collapse. If her body hadn't given out, she might still be doing it. And coming home to an empty apartment every night, with no Mira. "I used to work overtime a lot, though. I wrecked my knee doing it." Maybe it wasn't the worst thing to talk more about her own life. To be friendly.

Mira frowned. "How is it now? Is it better?"

Maybe it wasn't the worst thing to have someone concerned for her, either. "More or less. As long as I don't keep working too much."

"The apartment stairs don't bother you?"

"It takes a lot more than that. I'm fine."

"That's good. I'm lucky that I don't have to do anything harder than carry boxes of exams around." Mira didn't sound like she felt lucky. She rubbed her face. "I'm so tired."

"Take a day off next weekend."

Mira glanced at her pile of papers. "I don't know if I could make myself do it. I'd feel so guilty about not working."

Isabel knew that feeling, too. "Tell yourself you'll get back to it the next day. Your students will live."

"You're right. Ugh. My work isn't that important in the grand scheme of things."

"Your work is important," Isabel said with finality. Mira looked startled. "Don't say that it isn't. Just take a break." She had sounded more brusque than she'd meant to. In the silence that followed, she said, "You been to Astoria Park yet? By the river?"

Mira shook her head. "I haven't had time."

"You should go out and see it. I'll show you around if you want." Isabel's words caught up to her. Why on earth had she offered that? Maybe just to fill up space in the conversation, which she usually felt no need to do. Maybe because she had nothing else to do when she wasn't working.

Maybe because she was lonely. But Mira didn't need Isabel for finding her way around a park.

Mira seemed surprised. "That's kind of you to offer."

"You don't have to go. But it's nice." The park was a slice of green space on the East River, too rare around these parts. And Isabel loved the neighborhood. Hopefully she could stay after her lease on this place ended.

"Actually, I'd love to have you show me around, if you're not busy."

Isabel wasn't busy. She had a dead older sister, and a younger sister who hadn't spoken to her in months, and an ex who had chosen to move across the country rather than live with her miserable wreck of a partner for a second longer, and a sister-in-law who said she was "worried," and friends she didn't talk to anymore because they didn't know what it was like to lose the only person who had ever truly understood you. "Yeah, I'll be around."

Mira smiled sweetly. "I'm looking forward to it."

The coffee maker beeped, shaking Isabel from her thoughts. She'd gotten carried away. In the in-between hours of the morning, anything seemed possible, like Mira trusting her, like the two of them getting close. She needed to get a grip.

She got up and returned with a steaming mug of black coffee. Mira groaned. At that, heat rushed through Isabel's entire body, followed by a wave of guilt. "It smells so good," Mira said. "You're tempting me."

Isabel took a panicked, hasty sip, scalding the inside of her mouth. The pain made her wince. If that was what she needed to control herself, so be it. "Do you really want it? I can make you some decaf."

Mira gave her a stern look, her elegant eyebrows arching. "That defeats the purpose." She looked down at the paper in front of her, unenthusiastic about continuing. Then she stretched, letting out a soft, breathy moan as she winced. Isabel was *not* going to think about giving her a back rub, easing the knots in her back and making her moan like that again. Mira continued, "I'll just finish this one and go to sleep."

"I'll stop distracting you." Isabel uncrossed her arms and sat up, but she didn't stand. She was getting deeper into trouble.

"No, it's okay." Mira's gaze darted down. Isabel was suddenly very aware that she wasn't wearing a bra under her thin white T-shirt. And Mira was staring at her breasts.

Isabel went hot all over. She was really in trouble. Women had eye-fucked her at bars with more subtlety than this. The difference was that Mira seemed to be doing it unintentionally, her big, dark, curious eyes roaming slowly over Isabel's body, her soft mouth falling open.

It could mean something or nothing at all. But Isabel had to put a stop to it, or else she'd combust. Her nipples were painfully sensitive against her T-shirt, and her pulse pounded between her legs. It had been so long since her body wanted *anything*, and this was far too much, far too soon.

She could carry Mira to bed and get in with her. She couldn't—but her craving was a physical ache, sharp and unbearable. She could free Mira from that constricting blouse. She could strip off her own T-shirt and let Mira do more than just look—

Her alarm in her bedroom rang, and they both jolted in their chairs, Isabel bumping the table so hard that her coffee sloshed over the rim of her mug. It spilled onto the paper Mira was grading. "Shit," Isabel said. She scrambled to stand. "Sorry."

Mira looked at Isabel's face, then at the paper and the rapidly spreading coffee stain. Like she was only now remembering where she was. "Oh."

Isabel grabbed the paper towels from the kitchen and started blotting the stain. The alarm was still beeping, and it sounded ten times louder than usual. "Sorry, sorry," she said, feeling like she was apologizing for more than just spilling her coffee.

"It's okay." Mira was still dazed. "It wouldn't be the first time that's happened."

Isabel cleaned up as much as she could and threw the used paper towels in the trash. She rushed to her bedroom and shut the alarm off, ran a hand through her hair, and took a deep breath. What the hell was happening to her?

Mira could look if she wanted. Straight girls had a right to be curious, or however they felt. Isabel was a big butch lesbian who stuck out like a five-foot-eleven sore thumb wherever she went. Women, including straight ones, had all kinds of reactions to her: disdain, admiration, revulsion, desire. It wasn't her problem what other people thought of her.

What *was* her problem was that she was uncontrollably attracted to her roommate, who was straight, and skittish, and sleeping in the room that Isabel's ex used to paint in. And absolutely, unquestionably off-limits.

Isabel would just have to control herself. She had less than zero patience for any man who felt attracted to a woman and blamed her for it, and she wasn't a hypocrite. She was an adult with self-control and not a fucking creep.

It was almost November. She could endure living with Mira for two more months. Now that her alarm had gone off, she needed to hurry. She headed out of her room again to brush her teeth.

"I'm done with this one," Mira said, still sitting at the table. Isabel stopped in her tracks despite herself. Mira set her student's paper aside, and her gaze roamed downward again.

Right. Isabel was wearing the boxer shorts she slept in. They weren't revealing enough that she'd thought twice about walking around in them. But they still showed plenty of thigh, and Mira was thoroughly looking her over. It was even clearer that Mira was doing this with no self-awareness. No one in their right mind would try to flirt right now, when they were both frazzled and Isabel was rushing to work.

"You should go to sleep," Isabel said. She hurried to the bathroom.

When she returned, Mira was thankfully gone. Isabel finished off her mug of coffee in a few gulps, poured the rest of the coffee into her thermos, and got dressed.

She was rushing more than she had to. There was time to grind more coffee and make a new pot for when Mira woke up. She was pressing buttons on the coffee maker when Mira's door opened.

Mira stood in the doorway in a lacy pink camisole and a tiny pair of matching shorts. The fabric skimmed the soft swells of her breasts and let just a hint of her nipples show through. And those long legs, those lush thighs, all that bare skin... Isabel flushed, her heart pounding, desire piercing her like a red-hot poker.

"Oh!" Mira said. "You're still here."

Isabel tried to look nonchalant as she stared at a spot above Mira's head. She wasn't going to make Mira uncomfortable in her own home. She wasn't going to think about how Mira had been sleeping in that frilly pajama set all this time, right on the other side of the wall.

"I'm heading out," Isabel said, her voice strained. She turned back to the coffee maker and fumbled with the buttons. "I'm just, uh, I'm making coffee for when you wake up."

"Oh, you're so sweet," Mira said. "You didn't have to. Thank you."

Isabel shrugged. She didn't turn around. Mira walked behind her to head to the bathroom. "Have a nice day at work."

"You too," Isabel said, a second too late because she'd forgotten how to speak.

She laced up her work boots, grabbed her backpack, and left the apartment. Outside, she inhaled a lungful of cold morning air and exhaled in relief.

She tightened her jaw as she walked to the train, passing the occasional person getting off the late shift or starting the work day like her. She wasn't going to think about Mira sleeping under the covers in that tiny room, getting some much-needed rest. She wasn't going to think about crawling into that twin bed next to Mira and holding her close, about kissing her good night, about making breakfast for when she woke up. She wasn't going to think about slipping the straps of Mira's camisole off her shoulders, sliding those little shorts down over her hips...

Isabel dug her short nails into her palms. None of that would ever happen.

Two more months.

She was going to ignore the treacherous voice in her head saying that there was more to Mira's gaze than passing curiosity. That if Mira wanted her and she wanted Mira, then there was a chance. That unlike everything else in her life in the past two years, this would end in something other than her being left desolate and alone.

10

MIRA YAWNED and stretched in the open doorway to her bedroom. How long had it been since she'd slept in on a weekend? She'd needed that. The late morning sun filled the living room, making her squint. And Isabel was sitting on the couch, looking right at her.

"Oh!" Mira said, self-conscious. She was still in her pajamas and disheveled from sleep. "I didn't see you there. Good morning." The hem of her camisole had ridden up, exposing her stomach, and she tried to be inconspicuous in tugging it back down. Hopefully Isabel didn't think she was a total slob. "Do you still want to walk to the park? I hope I didn't keep you waiting." They'd settled on going in the morning, but Isabel probably had an earlier definition of *morning*.

Isabel looked down at the book in her lap. "It's fine. I'm ready when you are. Take your time."

Dressed, with some coffee in her, Mira set out with Isabel. The air was crisp, the sky a gorgeous clear blue. Isabel was wearing her leather jacket and moving with the same quiet self-assurance as on the night they'd met.

The memory of being wrapped up in that jacket had lingered with Mira. The weight and warmth of it over her dress, and how safe she'd felt for those few minutes.

Were the two of them friends? Mira didn't know where they stood. For two people who didn't talk much, they saw plenty of each other's lives. A few days ago, she had seen Isabel at four in the morning in nothing but a well-worn T-shirt and boxers, bleary before her coffee, her hair mussed from sleep. It had been nothing out of the ordinary, but Mira had kept replaying the moment in her mind, marveling at how big, tough Isabel could be so exposed and soft.

Mira had feared an awkward, silent walk. She'd had nothing to worry about. Isabel seemed at ease, walking at a leisurely pace, not forcing Mira to work to keep up this time. She pointed out a landmark on every block: the dive bar, the "good" hardware store, the Greek Orthodox church decorated with mosaics. A new apartment building that Isabel had worked on. "Shortest commute I ever had," she said. They passed an eyebrow threading salon—Mira would have to come back and see if it was any good.

Dry leaves crunched as they walked. The sidewalks were busy: There were joggers, clumps of teenagers, parents pushing strollers, grannies pushing grocery carts. An orange cat casually emerged from a bodega, and Isabel crouched down.

"She's friendly," Isabel said, clearly acquainted with the cat, who only had one eye. Mira bent down next to her. Isabel was stroking the cat's sleek fur, smiling faintly. Mira held her hand out, and the cat investigated and nuzzled Mira's hand. She was, technically, allergic to cats, but it never stopped her from petting them.

"She's so sweet," Mira said, charmed by the cat and

even more so by Isabel's tenderness. Isabel glanced at her, and the corner of her mouth quirked up.

Something about the way Isabel was crouched reminded Mira of a big cat, too: languid, powerful, not entirely domesticated. Dangerous in the right circumstances, like she'd been to Dylan and his friends. Her strong thighs were straining against her jeans—Mira had seen them bare the other night. Before that, she hadn't thought much about what a decade of physical labor would look like on a woman's body.

The cat—the small one—strolled back into the bodega. Isabel stood back up in one easy motion, and they continued on their way.

They approached the park. The leaves were blazing red and orange, and the late-autumn sun was bright. Despite the chill, a brave group was having a kids' birthday party, their banners flapping in the wind. In the distance was the East River, and then the Manhattan skyline.

"Oh, it's lovely," Mira said. They started down a tree-lined path toward the river, passing joggers and dogs on leashes. "Have you been in this neighborhood for a while?" Isabel had obviously put down roots here. It seemed incongruous with how much she liked being alone.

"I guess so," Isabel said. "I moved here five years ago, but I've been in Queens my whole life."

So Isabel was a lifelong New Yorker. Isabel was so sparing with information, and it made Mira want to collect every last bit of it and piece it all together. Isabel had lived with her ex in that apartment. Had they both lived there from the start? If they had broken up less than a year ago, they'd lived together for four years.

Mira couldn't ask about it, but her heart ached for Isabel. And there were other questions that were even more off-limits: Was Isabel heartbroken? Was she seeing anyone new? Did she want to?

The idea of Isabel being tender with someone, anyone, made Mira's stomach swoop like she was falling. It was too easy to imagine: Isabel taking a woman in her powerful arms, dipping her backward—the other woman would probably be shorter—and kissing her passionately, like a rugged hero in a classic film. What kinds of women did Isabel like? Did she have a type?

A couple was setting up for a picnic in the grass nearby. Mira felt a traitorous stab of longing. Being single was exactly what she needed. Even thinking about being trapped in a relationship again made her throat constrict. But in her two years with Dylan, he'd never done something so simple as laugh with her while trying to spread out a blanket in the park.

They reached the sidewalk along the river. It was windy, and sunlight glittered on the water.

"This is such a lovely neighborhood," Mira said, meaning it. She hadn't made any attempt at getting to know where she lived. After all, she would be moving again in a few months, and she was as likely to end up here as anywhere else. But in a fifteen-minute walk, she already felt more at home than she ever had in Dylan's neighborhood, with its endless boutiques and tourists. "I can see why you moved here. Maybe I'll try to stay in the area after your lease ends."

Just one more move. This one, hopefully, would be less stressful than moving from Vivian's couch, and less traumatic than collecting all her things from Dylan's apartment while he loomed over her, only barely restraining himself because Vivian was glaring at him with homicidal intent.

"Yeah, me too," Isabel said. How did Isabel feel about

moving out of her home for the last five years? Another question Mira would never know the answer to. "Where'd you live before this?"

Mira told her the neighborhood. "With my ex," she added.

"Sorry. Didn't mean to bring that up."

A happy running toddler weaved past them, and then another, followed by their parents. "No, it's okay. Although I'd rather be here, that's for sure."

"I worked on some of the high-rises going up along the old waterfront there." Isabel shrugged. "Nice view, if you can afford it."

"I lived in one of those." Isabel's eyebrows lifted. Mira, after all, was just a broke grad student. "Dylan had a condo. His parents were rich and he got his big break with his novel."

Isabel remained silent. Mira flushed. Was Isabel judging her?

She knew what it looked like. She'd been taken care of by her rich boyfriend. What was there to complain about? Isabel had had the worst possible first impression of him, but maybe she was changing her mind. "I mean, I did pay for half the utilities and groceries and some other things," Mira rushed to add. "But I never really felt like it was my home. It was his condo, and almost everything in it was his, even though I was always cleaning up after him. But on the bright side, not having anything meant that it was easy to move out after I dumped him, at least."

Hopefully she could change the subject now. Isabel's unreadable reaction made her anxious.

"You weren't paying any rent before you moved here?" Isabel said.

"No, I wasn't." This was bewildering. Was Isabel actually taking his side?

Isabel opened her mouth and closed it. Finally, she said, "Is it hard for you to pay rent? I mean, if it's too much. Because I figured—"

"What are you saying?" That came out more sharply than Mira had intended.

Isabel was startled out of her usual impassive expression. "I don't like the idea of you paying more than you can afford when you're getting started on your own again." She hesitated. "I thought if it was too much, you could pay less."

"No. That's okay." Maybe Isabel wasn't chastising her for being a kept woman, but the relief didn't come. Isabel didn't like the *idea* of it, as though the shape of Mira's life were up to Isabel to decide. "Thanks, but I don't need your help."

She took a breath and tried to calm down, to stop being so oversensitive. She shouldn't have brought up living with Dylan. It was never going to end well, and she was ruining their outing. God knew what Isabel thought of her now. "Sorry. It's kind of you. But there are so many other people who have it worse, and you don't need to help me."

"I just meant..." Isabel ran a hand through her long, thick hair, stirred up by the breeze from the water. "I just want to make things fair. If you're struggling—"

"I'm not." This was untrue in any sense of the term, but it didn't matter. "It's not fair that either of us, or anyone, has to pay this much money just to have a place to live. But I can take care of myself." She had to stay calm and reasonable. She had to suppress the rising tide of anger.

"I didn't mean to say you couldn't."

"Then what did you mean?"

"Things are easier for me financially. That's all I meant."

Anger crashed over Mira in a wave, and with it came the undertow of shame. Isabel was financially secure, strong, and in control of her life, and Mira wasn't any of those things. Isabel could be benevolent from on high, and Mira would remain where she was, struggling and vulnerable and grateful.

That had been how Isabel had viewed her all along. Mira couldn't be her equal or her friend. It was the truth, but Mira didn't want the reminder of it. "I don't need your charity."

"I didn't mean—" Isabel cut herself off. "Forget I said anything."

Mira sighed. The anger was draining from her, leaving behind hollowness and regret. Isabel was clearly being sincere. And a bit of extra money in her bank account every month would make a difference; a lot of her savings had gone toward buying new things after the move. Maybe it had been stupid to say no. But Isabel was already undercharging her, even though they'd never acknowledged it, and she was uneasy enough about that.

There was nothing wrong with Isabel's offer that Mira could articulate. But she was sick of being so powerless that even her roommate noticed and offered to help. She'd been feeling good about her union organizing, about getting her life back in order. But as long as she wasn't making more money, she'd be stuck where she was.

"I'm sorry," Mira said. Her jaw and shoulders were tight. She couldn't afford to get visibly angry. She knew how she'd come off to Isabel and all the passersby: aggressive, hysterical, threatening.

Isabel shook her head. "It's fine. I shouldn't have said anything."

"It really is kind of you to offer. But I don't need it. I managed to save some money while I was living with Dylan. And it helps to not be living in an expensive neighborhood and having to keep up with someone's rising literary star lifestyle." These days, thinking of her past life with Dylan was like recalling a surreal nightmare. "And, you know, it's not just me. This is how it is for a lot of us grad students, or at least the ones who aren't supported by their families. That's why we're trying so hard to unionize."

Isabel nodded. "Look, it's your business. I shouldn't have jumped to offering that." She ran a hand through her hair again. Mira realized, suddenly, that what she'd thought of as a suave gesture was something Isabel did when she was nervous. "Sorry."

"Thanks. I appreciate that." It was time to move on, before Isabel got the idea that Mira was unreasonable and difficult and that she'd had it coming to her. "I'm sorry I was"—she almost said *oversensitive*—"rude about it to you." She took another deep breath, trying to release the tension choking her. "This breakup has been hard on me."

It wasn't really the breakup. That had been the only good part. But she didn't want to elaborate.

"It's fine," Isabel said. "I met him. You don't need to explain."

That soothed Mira's nerves a little, even if she couldn't expect Isabel to fully understand. In Dylan's circles, a brilliant, brooding literary star could get away with anything. But Isabel hadn't known that version of him, and even if she had, she wouldn't have cared.

They kept walking in a strained silence. Finally, Mira said, "I can explain more. If you want me to." Isabel seemed willing to let this go. But Mira so rarely got to speak for herself on her own terms. She wanted to try, for once, instead of letting Isabel assume the worst about her.

A car drove by, blasting a pop song. After it passed, Isabel said, "Can I take you out to lunch? You can do it then. It's on me. I mean—" Isabel stopped mid-sentence.

Mira huffed a laugh. "Let's split it, okay?" She didn't have much room in her budget to go out for lunch. But she wasn't going to let Isabel pay for her.

Isabel was silent for a few moments. "You got anything in mind?"

"No."

"Let's go to the halal cart. It's nearby." Mira was relieved. That had been a calculation on Isabel's part, picking somewhere inexpensive without drawing attention to it. "We can talk in the park. It's nice out here."

11

THANK god for the halal cart next to the park. On their walk, Isabel had led Mira past half a dozen restaurants where she'd regularly gone with Reina. That was the thing about being dumped after a relationship of six years and staying right where you were.

Sometimes she envied Reina, who was all the way across the country at her artists' retreat in California. Free from her old life, free from the partner who couldn't be what she needed.

It wasn't that Isabel missed her ex, or that whatever happy memories she had remaining would overwhelm her. But today, of all days, she didn't want her surroundings to remind her of her failures.

Still tense, they unwrapped their pita sandwiches on a bench: shawarma for Isabel, falafel for Mira. "I moved in with Dylan because my landlord raised the rent on my windowless bedroom, and my stipend was so low that I couldn't afford to live there anymore," Mira began, looking out at the river. "At that point, we'd only been dating for a few months. He was a few years older and had a fancy condo, and I thought— I mean, I wasn't stupid. I had some idea of what it would mean for me to live with him. But compared to the alternative of scrambling to find an even worse apartment, it still felt like he was rescuing me."

Mira met Isabel's gaze. She seemed hesitant, but defiance burned in her eyes, too. She was daring Isabel to pity or condemn her. "He wasn't openly abusive to me. Not in an obvious way I could point to at the time. But I knew we weren't equal partners who happened to make different amounts of money. I was there on his largesse. And I felt like I had to be grateful, and to give him everything he wanted because I was indebted to him."

Mira was crumpling a napkin in her lap. Isabel had known Mira was angry. How could anyone not be? But in that moment, it was painfully clear how much anger Mira was holding onto, and how much it was killing her to hide it.

Isabel knew all about being angry at how the world treated you. She'd always been loud about it, and she couldn't hold back even if she tried. Mira's life was different and harder. But they had something in common, and that shared understanding went beyond words.

Isabel nodded. All she could do was stay quiet and let Mira say what she needed.

"He never said it overtly, either, so I felt like I was crazy for even thinking that there was something wrong." Mira's expression was unnaturally calm. "It only really came out when we fought. That's not really the right word. When he got angry at me, and I tried to stand up for myself at all. He'd say, 'What else are you going to do?' After hearing that two or three times, even if he pretended he didn't mean it later, I got the message." Mira took a shaky breath. "Who else was going to pay for my healthcare? Where else would I live?"

"My god, Mira." What was there for Isabel to say? "That's... I'm sorry. That's not right."

She wanted to find Dylan and throw him out his expensive floor-to-ceiling window into the East River. But her fury was mingled with guilt. She shouldn't have needed Mira to spell it out for her. A woman moving into a man's apartment because she couldn't afford rent usually wasn't a happy story. And when Mira had told her in the park, all Isabel had thought about was barging into Mira's business. Rescuing her, like her ex had pretended to do.

Had Mira ever seen anything good in Dylan? Or had she just been doing what she needed to do? Either way, Isabel wasn't judging. But if Mira had loved him even a little, if she'd hoped for something better and been let down... The thought broke Isabel's heart.

"No, it wasn't right," Mira said, echoing Isabel's words. She still sounded too calm, but the set of her jaw and the stiffness of her shoulders made it clear she was boiling with anger. "The truth is, I was relieved when I caught him cheating on me, because I finally had a good reason to leave him." She looked straight at Isabel, her defiance returning. "Even if I had no idea where I was going to go, or how I was going to be on my own. At least I didn't have to be with him anymore."

Isabel nodded. Mira was braver and stronger than she knew. Truthfully, she was even braver and stronger than Isabel had known from the start. And Mira had held on to her softness and her sympathy all this time, which made her even more remarkable. But she never should have needed to endure so much in the first place. Isabel wanted to rip the world apart for her.

"I don't know if he acknowledged to himself what he was doing," Mira continued. "Maybe he deluded himself into thinking that I didn't mind the power imbalance between us, and I just wanted to be his perfect, docile girlfriend who always did what he wanted and never inconvenienced him or had any needs of my own. And that's why he was so angry when I left him, like he thought I loved him so much I'd put up with anything." Mira's voice shook. "I wonder about it sometimes. Whether he knew how much he had taken from me."

The words rang in the space between them. "Christ, Mira. I'm so fucking sorry. That's awful." Isabel rubbed her face. "I— My god. He didn't deserve you. You didn't deserve that, is what I meant."

Mira looked down at her sandwich, still uneaten. "Thank you," she said faintly.

"I'm sorry for offering to..." There was nothing Isabel could say that was close to adequate, even if she hadn't known. "Sorry."

It was unbelievably selfish, after Mira had confided in her, for Isabel to even spend a second thinking about what this meant for *her*. But over the last week, she'd been nursing daydreams about Mira, knowing full well that they were impossible—that Mira might discover that she liked women, that Mira could return her feelings, that they could have a future together.

As though Mira would ever want anything more from Isabel while living in her spare bedroom out of necessity. She imagined herself in Mira's position: running from your abusive ex and finding out that the person who'd offered you a cheap spare room had been lusting after you, too. The thought of putting Mira in that position made her sick.

It wasn't as though she would have tried anything. Mira was straight, after all. But Isabel was going to have to be much more careful. No more letting her gaze linger too long. No more letting her guard down.

No more idle daydreaming. No more thinking about how if Mira lived with her as *her* girlfriend, she would treat Mira like a princess, protecting her and doting on her and giving her everything she wanted and needed. Isabel dug her fingernails into her palms. Someone was going to do all that for Mira someday, if there was any fairness in the world, and it was not going to be Isabel.

"It's all right," Mira said. "I told you it wasn't really about you." She hesitated. "Could I ask you something?"

"Go ahead."

"When we met, you said you needed a roommate to cover rent, or else you couldn't afford to live here anymore. So when you offered— To be honest, it's obvious that you're already undercharging me for the room. So I don't understand how you could have offered me an even bigger discount. I thought you didn't want a roommate in the first place."

Mira was suspicious and trying to be polite. Isabel said, "It's true. I wasn't lying when I told you that. It's nothing personal, I just meant..."

Mira smiled thinly. "It's okay. I don't think many people have roommates solely for the sake of it."

"I didn't know how I would afford it." Isabel shrugged. "I wasn't really thinking. I just had the idea. I'm close to spending my whole paycheck every month, but I could have used some of my savings."

"Really?" Mira said immediately. Then she winced. "I'm sorry. Please don't answer that. I don't mean to pry."

Mira's surprise was understandable. Isabel obviously wasn't living it up. "I help my parents and grandmother with their mortgage payments, and my little sister's wedding is coming up. So it's a little tight right now." The truth was that she'd set some money aside for Grace, but as long as Grace wasn't speaking to her, there was no way for Isabel to offer.

"You're paying for your parents' *and* your grandparents' houses?"

"My mom's mom lives with my parents. Alexa and I saved enough for the down payment for the house, and the plan was that we'd both help them with the mortgage payments." There was a deep well of pain underneath those simple facts. Isabel couldn't fall in, not right now.

Mira's gaze was gentle. "It sounds like you're a really good daughter. And sister."

Hearing that from Mira meant more than it should. Isabel's chest ached. She wanted to believe those words. She wasn't sure if she could.

Mira took a bite of her sandwich, letting Isabel remain in her silence. "Oh, it's good," Mira said. "Thanks for tipping me off about this cart. I'll have to come back."

Isabel smiled, the weight of grief lifting slightly. "No problem." After what Mira had told her today, it was nice to see her enjoying something, no matter how small. Even if Mira's happiness wasn't any of Isabel's business.

They ate in silence for a few minutes. Then Mira said, "I appreciate you explaining that to me."

"Explaining what?"

"When you offered to help me with rent, I didn't understand what was happening. I didn't know why you were offering, or if there was a catch, or..." Her eyes went wide. "I'm not comparing you to Dylan. That's not what I meant."

Mira had no idea. Isabel swallowed her guilt. "Don't worry about it."

"Well, I want to say that I'm grateful I ended up here. I

really am. It's been so nice to live somewhere where I can have some space to myself. Not just having my own room, but actually having freedom again. I'd forgotten what that was like."

Isabel's guilt rose again, stronger than ever. Reina must have felt just as free after she left, even though she'd been considerate enough to not say it outright. They were on good terms, in theory. Reina occasionally texted her photos of the wide-open Californian sky.

"I'm glad," Isabel said. She meant it. Mira deserved freedom, and that was far better than anything Isabel could give her.

It was sheer bad luck: The woman she'd run into who'd desperately needed a spare room was too beautiful and too hard to resist. And it was even worse luck that Mira was lovely and brave, that she asked Isabel questions and listened as though she cared, that she constantly tempted Isabel to let her defenses down.

This was torture. And there were two more months of this. Maybe she could give Mira the last month for free, to help her move out earlier. Isabel could find enough money to cover that.

Mira flashed her a sweet, conciliatory smile. If Isabel's heart hadn't already been crushed, the curve of Mira's mouth and the crinkling around her eyes would have done it. "When you helped me that night at the club, did you also do that without thinking?" Mira asked. "You were fast."

"I guess so." Isabel hadn't needed to think. She'd seen a man yelling at a woman who was clearly afraid. "I don't regret it."

"I could use more of that. Just doing things without overthinking, I mean."

Isabel shrugged. "It doesn't always work out."

"Yeah, you ended up with a roommate. No good deed goes unpunished."

Isabel laughed despite the dull, heavy pain in her chest. "I didn't mean it like that. Hey, seriously, it's been good," she added. Mira didn't owe her anything. She had to be sure that Mira knew.

They both looked out at the water again. "I'm sorry for ruining our outing with this argument," Mira said. "I'm grateful you showed me your neighborhood. It really is lovely."

"You didn't ruin it. It's good to be here." Isabel had taken so many lonely walks along the river, frozen and dulled to all emotion. What a difference it made to have Mira with her, no matter how much it hurt.

Mira leaned back against the bench. Her curls were exquisite in the autumn sunlight. "This is a better view of the river than the one from the high-rise."

"You don't have to say that."

"Oh, I mean it. It's better than being sealed in a glass box, looking down at everyone. I felt like I was in a cage." She casually turned toward Isabel, and the light shifting across her face made Isabel's breath catch in her throat. "The company is better, certainly."

Isabel's crushed heart was no one else's problem. "I'm glad it worked out."

12

When Mira opened the door to the apartment, she was greeted by the scent of scallions and garlic in a hot pan. Isabel was stir-frying something, her sleeves rolled up to expose her impressive forearms, her hair in her usual braid. She turned and gave Mira a small nod.

Mira hadn't seen much of her since their walk to the park two weeks ago. Yesterday, Isabel had told her that she could move out a month early if she wanted to, and had gone to great pains to clarify that it was purely for Mira's convenience and Isabel wasn't kicking her out.

Maybe it was nothing. Or maybe Isabel was avoiding her after that messy, painful conversation they'd had. Mira didn't exactly have high expectations for Isabel being open and friendly, but the possibility still stung.

Isabel could be a surprisingly good listener. In her silences, she made room for Mira, and she didn't say anything she didn't mean. It was tempting to think they could be an unlikely pair of friends, given more time.

But Mira was moving out soon, hopefully by the end of

the month. She already had a few apartment showings on her calendar. Isabel probably wouldn't want to keep in touch, to go for more walks in the park, to talk about herself unprompted for once. The truth was that there was no reason for Isabel to find Mira as compelling as Mira found her.

Mira dropped her bag on the dining table. "Do you mind if I heat up some leftovers in the microwave?"

"Go ahead."

Mira opened the fridge. There were no leftovers. She'd finished her lentils yesterday.

She groaned. It had been a long day. She hadn't had time to eat before the union meeting—which had ended late, as usual, because they hadn't figured out how to finish a meeting on time at any point in the last four years. Given the state of her bank account, getting takeout would be unwise. She surveyed her side of the fridge, but there wasn't much beyond two eggs, a mostly empty tub of yogurt, and a few sad-looking carrots.

"Something wrong?" Isabel said.

"No. Sorry. Just figuring out what I can have for dinner, since I don't actually have any leftovers." She could make a very small carrot omelette. The idea was not appealing. She closed the fridge.

Isabel was dumping the contents of the wok into a bowl: fried rice with vegetables and bits of red cured sausage. She didn't reply. Mira was on her own.

Then Isabel said, "Let me make you something. I owe you one."

"You do? I mean, thank you, but you don't have to."

"You cooked dinner for us a few weeks ago."

Right. She'd done that to thank Isabel for helping her.

But Isabel had been so grateful, and that had been its own reward, having her efforts in the kitchen be appreciated instead of taken for granted. And they'd had a nice meal together. Isabel didn't owe her anything.

But Mira was too hungry to argue about the ledger of what favors they owed each other. "Okay, I'll take you up on that. I really appreciate it. Um, I'm vegetarian, by the way."

"I know." Isabel had her back turned to Mira. She washed the wok she'd been cooking sausage in, which was rather thoughtful. "Excuse me," she said, heading for the fridge, and Mira took the hint and got out of the way.

She sat at the dining table intending to do some reading. Instead, she watched Isabel cook, in graceful, economical motions, her braid swaying as she worked. When she chopped scallions with a cleaver, the cuts were so fast that Mira couldn't tell them apart.

Isabel was as competent at cooking as she was at everything else—or at least everything that didn't require her to make conversation. And the domesticity of it gave Mira a forbidden thrill. She was privy to something intimate that few people would ever see: Isabel making dinner in house slippers, an apron, and an old pair of jeans so worn they'd molded to every curve of her body. Just an ordinary Thursday night.

The sound and scent of sizzling scallions filled the air again. A few minutes later, Isabel brought out two bowls of fried rice. Mira's had an extra fried egg on top, perfectly runny in the middle, scattered with finely slivered scallions.

They started eating. Mira couldn't imagine a more perfect dinner. It was so simple, but Isabel knew what she was doing, and even the frozen peas, corn, and carrots from a bag took on new life. "Thank you so much," she said, when she'd already finished more than half the bowl.

"It's nothing," Isabel said, rather gruffly. "How are you all doing on union cards this week?"

It was funny how her roommate took more of an interest in what she did at work than her ex-boyfriend of two years ever had. "We're doing well, thanks for asking. We have fewer than a hundred left to go, and we'll be over our goal by the end of the semester. It looks like we're on track to have the election next spring."

They talked about their days. Isabel was having a late dinner because she'd been translating for her aunt at the doctor's office. She was an exemplary niece, too, on top of everything else. Mira mentioned the apartments she was seeing this weekend, in her attempt to move out at the end of the month, and Isabel displayed no obvious reaction.

"Do you have any plans for the holidays?" Mira asked, after the lull that followed.

"I'll see my family for Thanksgiving. They're out in the suburbs on Long Island." Isabel's face had turned blank, and Mira realized, too late, that she'd brought up Isabel's family. "My sister died on December 5th two years ago. It's not an easy time."

"Oh, Isabel, I'm so sorry." Mira's heart broke for Isabel all over again. "I can imagine the holidays must be painful." She hesitated. Did Isabel even want condolences? "May her memory be a blessing."

Isabel blinked. "Thanks. That's nice of you." She looked down at her fried rice. "We'll visit Alexa's grave close to the day. Then I might see them on Christmas. That's not a big thing for us. At least not for me."

"Does it help to see your family?" Mira was taking a risk in asking questions. Maybe Isabel wanted to be left alone. If their roles were reversed, Isabel wouldn't say anything at all, and she'd simply let Mira talk as much or as little as she wanted. But, like Isabel had said, Mira had to find her own way of doing things.

Isabel sighed. "I think it helps my parents to see me. I just wish I could make things easier for them."

She looked stiff and somehow small sitting at the table, her eyes downcast. She hadn't actually answered the question, nor had she brought up the younger sister she'd once mentioned—presumably, the other bridesmaid in the photo Isabel had on her bookshelf. "It's good of you to be there for them," Mira said, treading carefully. "I'm sure they're happy you're there."

Isabel nodded. They ate in silence. It wasn't uncomfortable, exactly, but Isabel's mind was clearly elsewhere, leaving Mira to wonder about some things. Why did Isabel go to such great lengths to care for her relatives when she didn't seem to want to be around them? Did Isabel want to be around *anyone*? What did she do when she wasn't working or taking care of her family?

When they were done eating, Mira grabbed Isabel's bowl before she could object, headed to the sink, and started on the dishes. "Are you going to bed?" she asked. "It's a late dinner for you."

"Maybe in an hour. I might, uh... I might do some reading or something." Isabel stood up behind Mira. "Let me help."

"No, you cooked. What are you reading?" Isabel was always holed up in her bedroom when she was at home, and what she did in there was yet another mystery.

Isabel came over and started drying dishes next to her anyway. Her forearms were distractingly thick, flexing as she moved, tanned by the sun. There was barely any space between the sink and the countertop next to it, so they had to stand close together. It was one of the many quirks of their kitchen, which wasn't quite big enough for two. "Nothing right now," Isabel said. "I finished *The Left Hand of Darkness* again." She paused, not looking at Mira. "It's different, reading it after Alexa died."

Mira had wept the first time she finished the novel years ago, and she'd never lost anyone close to her. A friendship between two very different people who came together as equals, sublime in its intimacy and love—maybe Isabel had had that with her sister. "It's devastating, isn't it?"

Isabel gave the smallest nod, one Mira might not have seen if she weren't standing only a few inches away. That was answer enough.

They went on washing and drying the dishes, settling into a rhythm. Standing this close together, Mira sensed every one of Isabel's movements as they worked. There was something about Isabel's self-assured, solid presence that set Mira thrumming merely from being nearby, like a tuning fork resonating at exactly the right pitch. A little excited, a little buzzy, but calm, too, like she was where she was meant to be.

And she was. It felt good to wash Isabel's homey, mismatched dishes together. It felt good to come back to the apartment after a long day, turn on the lamps in the living room, and let herself decompress before starting on her work again at the familiar table. This was how being at home was supposed to feel. Like she was warm and safe, like she could breathe.

But she was leaving soon. Maybe in just a few weeks.

Once they were done, Mira said, "I hope I'm not bothering you by working at the table all the time—"

"You're not."

Mira smiled as she dried her hands. "What I was going to say is, you know I wouldn't mind if you read or did other things in the living room. Not that you have to, of course. I just hate to think I'm crowding you out."

"No, you're not." Isabel looked at the living room, as though seeing something that Mira didn't. "I don't have anything against it. I could use a change of pace."

13

Isabel settled on the armchair with an old sci-fi paperback, with Mira halfway across the room grading papers. When was the last time she'd sat in her own living room just to relax? She couldn't remember. And she hadn't expected both how familiar and how unfamiliar it would be.

The apartment had changed. In the last few months, slowly but surely, it had turned back into a real home. This wasn't the dark, empty apartment she'd been used to, but it wasn't the one she'd shared with Reina, either. Mira's fingerprints were everywhere: the plants thriving thanks to her friend Frankie's advice, her jars of lentils in the pantry, her hair clips and forgotten mugs of tea spreading to increasingly unlikely places.

Most of all, there was Mira herself, sitting at the table with her glasses perched on her nose and the end of her pen resting on her lower lip. Occasionally a smile or a frown would flit across her face, and she would write something down on her student's paper. She was so lovely that it hurt to look at her. But Isabel looked, anyway.

She'd tried to avoid Mira for a while. It hadn't dampened her feelings. It had just made her lonely, and with her looming family obligations, she couldn't handle spending another evening alone. If that was selfish...well, she was weak. But being in the same room as Mira was stirring up the emotions she was having trouble keeping on a short leash. Or any leash at all.

Mira looked up, caught her gaze, and quickly looked down. Isabel was chastened. She returned to her book and ended up reading the same technobabble-filled sentence for several minutes. Classic hard sci-fi had always been her escape from the real world. But it wasn't doing its job tonight.

Once again, she found herself looking at Mira, who was shuffling her papers. Mira noticed. "How's the book?"

Isabel shrugged, her heart racing. "I don't think I'm in the mood for this. Reading about a bunch of tough guys and maybe one woman on a space station. I should start going to the library again."

"Hmm." Mira's lips pursed in thought. "Well, if you're a purist for physical books, you can read any of mine."

"I don't have to take your Latin class first?"

"I do have novels. In English. If you want to read them." Maybe Mira was eager for a distraction from grading. She took her glasses off—how Mira looked so sexy both putting her glasses on and taking them off, Isabel couldn't say—and got up. They crouched in front of the bookshelf.

For the second time this evening, after they'd been torturously close while washing the dishes, Mira's coconut shampoo wafted to Isabel's nose. Her curls were stunning, bouncy and lush and the deepest, darkest brown. Isabel wondered, for the millionth time, how it would feel to gently run her fingers through Mira's hair.

"Have you read *Parable of the Sower*? You don't have

that one," Mira said. Isabel snapped back to reality. Mira was examining the Octavia Butler books in Isabel's collection. She shook her head. "It's my favorite of hers," Mira continued. "I'll get it from my room. You can come with me and see my other books."

Isabel followed Mira through her doorway, roiling with curiosity, wracked by guilt. And she had good reason to be. There was Mira's unmade bed. And there were her pajamas, in a heap of pink cotton and lace on the bedspread.

Isabel's face burned, her heartbeat pounding between her legs. Mira had pulled those pajamas off herself this morning before putting on the sweater and skirt she was wearing now. Isabel absolutely couldn't be thinking about that, not after Mira had invited her in for the most innocent reason imaginable. Let alone picturing it in detail.

So many things she shouldn't be thinking about. Like how if Mira wanted some stress relief, the kind that involved Isabel's face buried between her thighs, Isabel would be on her knees on this wood floor in an instant. There must be some way Mira loved to be taken care of, some way to make her go from buttoned-up to fully unraveled, flushed and panting—

If there was, Isabel was never, ever going to find out. Thank god Mira was looking through her piles of books and couldn't see Isabel's face.

"Sorry that all my books are on the floor," Mira said. "I figured it wasn't worth it to organize them, since I'm moving out soon anyway."

Isabel bit the inside of her cheek. Hard. "That's fine."

She rubbed her face, exhaled, and took in the rest of the small, bare-bones room: the familiar blouses and skirts hanging in the closet, the alarm clock and prescription pill bottles on the windowsill that Mira was using as a makeshift nightstand. Someone who walked into Mira's room knowing nothing about her might think she was just an academic whose entire world was in her books. But there was so much more to her.

Isabel took a small book from a pile on the floor. It turned out to be in Latin, but she idly flipped through it anyway. Mira had written notes in the margins, and seeing them was somehow more intimate than being in Mira's bedroom—it was like being inside her mind. Isabel brushed her thumb over a line of Mira's writing, her hand trembling slightly.

"Found it," Mira said. Isabel, startled, closed the book she held. Mira stood up and handed over her copy of *Parable of the Sower*. It was an older edition, clearly well-loved. "Let me know what you think. I first read this in high school, and I thought it was astonishing. So clear-eyed and so hopeful. Before that, I didn't realize that science fiction could be so much more than..." Mira stopped and frowned.

"Books about a bunch of tough guys on a space station?"

"I didn't mean..."

"Don't lower your standards just for me."

Mira rolled her eyes playfully. "I don't mean it like that. Let me put it this way. If we ever go to space, I'll be an alien linguist. *You* can build the spaceship."

"Deal. You brought a lot of books with you." A few months ago, Mira had moved into her apartment with a small suitcase and two big boxes of books. It seemed like a lifetime ago.

"I have a hard time getting rid of them. Sentimental value, and all that." Mira picked up a slim novel from a pile. "My boyfriend in college gave this to me. He was sweet, even if it didn't work out. He was a gay boy and I very much wasn't."

Emotions swirled within Isabel. Relief that someone had once been good to Mira, and regret that she herself would never get to be. And a prickle of jealousy that she didn't like in herself. Mira picked up another book, a much thicker one. "This was from the 'literary criticism for classicists' seminar I took in my first year of grad school. My French wasn't really good enough at the time. But I was new to the city, and I felt so sophisticated, lugging around my big books and doing my reading in cafes like I was finally a *real* intellectual. But now I'm rambling."

"No, no." Isabel was parched. She could keep drinking up every detail of Mira's life for hours. She held up the book in Latin that she'd picked up originally. "What's this?"

"Oh, that was the edition of Catullus I used in under-grad. I had— I'm not boring you?"

Isabel shook her head. Mira went on. "The professor I had for that class terrified me. I was one of those insufferable students who breezed through the intro classes and thought I knew everything. And on the first day, she made sure I knew, in front of the entire class, that using big words wasn't going to cut it anymore."

They shared a smile. Mira continued, "She gave me a B-minus. And she wrote me a letter of recommendation for grad school, and I got in everywhere I applied. Last year, she sent me a long email about an article I'd published, rebutting everything she disagreed with, and it felt like the highlight of my career so far, that she took me so seriously."

Isabel leaned against the foot of the bed. "I had a journeyman like that once. Steve, the one I told you about. The first time I showed him a panel I wired, thinking I was hot shit, he made me take it apart and do it all over again. Took me hours. He told me that anyone who sees my work should know immediately that the union electricians in New York City are the best in the world."

"Do you tell that to your apprentices?"

"I do. I try to go a little easier on them, though."

"Not everyone can be you, right?"

Isabel snorted. Mira leaned against the wall, mirroring her. "I've always thought that if I ever got to be a professor, that's the kind of professor I'd want to be. Not that I'm counting on it. But last week, one of my students said something, and I found myself frowning and leaning forward and asking her to clarify her argument in the exact same way. It's like how we all become our parents. Though I'm sure I wasn't nearly as intimidating."

"I don't know about that." Mira was probably underestimating herself.

Mira smiled like Isabel was joking. "Maybe I'll get there someday. I do try to take my students seriously, which is why I push them. I think that's more important than any specific thing I can teach them, ultimately."

The two of them had plenty in common. Mira took real pride in her work, and she knew she was meant to be an academic and a teacher, no matter what people threw at her. Maybe Mira wouldn't put it that way, but Isabel knew conviction when she saw it. "I've had people have a problem with me, and point out every little unimportant thing or ice me out because they thought I shouldn't be on the job site in the first place." Mira nodded. She obviously knew all about that too. "It's different when someone's pushing you because they believe in you."

"Oh, absolutely," Mira said. "Also, I don't think I'd ever... Well, Catullus can be seamy. Before that class, I'd never heard a professor say the word *face-fucking* before."

Isabel nearly choked. Her face flushed again. Hearing

Mira say that word in a completely dry tone was doing something to her.

Mira smiled slyly. "Here, let me find you an English translation. Unless you're too scandalized. In which case I'll dig up one of those Victorian translations that left the good parts out."

"I think I can handle it." Isabel wasn't sure if she could.

Mira took another book out from the middle of a stack. It wobbled, and Isabel rushed to keep it upright. "Thanks," Mira said, standing back up. She flipped through the book, opened it to a page, and gave it to Isabel.

It was eyebrow-raising. "Huh," Isabel said, still blushing like she was a prude.

"There's a lot to say about that little poem," Mira said. "Gender roles, sexual mores, the relationship of a poet to their work, and so on. Anyway..." Mira's expression turned serious. "Well, he had quite the range. I don't know if you're familiar with his elegy for his dead brother."

Isabel shook her head. Mira looked uncertain. "Tell me about it," Isabel said, not wanting the conversation to end. She hated dealing with other people's fumbling attempts to talk around her grief. Mira's gentle matter-of-factness was different.

Mira took the book from her. Their fingers brushed, and sparks lingered on Isabel's skin. Mira flipped through it, dog-eared a few pages—apparently she wasn't precious about her books in that way—and handed it back to Isabel. "A few of his poems mention his brother, and 101 is the most well-known—*and forever, brother, hail and farewell*— but this portion of 68 is the most moving, to me. I don't know if... Well, if you do read them, and you'd like to share with me, I'd love to hear what you think. You don't have to look now, if you're..."

Isabel wanted to. She was tired of shutting herself away. She wanted to get closer to Mira's world, and she wanted to see what Mira wanted her to see.

She opened to one of the dog-eared pages. *My brother, you have shattered my comfort. Together with you, our whole house was buried. Together with you, all our joys have passed away...*

A surge of something vast from the depths over-whelmed Isabel before she could keep it down. Her face wobbled and her throat ached. Tears threatened to break through.

Isabel took a shaky breath, keeping the threat contained. She closed the book. Mira put more hairline cracks in her composure every day. Now, with this offering, Mira had almost split her open.

What if she allowed herself to crack?

She couldn't. Not when she had to see her parents and Grace in a few weeks. She had to stay strong for them. But maybe there would be a time when she could pour herself out and let something new in.

What was Mira doing to her?

"Thank you," Isabel said, with a tight hold on her voice. She clutched the books close to her. But she'd have to return them soon—Mira would probably be gone in less than a month. That realization nearly broke the dam. She swallowed around the lump in her throat, trying to control herself. "I'll give these back before you go. I don't know if... If I'm ready for the poems. But I appreciate it."

"You can keep the books," Mira said. Isabel looked away before she fell apart. "It's a gift, okay? Take as much time as you need."

14

THE WEEKEND SUBWAY schedule truly had it out for her. Mira emerged into the gray November drizzle after an hour and a half, two boroughs, and three transfers. She took out her phone, trying to get her bearings in this unfamiliar neighborhood.

There was a text from one of the people whose apartment she was about to see. Raindrops beaded up on her phone screen. *Hi, we're sorry, but someone just put down a deposit for the room. Apologies for the last-minute update.*

Mira made a hopeless strangled noise. She tried to quell her frustration. They'd probably had dozens of applicants for the room and had just wanted to pick someone as quickly as possible. At least they weren't going to give her a tour while knowing they were wasting her time.

But this was a bad start to her second day of looking at apartments, after a bad first day of meeting a scammer, meeting a creep, encountering a bizarre intra-apartment love triangle gone wrong—hence the need for a new room-mate—and, finally, meeting a different type of scammer.

She stopped for a coffee, as though that would make the trip less fruitless, and went back into the subway station.

The next apartment, an hour away, was promising enough that Mira allowed herself some optimism for once. It was on the fifth floor with no elevator, and the room wasn't much bigger than her current one, but at least it was close to campus.

She met the roommates, all around her age, who were superficially polite and questioned her with such obvious, barely veiled suspicion that Mira shook with anger as she made her way back down the stairs. She knew what it meant when people looked at her like that. They didn't want her there, couldn't admit to themselves that it was because she was trans, and were scrambling to invent other reasons to disqualify her.

A familiar instinct had reared its head, to make herself as meek and small as possible, even as she'd known that they were in the wrong. She'd managed to resist: She'd stood up, curtly thanked them for their time, and walked out.

That was something she might not have done back in September, when she'd been crushed by the breakup and by the last two years. At least she'd had these precious months to start picking herself back up. It was a bitter victory. But her shoulders relaxed only after she walked back out into the cold rain and let herself breathe.

She longed to go home—which was to say, back to Isabel's apartment. Isabel wasn't superficially polite; she was barely polite at all. But she was honest even when she was gruff, and she had always been fundamentally decent to Mira in a way no amount of overcompensating niceness could substitute for.

There was more to Isabel than basic decency. But it was infuriating that the bar was so low.

On to the next apartment. The bedroom had no window, which had not been clear from the photos but did explain why it was so affordable. *Not again.* In a better mood, Mira might have considered it, but she wished the current inhabitants good luck and went on her way.

Another subway ride, and then an artist with three beautiful, cuddly long-haired cats who hadn't been mentioned in the ad. They climbed all over Mira as she introduced herself for the third time that day, eyes watering. She sneezed profusely on the train to the next apartment, cat hair clinging to her clothes. Allergy meds weren't going to cut it. She was going to be sneezing for days.

On the train, a text from Isabel arrived. *When are you getting home?*

Mira was overcome by longing so hot it bordered on frustration. She could have gotten used to grading papers while Isabel read on the couch, and waking up to good coffee every morning, and occasionally having dinner together and going on walks to the park. It was the quiet life she'd wanted, forever out of reach.

Mira texted her back. Another notification popped up. The apartment she was about to see had "just been taken." But was Mira free to see a different apartment all the way across the city?

No, she was not. Someone had tried to pull this scam on her yesterday. Who the hell did they think she was? After the day she'd had, she let herself indulge in some righteous anger. But she was relieved, too.

She opened up her texts with Isabel again. *Actually, I'll be back earlier than that.* She could finally go home.

. . .

Isabel had been too ambitious. She was a competent cook. But it had been too long since she'd put in the effort, and Mira had put things back in the cabinets seemingly at random. Dinner was coming together more slowly than Isabel wanted.

The door unlocked behind her, and she turned around. Mira entered, soggy from the rain, worn out after another day of apartment hunting. She greeted Isabel and slipped her coat off. "That smells good. What are you making?"

Isabel hesitated. The answer was that she was cooking for Mira again. It had been embarrassing to make her the most basic fried rice imaginable the other night with whatever vegetables Isabel had scrounged up from the freezer. It was one thing for Isabel to make it for herself, and another thing to serve it to Mira, as though she couldn't do any better.

And it was about time that something was easy for Mira. She deserved to just come home and sit down to a nice dinner, for once, no matter what else was going on in her life. "I, uh... I was just making dinner for myself. You can have some if you want."

"Oh my goodness, you're wonderful," Mira said. She was joking, but Isabel's chest fluttered regardless. This was why being around Mira was dangerous. "I don't intend to make a habit of having you cook for me," Mira continued. "I've just had an awful weekend."

"That bad?" For months, all Isabel had looked forward to was moving out. But reality was looming for her, too. Soon, she'd have to pack up everything and move into some barren new apartment. She'd be living alone. That didn't comfort her the way it used to.

"Yeah, it was. Can I help you at all?"

"I'm fine," Isabel said instinctively. Then she glanced at

the pea leaves and bitter melon yet to be washed and chopped. She hadn't started the rice, either. She sighed. "Actually..."

"I do know how to cook, you know. I don't just eat whatever my roommate makes for dinner."

Isabel smiled. "Do you want to wash and roughly chop those?" She nodded toward the big bundle of pea leaves.

The kitchen wasn't big, and Isabel didn't usually like to share. Her ex had hated cooking, so it hadn't been a problem, but she had sometimes shooed even her mom and sisters out of the kitchen during their visits. No matter how much she craved being around Mira, she was preparing to grit her teeth at least a little.

But they made room for each other, Mira washing the pea leaves in the sink in the big colander as Isabel scooped rice into the rice cooker. It was such a simple pleasure to measure out enough for two people. She stepped to the side as Mira started chopping the pea leaves next to her, their arms and hips almost touching.

Mira was sneezing more than usual. Hopefully she wasn't getting sick. But if she was, at least Isabel would be around to take care of her.

"Do you want it smaller than this?" Mira asked, holding up a piece. "What are these greens, by the way?"

"No, that's good. They're pea leaves." Isabel walked behind her to rinse the rice in the sink, and Mira made room. Isabel let the milky-white water run down the drain, distracted by Mira's elegant hands and her dark blue nails as she worked. "They taste like peas. You'll see."

She turned on the rice cooker as Mira continued chopping. Once Mira was done, she turned to the knobby bitter melon. "I haven't had pavakkai since my dad made it for me.

You know, I haven't really thought about what it's called in English, since I've never tried to buy it."

"You don't like it? I didn't know it's used in Indian food. I was wondering what you'd think." Isabel wasn't doing a great job of pretending she hadn't made all this for Mira, but maybe it didn't matter.

"I don't mean that," Mira said. She cored the bitter melon and started chopping it into half-moons. Not what Isabel would have done, but that was fine. "I'm sure I'll like the way you cook it."

Isabel smiled. She leaned against the counter, taking a break to watch Mira work. Her hair was damp and frizzy from the rain, and she had on a silky blouse, a pencil skirt, and dark tights, slightly sheer in that way that highlighted every curve of her legs. She'd been trying to make a good impression today, not that it had done her much good. Her feet were otherwise bare on Isabel's scuffed kitchen floor.

Isabel wanted to get her out of those constricting clothes and wrap her in a fluffy robe. Unwrap her once she was warm and dry. Make her feel nice and relaxed like she had nothing in the world to worry about. Kiss her good night, let her sleep, wake up to her in this apartment every morning.

Isabel's fantasies were spiraling out of control again. She mentally caught back up to their conversation. "So, do you speak— What language does your dad speak?"

"My dad speaks five or six languages. He has family all over South India, and he has a Ph.D. in history. But he made sure I learned Tamil. Not that I speak it as well as I want to." So everyone said. Isabel was lucky she could still talk with her grandmother easily. "He's always getting on my case about how Tamil is the oldest classical language. Older than Greek and Latin."

"Huh. Did you ever think about studying that?"

"Maybe once I get tenure." Mira's smile was sardonic. "Right now I'm just trying to get through the next year."

Mira made quick work of the bitter melon. She sliced the mushrooms while Isabel tossed the pea leaves in a hot wok with garlic and they turned a glossy, vivid green. Next came the bitter melon, stir-fried with the mushrooms—Isabel had never made this without beef, but she could probably stand to eat less meat. "Thanks for letting me cook with you," Mira said, as though she needed to thank Isabel for that. "I could use the distraction."

"What happened?"

Isabel had forgotten how awful apartment-hunting could be. Mira wasn't done talking by the time they carried the food to the dining table: the rice, the pea shoots, the bitter melon, and braised tofu in a sticky red-brown sauce that Isabel thought might work as well on tofu as on meat. It was all Cantonese food you'd have at home on a regular night. Nothing special, Isabel told herself.

They sat down to eat together for the second time that week. Isabel could get used to this. She pushed the thought down. "Oh," Mira said, "I forgot to mention the love triangle from yesterday. Probably because I was trying to forget about it as fast as possible."

Isabel raised an eyebrow. Mira grimaced. "I met these two women who were sharing one of the two rooms in the apartment. They wanted someone to fill the empty room. It seemed promising at first. Until I asked them why their current roommate was leaving. And it turned out she'd been dating one of the members of the couple until a few weeks ago. *They'd* been living in a room together, and when they broke up..."

Understanding dawned on Isabel. "So she replaced her

girlfriend with her other roommate. And they all had to switch rooms."

"Well, when you put it that way...yes." They exchanged mock-horrified looks. "And then the ex-girlfriend came home while I was there."

Lesbian drama was the one constant of the universe. Mira told the rest of the story—angry words, wild accusations, Mira managing to calm everyone down simply by being the only reasonable person there—more generously than Isabel would have told it. "They were nice otherwise, believe it or not." Mira shook her head. "The new couple was very much in love. Making eyes at each other the entire time."

Isabel laughed. "No."

"They were."

"You'd better not seduce either of them, then," Isabel said, before she could stop to think. For a heart-stopping moment, she was terrified—had she gone too far and revealed herself? Then Mira let out a loud, undignified laugh, her face lighting up, her curls bouncing.

Isabel was so screwed. She was digging herself deeper into this hole. Her only hope was that after a few more weeks, she'd never see Mira again.

Mira recovered, but she was still smiling. "Don't even joke. Oh my goodness, can you imagine?"

Could Isabel imagine one of Mira's roommates falling for her and blowing everything up? Yes, she could. "So you said no to them."

"Well...I didn't." Mira sighed, slumping forward. "I don't have a lot of choices. The bedroom has a window, and they weren't scammers, and neither of them was a creep. Anyway, it's down to these lovebirds and Vivian's friend in Bushwick. Apparently the cats liked someone else more. I would have been too allergic to live with them, but it really adds insult to injury."

Isabel sobered up. "Good luck." Looking for a new place would be a pain for her, too. But at least she had enough money to live by herself, and she would have better choices. None of this was fair.

She'd keep taking care of Mira in whatever small ways she could. The food they'd cooked together was delicious, and Mira had helped herself to seconds of everything, even the bitter melon, which was gratifying.

This wouldn't last. But for now, they could still share a homey dinner on a cold, rainy night, and Isabel was going to savor it while she could.

Mira's phone buzzed. "Sorry," she said. "Do you mind if I... I'm anxious to hear back."

"Go ahead."

Mira picked up her phone. Judging from her expression, the news was bad. "Vivian's friend found someone else." She put her head in her hands.

It hurt to see Mira struggling when there was nothing more Isabel could do to help. She had already asked everyone she could think of. She had even texted Grace, swallowing her pride after they hadn't talked for months. They still weren't talking, but it had been a relief that Grace had curtly responded at all. "Sorry," Isabel said.

"It's okay." Mira didn't even bother trying to sound convincing.

Her phone buzzed again. "Oh. It's the love triangle apartment." She scoffed. "They want to offer me the room." She stared at her phone screen, then shook her head. "I'm not going to take it. I have a bad feeling about it. I mean, what if they *do* break up?"

She started typing on her phone, and then put it down.

"I can't text them right now. I'm in too bad of a mood to be nice to them."

"I doubt it," Isabel said.

"What do you mean?"

"You probably won't be rude to them unless you're trying to be. You're too nice for that." Mira frowned. "I didn't mean it in a bad way," Isabel added. "You'll feel better if you get it over with."

"That's true. And I don't want to second-guess myself." Mira picked up her phone again, and typed and retyped for over a minute before setting it down. "And now I'm right back where I started. Maybe next weekend there'll be openings for December 15th, too. I'll just have to keep trying."

Isabel nodded. They continued eating. Then Mira said, "I was thinking... I don't know if this is a bad idea."

"What is it?"

"What if I stayed in the apartment, and found someone else to take your bedroom? I know that's easier said than done. Especially because, honestly, I think I'd have to start paying more in rent. You've been really generous." Mira smiled weakly. "You wouldn't have to deal with the landlord showing people the apartment while you're trying to pack. Just me doing it."

Isabel gaped at her. There was another solution staring them in the face, so tempting that Isabel was afraid to think about it. She couldn't hurt Mira if Mira was moving out in a few weeks.

But if they lived together for the next *year*...

She had to calm down. Mira wasn't asking her to stay. Maybe Mira had assumed, reasonably, that Isabel didn't want to. Or maybe she didn't actually want Isabel as a roommate any longer. Mira could get along with just about anyone, and she might want a nicer roommate with less baggage. Isabel wasn't going to put her in the position of having to say which it was.

"Sure," Isabel said. "If you want to find someone else to renew the lease with, I won't stop you. It might make it easier for me if you took some of my things. I have a lot I don't need."

"I can do that. That's kind of you."

"I'll call the rental office, but you'll have to find someone soon. They'll start showing the place on December 1st."

Mira opened her mouth as though to say something, then closed it. Finally, she said, "Okay. I'll try my best."

15

On the train back to the city, Isabel came closer to crying than she had in a long time. Her grief was just below the surface, raw and frightening and unmanageable, threatening to break through her numbness. But the tears didn't fall.

It was a long ride back to her stop, and the sky darkened as the train rumbled through Long Island. Isabel hated this time of year. She hated how the nights grew longer and the cold worked its way into her bones. She hated counting down the days until the anniversary of Alexa's death. This was only the second year of the rest of her life without her sister. How was she supposed to go on living like this?

Seeing her family had been as painful as she'd feared: Grace pointedly not speaking to her while their parents and grandmother looked on with disappointment. All of them silently remembering Thanksgiving two years ago, the last time they would all be together ever again. Staying the night at her parents' invitation, knowing it was more for them than for her. Seeing her mother's hair turning gray and her father struggling with his back pain. She had done some repairs around the house for them this morning, grateful for the opportunity to be useful, trying to not think about how her parents would need her even more as they got older.

She wanted to be home. At her stop, she trudged to the subway, gritting her teeth at the loud, excited people with their Black Friday shopping bags.

Would Mira be home? Did she *want* Mira to be home? She didn't want Mira to see her like this. But coming home to a dark, empty apartment might be even worse.

When she turned onto her block, the light was on in the window. Isabel was relieved, and then surprised by her own reaction. At the door to the apartment, she took a second to pull herself together.

Then an unfamiliar voice came from inside.

Right. Mira was showing the apartment to people this evening. Isabel's jealousy surged. That was *her* home, and Mira was *her*—

Mira wasn't her anything.

Frustration and exhaustion overwhelmed her. She had no idea how she felt about seeing Mira, but facing a stranger would be unbearable. The ladder to the roof hatch was just outside their door. It was narrow, rickety, and probably not up to code, to the point where it always made Isabel nervous. But now, without stopping to think, she started climbing.

At the top, she unlatched the door with one hand and pulled herself up through the hatch. The wind was bracing. She closed the hatch most of the way and sat on the elevated rim. It was too cold to be comfortable, but maybe Isabel deserved it. She was alone in the darkness, cut off from the world below.

She'd been so eager to leave the apartment and its memories behind. But now all she wanted to do was take refuge inside it. Thinking about Mira finding someone to take her place felt like prodding at a bruise.

She was going to miss hearing about Mira's union organizing—something that gave Isabel hope, even from the sidelines, when so little else in her life did. She was going to miss having someone to cook for. She knew herself well enough to know that she'd go back to eating fried rice and ramen every night.

She was going to miss Mira. The way she could be so soft, and then so sharp and funny in an instant. The way she made Isabel ache, which was better than being numb for all those months before she'd caught sight of Mira under the streetlights. Isabel hadn't known it then, but it was the moment when her life as she knew it had begun to come apart.

There was a thump below her like someone was trying to climb up. Isabel stood up, shaken from her thoughts, and opened the hatch. Mira was more than halfway up the narrow ladder, clinging to it like she'd never climbed a ladder in her life. Her eyes widened when she saw Isabel.

Isabel called down, "What are you doing up here?"

"Sorry," Mira said. "I thought you might have come to the door, so I came out and saw that the roof hatch was open. And I texted you but you didn't reply." Isabel had been too deep in her thoughts to notice. "I wanted to see what was going on. Are you okay?"

Mira had cared enough to check up on her. Isabel was rattled, and more grateful than she could say. "Yeah. Sorry to make you worried. Can you get down by yourself?"

Mira looked down and recoiled. "I think so. I'm a little afraid of heights."

"I don't want you to fall. Come up and I'll help you down."

Mira nodded grimly. She climbed until she was gripping the spindly top rung. Isabel held out her hand. "Hold on to me."

Mira took her hand cautiously, and the contact sent heat all the way down Isabel's body. Mira's grip was tentative at first, but she put more weight on it once she sensed Isabel's sturdiness. Isabel braced herself, and together they got Mira through the hatch.

The warmth of Mira's hand lingered after she let go. Mira was still the only person Isabel had touched in months, apart from when she'd hugged her parents hello and goodbye.

Mira was breathing hard, clouding up the chilly air. She gingerly turned around. "This is a gorgeous view." Considering that she'd lived in a high-rise, her appreciation sounded surprisingly genuine. "Oh, the moon's out."

Isabel turned too. The moon was a crescent low in the sky, bright through misty clouds. She had missed it earlier.

"Did you come up here because I was giving someone a tour?" Mira asked. "Sorry about that."

"It's fine. I just wanted some fresh air." Isabel inhaled deeply, letting the chill settle in her lungs.

"How was Thanksgiving?"

Isabel opened her mouth, but nothing came out for several seconds. Mira said, "I can leave you alone. Though I think I need some help getting back down."

"Stay if you want. It's up to you." Mira was dragging her into the land of the living, and Isabel didn't want to admit how desperately she needed it.

Mira looked hesitant. Isabel lowered herself to sit on the edge of the hatch again, going slowly to avoid irritating her bad knee in this weather. After a moment, Mira sat next to her. There wasn't much room. Mira settled in, and then their arms were resting against each other.

Isabel's heart sped up. All her senses were overwhelmed by Mira—the pressure of Mira's arm through their thick coats, the scent of her shampoo, the heat of her body. Isabel had been starving for the most basic physical touch, and every fleeting contact made her want more. Not just sex. Even being able to hold Mira, to feel her warmth skin-to-skin on these winter nights, would be everything in the world.

Isabel sucked in a breath of icy air. She had to calm down. Such stupid, unbearable yearning. "How was your Thanksgiving?" she asked, not wanting Mira to feel unwelcome.

"Same as always. My mom was in town very briefly. She had a layover before she went off to report on migrant workers in Spain. It was nice to see her for the forty-five minutes she was at dinner." Mira shifted her long, graceful legs, making herself more comfortable, and Isabel was jolted by every small movement of Mira's arm against hers. "My bubbe always makes Tofurky for me and my vegetarian cousin, even though we always tell her she doesn't have to and we can eat sides. So we have to eat it to be polite. And I had to take the leftovers home this time because my cousin did it last year. I had Tofurky sandwiches for lunch and dinner and there's still more."

Isabel laughed. The weight on her chest eased slightly. "You should let me try it. I haven't eaten yet."

"It's all yours. Don't say I didn't warn you."

They sat in silence, looking at the city lights. Isabel said, "Aren't you cold in those tights?"

"I've gotten used to it." Mira pursed her lips. "Well, maybe a little."

Isabel unwound the thick wool scarf from her neck, zipped up her coat to compensate, and draped the scarf over Mira's legs. Mira smiled. "Okay, you got me. That is better. Thank you." She edged closer, pressing her leg close, and draped the other end over Isabel's lap. "You must also be cold. Your jeans can't be that much warmer."

That was true. But Isabel was burning everywhere they touched. Her heart thudded so loudly that she worried Mira might hear it.

Mira said, "I'm guessing you didn't have a good time with your family. I'm sorry."

"Don't be. It's my fault." At that, Mira frowned. Isabel continued, "I got into an argument with my little sister Grace a few months ago. It's why I've been so..." She didn't have the words to describe what the last several months had been like for her. She shook her head.

"I'm sorry," Mira said. "I know how much you love your family. This must be terribly difficult for you."

Isabel looked away. She didn't deserve Mira's tenderness. Mira didn't know the first thing about her and her family. "Grace deserves a better older sister than me," she said, with so much venom that she surprised herself. "But I'm all she has now, and it's not fair to her, and there's nothing I can do about it."

Mira was silent. Then she wriggled under the scarf, took out her phone, and said, "I'm going to cancel on the other people who were going to visit the apartment tonight. And then you can tell me more."

"No, don't," Isabel said, but Mira was already texting.

"I just did." Mira put her phone back in her pocket. "Why are you saying that?"

Mira was being too kind. Isabel had to tell her the truth and put an end to it. "Grace is getting married to her boyfriend Kevin in June. Her fiancé, I mean. I don't like him. They're both a couple years out of college, and she's been working hard as a vet tech to support herself. Kevin doesn't do anything. He works part-time and lives with his parents and streams himself playing video games online. When *I* was his age, I was making 30 percent wages as an apprentice and working a second job after night school."

Isabel's indignation was rising dangerously. She was getting off-track. "Anyway, my sister loves him, and I respect that." She didn't even sound convincing to herself. "When Grace told me they got engaged, I tried to raise my concerns about him and told her that she should be with someone who'll pull his weight and act like a grown adult."

Mira nodded, frowning.

"It was bad. And I didn't mean for it to become so ugly. But I said..." Isabel looked away, unable to meet Mira's gaze. "I told her that Alexa wouldn't want her to marry him either, if she were still here." The shame of the memory burned. "I knew how bad it was as soon as I said it. I don't know what I was thinking."

She kept her gaze on the rooftops. "I fucked up so badly. Grace is the only sister I have left, and she's getting married and starting a whole new life with him, and she won't let me apologize and didn't tell me when she scheduled her wedding. And she wouldn't talk to me at Thanksgiving, and she didn't ask me to be her bridesmaid even though we all— We all promised each other—"

She took a few shaky breaths, forcing everything back down. She couldn't cry in front of Mira. She could not.

"I'm so sorry, Isabel," Mira said.

Mira's unrelenting kindness was too much. It might have hurt less if Mira had just gotten up and left her alone. "I don't need you to pity or coddle me. I know I fucked up."

"I'm not pitying or coddling you." Mira's tone was still gentle, but with a sharp enough edge that Isabel turned to look at her.

Mira's beautiful dark eyes were full of concern. Isabel was exhausted, and she was weak, and she wanted to drop to her knees with her head on Mira's lap. She was losing control of herself.

Mira said, "Do you want me to tell you that you shouldn't have said that?"

"You'd be right."

"You shouldn't have said it." Mira sounded sincere, but there was no reproach in her voice. "I'm sorry. I know you love her and you want the best for her."

"I do." It was ridiculous to tell all this to Mira. But she had no one else to talk to aside from Cat, who was equally close with Grace and hated being their go-between. Now that Isabel had started, she couldn't hold herself back from spilling everything. "Alexa would have wanted the best for her, too. That's what I meant to say. But I said it in the worst way possible and I don't blame Grace for anything."

The moment Isabel's life had truly changed had not been hearing the news. It had been seeing her family at the funeral, her parents looking older and frailer than she had ever imagined, Grace looking afraid and lost, all of them desolate. She had understood, in that moment, that she would be the one taking care of all of them from now on. There was no one else. And she wasn't good enough.

"I don't even know how to apologize to her." Isabel ached from the effort of holding back tears, but she needed to say this. Part of her craved more of Mira's tenderness, and part of her wanted Mira to run away after learning the truth. "I know Grace doesn't just want me to apologize for what I said about Alexa. She wants me to apologize for saying what I said about her fiancé in the first place. And I can't, and I told her I wouldn't. I can't lie to her."

"Is that how you see it?" Mira said gently. "Either you're honest with your sister, and you make her upset by telling her the truth she needs to hear, or you're lying to her?"

When Mira put it that way, Isabel's reasoning somehow seemed flawed, too simple. But what other option was there? "I guess so. I don't know what else to do."

"Do you think your sister is in danger with him?"

"No. He's lazy, not abusive." Isabel sighed. Maybe she needed some perspective. "I know it could be much worse. I should be grateful for that."

"That's not what I meant."

"Well, I should keep that in mind, anyway. I know I'm alone in this. Even my parents have basically come around to him. God knows what they see in him. It's not as though he has a great personality, as far as I can tell. Every time I've tried to talk to him, he hasn't spoken more than five words." At that, Mira smiled. "What?"

"Nothing." After a second, Mira continued, "It's just that if I were in his position, I would find you intimidating."

Isabel couldn't help laughing. The shame, the despair, the self-righteous anger loosened their grip on her. What remained was sadness and doubt. There was no easy way out of this, whatever she did.

"I just want Grace to have a good life." Isabel faced Mira, who was still patiently listening. "She's been through so much. She was just a few months out of college when Alexa died, and I know she misses her as much as I do, even though she rarely talks to me about it. I just want her to have a husband who will take care of her, not someone she has to spend all her time supporting. That's what she deserves."

"I know." No judgment, no reproach, no false plati-tudes. It would have been easier if Mira had told her she was an irredeemably awful sister and person. Or that Isabel was right about everything—but she knew she wasn't, even if she didn't know how to fix it, and Mira wouldn't lie to her.

Mira continued, "I was about the same age as Grace, it sounds like, when I started seeing Dylan. And Vivian and Frankie knew from the very beginning that he was terrible, and they tried to talk me out of it. But, ultimately, I think it's hard to protect the people we love from that kind of pain, even though my friends did their best. It doesn't sound like Grace's fiancé is that bad, or at least I really hope not. But I think he could step up and surprise all of you. Or he could have seemed wonderful at first, and then turned out to be awful. Or something else could happen that's entirely out of your control or anyone else's."

Isabel nodded. She knew that all too well. She was reminded, too, that Mira's sweetness didn't come from being naive. "I know you want to protect Grace," Mira said. "To be honest, I'm not sure there's anything Vivian and Frankie could have said that would have convinced me to not move in with him. What would have made a difference was not being broke." She smiled ruefully. "But they did decide to be there for me the whole time I was with him, and they made sure I knew that."

The message was clear. Isabel put her face in her hands. "I need to apologize to her." Despair crept back in. How the hell was she going to do that? "I want her to know I'll always be there for her. But maybe she's right to not think so. Because I haven't been. I don't know what to do."

"I'm so sorry," Mira said. So good, so kind. "I know how much you care about her. I hope you'll find a way."

Somehow, while talking, they'd leaned further into each

other. Now they were pressed together from their shoulders down to their calves. Isabel didn't want to move, didn't want to lose Mira's warmth, didn't want to stop touching Mira. If only she could have all she wanted. Holding Mira and being held, letting herself be understood.

She was afraid to look at Mira—it might shatter the fragile moment. Instead, she stared at the city below, unseeing, as Mira warmed the left side of her body like a furnace.

She felt lighter. Telling Mira about the shame that'd been festering in her for months had helped ease it a little. She'd told Mira, and Mira hadn't run away.

Mira shifted her limbs. Isabel was taken by surprise. How long had they been sitting here? The last of the sunset had vanished, and it was fully nighttime.

She turned toward Mira at last. Mira was looking at the rooftops, and Isabel studied the features she knew so well: Mira's deep brown eyes, her long lashes made even more dramatic by mascara, the elegant line of her nose, the soft, full curve of her mouth. Isabel was used to stealing glances. But then Mira turned, too, and their eyes met.

The clouds of their breaths mingled in the cold air. Isabel's heart quickened. She had gotten used to Mira leaning against her, but now she was acutely aware of it again, and electricity tingled everywhere they touched. Mira's lips parted, and Isabel caught herself staring. She looked back up at Mira's eyes after a moment too long.

"So, I was thinking," Mira said, startling Isabel. For a second, she'd wondered whether something else might happen. Like Mira kissing her. She was losing her mind.

Thank god Isabel would be out of here soon. The thought gave her no joy at all. She caught up to Mira's words. "Yeah?"

CHAPTER 15

"Would you consider staying in this apartment for another year?"

16

ISABEL SAID NOTHING. With every passing second, Mira's stomach sank further. She had ached for Isabel—for her seriousness and devotion toward the people she loved, for her guilt and pain at the very real mistake she'd made, for the vulnerability she had let Mira glimpse.

And when they'd looked at each other just now, there had been a spark Mira didn't know how to describe.

A shared understanding, maybe. A sense that they could be more than roommates to each other. A hope for a quiet, stable friendship and the assurance that they could look after each other even as they lived their own lives. And a wild craving—one that unsettled her—to have *more* of Isabel, to peel off more layers and see what was underneath. Mira couldn't explain or justify any of it.

At the end of the day, they were roommates, and Isabel had her own reasons for moving on.

"Never mind," Mira said. "I know why you wanted to leave this apartment. You're free to say no. I'm sorry. It was just an idea."

Isabel moved away. Without Isabel's warm, solid body

against hers, the cold set in. One last unpleasant reality check. Mira took the hint and moved away too.

"I don't know," Isabel said.

"Never mind. Forget I asked."

Isabel hunched into herself. "I'm not saying no. I really don't know."

Mira remained silent. Even if Isabel was considering it, she wouldn't want to decide now, after she'd had such a hard day. Some part of Mira longed to put an arm around Isabel, but it clearly wouldn't be welcome. Isabel was only a few inches away, but she was far out of Mira's reach.

"Thanks for the talk," Isabel said, not looking at her. "Let's go back down."

So Isabel wanted to be alone. Mira didn't begrudge her that, even if it was now clear how much Isabel tormented herself in private. "Of course. Any time, okay?" She gave Isabel her scarf back, and Isabel wrapped it around her neck again. "Thank you for the scarf. Um, how do we—I should say, how do I get back down?"

"I'll go ahead of you. You can watch me get back on the ladder, and then do what I do." Isabel opened the hatch, and light spilled out from below. "If you fall, you'll have something to fall onto."

"But I don't want to crush you."

"Then you'd better not fall."

Mira smiled. She stood up, her legs stiff. Isabel swung one leg over the edge, followed by the other, and disappeared down the hatch. Once again, Mira was startled by the nimble, powerful way she moved. She'd been standing on the roof just a moment ago.

"Your turn," she yelled from below.

This was much harder than Isabel had made it look. Mira crouched down, gripped the metal edge of the hatch with frozen fingers, and forced herself to get her leg over the edge. She waved her leg around for a few nerve-wracking seconds, with nothing underneath her, until her foot found the rung.

She wasn't as stable as she would have liked. Her ankle boots with a bit of a heel had been a bad choice. But when she'd seen the hatch open, she'd been so worried that she hadn't stopped to think.

"You got it," Isabel said, a few feet down.

Mira held on to the edge for dear life, got her other leg down, and flailed until that foot caught a rung, too. She took one hand off the edge and gripped the ladder, then did the same with her other hand.

"Looks good," Isabel said. "That was the hardest part. You can come down now."

Mira glanced at the open hatch. "Should I..."

"I'll get it later."

Mira moved one foot down, and then another. She looked down—there was Isabel, and beyond her, the floor of the apartment hallway very far away. Mira's terror spiked.

"Don't look down if you're nervous," Isabel said. "I'm right here."

Mira breathed in, then out. No need to look down. Isabel was right there. She took it one rung at a time as Isabel descended below her, the rungs wobbling from their weight.

She heard Isabel get off the ladder. If Mira fell now, she'd fall right onto Isabel, and Isabel would catch her— The thought made her so woozy she almost slipped. She held on. A few more rungs, and then she was on solid ground again, her legs wobbly.

At least she hadn't embarrassed herself too badly. She gave Isabel a shaky smile. "Thank you."

Isabel nodded, clearly preoccupied. She went up again to close the hatch. Mira stole a glimpse of her ascending, rugged and graceful at once, before unlocking the door and going back inside.

She took a few more breaths to settle her nerves, then started making tea in Isabel's beautiful glass teapot, the one Alexa had given her. Isabel had been using it more often these days. It was the perfect size for two. Isabel could drink her tea in her room if she wanted to be alone.

But when Isabel returned, she didn't retreat into her room. She lingered in the living room, standing with her hands in her pockets, as though she couldn't make up her mind. That was rare for her. A strange silence filled the apartment, less comfortable than what Mira had grown used to.

Isabel said, finally, "Can I ask you something? You don't have to answer."

"You can always ask." After a moment, Mira added, "If I don't want to answer, I'll let you know."

Isabel hesitated, drawing out the silence. "Why'd you start dating Dylan in the first place?"

Was that what Isabel was so preoccupied with? It was unlikely. "Are you asking because of your sister?"

"It's not that." She looked at the floor. "When you were talking about him earlier... I was just wondering what you saw in him, if there was anything."

Mira had been asking herself that, too. The question was so tangled up in her self-blame that she didn't know if she could answer for her own sake, let alone for Isabel's.

But she wanted to try, if only for herself. Maybe Isabel wouldn't understand. But for all her rough edges, she'd never secretly pitied or condemned Mira for her choices.

Isabel was a straightforward person, and that wasn't how she operated. Mira understood that now.

And this was a night for sharing messy secrets. It was just the two of them—and the grief and guilt that haunted Isabel, and the shame and doubt that haunted Mira, and this strange silence between them.

"You can ask," Mira said. She sighed. Where to even start? "I met him at a party in my third year of grad school. It was mostly, you know, 'cool' grad students and artists and literary people in a loft somewhere. He saw me and started talking to me." Dylan had gotten too close, asking her questions that were too personal. She still remembered the heady, frightening realization: *He's acting like this because he wants me.* "I'd read his novel. And I didn't think much of it. But everyone else had loved it, and I thought..."

Isabel nodded solemnly. Mira had to go on. The truth was lodged in her like a thorn, and she had to pull it out. "I thought that if a real writer like him was interested in me, it meant that I mattered. That I was this beautiful, sparkling, clever girl at a party and he wasn't hopelessly out of my league. And that he thought I was attractive because of what I had to say, about my research, about books, about whatever else we talked about. Not just because he saw how vulnerable I was."

She clutched the table behind her and took a shaky breath. She was at home, and she was safe, and she would never, ever have to go back to him. "I wasn't stupid. I knew that was part of it. And I knew I would never be allowed to be as clever, or as important, or as much of a person as he was. I just didn't know how bad it would get. I couldn't have known."

Isabel shook her head. "I'm sorry," she said quietly.

The kettle turned off. Mira poured hot water into the

teapot, still on edge from all she'd said. Isabel remained silent, which Mira was grateful for. Right now, she didn't need Isabel telling her she hadn't deserved it, or that she'd been too good for him. She already knew. That wasn't what was at stake.

Somehow, the fact that she'd wanted Dylan was the hardest thing to face. It meant admitting that she'd ever wanted anything at all. To have someone see her as both smart and beautiful. To be taken care of, to matter, to be loved.

She wasn't ready to date again. She needed to be single for a good, long time. But some stubborn, reckless part of her couldn't stop wanting. She had more than enough reason to be cynical. But she *still* yearned for someone who would sweep her off her feet and take her seriously at the same time. Someone who would laugh with her, cook with her, talk about books with her, share easy, quiet nights with her. Someone like—

Isabel said, "There's something I need to tell you."

Her voice was so strained that Mira turned around. Isabel was stiff, her face unreadable. Which meant she was hiding something immense.

Mira racked her brain for possibilities and came up with nothing. "What is it?"

"I want to make it clear I'm not asking anything of you."

"What are you saying?"

Isabel's face twitched as though she were in pain. "I have feelings for you. And I know that's my responsibility. I don't want to cause you any problems."

Heat rushed through Mira's body. What had Isabel just said? Mira couldn't have heard that correctly.

"I'm not asking anything of you," Isabel repeated in a monotone. "I just thought it would be unfair to you if you didn't know. If you don't want to keep living with me, I get it."

Mira stared. Emotions churned within her, too confusing to name. "For me?"

Isabel nodded like she was breaking horrible news.

"Okay. I, um, I didn't expect this." That was an understatement. Isabel could obviously have anyone she wanted. Any woman who actually liked other women would be all over her in an instant. In a sense, it was a tremendous waste that Mira wasn't into women.

A long time ago, she'd had a few short-lived relationships with straight women; each time, the unspoken expectations had wrapped around her and choked all the air from her lungs. Years later, panic still gripped her when she remembered trying to be someone she would never be. Being with men had been a relief, though she had never fit into the small, insular, mostly white gay scene in college, either. And after she had transitioned, that was gone too.

When she'd gotten serious with Dylan, she'd thought everything was falling into place. She was a woman with a long-term boyfriend—something that, for her, had been terribly hard-won. And, slowly and inexorably, he'd squeezed her to fit into his life—as a devoted girlfriend, a muse, a plaything, but never a partner or a human being. There was no more room for the question of what she wanted.

She'd been told her whole life, in a million overt and covert ways, that women like her didn't deserve better. Dylan hadn't needed to say it aloud to her. He'd said it in everything that he did.

Now Dylan was gone. What was left for her? Mira was lightheaded. The momentary terror of climbing down through the hatch returned, when she'd found nothing beneath her but air. "Um, do you want to sit down?"

Isabel sat down on the couch. Mira got mugs from the cabinet—her favorite, and Isabel's—and poured them tea, grateful she had something to do. "It's just about the apartment," Isabel said. As though that were true. "It's fine if you don't want me to stay. I won't take it personally."

Mira's head was still spinning. She hadn't been remotely prepared for this. Isabel wanted *her*? "It's okay. I don't hold it against you or anything. But, um, you know I'm straight. And I'm not looking for a relationship right now." Who was she trying to convince? These were obvious, irrefutable reasons, weren't they? Then again, why would her reasons even matter? Isabel had made it clear that she wasn't asking for anything. Having *feelings* could mean anything. It would be mortifying to ask, and there was no reason for Mira to wonder or to know.

"You don't have to let me down easy." Isabel gave her a small smile. If she was joking about it, maybe this wasn't a big deal. Isabel didn't want anything between them to change. Mira was overreacting.

"Well, I appreciate you telling me." Mira was proud of how level her voice was, considering that she'd had her head split open. "It's just unexpected for me. You can stay in the apartment if you want. I don't see why you shouldn't."

"Don't say that because you feel like you have to."

"I'm not." Isabel was too honorable for her own good. It was sweet that she was trying to protect Mira, as though Mira were in any danger. Her mind drifted to that night at the club—her sheer relief, her sense of safety. Maybe that was how Isabel's girlfriends felt all the time with her.

"You can take some time to think about it," Isabel said.

"We have until the end of the month to tell the rental office."

Right. They had practical things to discuss. "If you let me say yes now, I can cancel all my showings for tomorrow," Mira said. "I can give you a tour of the apartment. It's a nice place. You'd get the big bedroom."

Isabel smiled, her stoic facade crumbling. "Yeah?"

"Yeah. But it'll be about as tidy as it is right now, with all these books and papers and hair clips everywhere."

Isabel laughed, which was always a pleasure to hear. Then she sobered up. "I thought, with your ex..."

"That's different," Mira said quickly. "This is nothing like that. We're not together."

"I guess. I mean, of course not." Isabel looked stricken.

"Please don't worry about it," Mira said. "You're a good roommate and a good friend. I want to keep living together, if that's what you want." This had been a rough day for Isabel. The least Mira could do was comfort her.

Tea would help. Mira had almost forgotten. She jumped up. "Be right back." She returned with mugs of tea for them both. "It's a bit strong. Don't drink too much."

Isabel took a sip and sighed. "Thanks, Mira." Her stiffness was mostly gone. "I do want to stay. I'm glad this worked out."

"Me too." They had a good thing going. Isabel's revelation wouldn't change anything.

"Are we good?"

Mira smiled. "That's up to you."

Isabel didn't quite meet her gaze. "Then I guess we are."

17

ISABEL HAD either the best or the worst sense of timing. She'd come out with her feelings to Mira right before the most unbearable day of the year. Maybe the honesty had been necessary, or maybe she'd just made Mira uneasy for no good reason. Either way, she was too frozen now to feel anything at all.

She was exhausted as she trudged up the stairs to the apartment. It had been a day of work like any other. She had called her parents during her lunch break and replied to the few texts she'd gotten. She hadn't had the appetite to eat. What she wanted was to sleep and only wake up when it didn't hurt anymore, and she might be waiting a long time for that.

It was only five o'clock, though the sky was already dark. She just wanted the day to be over. At least Mira wouldn't be home for another few hours. Her union meeting was tonight.

No. The lights were on, and Mira was in the kitchen. She turned around when the door opened, and it was clear from her expression—serious, hesitant—that she knew.

Isabel had mentioned the date to her just once, and she had remembered.

"Good evening," Mira said. "I made dinner, if you'd like to have some. But I understand if you'd rather be alone."

Isabel came closer to crying than she had all day. After doing so many things to drive Mira away, she still had no idea what she'd done to deserve Mira's kindness. But her body acted of its own accord. She dropped her backpack on the floor and staggered to the dining table.

Deserving or not, she couldn't spend tonight alone.

She sat down, still in her dirty work clothes, and put her face in her hands. Part of her was where she had been two years ago. Getting the call that Alexa and James had been in an accident. Sitting in the car to the hospital, shaking as the heavy rain blurred everything around her.

Mira's hand was soft on her shoulder. Isabel came back to herself, sitting at her dining table, the scent of something delicious wafting from the stove. She was suddenly weak with hunger.

"Do you want dinner?" Mira asked.

"I should shower and change." But Isabel didn't stand up, didn't move. The candles flickered in the menorah on the windowsill. Mira must have lit them right before Isabel came home.

"You can do that after you eat." Mira set something in front of her. It was a bowl of stew, thick and colorful with white beans and vegetables: winter squash, greens, carrots. A mug of green tea followed.

Isabel's vision blurred from tears. Maybe she wouldn't have the strength to hold them back in front of Mira. Maybe she didn't want to bother trying anymore.

"There's something else," Mira said. She took a casserole dish from the oven and set it on a trivet on the table.

"What is that?" Isabel's throat was tight.

"I made noodle kugel. My mom made it for my aunt Miriam's yahrzeit, which is her death anniversary, every year after we attended services. It's one of maybe three things she ever cooked. But, um, I thought you might..."

"Your mom also lost her sister?" Isabel almost couldn't say it aloud. Mira nodded.

Isabel was fighting a losing battle. A tear rolled down her face. She numbly wiped it away in full view of Mira.

"You should eat," Mira said.

Her gentle voice was a balm. Isabel picked up her spoon and started eating mechanically. The stew was hearty and filling, and it warmed her through. Her hopelessness was loosening its grip.

Mira put a plate of the beige noodle pudding, studded with what looked like raisins, in front of her. Isabel glanced up. "You should eat, too," she said, trying to regain some control over the situation.

"I will. Do you want me to stay?"

Isabel nodded. *Please.*

Mira sat down. They ate in silence. Returning to a dark, empty apartment would have been unthinkably awful. Isabel was quietly overwhelmed by gratitude. Mira's kindness went far beyond a simple favor that could be repaid.

Mira said, "Will you tell me about her sometime? It doesn't have to be now."

Isabel nodded again, not trusting herself to speak. Out of all the things she hated about losing Alexa, one of the worst was knowing her memories were fading with time. Eventually, they'd slip away, and she would never have new ones to take their place.

On her own, there was only so much she could do to hold on to her memories. What Isabel needed was someone to listen. She was desperate for it, even more than she'd realized, and Mira had sensed it in her and understood.

Isabel took a bite of noodle kugel. It was creamy, rich, and shockingly sweet, totally incongruous with the rest of her dinner. "Oh my god, that's sweet," she said. "Sorry. It's good. I just wasn't expecting that."

"Is it?" Mira looked puzzled. "You know, I never really thought about that. I guess it is."

Isabel remembered that Mira took her coffee and tea with a small mountain of sugar each time, and she smiled in spite of everything. "It's delicious. Thank you." She tried to convey what she couldn't find the words for yet: She was grateful that Mira had remembered, grateful for Mira's care, grateful that Mira had seen what Isabel would never admit to needing.

She said, "I can tell you about Alexa now. If you want."

"Please."

Isabel was going to fall apart completely once she started talking. Maybe that was nothing to be ashamed of. Mira had cried in front of her weeks ago at the dinner table, and Isabel hadn't thought she was weak. There was no reason why Isabel should be too proud to do the same thing.

She braced herself. Where would she even start? In some of Isabel's oldest baby photos, three-year-old Alexa had held her infant sister with tenderness and wonder. Alexa had simply always been there, until she wasn't anymore.

"She was the first person I came out to, when I was thirteen," Isabel said. That was as good of a place to begin as any. "Even then, I acted like I wasn't scared of anything, but I was. She asked me if I was sure, and I said yes, and she told me that she was so happy for me and I knew I was going to be fine. And she came with me when I told my parents. They weren't happy about it at first, and Alexa argued with them nonstop about it. She really went to bat for me."

A few tears fell. "She always did that for me. My parents didn't like it when I dropped out of college, and she stood up for me then, too. And I was working a second job and scraping by because I didn't want to ask my parents to live with them, and she'd come over with groceries and we'd cook together—"

Big, heaving sobs rose in her, and she let herself cry, throwing herself into the bottomless pit of grief. It was perversely, overwhelmingly good to let go. She cried and cried, and Mira pushed a box of tissues toward her—the same tissue box she'd once given Mira—and she blew her nose and wiped her disgusting face and kept crying.

When she'd run out of tears, she was light and unmoored, as though a terrible weight had been lifted from her. Her nose still leaked, and her throat ached. When was the last time she'd felt so unburdened in the last two years?

She had rarely cried in the first few months. Between helping her parents with funeral arrangements and trying to win the union election at work, it had been a matter of treading water so she wouldn't drown. After that, the wellspring of tears had frozen solid. She had thought she was sparing Reina. So much for that. After Reina had left, Isabel had occasionally cried at home, curling up in embarrassment from ingrained habit even though there had been no one to see.

None of those times had been as cathartic as today. She was a mess, utterly broken down. And Mira was still here with her.

Last year, she had worked a ten-hour day, returned to the apartment, and collapsed in her bed. She hadn't said anything to Reina, and Reina, following her lead, hadn't brought it up. Everyone grieved differently. That was what well-meaning people said. So what if Isabel didn't want to talk about it?

But all it had taken was a few questions from Mira for her to pour everything out. The dam holding back her grief had been so fragile.

Isabel shoved those thoughts aside. She couldn't get in the habit of comparing Mira to her ex. She would never have that kind of future with Mira.

"I'm so sorry, Isabel," Mira said. "Alexa sounds like an extraordinary person."

Isabel took a shuddering breath. "She was the one who taught me what it meant to take care of other people. It was in everything she did for our parents and grandparents, and her patients, and for Grace."

"And she took good care of you, too."

Isabel nodded. It was a bittersweet truth. No one had ever taken care of her the way Alexa had, and no one ever would again. She was the one caring for her parents now. She'd been older and more financially stable than Reina, and she'd played the role she needed to. Taking care of people, accepting responsibility—that was what being an adult meant, didn't it? That was what being the oldest daughter meant, and the title was now Isabel's alone. "I just wish I could be nearly as good as Alexa," Isabel said. "I wish I could be for Grace what she was for the two of us. I wish —" She sobbed again.

Mira put a tentative hand on her shoulder. It was what Isabel needed, and it wasn't enough. She wanted Mira to hold her, and that was more frightening than any fantasy she'd ever had about holding Mira.

She wept. Mira rubbed slow circles over her shoulder

and back. She told Mira how happy she'd been at Alexa's wedding to James, the love of her life and one of the few straight men Isabel liked. How Alexa had given her strength when she'd nearly quit her apprenticeship out of justified rage, and how proud Alexa had been when she had turned out as a journeywoman at last. How Alexa had always been there to talk, no matter what time of night it was, no matter how busy and sleep-deprived med school and her residency had made her. Sometimes Isabel still felt the vestigial instinct to pick up her phone and call her sister.

Mira listened. It was so simple, and it meant everything. She didn't pretend things were fine or ever would be. She didn't try to tame Isabel's uncontrollable, unbearable grief. She just listened.

Isabel had another bowl of vegetable stew, and another big slice of kugel, and a few more mugs of tea. At some point, Mira dragged her chair closer and slung her arm over Isabel's shoulders, and Isabel cautiously let herself relax into the touch, into Mira's soft cardigan and the familiar coconut scent of her hair, into her warmth. It was as close as she would ever get to Mira holding her.

At last, she was emptied out, light as air. "Thank you," she mumbled, as though she could thank Mira enough. She didn't want to imagine looking back on this after she'd put herself together again.

"I should be thanking you." Mira was rubbing her shoulder. "I'm so grateful you told me these stories. I wish I could have met her."

Isabel hadn't allowed herself to imagine it. In another world, she would be introducing Mira as her partner to Alexa, and the two of them would be sisters-in-law, and... Apparently Isabel wasn't done crying.

"Me too," she said, through her fresh tears.

18

"HEY, MIRA." Mira looked up. Isabel had emerged from her room, wearing her weekend clothes: a soft, faded flannel shirt and jeans with a few smears of white paint. "Do you have time to help me with something? Doesn't have to be now."

Mira set her laptop aside on the couch. "Of course. Now is fine."

This was how it was going to be: an ordinary Saturday morning. A few days ago, she'd sat with Isabel at their kitchen table as Isabel had poured out an extraordinary account of her sister—and of her own life, too, as a sister, a daughter, a granddaughter, a partner, someone who loved and grieved deeply. They hadn't talked about it since, but Mira hadn't stopped thinking about it. Isabel was so much more than a pillar standing alone.

Isabel had returned to her usual laconic ways. She'd made dinner for Mira last night, and they had chatted about their days and laughed and shared stretches of easy silence. But Mira would never forget the way Isabel had wept for hours, her strong frame shaking as Mira stroked her back.

And then there had been Isabel's confession before that. Her mysterious, unspecified *feelings*. They certainly hadn't talked about that again. But Mira had not, for a single second, stopped thinking about that either.

"I'm free all day," Isabel said. "If you're busy..."

"Please give me something to do other than edit my thesis chapter." Mira had spent the last ten minutes adding, deleting, and re-adding two words. She stood up and stretched, and winced as her back creaked. "What do you need help with?"

"I need to hang those shelves, and it's easier with two people." Isabel nodded toward the shelves propped up in the corner that had appeared yesterday. "Shouldn't be more than twenty minutes."

"I'll try my best, but I'm not sure how much help I'll be." It was strangely easy to talk to Isabel the way she always had, all while this new knowledge lived between them.

"You'll be fine. One second."

Isabel went to the closet and returned with her toolbox. "I never got around to this. But now that we're sticking around..." She shrugged. "It's a two-person job. One of us holds the shelf and makes sure it's level, while the other person marks where it goes and where the brackets go. The shelves are going up over there." She pointed to a stretch of empty wall opposite the couch. Mira nodded.

Isabel rolled up her sleeves, exposing her thick forearms. Mira was lit by a spark of excitement. She'd finally get a glimpse of Isabel working, wielding all that competence and strength. She knew now, more than ever, that Isabel's toughness hadn't come easily, and it hadn't diminished Isabel at all in her eyes.

What could someone like Isabel see in *her*? What was it

that Isabel wanted and wasn't asking for? Maybe for Isabel, none of this amounted to much—she'd just had a passing thought she'd felt duty-bound to disclose. Even the idea of that gave Mira butterflies. If Isabel had ever looked at her like *that*, even for a moment...

Her thoughts had wandered. There was no reason to keep dwelling on this.

Isabel took a small device from her toolbox and swept it over the wall. It stuck to a particular spot. "What's that?" Mira asked.

"It's a magnetic stud finder. We're going to drill into the wooden studs in the wall—that's what the drywall is attached to—so that they'll hold up the weight of the shelves." All this was probably painfully obvious to Isabel, but she didn't seem impatient. She took a pencil from her pocket and marked the location of the stud finder on the wall, and then did it again for another stud with the ease of long experience. Some woman was going to be fortunate, someday, having Isabel put up all her shelves. Isabel said, "Can you get one of those and hold it up? We'll do these top to bottom."

Mira grabbed one of the shelves propped against the wall. It was more awkward to balance than she'd expected. Mira wasn't weak, exactly, but a lifetime of living inside her head had made her uncoordinated. She held it horizontally at eye level. "How high should it be?"

"Depends. How high do you want to reach once the shelves are up?"

It was nice of Isabel to accommodate the shorter people in her life. "This is fine."

Isabel set a level on top of the shelf, and it was obvious, after a second, that Mira needed to tilt the shelf to center the bubble. It was satisfying to do something physical, as basic as it was, after typing and deleting words all morning.

"That's good," Isabel said. "Keep it there. Now watch me."

Isabel came closer. She marked one end of the shelf, lined up the bracket in the right place, and marked the holes with her pencil, making running commentary. Then she did the same on the other side. Mira took in Isabel's silver earring, the delicate wisps of hair around her ear, the dusting of dark speckles on her cheek from working in the sun.

"Thanks," Isabel said. Mira had gotten distracted again. She might have missed a step while she was at it. "You can mark the brackets for the next one."

Apart from Mira's failure to stay on task, it was nice to work on something together. No matter how inexperienced she was, Isabel took for granted that Mira was capable of helping out. Isabel held the next shelf in place far more effortlessly than Mira had, and Mira hesitantly placed the bracket. "That's good," Isabel said. "Oh, wait. You can get my pencil from my back pocket."

Mira flushed. Hopefully Isabel didn't see it. She reached at an awkward angle and plucked the pencil sticking out of Isabel's pocket, holding her breath as her hand shook slightly, trying to not think about the curve of Isabel's backside or how tight her jeans were when she was bent at the waist. Trying to not touch anything.

Isabel stiffened as though she'd realized what she'd asked Mira to do. Then the moment passed. Mira concentrated on making her pencil marks. Not on Isabel holding the shelf against the wall with those sturdy forearms.

They dealt with the last shelf quickly. Mira was getting the hang of this. Thank goodness she had something to focus on besides her own thoughts. Then Isabel crouched next to her toolbox. "Come here."

Mira crouched down next to her, their thighs nearly touching, and watched Isabel put the drill bit into the drill. "Is this what it's like to be your apprentice?" Mira asked.

"You're a faster learner than most of them." They shared a smile and stood back up. Isabel drilled the first few pilot holes with unhurried ease. It was thrilling to watch her work with those big, confident hands, all her experience distilled into a few quick motions.

"Your turn," she said.

Mira took the drill, and Isabel stood to the side. It occurred to Mira that this part wasn't a two-person job. In fact, aside from leveling the shelves at the start, Isabel could have done all this herself in a tenth of the time.

Mira lined up the drill bit with one of the pencil marks. "You want it at a right angle to the wall," Isabel said. Mira adjusted the drill. Isabel didn't seem satisfied. "Here, let me..."

Mira made room as Isabel came closer. "Excuse me," Isabel murmured. She didn't look at Mira as she repositioned the drill, her calluses brushing against the back of Mira's hand. Isabel's fingernails were trimmed short and filed smooth. And her hands were moisturized, well-kept, surprisingly elegant. She had thick fingers, thicker than Mira's.

Isabel stepped aside, satisfied. "Thank you," Mira said, a moment too late, her voice unsteady.

She was overthinking this, as usual. She was thinking about Isabel more than Isabel had ever thought about her. Isabel was a responsible adult; she hadn't made a big deal out of it. It was time for Mira to do the same thing.

She pushed the trigger, but the drill made a feeble

sound and went nowhere. "Go faster and push harder," Isabel said. "You have to commit to it."

Mira did, and a mild thrill went through her as the bit sank into the wall. "Not bad," Isabel said. "You've never done this before?"

Mira shook her head. She wasn't one for home decor in general. That was the thing about constantly moving from place to place, never knowing if she'd be able to put down roots. "Is it not completely obvious? I'm flattered."

"It's a good thing to know. In case you want to hang shelves at your next place."

Mira drilled another hole. It was easier this time. "I can't just call you to do it for me?" On second thought, she didn't want Isabel thinking Mira actually took her help for granted. "I'd pay handsomely. Maybe not in money. We could work something out."

Isabel's eyes widened for just a moment before her poker face reappeared. Mira hadn't meant to flirt—hadn't meant to suggest she'd offer up whatever Isabel might want. She turned hot from her cheeks all the way down to the tips of her toes.

"I don't do non-union work for pay," Isabel said. She was joking, too. Mira relaxed. "I'd do it for free. But you don't need me. You got the hang of it."

"Well, it's kind of you to go out of your way to teach me. Thank you." Mira had caught on to Isabel's agenda.

"If I'm asking for help, I might as well give you something in return."

"But you didn't have to. That's what friends are for." The word *friends* stuck in Mira's throat.

"I like to be useful."

"I've noticed that." Mira drilled one more hole, and then another. "I'm enjoying this. I'm sure you're rolling your eyes because it's not fun when you do it all day for a living."

"Not always. But you'd be surprised."

Mira stood back up. When their gazes met, Isabel's smile was warm and bright. She was usually so rigid that every quirk of her mouth and eyebrows spoke volumes. Whenever she smiled—genuinely, amusedly, happily smiled—it transformed her.

Isabel was gorgeous. She was *hot*. The knowledge hit Mira like a physical blow. All her senses were fully dialed up—keenly, painfully sensitive to all those thick curves under Isabel's clothes, her quietly radiant smile, the sheer magnetism of her presence. Every passing thought Mira had been too afraid to examine, every flicker of curiosity, every burst of affection, every flare of heat—they all added up to one fact. She wanted Isabel.

Desire melted Mira's insides and made her quiver. Her wanting was too wild and unformed to put into words. Isabel had *feelings* for her, which could mean anything at all. What was she supposed to do now?

Isabel now looked concerned. "You okay?"

"Yeah. Um, are we doing the brackets?" Mira was dizzy. This wasn't supposed to happen.

"Yep." Isabel eyed her for another moment, then crouched down. "Here, you put in the driver bit."

Mira would have done this clumsily in the best of times. With her heart thumping and her hands shaking, she stood no chance. She fumbled with the driver bit until Isabel put her hands over Mira's again and all but did it for her. Each brush of those rough palms against her skin sent sparks through her. Mira was a bundle of kindling about to catch fire.

She stood up unsteadily. Isabel installed the first

bracket, and Mira forced herself to pay attention. When it was her turn, she took deep breaths as she worked. One screw at a time.

Finally, the shelves themselves went up, and all Mira had to do was drive in the tiny screws that held them in place. They both stepped back. Isabel asked, "What do you think?"

"Oh, um, I like them." Mira was too scattered to be articulate. But the shelves were elegant, and they made the living room less bare. More than that, Mira had rarely given any thought to how the space around her had been built. Shelves and cabinets were simply there.

The fact that Mira was capable of altering her space, just like that, subtly changed the way she viewed everything else. Maybe this was how Isabel saw the world: how it had been built, who built it, and what she herself could change.

Mira had had enough ground-shaking realizations for the day. "What are you going to put on them?"

"I thought you could put your books here."

Mira gasped. "Oh my goodness." This was unbelievably kind, and thoughtful, and...sexy. She wanted to swoon. The unnameable longing from when she'd been up on the ladder returned—to let herself fall right into Isabel's arms. What was happening to her? "That's why you wanted to put the shelves up?"

Isabel shrugged. "You want to get your books yourself, or should I help?"

Mira laughed shakily. "Okay, you can help." She led Isabel to her room, still flushed, grateful that Isabel couldn't see her face. They each carried a stack of books back to the living room. "You didn't tell me," Mira said.

"You would have told me I didn't have to." That much

was true. "I figured if you didn't want to put your books there, I'd come up with something else."

"Like what?"

"I need some new hobbies. I could start making those ships in bottles or something."

"I could see that, actually," Mira said. "You getting into dad hobbies." Isabel scoffed. "You're so sweet, Isabel. I'm so grateful." That was true, but it wasn't the entire truth, which was that Isabel was making her heart pound and her body run hot, every part of her vibrating with confusing, unfulfilled need.

"Uh, anyway." Isabel put her hands in her pockets. "I wanted you to know that this apartment is yours. You can take up as much space as you want. It's yours as much as it is mine. I don't ever want you to feel any other way."

Isabel's words sounded semi-rehearsed, which made them all the more sincere. "You're so kind to me," Mira said, bubbling over with emotion. Over the last two months, she'd gone from being a complete wreck to mostly having her life together, and now Isabel was taking her apart all over again. "Thank you so much. You don't know how much this means to me."

Isabel looked at her feet. "You did most of the work."

"'It's nothing,'" Mira said, imitating Isabel's gruff cadence. "You know, if you do something kind for someone, you're just going to have to accept it when they thank you."

Isabel gave her a gently amused smile, as radiant as any other. "You're very welcome, Mira."

Mira shivered at the sound of her name. Their gazes met, and the charged silence went on for a beat too long. Isabel looked away first.

"I'll let you put your books in order," she said. "I'll get more from your room."

With Isabel in the other room, Mira was left with only the roar of her heartbeat in her ears. She began putting her books on the shelf—separated into fiction and nonfiction and by language, and alphabetized—and let the process distract her.

Women were interesting and beautiful. Mira was often captivated by specific women, and it was because she admired them and wanted to emulate them. Of course she wanted to be like Isabel. She could appreciate Isabel's strength and competence and gorgeousness without being *attracted* to her.

She'd solved this puzzle long ago. She just wanted to be *like* other women. Right?

That was all true in theory. Reality was something else. Mira wasn't ready for that right now. She focused on putting all her Loeb editions—green for Latin, orange for Greek—on the bottom shelf. At least her bookshelves could be well-ordered.

After two trips by Isabel, all of Mira's books were in one place. "Thank you," Mira said. "I appreciate it. I can take it from here." She was afraid to look at Isabel. It would be too much like looking at the sun.

19

Mira turned underneath the covers again, overheated and restless.

She was turned on. Even admitting it to herself made her face burn. That was why she'd been feverish all day after she and Isabel had put up the shelves. It had been so long since she'd been truly aroused, not just lukewarm and willing, that she'd almost forgotten what it was like.

Sex had never been very interesting to her. With Dylan, it hadn't been terrible. He hadn't coerced her or hurt her. She had liked being desired; as long as he wanted her, she had a place in his world. Sometimes she had thought about her research while he did what he wanted.

She rarely ever touched herself, either. She was more or less at peace with her body these days, but there was never any particular reason for her to seek out pleasure. She had always retreated into her intellect to escape her bodily existence, and old habits died hard. Wasn't there always something more interesting to think about?

Right now...there wasn't. Her skin was hot and sensitive, caressed by her pajamas and by the cotton sheets. The memory of Isabel's body a few inches from her own—all those powerful muscles shifting under Isabel's clothes—was making her burn up. Isabel wasn't a statue. She was a person with a thick, gorgeous body, curves and muscles that you could touch...

Mira squeezed her thighs together, and the dull ache between her legs grew so sharp she gasped. She needed more.

She slipped a hand between her shorts and her underwear, a thrill running through her as though she'd never done this before. She pressed the heel of her hand against her clit and quivered in relief. Isabel's hands had been so big, so deft, so careful... Mira cupped one of her breasts through her camisole, and her nipple tightened as a pure, sweet shiver of pleasure coursed through her.

She twisted herself under the sheets to get a better angle. She was giddy, flushed, and by her usual standards, wildly out of control. This time, she pressed her fingers against her clit, indistinctly imagining Isabel touching her—and the searing jolt of arousal made her moan, hips lifting off the bed, the bed frame creaking.

Mira went still, her heart racing. She'd been far too loud in this very quiet room. Isabel was on the other side of the wall. Oh, god. Mira had been fantasizing about her.

She wasn't into women in that way. Maybe she was. Mira rolled over and groaned into her pillow. Now wasn't the time to be reconsidering everything about her sexuality, her relationships, her desires...

She took a long breath in, then out. It slowed her thoughts but didn't make her any less desperately turned on.

Time to face the obvious truth. This was not what platonic friendship or admiration felt like. She rarely had orgasms during sex, or even on her own. But now she was so needy that she could barely recognize herself—and if she kept touching herself and thinking about Isabel touching her, she would come from it, and it would be good to the point of being unendurable. Then all the questions would flood back in.

She lay unmoving in bed, taking more deep breaths, willing herself to cool down. Somehow, after an unbearably long time, it worked.

The embarrassment set in. Maybe she did like women. She could take some time to consider it. Maybe put it off for another few months or a year while she got the rest of her life sorted out. There was no reason to lose control like this, tempting herself with desperate measures while her room-mate was sleeping in the other room.

She could use a shower. She was sticky. And she needed to metaphorically wash everything off.

She slipped out of bed. It was chilly, and her nipples tightened and rubbed against her camisole, making her quiver with arousal again. It was too much. She tried to ignore her body screaming at her and opened the door.

And walked straight into something big, soft, and warm. She yelped as Isabel inhaled sharply.

They both stepped back. Isabel's... Isabel's breasts had been pressed against hers, and Mira's were still aflame from the contact. She almost wept from frustration. There was nowhere safe to look. Even when she dropped her gaze, there were Isabel's solid thighs, her well-built calves...

Mira's eyes wandered wildly. Isabel's breasts were incredible under that thin cotton T-shirt, so lush and heavy —and Mira knew, because she had *felt* them. And Isabel's nipples were right there, in light and shadow, and the fabric draped over them somehow made it worse—

In sheer panic, Mira jerked her head up. Isabel looked terrified. She ran a hand through her hair. It made her T-shirt ride up, the thin material shifting over her breasts. Her eyes flicked downward for a moment.

Oh. This was real. Mira had been thinking about it all week, lying awake in bed, her brain constantly buzzing. But she hadn't seen it before. Yes, Isabel really did look at her like *that*. Her body knew it now, too—her clit throbbed from Isabel's gaze, and her face and breasts and thighs tingled with heat. She was beyond reason. She was going up in flames.

Isabel closed her eyes, inhaled and exhaled through her nose, and opened her eyes again. She stared at something right above Mira's head.

Mira found the wherewithal to speak first. "I, uh... I..." Maybe she hadn't. "I needed to shower. Are you— You're not usually up. At this time."

Isabel ran a hand through her midnight-dark hair again, exposing her ear and the line of her neck in the dim light. Mira couldn't believe it. She, of all people, was doing this to Isabel.

"Couldn't sleep," Isabel said.

"Me neither," Mira blurted out. She couldn't look any lower. Not at Isabel's parted lips. Definitely not anywhere lower than that.

Isabel might have heard her. Her gasps and moans, the creak of the bed frame. Mira winced. The embarrassment was a splash of cold water. Not cold enough to make her stop overheating.

Isabel frowned. "Everything okay?"

"Oh, yeah, it's fine. I just— I need to shower."

Why had she said that? Before she could embarrass herself further, she ran past Isabel to the bathroom. She'd forgotten to bring a towel, but she couldn't go back and risk running into Isabel again.

She shut the bathroom door, turned the light on, and exhaled. Her reflection in the mirror was a mess. Tossing and turning hadn't done her hair any favors. Her camisole was askew, one strap nearly falling down.

And there was a flushed glow to her skin, and her eyes were wild, and her nipples were straining against her camisole. Maybe Isabel hadn't seen in the dark.

What if she had?

Mira was dizzy. She turned and sat on the hard edge of the sink, waves of need rolling through her body. The bathroom was on the other side of the apartment from where they slept. Could she—

Isabel was surely still awake. But Mira didn't hear anything. Still, she turned the shower on. The noise drowned out her thoughts, especially the ones about how bad of an idea this was.

She slid her hand inside her underwear this time and found her clit again. A fantasy came to her. Usually, Mira never fantasized about *anything*, and this one didn't make any sense, and in her right mind she'd be embarrassed, but she was in no state to care.

When she'd said what she'd said earlier—that she'd repay Isabel however she could, in exchange for Isabel putting up shelves for her—Isabel's mask had slipped for a moment.

The idea was absurd. Isabel would never, ever ask Mira for sexual favors as compensation. But Mira was in the relative privacy of her bathroom, alone with her fantasies, and she was so turned on it didn't matter. What if she offered herself up? She'd be wearing something cute, maybe a blouse and a short skirt, and she'd unbutton her blouse and let Isabel decide if she liked what she saw...

Mira moved her fingers and rolled her hips, sparks of pleasure arcing through her. She sped up. Picturing Isabel looking at her, no longer bothering to hide the smoldering heat in her gaze.

Mira tugged her camisole down, as though she were baring herself to Isabel, and the cool air against her sensitized skin made her gasp. She rolled a nipple between her finger and thumb as she rubbed her clit, squirming at the jolts of pleasure from two places at once. Isabel's hands had set her on fire merely from brushing against hers. If Isabel palmed her breasts, cupped her bare pussy, made sure Mira felt those calluses—

Mira moaned, unable to help herself. She had to do something to muffle the sound, but she couldn't take her hands off herself, couldn't stop, not with this sweet, searing tension coiling inside her.

Isabel would pin her against the wall as easily as she'd held up those shelves. She'd lift Mira's skirt with one hand and push her underwear to the side, teasing Mira's nipples like *this* with the other—oh, that was good—and turn Mira into a desperate, sticky mess pinned to the living room wall. Squirming like she was squirming against the sink now, her most soft, wet, sensitive places yielding to Isabel's hand.

And then Isabel would sling Mira over her shoulder and carry her to Isabel's own bedroom. She'd spread Mira's thighs open and sink her fingers into Mira where they belonged. She'd would take what she wanted from Mira, but she'd make it good for Mira, too, taking control but being so careful—

Mira's orgasm tore through her so hard and fast it hurt. She let out a desperate, choked-off moan, her knees buckling, her toes curling against the cold tile. It was too much, but she kept going until she was wrung out.

She went limp against the sink. Too sensitive all over, too vulnerable, and somehow still unfulfilled.

And she was. The woman she wanted was a few rooms away, and Mira had just made herself come while thinking about her. Mira squirmed, this time from embarrassment. She pulled her camisole back up over her breasts, still so tender that the soft cotton felt like sandpaper.

She still couldn't make sense of this. Her anxieties about wanting and being wanted were catching up to her fast. She'd indulged in a silly, illogical heat-of-the moment fantasy—and, yes, it had been unbearably hot. Which could mean anything or nothing at all.

It wasn't like Mira had a problem with being queer. Before she'd realized that she was a woman, she'd quietly accepted that she liked men. And even before that, people had sensed something in her that they didn't like, singling her out before she'd had the words and ideas to understand herself.

And Mira had known Vivian and her circle of queer trans women for years. She cherished her friends, but their lives weren't quite the same as hers. Most of them didn't date men or didn't date them often. They had their own vocabulary and parties and dating drama that Mira wasn't fully in on. They had their battles to fight, and Mira had hers, on top of what they all dealt with. Most of them had always liked women, and Mira had not.

She'd thought that was all there was to it. Saying yes to the men who pursued her, both the ones who'd treated her well and the ones who hadn't, had always been good enough. Hadn't it?

She hadn't expected her life to take this turn. Desperately making herself come in the bathroom from the thought of a gorgeous butch touching her. Imagining herself with a woman, not suffocating in a man-shaped prison but as *herself*. Being forced to confront that she might want something different, something more.

She didn't know how to be a queer woman, if she even was one. But one question crowded out all others—one she'd never been good at answering, one she'd spent the last two years pushing down until it had gone silent within her. What did it mean to want something for herself?

Isabel hadn't asked anything of her. She hadn't even put anything on the table. Evidently, she was planning to never bring up her so-called feelings again. If something was going to change, it would have to come from Mira herself.

This was the freedom she'd wanted. It was terrifying, and she had no idea what to do with it.

She took another deep breath. Washed her hands in the sink. Avoided her reflection, since she'd be even more of a mess now. She turned off the shower—guilty about the wasted water, but she'd taken barely any time at all—and listened for sound from outside, trying to ignore the pounding of her own heart.

The coast was clear. She tiptoed back into her room, grabbed her phone with shaking hands, and texted Vivian.

20

"OKAY," Vivian said, after a few seconds to process Mira's rambling account as they walked through the park. "I'm a little worried about this situation."

"What specifically?"

"I don't like that she's coming on to you."

"She's not. Isabel isn't like that. She didn't ask me to date her or sleep with her." Mira flushed. Her torrid fantasies from last night were embarrassing in the light of day. "She just told me how she felt. It was pretty obvious that she saw it as a problem more than anything else. Her problem, not mine."

"And you're fine with that?"

"I guess so," Mira said. Vivian frowned. "No, I mean, she doesn't make me uncomfortable. It's me. I think I like her too much. And I don't know what that means or what I should do about it. For one thing, I don't know if this means I'm actually bi?" She looked out at the East River, reflecting the gray sky, and didn't find any answers. "I don't think I've ever felt this way about a woman before. Maybe I have. I don't know."

Vivian was silent. Mira let out a frustrated groan. "I don't know what's happening to me." She was usually more articulate than this. Isabel had her at a loss for words.

"Well, she did express interest in you."

"I don't think I'm just responding to that. To be honest, I think I've felt this way about her for a while now." Mira had never trusted her own memories or judgments much. She tended to second-guess herself, to talk herself into or out of things, and Dylan had worn away what little trust in herself she'd had. But even she could see it now: Every time she'd felt a tug toward Isabel in her body or her mind or her heart, she had talked herself out of considering the most obvious possibility.

Until the smile Isabel had given her yesterday. In one ordinary moment, Isabel had changed everything.

Still, the second-guessing was a hard habit to break. "Although, now that I think about it, I guess I have felt this way in the past. Not this strongly. Mostly with my female professors and TAs, and trans girls I really looked up to. Which makes me think that maybe it's not..."

Vivian smiled. Mira said, "What?"

"I think this is the gayest thing you've ever said to me," Vivian said. "I mean, aside from the fact that you U-Hauled with this woman before you even realized you liked each other. I'm convinced now."

Mira snorted. Though the reminder that she and Isabel already lived together was ominous. "What are you talking about?"

"Listen to yourself. You're obsessed with this question of whether you want someone or want to *be* her."

"But I do want to be like Isabel. She's amazing. I'm just saying, that doesn't necessarily mean—"

"Yeah, the fact that you think about how amazing she is

all the time doesn't mean anything." Before Mira could reply, Vivian went on. "You know I'm worried about you—"

"I know."

"—but I do feel like it's my responsibility to help you figure out if you like women. You know, for the community." Mira smiled at that. "I don't know, Mira. Do you only want to be *like* her? I can't answer that for you."

No, Mira did not. She wanted Isabel's bravery and integrity. But when she saw Isabel's broad shoulders and capable hands and thick thighs, her flannel shirts and work boots, Mira didn't want those things for herself. She wanted to strip those clothes off and feel those muscles flexing and let those strong thighs spread her legs apart...

"And for what it's worth," Vivian said, "you can have both. You can have everything. I mean, you can have women as friends who are there for you no matter what, and you can be around women who help you do all the things you want to be brave enough to do, and you can have your little homoerotic crushes, like you did with your professors—"

"That's not—"

"—*and* you can also date women and fuck them and fall in love with them, and get married, live happily ever after, have a bunch of lesbian drama, whatever. You don't need permission from anyone. Especially not from me. You can have all that, if that's what you want."

Mira took a breath of chilly air. The river rippled, as unanswering as ever. Bare branches rustled overhead.

She'd gotten used to telling herself that she'd simply admired all those women from a distance. Just as the world constantly reminded her that she couldn't demand better from the men she dated, it had tried to extinguish the part of her that ached to love women and be loved by them. But she didn't have to accept it.

Maybe she could just have what she wanted. It sounded like the easiest and the hardest thing in the world.

It wasn't easy, but it wasn't out of reach, either. In the last few months, something within her had changed. She was learning to treat herself like she mattered, like what she wanted mattered. Isabel had treated her that way from the moment she'd stepped between her and Dylan at the club. *That* was what Isabel had done for her. And Mira was finally starting to believe it, too.

"I guess I do like women," she said. It was so obvious, in retrospect, that it hardly felt new at all. This precious part of her had been there all along.

Vivian put an arm around her as they walked. She held Mira close, almost tilting her off-balance. "Welcome."

Mira laughed. This wasn't a big revelation in the grand scheme of things. Transitioning in the first place had been the big upheaval in her life, and this was a small one in comparison. But she knew now that she was a woman who loved other women, and it felt good and right—like coming home to her apartment at the end of a long day.

But this left her with as many questions as answers. "I still don't know what to do," Mira said, leaning against her taller friend.

"About Isabel?"

Mira nodded. "It was easier when I didn't know I liked her. I know she's not Dylan. It's just... I promised myself I wouldn't date again for the foreseeable future for a reason. And, you know, I'm living in her apartment. I know it's different, because we both pay rent and we're both on the lease. And when she put up those shelves with me, I think I knew what she was trying to say. But ultimately, she's older, and she makes more money than I do, and she's just more secure in life than I am."

Vivian didn't argue with that. Mira sighed. "I just know that if something happened, she would survive. And I'm not sure I would. I'm scared that it would destroy me again." She'd been afraid to voice the fear to herself, but now it was out in the open.

"Anyway, this is all presumptuous of me," she added. Maybe she had been working herself up over nothing again. "I mean, just because Isabel has *feelings* for me, and I, um, I do for her, doesn't mean anything's going to happen. Isabel obviously has bigger problems to deal with. Maybe she just sees her feelings as a problem." Isabel didn't seem ashamed of being attracted to her, but the thought still hurt.

Something heated and raw and confusing had crackled between them last night. Mira could pretend it hadn't happened. If she tried, Isabel would let her, and life would go on. But Mira wasn't sure she wanted that, and now everything was infinitely more complicated.

Vivian squeezed her tighter. They were taking up most of the sidewalk, but Vivian was unfazed. "Whatever happens, I hope you're not asking if it's possible for this butch lesbian to fall in love with you and want to take care of you. Or whether you deserve it."

Mira might have been asking herself that. "Isabel is not in love with me."

"And you won't be destroyed by it," Vivian continued. "I don't want Isabel to hurt you. But Dylan didn't destroy you. He was just a pathetic, spineless loser at the end of the day. And, worst comes to worst, Isabel won't, either."

Mira stayed silent. She could believe in her own strength, more or less, on a good day. Hearing it from Vivian helped. Hearing it from Isabel had helped too. But ultimately, Mira had to believe it for herself.

"Anyway." Vivian let go of her. Something else was coming. "Just because you like women doesn't mean that you have to get married to the first dyke who's nice to you and knows how to hang shelves."

Mira laughed, but she bristled, too. "Are you saying I have low standards?"

"No. Not exactly." Vivian pursed her lips. "I want you to have high standards for yourself. You can set the bar a lot higher than Dylan."

"Isabel is actually really wonderful." Mira was still hurt. "I'm not just—"

"I know."

"You don't."

Vivian paused. "You're right. I'm sorry. I didn't mean it like that. But you're right to be worried. It would be messy if it didn't work out. Although you're always welcome to our couch." Mira smiled faintly. "Here's what I'm trying to say," Vivian continued. "There are plenty of other women out there who would love the chance to treat you well. And some men, for that matter, though I'm not going to give you that speech again. This isn't your only shot, is what I'm saying."

"I guess so." How could someone like Isabel want her? It was still sinking in. "It's hard to think of myself that way right now."

"You can take some time to get used to it. And, you know, if you just want to be with a bunch of other bi girls and lesbians, you can come to Volume with us again. You can stick with us, and we won't let anyone bother you."

"I'm not worried about seeing Dylan again." Nearly all the fear had drained from her memory, and what remained was how comically pathetic he'd looked. That was a victory to savor, as small as it was. "That's not what I'm afraid of. I felt like I didn't fit in when I was there. Everyone else was so..." She sensed there was *something*, but she couldn't point to any specific thing she lacked.

"I don't think you should be worried about that," Vivian said. "You should probably worry about being swarmed, instead."

"What are you talking about?"

"Were you not paying any attention? I guess you weren't. You were distracted and completely unapproachable when we went last time, which was understandable. And there were still probably half a dozen girls checking you out. You were just too sad and too straight to notice."

"Really?" Mira didn't dislike that news. It was flattering. But Isabel didn't just look at her. Isabel *saw* her, and she couldn't imagine anyone else's attention mattering. And the way she had looked at Mira last night...

Vivian rolled her eyes. "You can come out and see for yourself, if you don't believe me."

Mira must have looked unconvinced. "I know you really care about Isabel," Vivian said, more gently. "And I believe you when you say that she cares about you. I'm not telling you to come out to meet someone else, though you can, if you want. I'm telling you to come out, be around other girls like you, and take your mind off it for a while."

Mira sighed. "I want to know something."

"Yeah?"

"When I was with Dylan, you and Frankie always hated him, but you still listened to me and supported me the whole time I was with him. Instead of, I don't know, just yelling at me every day to break up with him. And I know why. Because I wasn't in a place where I could listen."

Vivian nodded. Mira went on. "But I want to know—are you keeping something like that from me? I want to know if you think there's something I should be doing, and you're not telling me because you think I can't handle it right now."

They walked for a few steps in silence. Then Vivian said, "No."

"Are you sure?"

"You know why I'm worried about you. But I think you should do what you want." At that, Mira scoffed. "Just make sure it actually is what you want," Vivian added. "I don't think you actually wanted to be with Dylan, as opposed to some idea of Dylan you had in your head, and I said that to you at the time."

"I don't know what I want. That's the whole problem."

"What were you hoping I'd tell you to do?" Mira was struck by the question. "Maybe you should start with that."

21

HALF A BLOCK AWAY FROM VOLUME, the thumping bass rattled Isabel's bones and numbed her to everything else. She needed this. She hadn't been back since the night she met Mira, and now she was trying to do the impossible: to forget about Mira, at least for a few hours. Cat's set would be starting soon.

She'd made a mess of this. So much for staying away from Mira and not looking at her. Mira had worn down her walls so slowly and persistently that Isabel hadn't even noticed until it was too late. She'd spilled everything—her dangerous feelings, her endless grief—and Mira had taken it all surprisingly well. But Isabel still felt too exposed, as though she'd peeled off an outer layer of skin.

And...that night last week. Lying awake for hours, all her senses magnified, her imagination tormenting her over the innocent sighs and creaks she'd heard from Mira's room. And then walking right into Mira...

Isabel hadn't slept much after that, either. Curiosity was one thing, but no straight woman on the planet had ever looked at another woman like that, Isabel was certain. Or maybe her imagination had run wild again. Wishful thinking.

In any other situation, she'd buck up and ask Mira what she wanted. But Mira was living in her apartment for another year.

If there was even a chance of hurting Mira, Isabel wouldn't risk it. She burned with frustration. Not at Mira, never at her, but at everything that kept them apart. Even if Mira didn't have a million good reasons for not getting involved with her roommate...well, just because she thought Isabel was worth looking at didn't mean she wanted Isabel's baggage.

Isabel had been frustrated that night, too. She'd been so out of her mind that she'd almost taken out her vibrator while Mira was in the shower. Knowing Mira was naked at that very moment, water sluicing down her body—that hadn't helped, either.

She'd made herself a promise to not touch herself while thinking about Mira. A meaningless line in the sand, maybe, but she'd needed to draw one somewhere. And after months of pent-up longing, she'd broken her promise yesterday in the shower, shaking and muffling herself in her elbow, slick and dripping down her thighs. It hadn't taken the edge off. She'd sensed the thick, syrupy tension between them during dinner, worse than ever. Or maybe she'd imagined that too.

How was she going to get through a year of this?

She reached the front of the line, showed her ID, and went through the door. Time to leave all that behind. Isabel used to meet women here, and at other bars and clubs where queer people cruised each other. She'd done it often when she was younger, heady with the awareness of how many girls wanted a big blue-collar butch to take them home and take charge. With Isabel, you knew what you were getting.

She hadn't picked up anyone since she started dating Reina, and she didn't want to tonight. She probably wouldn't want to for a good, long while. She couldn't even imagine being so over Mira that she'd bring another girl home. But it was good to be with her people, and a little dancing, maybe even a little flirting, wouldn't kill her.

Within the first hour, she spotted an old ex she was still friendly with and another one she didn't talk to anymore. She was disintegrating into Cat's music and into the masses of people, all with their own problems and their own needs. Women looked her over and tried to come closer, and she didn't discourage or encourage them.

Then, far away in the crowd, there was a flash of curly dark hair. Isabel's heart clenched.

The person turned around, and the strobe lights illuminated their face. No, that wasn't Mira—Isabel had memorized her face and the way she moved. Isabel's alarm turned to a strange sense of disappointment. She didn't want to find Mira here, did she?

She was thrown off, no longer part of the crowd even if she was in the middle of it. The music was infinitely far away and too loud. She had to clear her head. She looked around, found the exit sign, and started weaving through the crush of people. At the coat check, she grabbed her leather jacket, barely paying attention.

The too-cold air was a relief to her face and lungs. She rubbed her face, ran a hand through her hair, and froze.

Mira was standing on the sidewalk.

She spotted Isabel a moment later. Her dark eyes widened, and her lips parted. The pounding music disappeared along with every other person outside. So many beautiful women at the club, yet the only one Isabel truly saw was Mira.

They approached each other. Mira was stunning. Under the streetlights and the club's neon sign, her skin subtly shimmered and her curly hair shone in every color. She wore a puffy jacket, but underneath it was that unforgettable slinky black dress.

Isabel couldn't hold back anymore. She stared—at the long lines of Mira's legs in her tights, her dramatic eye makeup, her lush lipstick, the hint of cleavage under her half-unzipped jacket. Isabel usually saw her prim and put-together for work, or soft and cozy in her house clothes, and it was a treat to see her no matter what. But now Mira was gorgeously done up, standing taller and more self-possessed than on the night they'd met, and Isabel was going to faint.

They were close now, so close that she could make out Mira's individual mascara-coated lashes. Mira had on a delicate gold necklace, the pendant pointing straight down between her breasts in that low-cut dress. Isabel swallowed.

Mira spoke first. "What's a nice girl like you doing in a place like this?"

Isabel laughed. As always, Mira could disarm her in an instant. She was exquisite, playful and sparkling, her cheeks glowing from the cold.

"I'm not nice," Isabel said. It was true. Her self-control was fraying. What she wanted from Mira could ruin them both, and Isabel should be pushing her away.

But they both stayed right where they were. Mira's eyes widened—and in them, desire blazed, hot and wild. Isabel's words could have been a joke or a warning. She wasn't sure herself. Apparently, Mira had taken them as a challenge. "What do you call it when you rescue girls from their bad exes and make sure they get home safe? Are you just being honorable? Like a knight?"

Isabel had leaned closer unthinkingly. Mira had to tilt her head up. Her lips were painted dark red, and her breaths were coming fast, forming clouds in the chilly air. She was vibrant, delicate, alive. And nervous, too, which made her boldness even more alluring. A few more threads of Isabel's self-control snapped. "I'm not that honorable, either."

"So you have ulterior motives for coming here?"

"Yeah." Isabel glanced at that gorgeous mouth again. The beating of her own heart drowned out everything else. "You could say that."

Mira smiled. "Then it's a good thing I'm not a pure maiden, either."

They kissed. Hot, messy, surprisingly slow. Electric heat flooding through Isabel's body, stars behind her eyes. Mira's mouth was so soft, and the kiss was so perfect it hurt, and Isabel was so ecstatic she could die. Finally, finally, finally—Isabel had found an oasis in the desert, and she'd never drink deeply enough.

They broke off the kiss, panting, Mira's expression wild and desperate. Then Mira lunged at her, and Isabel grabbed Mira with both hands, fingers tangling in Mira's lush hair, and kissed her again.

No matter what, Isabel would always have this—Mira moaning needily as she squirmed with abandon against Isabel, her clear hunger the hottest fucking thing about it. She pulled Isabel down by the collar, and Isabel's hand went to the small of Mira's back, slipping under her jacket, feeling the furnace of her body through that thin dress and pulling her in tight. Isabel wanted so much, too much. She wanted to spend all night making Mira moan like this, wanted to kiss Mira like this every morning when they woke up. She was so far gone.

Then Mira broke off their kiss. She looked dazed, then uncertain. Isabel let go of her, panic rising.

For a few seconds, neither of them spoke.

"I'm sorry," Mira said, looking closer to the scared girl from that first night than the siren she'd been a minute ago. "I'm sorry. I don't know what I..."

She ran past Isabel, toward the subway station, and then she was gone.

22

It was a long train ride home, but Mira barely noticed it. She would never forget that kiss for as long as she lived. And the way Isabel had grabbed her... She'd forgotten how *good* it could feel to be touched. She'd sizzled at the contact. Even now, the memory of Isabel's hands lingered all over her skin.

Her phone buzzed once every few minutes. She ignored it, and tried to ignore her guilt, too.

For one moment, she had done what she wanted, like Vivian had told her to. And now she couldn't blame anyone but herself. The consequences were hers, and she had made everything worse. Life would be easier if she never wanted anything at all.

The kiss had been searing. At least Mira would never, ever doubt again that she liked women. But it hadn't changed what mattered. Not the fact that Mira had no business getting into another relationship, let alone one with someone she lived with. Not the fact that they'd just signed a year-long lease together. Not the fact that they'd built a sweet, tentative friendship, one Mira had started to rely on, and Mira had just ruined it, because she couldn't imagine simply being friends and roommates again after this kiss that had overturned her life.

She was deposited at her own train stop too soon. She couldn't go back to the apartment; sooner or later, probably sooner, she'd have to face Isabel there. Better to avoid the consequences of her actions for a little longer.

Despite the cold, she walked past her apartment and continued toward the river.

Every awful scenario played itself out in her head. All variations on a theme: Isabel might be good to her now, but eventually she'd realize she didn't have to be, whether that had already happened or would happen in a week or a month or a year, and then Mira would be trapped. And this time, it would hurt so much more. She had kept her wits partially about her with Dylan. But she had fallen too fast for Isabel, diving into the deep end, and now she was in danger of drowning.

Maybe it wouldn't happen that way. Maybe Isabel would continue being good to her. Maybe her heart would be broken for one of a million other reasons. But her worst fears were coming to feast on the moment of joy she'd found outside the club, and now there was nothing left.

The park was deserted. Cars passed by with their blinding headlights, but no one would take a walk at this time of night in December. Mira's breath fogged up as she walked along the river path. The lights of Manhattan glittered, remote and cold.

Her phone rang. Mira was paralyzed by guilt once again. Before she could decide whether to pick up, it went to voicemail.

She walked another few steps, then took out her phone

with frozen fingers. She played the voicemail as she looked out at the dark, rippling water.

"Mira, I'm sorry," Isabel said, her voice stiff. It was clear even in the tinny recording how much emotion she was suppressing. Mira was shaken. She liked seeing Isabel best in her moments of openness, laughing or crying, not holding back. Not like this. "I'm worried about you. Please tell me if you're safe. Even if you don't want to come home." She inhaled shakily. The voicemail cut off.

Mira was a coward. Everything fell into place. Kissing Isabel at the club had been reckless, but it wasn't the end of the world. Running away and ignoring Isabel's messages, knowing how much Isabel cared about her safety, was so much worse.

The problem wasn't that she'd done what she wanted. She hadn't known what she wanted, and she'd done something halfway without following through, and now she'd hurt Isabel as well as herself.

Mira stared blankly at the river and the Manhattan skyline. The chill set in alongside her remorse. She wasn't ready to go home yet.

But she could at least be brave enough to call.

Isabel picked up immediately. "Are you okay?" Her voice was threaded with panic.

"Yes, I'm okay. I'm so sorry for making you worried about me. I'm okay."

Isabel exhaled. Her palpable relief made Mira's insides twist in guilt. "I'm sorry, Mira. I shouldn't have done that. I'm so sorry. If you don't feel safe with me, I—"

"What are you talking about?"

Silence on the line. "I thought you didn't want me to kiss you. Or that I rushed into doing something you'll regret, or—"

"Isabel, I wanted it." It was exhilarating to finally own up to what she wanted. No more second-guessing. "I wanted it so much. You have nothing to apologize for. I wanted to kiss you, and I don't regret it." She might not like all the consequences. But she'd never, ever regret that kiss.

"Oh." Isabel's voice trembled. "I was so afraid. Oh, god, I don't want to hurt you."

"You didn't hurt me, okay? I ran away because I didn't know what I wanted and I was scared. Not scared of you. Are you in the apartment?" She could think through all this in the fifteen minutes it took to walk home, and then she and Isabel could work it out together. Maybe there was no way to make this work. But she owed it to Isabel, and herself, to at least figure out what she wanted.

"Yeah," Isabel said. "Where are you?"

"I'm at the park." At that, Isabel sucked in a breath. "Please don't come get me, okay? Stay where you are. I'm coming home."

ISABEL SAT STIFFLY on the couch, relief and fear both written on her face. Mira rushed to her and sat down. After a moment's hesitation, she flung her arms around Isabel's shoulders.

Isabel softened slightly in her arms and turned toward her. "I was worried about you." Her thick, silky black hair brushed against Mira's face. Her voice was level, but Mira knew better. There was panic underneath, and even anger.

"I know." Mira held on tight. "I'm so sorry, Isabel. Please forgive me."

"I'm just glad you're okay," Isabel said quietly.

It wasn't enough. Isabel had truly been afraid for her, and afraid for what this meant for them. Mira simply hadn't imagined this possibility: Isabel caring enough about her to be devastated when she'd disappeared. Her own fear had made her thoughtless, even cruel.

"You don't have to say that," Mira said. "I'm sorry for running away." Isabel acknowledged that with the smallest nod. "I'm so glad I'm back here with you."

Reluctantly, Mira let go and slipped her coat off. Isabel uncurled her limbs, and they wordlessly slid their arms around each other side-by-side on the couch. Mira tipped her head forward so their foreheads touched. If this was all they'd ever have, Mira would remember this moment even more than the kiss: holding Isabel, and being held.

But first, she had a lot to say. She disentangled herself from Isabel again. "I've been thinking about what I want." It hadn't been difficult to figure out. "I want to be honest with you."

Hope and terror flared on Isabel's face, making Mira ache. "What is it?"

"I want to give this a try." Mira's heart was pounding. "I'm scared, to be honest. I didn't expect this to happen so soon. But I know I want you." She flushed and dropped her gaze. Then she looked Isabel in the eye again. She needed to be brave. "I can't pretend this didn't happen and go back to the way things were. I don't know what this means or what we're going to do. But I really, really want you. You're so strong and capable and caring, and I've never met anyone like you. I don't think I've ever wanted anyone this much."

Isabel turned away. The words rang between them. "Are you okay?" Mira asked.

She didn't know what Isabel wanted. So much was still unspoken between them. If Isabel didn't actually want this —well, at least Mira would have been honest, both to Isabel and to herself, and she would survive.

"I don't want you to get hurt," Isabel said flatly. "I want to be with you, too. You have no idea. I want you so much it scares me." She still wasn't looking at Mira. "You didn't know this would happen when you moved in with me."

"Neither did you." Mira smiled. "Unless you really did rescue me just to seduce me, in which case I wouldn't complain."

Isabel smiled back, but only for a moment. "I mean, with your ex. I'm worried you're going to feel trapped here, like you did with him, and that it won't be easy for you to leave. I hate knowing it's not fair to you."

"I've thought about this, too. Let's just talk about it honestly, okay?" Mira took a deep breath. They were getting to the hard part. "I do really want to try this. But I also need to be able to leave. Leave this apartment, and leave you." Isabel tensed up—almost imperceptibly, but Mira was attuned to her every movement. "I trust you. I know you won't abuse me or try to control me with your money. But I need to know the option is there."

"Of course." Isabel's expression was familiar: in pain, and trying to not show it. "I'll do everything within my power that you ask me to do, if it comes to that. I promise that to you." She hesitated. "I know you don't want my money. But I'll help you move, I'll help you find a new place, I'll find someone to take your room. Anything."

She spoke calmly about the logistics of Mira leaving her, as though she'd thought about it too. Mira slipped an arm around her broad shoulders again. Promises could be broken, but Isabel had given her enough reasons to trust her, and Mira couldn't live in fear forever.

"I believe you," Mira said. Isabel relaxed against her. "You've been so good to me, Isabel. You've been a good friend. You make me feel safe, and you've made me stronger and braver, and I've healed so much since I moved in." She didn't want Isabel dwelling only on how she could hurt Mira. "I didn't know how much I needed it until I met you."

Saying what she needed even though she was afraid—she couldn't have done this three months ago. The seed of that change had been inside her all along, but Isabel had watered it, too. Isabel had reminded her that she owed it to herself to talk to her coworkers, no matter how much it terrified her. Isabel had taken her seriously from the beginning, and Isabel was taking her seriously even now.

"What do you want from me, Mira?" Isabel asked.

Mira steeled herself. She owed both of them her answer. "I think we should take things slow. And I know we already live together, which makes that difficult." They exchanged uneasy smiles. "You know I just got out of the worst relationship of my life. I can't handle anything serious or committed right now. I guess that means...we should keep things casual." The word wasn't right. She yearned for Isabel, and she was afraid for herself, and *casual* was such an inadequate way to split the difference. But it was all she had.

Isabel nodded solemnly. "But I want to keep spending time with you," Mira continued. "I, um, I loved kissing you." She was understating it, and blushing like a schoolgirl, too. She'd kissed lots of people. Discussing it like this was something else. "I think I would need to ease into the physical side of things. It's not easy for me to have sex with anyone new. But I do want it. I want to try it with you."

Even saying the words made heat spread through her body. She wanted to feel safe and cared for during sex, and she wanted Isabel to fuck her until she couldn't stand. Maybe she could actually have that, and not only as a fantasy locked up in her head.

"I want that too," Isabel said, a low, urgent note in her voice. She added, "If you just want sex..."

She didn't sound happy about it. "That's not what I meant," Mira said. Asking for kissing and sex was already extravagant, but she wanted even more. "I want to spend time with you and get to know you. In the way people date and get to know each other when they don't, um—don't already live together." She hesitated. "If we need to discuss apartment things, then we can do it as roommates. But other times..." How much more did she want? Maybe she could figure it out along the way.

"Do you want to keep things the way they are, aside from when I take you out?" Isabel asked.

No. Mira didn't want that either. The prospect of Isabel taking her on dates was wonderful. But the idea of not being able to kiss Isabel at home at breakfast, at dinner, before bed, whenever she wanted was unbearable. "No. I don't think I'd be able to keep my hands off you."

Isabel's eyes widened. So did Mira's. Had she just said that aloud? Isabel smiled—her first real smile tonight, and such a lovely one, too. Now that Mira allowed herself to do it, every moment of looking at Isabel was a gift.

"Can I kiss you right now?" Isabel asked.

Mira nodded. They kissed again. It was sweet and slow, and the way Isabel cradled her jaw was delicious, making her whimper and melt. Isabel was clearly restraining herself, and Mira matched her even though she wanted more.

Then Isabel pulled back like she was rationing their kisses. "You can keep going," Mira said.

"Later." Isabel didn't seem like she wanted to wait any more than Mira did. "After we're finished." Her face turned serious again. "You can decide whenever you want that we're done. And you can move out whenever you want. I mean it. I won't ask anything else of you."

The pain in her eyes had returned. Mira didn't like thinking about leaving, either. But the words reassured her, and they made her want to get closer, knowing she could walk away. Isabel would be good to her through the end.

"Thank you," Mira said, truly grateful. Something occurred to her. "If I leave, I won't do it like when I ran away from you tonight. That wasn't fair to you."

Isabel looked away. "You don't owe me anything."

Mira tugged her hand, urging her to make eye contact again. "I'm going to try to be as good to you as I can, even if it doesn't work out." She wished she could promise Isabel more. Not just for Isabel's sake, but for her own. But it was too easy to be pulled under, and she had to keep her head above water. "I want this to work."

Isabel was silent for a few seconds, her face hinting at emotions Mira couldn't discern. "I do, too," Isabel said finally. "Can I kiss you again?"

The way she asked for permission was so gentle. She didn't have to, but Mira liked it. She nodded.

Isabel turned her body toward Mira, and Mira cupped her face, and they kissed again. It was a slow, hot kiss, heating Mira to her center and making her ache for more. When they pulled apart, they were both panting. Mira was as wild as she'd been earlier tonight, seeing Isabel in her leather jacket outside the club again and boiling with desire she finally had a name for.

"I want you so much," Mira said. Isabel's breath hitched. She leaned in, their lips brushing together. "I want you—" Mira was muffled by a kiss. "I want you to teach me everything. I want you to do everything to me." Saying it aloud was making her desperately turned on.

Isabel growled. She pushed Mira against the back of the couch, tipped Mira's head back, and kissed her neck, swirling her tongue and gently nipping at Mira's skin. Mira gasped, her body lighting up, her nipples tightening against her lacy bra. She squirmed and squeezed her legs together. Isabel hadn't even gotten her clothes off, and she was already molten with pleasure.

"I went out tonight to try to take my mind off you, but I couldn't think about anything else," Isabel murmured against her sensitive skin. Mira quivered. She needed Isabel to tear her clothes off and put that mouth all over her. "You're so gorgeous, Mira. I..."

She caught Mira's mouth in a kiss again, saying whatever she couldn't say in words. For all her hardness, her mouth was wonderfully soft, and she knew exactly what to do with her tongue. Jolts of electricity raced up Mira's spine, and the ache between her legs surged.

She ran her hand through Isabel's luxurious hair, then over the powerful, shifting muscles of her back, then over the hot, exposed strip of skin between her T-shirt and her waistband. Isabel moaned against her mouth—such a gorgeous reaction. Mira's hand wandered back up, and she gently stroked the underside of one of Isabel's soft, heavy breasts. Isabel let out a surprisingly high whimper. Then Mira found Isabel's nipple, hard through her bra, and Isabel made that delicious sound again—

She pulled away. Mira blinked, hazy with arousal, still thinking about pulling Isabel's T-shirt off. "Sorry," she said, after a second.

Isabel's breathing was ragged. A sweet rosy blush had risen on her cheeks. "It's fine. It's just... You said you wanted to take things slow."

"I guess so." Mira was flushed, too, and her heartbeat

pulsed between her thighs. Self-consciousness came over her. She never acted or talked like this. Had she ever wanted sex so badly in her life?

"I want you so much, Mira." Isabel's gaze burned. She leaned in for one more tender kiss, which turned into a few desperate, hot kisses, and then a series of more small kisses when they couldn't bring themselves to pull away.

"Do we have to stop?" Mira said, her mouth an inch from Isabel's, their foreheads touching. A line of Catullus drifted into her mind, and she smiled to herself—of course a thousand kisses wouldn't be enough.

"If you want to go slow, we should wait." Isabel didn't look like she wanted to.

"How long?" Truthfully, Mira wasn't sure if she could wait another five minutes.

"Will you let me take you out to dinner first?"

Mira laughed. Isabel saying she wasn't honorable had been an absurd lie. "You don't have to be chivalrous about it. You can do whatever you want to me right now."

Isabel closed her eyes, took a deep breath, and opened them again. "Next Friday. I want to have plenty of time for you."

Six days. Isabel might as well have said six years. "Can we still kiss?"

Isabel grinned. She leaned in and gave Mira a teasing kiss. Then came another, and another...

Isabel pulled away. "You're not making this easy." Her lips brushed Mira's cheek, and Mira shivered. "We should talk about a few more things first. And it's been a long night." Another gentle kiss on the cheek. "I promise I'll make it worth your wait."

23

ISABEL RAN her fingers through her hair in front of the mirror. She felt like a teenager again. Giddy and anxious, and trying to project enough butch swagger that her date wouldn't notice. She adjusted the collar of her button-down shirt, tugged at the cuffs to make sure they showed under the sleeves of her suit jacket, and tweaked her shirt collar again.

She'd gotten the suit made for Alexa's wedding. Her body had changed after a few more years of hard work, but it still fit. Even if she felt like an entirely different person inside it.

If she waited any longer, she'd be late. She smoothed out her suit jacket one last time, left her room, and found Mira standing just outside. Mira smiled shyly.

Isabel stopped in her tracks. Mira's makeup brought out her stunning eyes, and she was wearing that wine-colored lipstick Isabel liked so much and wanted all over her shirt collar. Mira's dress was plum velvet—demure but fitted, the fabric darkly shimmering where her curves caught the light, practically begging Isabel to touch. She had on those sheer black tights that showed off her sinuously long legs. Delicate, bell-shaped golden earrings glittered against her hair.

Isabel was dizzy. Mira was perfect, in that exquisite femme way that made Isabel want to drop to her knees and beg and weep.

Mira came to her first. "Oh my goodness, Isabel. You look beautiful." She ran a manicured finger down Isabel's suit lapel. Just that light touch through layers of fabric set Isabel's skin ablaze. "Could you zip me up?"

She turned and lifted her hair out of the way, exposing her back and shoulders, her skin burnished in the low light. A thin gold chain and its clasp gleamed at the nape of her neck.

Isabel's heart skipped a beat. She itched to press a kiss to that exposed triangle of skin between Mira's shoulder blades. Reluctantly, she pulled the zipper all the way up and latched the hook. When her fingers grazed Mira's back, Mira shivered.

She turned around. Isabel's throat went dry. "You're gorgeous, Mira." She tucked a loose ringlet behind the curve of Mira's ear and brushed a thumb against her dangling earring. "I like your jewelry."

"Thank you." Mira beamed. "My dad's sister gave a lot of it to me. I wish I had more chances to wear it."

"You can leave that to me." Isabel took Mira's hand in her own and kissed the back of it. Mira's bangles jingled softly. Gold jewelry was lovely on her.

Mira laughed. "You're trying to seduce me."

"Is it working?"

"Yes." Mira pressed her body close and slung her arms around Isabel's neck, and Isabel bent down to kiss her.

They had been kissing and talking things out all week, making time when they could around Mira's end-of-semester work, trying to take things slow. Last night they'd kissed each other good night for twenty minutes, with Mira pressed up against Isabel's bedroom door frame, neither of them able or willing to stop.

If they didn't restrain themselves now, they'd miss their dinner reservation. After a few more heated kisses, Isabel pulled away. "I don't want to smear your lipstick."

"It's waterproof." Mira smiled. "Although I suppose we'll see about that."

Isabel's face turned shockingly hot. She swallowed hard. They were in danger of not making it out the door. "Let's go."

THEY WENT to a little Greek restaurant with a view of the park. Isabel had agonized over where to take Mira—somewhere fancy but not too fancy, somewhere where she and her ex hadn't gone a million times, somewhere with good vegetarian options, somewhere not too close but not too far, somewhere special. In the end, Mira had suggested this place. Sitting in this cozy neighborhood spot with table-cloths and candles, Isabel hoped it would become *their* place.

Isabel was captivated. She was completely gone. Half a year ago, she wouldn't have thought she was still capable of this kind of wild, helpless delight. But here she was, across the table from beautiful, brilliant, wonderful Mira looking like a dream in candlelight, the murmur of the restaurant fading away.

Isabel wasn't going to screw this up. As hopeful as she was, she couldn't forget the truth: This was a new chance at happiness she'd done nothing to deserve. And she couldn't take it for granted. Mira hadn't promised her anything, and Mira didn't owe her anything.

She was going to do right by Mira for as long as Mira wanted her.

"I read some of the poems you gave me," Isabel said. She'd read about half the poems in the book, trying to get closer to Mira's world. She'd been surprised. She'd found grief, but also heartbreak, anger, envy, and love. And plenty of obscenity. At times, it had seemed like the poet was just rambling to his friends. Mira was listening patiently. "I didn't expect to get a sense of his entire life. He's tortured over whether that woman loves him. He's grieving for his brother. And he's also caught up in his day-to-day life and talking shit about people he doesn't like. It's what you said about his range. The way it's all mixed together." The best and the worst of what life could throw at you, woven together with the mundane. She shrugged. What she had to say was probably far beneath Mira's level.

"No, that's exactly right," Mira said. "Isn't it wonderful? What you're saying is why I became interested in lyric and elegiac poetry in the first place. It's the human scale of it. Two thousand years later, all that sorrow and joy and envy still leap off the page. I think most of us can recognize ourselves in Catullus's poems. Including, frankly, the parts of ourselves we may not want to admit to."

Mira's eyes were bright. Isabel could listen to her forever. "It's part of why teaching matters so much to me. I want my students to understand that studying Classics is for everyone, because it's so deeply human. Anyone can put in the work and find themselves in a shared conversation that's been ongoing for thousands of years, and I don't want any of my students to feel like it's not for them because of who they are." Mira paused. "I haven't talked to you much about my research, have I?"

Isabel shook her head. "I asked when you visited the apartment for the first time." That was an eternity ago. "You said you didn't want to bore me. I figured you thought I wouldn't get it."

"Oh, no. You know I can't abide that kind of elitism. I assumed you were just asking out of politeness." At that, Isabel snorted. Mira smiled. "I thought that if I went on about it, you wouldn't care. I'm happy to tell you as much as you want. If not more."

"I do care. I found some of your papers online." Isabel flushed. "I figured you should explain it to me yourself."

Mira's smile grew. "I guess there aren't a lot of classicists named Mira Srinivasan-Levin, huh?"

"I guess you're special." Isabel's face went red-hot. She wasn't even trying to be smooth. She just adored Mira so much, and Mira was so sexy when she talked about her work. Isabel was out of her mind.

"Oh my goodness, Isabel. Stop." Mira's calf brushed against Isabel's under the table, sending a warm jolt through Isabel's body. That might have been an accident. But then Mira did it again.

Isabel's breath hitched. Mira's expression was perfectly innocent. "Anyway, as you might have seen, I study Latin lyric poetry and its relationship to Greek lyric. I'm interested in how the Roman poets took a tradition that was oral and musical and turned it into a literary genre for their own time and place." She paused. "Did you read Catullus 51? Where the speaker sees their beloved sitting next to a man?"

Isabel took a moment to recall it. "I think so."

"It's a Latin adaptation of a Sappho poem. She sees the woman she's in love with sitting next to a man, and admires his composure. Because she knows if she were the one sitting next to the woman, she would be at a loss for words." She recited a few lines of poetry in Greek, in a lilting rhythm that sounded like music. She was entrancing. "'For when I look at you, even for a moment, none of my voice remains. But my tongue has broken, and at once a delicate fire has run under my skin.'" Mira looked shyly at Isabel through her lashes. "Speaking of recognizing ourselves in poetry."

Isabel shivered with desire. The things Mira could do to her just with words, sitting across the table... "Do you memorize every poem that you study?"

"I don't go out of my way to do it. But the poems I've read and studied and taught for years stay with me."

"And you never thought you might like women yourself?"

Mira laughed—a bright, pealing sound. "You know, for a long time, I was averse to any kind of personal identification with my work. I got tired of people assuming that I must study gender or South Asia or something. But all this time, I could have just been learning from Sappho herself."

Her leg pressed against Isabel's again. No, that was Mira's foot, deliberately running up and down Isabel's calf, insistent and warm through Isabel's slacks.

For a second, Isabel entirely forgot what they were talking about. "Let's get the check."

THE WALK home from the park had never been so torturously long. By the time they stumbled through the front door, holding hands and giggling like loons, Isabel could barely think. She slammed the door shut and pulled Mira into a kiss. They warmed up fast from the cold, and

Mira whimpered urgently as her lipstick slid against Isabel's mouth. Isabel wanted to get lost in kissing this woman senseless forever.

Then Mira stumbled and yelped, and Isabel rushed and caught her before she fell. "These heels," Mira muttered. She kicked them across the floor. Then she yanked Isabel down to her height for another kiss.

Isabel had to slow down before she got swept away—she had to make this last. She broke off their kiss. "Mira, sweetheart," she said, their faces an inch apart. Mira looked startled. Isabel had let the word slip out. "Let's take your coat off."

Mira fumbled with her buttons, clearly impatient. Isabel leaned forward, cupped Mira's face, and kissed her on the cheek again. "Take your time. We have all night, okay?"

Mira nodded. When she was turned on, she was unbelievably, adorably sexy, all pleading doe eyes and flushed skin and the sweetest needy sounds. Isabel was going to keep her promise from last week. She was going to give Mira the best night she'd ever had.

Mira finished unbuttoning her coat, and Isabel slipped it off her shoulders and hung it up. She did the same with her own coat and turned back to Mira, already mildly debauched with her hair tousled and her lipstick a little smudged. Not so waterproof after all.

It was hard to be patient. Isabel wanted to mess her up thoroughly, to unzip her out of that dress and tug those tights off... But she had to focus. She indulged herself in one more kiss. This time, Mira tugged at her suit lapels, and Isabel went weak in the knees.

"I've wanted to do that ever since I saw you in this suit," Mira said, when they came up for air.

Isabel shivered. This was going to be the end of her. "Mira." She ran a thumb along Mira's jaw and took in the way her eyes widened. "Let's get to my bed before I do all the things I want to do to you right in this hallway."

Mira squirmed against her. "You could."

Isabel grinned. "Don't tempt me. Here, hold on." In one swift motion, she crouched and scooped up Mira like a bride. Mira shrieked and laughed and held on tight. Isabel would never have anything more precious in her arms. "Let's go."

24

MIRA NESTLED her head against Isabel's shoulder as she was carried across the threshold. This was where she belonged, safe in Isabel's arms, warm and melty and so, so turned on. "Turn the light on for me," Isabel said, her voice velvety and low.

Mira reached out and flipped the light switch. She had only been in Isabel's bedroom while showing strangers the apartment, looking around the room with a longing she couldn't name. Now she knew what she wanted, and she was exactly where she wanted to be.

Isabel set her down with exquisite carefulness on top of the covers. Mira stretched out on the flannel bedspread, which was thick, rugged, and surprisingly soft against her bare skin. Not unlike Isabel herself. Mira reveled in the intimacy of it. Isabel slept in this bed every night, and soon she was going to fuck Mira in it.

Isabel shut the door, which made Mira smile as she shivered in anticipation. They had this cozy apartment all to themselves, and it wasn't as though anyone else would bother them. Isabel turned the bedside lamp on and the overhead light off, casting the room in a soothing glow.

"Can I unzip you?" Isabel asked.

"Yes, please. Let me take my earrings off, too." Mira sat up in the center of the bed, kneeled with her back to Isabel, and slipped the hooks out of her earlobes. She had thrifted her dress earlier in the week, wanting to wear something Isabel would be the first to unzip her out of—and now she was vibrating with impatience, squeezing her thighs together, struggling to keep still. The bed dipped behind her, and she put her earrings and bangles onto Isabel's outstretched palm.

Her necklace could stay on. Isabel would probably like her in that and nothing else.

Isabel parted her hair down the center and pushed it to either side of her neck. "I love your hair," she murmured. She undid the clasp at the top of Mira's dress, undoing what she'd done earlier, her fingertips tickling Mira's bare skin.

Isabel pulled the zipper down very, very slowly. Then her breath was on the newly exposed part of Mira's back, between her shoulder blades, and then came a teasing kiss that left Mira tingling.

"I've been thinking about this ever since you asked me to zip you up." Isabel's breath was warm against Mira's skin. Then came another kiss, open-mouthed this time, wet and white-hot against her spine. If Mira weren't already kneeling, her legs would have buckled. It was both frustrating and wonderful to be slowly teased like this—to be handled with care, as though she were precious, by someone who knew exactly what she was doing. "I thought about unzipping you instead and having you right there in the living room. I almost couldn't wait."

She pressed more kisses all the way down Mira's back,

and once the dress was fully unzipped, she coaxed it off Mira's shoulders. Mira couldn't wait any longer, and she got her arms free and twisted around. Isabel's eyes were blazing with desire, and Mira tangled her fingers in Isabel's thick hair and kissed her. They tumbled onto the bed, Isabel on top, kissing like they needed each other more than air.

They only broke apart to get Mira's dress off her hips and peel her tights off. "God, Mira, you're so fucking gorgeous," Isabel said, panting, both of them fumbling with her clothes. They finally came off, and then Mira was down to her lacy lingerie, her prettiest, skimpiest matching set.

Isabel stared down at her, mouth hanging open as though she'd forgotten how to breathe. Her gaze scorched Mira's skin. It was shockingly hot to be looked at by the right person, to feel exposed and beautiful and seen.

"Oh my god," Isabel said. She dove in again—this time with searing kisses just below Mira's jaw, using a little bit of teeth, making Mira squeal. Isabel's thigh slid between her legs, and Mira bucked her hips and moaned at the delicious friction. Her nipples were straining against the lace of her bra. She was going to make a mess of Isabel's nice slacks if they kept this up. "You're so beautiful, Mira," Isabel said, her breath hot against Mira's earlobe. "I can't believe—"

"Wait," Mira said. She clutched Isabel's lapels. "Let me take this off you. I've been waiting too."

Isabel laughed. It was impossible to stop kissing each other for long, and Mira let her lips brush against Isabel's as she slipped Isabel's suit jacket off her broad shoulders. She worked on Isabel's shirt next, impatience making her clumsy as she undid each button, both of them breaking out into giggles. It was wonderful to see Isabel having fun in bed.

Four buttons in, Mira had revealed a lot of delicious

cleavage in a sensible nude bra, and she was about to weep from frustration. She had never despised an article of clothing more. Isabel helped her out, and finally, *finally*, Isabel's bra and pants came off too.

Isabel's body was a marvel. Mira had seen those powerful arms and thighs before, and they were somehow even more luscious up close. Isabel's stomach spilled a little over the waistband of her boxer briefs, with a hint of rippling abdominal muscles underneath. The newly exposed parts of her skin were lighter than the rest, less tanned by the sun. And her breasts were so generous and lush that Mira went lightheaded.

She was desperate to lick every single square inch of Isabel, to bury her face in those breasts and take those nipples into her mouth... How had she ever thought that she didn't like women?

"You're so hot," Mira said, so turned on she struggled to find words. Isabel grinned, not shy in the least. Part of what made Isabel so fucking hot was that she *knew* she was hot. She got on top of Mira—and then their bodies were pressed together, bare skin to bare skin, and Mira couldn't think about anything at all.

Isabel's gorgeous black hair covered them like a curtain, and her breasts were deliciously heavy resting against Mira's own. She lit up every nerve in Mira's body with kisses, over her ears, her neck, her collarbones. Then Isabel's mouth wandered to the lacy edge of her bra. "You look good in pink lace," Isabel murmured. "I like this even more than your pajamas."

Mira flushed. "My pajamas?"

Isabel looked up, flustered. "I drove myself crazy looking at you in them. I didn't mean to, I just—"

Mira giggled. "It's okay. You can look. Actually, you can do more than that." Her face burned even hotter.

"Are you asking?"

Mira shivered. "Yes. Please touch me."

Isabel gently cupped her breasts—one in each warm, comforting hand—and rolled her thumbs over Mira's nipples through the lace. Arcs of pleasure raced down Mira's spine, and she gasped. "You can take it off. Please."

"You don't have to be so polite." Isabel slipped a hand under Mira, unhooked her bra with one hand in one easy motion, and tossed it aside. The air was cool against her nipples, and she drew a sharp breath.

"So gorgeous," Isabel said, her voice a low rumble. Mira was never going to get tired of hearing it. Isabel cupped her breasts again, and this time, there was nothing at all between her achingly tender nipples and Isabel's palms. She moaned and arched her back for more. "So sensitive," Isabel murmured. "You're adorable." She lowered her head and closed her mouth over a nipple, and Mira squealed.

Oh, this was good, too good. Isabel's sturdy thigh slid between Mira's legs again, and Mira writhed and whimpered and desperately pushed her breasts into Isabel's mouth, one after the other. Could she come like this? Probably not, but this was the closest she'd come to having an orgasm with someone else in a very, very long time, and she'd forgotten what it was like to lose herself in genuine, overwhelming need.

Isabel slipped a hand between their bodies. "Do you want me to touch you?" she asked, her breath warm against Mira's nipple, her eyes dark with desire.

Mira tensed up. The full-body glow faded. "Um, I think so."

This was what she'd been dreaming of, but some part of her still warned her to not expect too much. Isabel had been good to her tonight, but that couldn't undo years and years of being treated as an object of other people's commingled desire and contempt. Like she was nothing more than her body, and her body didn't belong to her.

Isabel had raised her expectations. But maybe that only opened her up to being hurt more. She had tried to explain all this to Isabel—that sex wasn't easy for her—and she had felt understood. But she'd been wrong in trusting people before.

"We don't have to," Isabel said, propping herself up and easing off. "I'd love to just keep kissing you."

Mira took a deep breath, returning to the moment. It was all up to her.

"I want you to," she said. Excitement rushed through her just from saying the words. "Um, I probably won't be able to come from it. But I still want you to touch me."

"That's okay." Isabel kissed her on the cheek again. Another thing Mira would never get tired of. "I'll do it for as long as you want, okay?"

Mira nodded, relieved that Isabel hadn't taken it as a challenge to try to make her come. "Will you kiss me while you touch me?"

Isabel pounced and hungrily kissed her mouth again. The heel of Isabel's hand slid between Mira's thighs, letting Mira set the pace and easing her into it, and Mira felt wanton as she rolled her hips upward harder and harder— and soon that wasn't enough. When Isabel hooked a thumb under the waistband of her underwear, asking a question, Mira whimpered in relief and nodded.

More impatient squirming as she got her panties off,

and now she was completely bare, and raw and vulnerable. But when Isabel's lips brushed her cheek, Mira knew everything she needed to know.

She was cared for. She was safe. She smiled up at Isabel. "I'm ready."

Isabel responded with a languid smile of her own. She sucked two of her own fingers into her mouth, getting them wet—and Mira was as wet as she ever got, but she appreciated the help, and it was so hot Mira almost fainted. "Let me." She took Isabel's fingers and put them in her own mouth, and traced the grooves and calluses with her tongue, heat pooling between her legs as she sucked.

Isabel's eyes widened. "Oh, you're gorgeous like this." Her voice was thick with desire.

She pushed her fingers in deeper, and Mira's entire body lit up at the thrust, her pussy aching. She could suck Isabel's fingers for hours, but right now, she needed those fingers where they belonged. She pulled them out of her mouth, slick and shining. "I think that's good."

Isabel slipped her hand between Mira's thighs again, and the first contact, fingers sliding through her sensitive folds, made Mira tense and gasp. Then came a brush against her clit, too light—and then more motions, all different, all deliberate, as Mira whimpered and let her hips move in response. Isabel was learning her body. And then Isabel did something that was just right, and a hot, electric pulse raced up Mira's spine as she cried out.

Isabel hummed in pleasure. She kissed Mira on the mouth, slow and sweet, and did the same thing again and again and again. Of course she was devastatingly good with her hands.

Mira dissolved into the sensations, moaning against

Isabel's mouth and moving her hips in time with Isabel's hand, riding out each delicious jolt of pleasure while the tension grew like a rising tide. Isabel's mouth moved to her neck, honing in on her sweet spots relentlessly. She'd kissed Mira's neck enough to know what made her squeal.

"Do you want me inside you?" Isabel asked, her lips hovering above Mira's collarbone.

Mira nodded, instinct taking over. She wanted more, more, more. Isabel twisted her hand, and then there were what felt like two fingers circling Mira's entrance, slick and teasing, not pushing in. Isabel's thumb returned to her clit, and the angle was different, but it was every bit as good. But those fingers were tormenting her. She needed Isabel inside. "Please," she said, arching her hips. She'd been waiting for days, for months.

"I like when you ask for what you want," Isabel said. She pressed her mouth to Mira's again and slid her fingers home.

The sheer relief of being filled was so sweet that Mira cried out, losing control. She couldn't stop moaning as Isabel curled her fingers and pumped them in and out, learning exactly how Mira liked to be fucked. Isabel's thumb on her clit never slowed down, and every kiss on her overheated skin made her shiver. Isabel was so intense, so deliberate, so careful, and Mira surrendered to the over-whelming pleasure. As her hips chased more of Isabel's hand, the first pang of what might turn into an orgasm hit her.

"I think I might be close," she said, shocked by her own body, by what Isabel could do to her. "I don't know how close."

Isabel hummed like she was savoring Mira. "Take your time, sweetheart."

She sped up, and a shockwave of pleasure tore through Mira so intense it almost hurt. She cried out, arching her back, digging her heels into the mattress, and then whimpered, as much as from embarrassment as anything else.

"You okay?" Isabel asked.

Mira nodded. She didn't want Isabel to stop. She wanted to trust Isabel, and to trust her own body. She just hoped she could.

Isabel's other hand found Mira's, and she interlaced their fingers and squeezed, as if to say *I've got you.* The reassurance unlocked something inside Mira, and she surrendered to the rising tide and was overcome by the shivery, elusive sensation of an impending climax. "Don't stop, please, please, please," she said, gasping. "Please—ah—"

Her orgasm rushed through her, hot and exquisite, as she moaned and writhed against Isabel's hand, needing more, never wanting it to end. As the sensation crested and receded, she squeezed Isabel's hand tight, as though she could communicate just through that—and Isabel kept up with her, somehow knowing just what she needed. When it became too much, Isabel sensed that, too, and eased her fingers out of Mira's body.

Mira went limp. In the afterglow, she was unbearably tender. Isabel lay down next to her, wrapped those strong arms around her, and held her close. Mira melted into a puddle against all that bare skin, that comforting solidity. "You're so precious," Isabel whispered, stroking Mira's back, sending showers of warm sparks through her.

Mira tangled her legs up with Isabel's, craving more touch. Inexplicably, she nearly teared up, and burrowed her face into the crook of Isabel's neck to take refuge. Mira had never let herself be so unguarded during sex before. Was this how it was supposed to be?

"How are you feeling?" Isabel asked.

"I'm good," Mira mumbled. She lived a life full of words. It was rare that she ever lost herself in raw, indescribable sensation. "Really good." The tears were threatening to overflow—happy, overwhelmed tears. She didn't want to frighten Isabel, so she held them in.

"You were wonderful," Isabel said. Her voice quavered. "I don't even know what to say."

Mira wriggled so she could look into Isabel's beautiful dark eyes, at that serious, striking face unraveled by emotion. "*You* were wonderful," Mira said. She kissed Isabel on the mouth and ran her hands through all that thick, lush hair.

Isabel moaned. When they broke apart, she said breathlessly, "Your nails."

"Oh, I'm sorry!" Mira had been raking Isabel's scalp. She pulled her hand away. "I wasn't thinking. I'm sorry."

Isabel smiled. She took Mira's manicured hand. "I didn't say I didn't like it." She took two of Mira's fingers and sucked them into her mouth, long nails and all, and ran her tongue over the sensitive pads of Mira's fingers.

Mira whimpered, flaring with arousal. She'd never investigated whether she could have multiple orgasms, but now she needed to find out. She pulled her fingers out, kissed Isabel again, and deliberately grazed Isabel's scalp with her nails. Isabel let out a sweet moan again, urging her on.

Mira's hand wandered lower. She cupped one of Isabel's soft, unbelievably lush breasts in her hand and gently pinched a nipple, and reveled in the throaty noise she drew out in response. She took Isabel's stud earring into her mouth and worked it with her tongue. Isabel squirmed, her breath hitching. "Oh, god, Mira."

This was intoxicating. Mira wedged her bare thigh between Isabel's legs, making her groan. The soft cotton of her boxer briefs was soaked through.

"You're so wet," Mira said, stunned into stating the obvious. *She* had done that to Isabel. "Can I do anything for you?" She kept her thigh exactly where it was. Isabel might have to teach her, which was just fine.

Isabel closed her eyes and exhaled shakily, then opened them, looking more composed. "Do you want to go again? I'd rather do that for you first."

"Well, um, I do," Mira said. "But—"

"How do you want it?" Isabel asked, her mouth close to Mira's ear—a deliberate distraction. "I can eat you out. Or you can have my strap."

Mira flushed, her pulse pounding everywhere. She wanted to make Isabel feel just as good, but apparently she'd have to wait, and of course she'd respect that. And she desperately wanted what Isabel was offering. If that was Isabel's answer, so be it.

If Mira wanted it so badly, she was going to have to ask for it. Her face burned. "Um, I don't know. I think I want your strap."

Isabel grinned. "You can have it."

She got out of bed and pulled her boxer briefs off. Mira propped herself up, taking in the thick dark curls between Isabel's legs, the incredible curves of her hips and ass and thighs in the soft light. Mira's mouth watered. She was a mess, roiling with arousal again, needing Isabel's comforting weight on top of her. Needing to be filled up. "I want you so much."

"You can have me however you want." Isabel reached down and caressed Mira's face, and Mira leaned into the touch. Then Isabel bent over her nightstand, and took out a black leather harness, a bottle of lube, and...a substantial dildo. Mira squirmed. She was going to die before Isabel even got inside her.

Isabel stepped into the harness, put the dildo into the ring, and tightened the straps with a few practiced motions. "Lie back, sweetheart," she said. "Let me take care of you."

25

ISABEL'S HEART was full to bursting as she closed the bedroom door behind her, with Mira sleeping peacefully inside. The earliest rays of sun filtered through the window as she started the coffee maker.

She couldn't stop smiling as she drank her coffee. Taking Mira to bed had been beyond her wildest dreams— the way she'd arched and trembled and writhed in Isabel's hands, the way she'd gasped and cried out like she was astonished by her own pleasure. Her scent, her taste, her softness. Most of all, the way she'd snuggled against Isabel after coming a third time, and cried a little and reassured Isabel that they were happy tears, and asked, "Could I sleep here tonight?"

It was precious to receive Mira's trust, precious to see her unwound and open, precious to be with her at all. Isabel's throat was lumpy as she sliced the loaf of challah on the counter. Being with Mira was the best thing that had happened to her in years. She wanted to wake up next to a beautiful, naked, sleeping Mira every morning, her dark curls spilling over Isabel's pillow, and fall asleep next to her every night.

Isabel absolutely couldn't fuck this up. After so much loss, it was terrifying to have something she desperately wanted to hold on to again. She had worried so much about hurting Mira that she hadn't thought about how badly she could be hurt, too.

And she could be hurt very, very badly. Because she didn't want Mira to leave.

She took a shuddering breath. If she wanted Mira to stay, if she wanted a chance at all, she'd have to be worth staying for. She had to be better than the partner she'd been —silent, walled-off, destroyed by her grief—when Reina had packed up and vanished.

Things were better now. Isabel was stronger, and life was more bearable. She just had to hope she would be good enough.

She cracked a few eggs into a bowl, added milk, sugar, and cinnamon, and distractedly stirred.

Even after months of longing for Mira, she'd been afraid to let Mira really touch her. She had come while fucking Mira with her strap for a second time, which was more than fine. She wasn't a stone butch, and she didn't always have to top, but falling apart under Mira's attentions would have been too much last night. She would have to ease into it and hope that Mira was willing to wait.

She put a generous pat of butter in the cast-iron pan, turned the stove on, and dredged the slices of stale bread in the egg mixture. When they'd gone limp, she put them in the pan and let them sizzle. The sweet fried scent filled the kitchen.

The door to her bedroom opened behind her. Isabel turned around.

Mira stood in the doorway, her hair tousled and wild, wearing one of Isabel's old T-shirts that hung off her small, perfect breasts like drapery on a statue. It was *barely* long enough to cover her. Was she wearing anything underneath? Isabel swallowed hard. Those legs had been wrapped around her hips last night, heels digging into her lower back—

"Good morning," Mira said, looking at Isabel from under those long eyelashes. There were faint bruises on her neck.

Isabel's knees went weak. She clutched the counter. "Morning."

"Sorry I took one of your shirts." For once, Mira didn't actually seem sorry. "I was going to my room to get dressed."

"Don't," Isabel blurted out. She flushed.

Mira laughed. "Okay, I won't. That smells good." She walked to Isabel, stood on tiptoes, and kissed Isabel on the lips gently. A second kiss followed, not nearly as gentle.

The scent of sizzling French toast became insistent. Isabel pulled away reluctantly. "Sorry. I need to..."

She flipped over the pieces in the pan. Behind her, Mira said, "It's all right if it gets crispy. I like that."

"Good to know." Isabel turned down the heat, pushed Mira against the fridge, and kissed her again. There was nothing like slipping her hand up under her own T-shirt worn by a beautiful girl in her own kitchen. And...no, Mira was not wearing anything underneath, and she was just as sensitive as she'd been last night.

Mine. The thought was loud, clear, and dangerous. Mira belonged to no one but herself. *Mine, mine, mine.* "I'm still a little sore," Mira said, panting. "Go easy on me. Not too easy."

Isabel tried to not get too carried away, but the French

toast still ended up with plenty of crispy bits. "You can give them all to me," Mira said, her face still prettily flushed as Isabel put their food on plates.

At the table, she poured a shocking amount of maple syrup over her stack and took a bite. Her eyes closed. "Oh, it's so good. Thank you so much. You are so sweet." She ducked her head and smiled. "I can't believe how good you are to me."

Isabel's chest fluttered with pleasure. She shrugged. "It's nothing. You know I like cooking for you."

"Stop saying that. I've never woken up to anyone making me breakfast before."

Isabel wasn't surprised, exactly, but how someone could live with Mira for two years and not do the simplest things for her was unimaginable. Isabel wasn't going to dwell on that. It made her angry in that instinctual way when something just wasn't right. She'd have to channel it into treating Mira how she deserved to be treated.

It still didn't seem real. She'd resigned herself to never being able to have Mira—and now Mira was happily eating breakfast at their kitchen table after she'd spent hours last night moaning and pleading and coming under Isabel's hands. Isabel had missed feeling wanted, missed feeling *needed*.

She wanted to give Mira everything. She couldn't protect Mira from every bad thing in the world, as much as it hurt to admit it. But she could provide the basics: good food, good sex, a shoulder to cry on, a warm, safe home to come back to every night. More than that, she wanted to be a partner Mira could rely on for the rest of her life.

Isabel's throat was lumpy again. It was too soon, and she had to take things slow for Mira's sake, and maybe she wasn't worthy. But she was in love. She wanted this to be forever.

They could be so good together. As long as Mira didn't leave.

Halfway through their breakfast, Mira started running her foot up and down Isabel's calf again. By the time they finished eating, Isabel was fully prepared to leave all the dishes in the sink, something she never did.

"We were doing something before we got interrupted," she said. There were some things she was good at, even if facing her emotions wasn't one of them.

"I think you're right," Mira said. She stood and took Isabel by the hand, leading her to the bedroom. Then Mira stopped short. "Can we go back to your bed?"

Isabel kissed her on the cheek. "Of course. You don't need to ask." She didn't say what she wanted to say. *My bed is yours. I'm yours. Everything I have is yours. And you're mine.*

"Are you still feeling nervous?"

Isabel nodded. Mira knew her well enough now that it was almost impossible to hide her state of mind. It made things easier and harder.

Mira leaned closer so she could be heard over the roar of the subway. "My friends will love you. You don't need to worry." She slid her hand into Isabel's hand.

After a blissful week of sleeping in, cooking together, taking long walks around the park, and making love to Mira in every room and on every surface of the apartment, Isabel felt human again. For now, she could devote herself to making Mira happy. And it made her happy, too, deeply content in a way she hadn't been in a very long time.

But she needed to win over Mira's friends, too. She had to make them see that they were good for each other, that Isabel was good for her. She was rusty on the winning-people-over front these days, unused to meeting people other than other electricians on her crew. She just hoped she'd be able to make her case.

And she hated the so-called holiday season. After being subjected to endless holiday cheer after Alexa had died, she never wanted to hear a Christmas pop song again in her life. At least her parents were having Christmas dinner with their church friends, removing that responsibility for her. She wasn't ready to see them again so soon.

Mira knew all this, and knew that Isabel didn't want to talk about it. There was nothing to say. Grief was monotonous. She just had to endure these darkest months of the year.

They got off the train in Chinatown and walked to one of the dim sum places. Mira and her Jewish friends gathered there every Christmas—so she'd explained—along with whoever else wanted to come, if they didn't celebrate Christmas or didn't want to visit family. The restaurant was well-lit and full of big groups, mostly families, talking and laughing. Isabel tensed up. Mira squeezed her hand and looked at her, asking a silent question.

"I'm okay," Isabel said. She opened the door for Mira, and they went in.

She spotted Mira's friends sitting around an enormous round table, waving at them—mostly about her age, and a lot more low-key than her ex's artist circle had been. Frankie and her girlfriend Vivian were there, and Shreya from Mira's union, and several other people whose names Isabel tried to remember as they introduced themselves. She was good at that, if nothing else, since she didn't like to forget apprentices' names.

They sat down. More people arrived, and they got through the usual gauntlet of ordering several dozen dishes for a dozen people. Isabel let the conversation wash over her. She chatted with Shreya, sitting on Mira's other side, who was straightforward in a way that put Isabel at ease. If Shreya thought it was strange that Isabel had reappeared as Mira's girlfriend—if that was the right word—she didn't say anything.

The food began to arrive. She tore into a fluffy char siu bao and talked to Mira's friend Noah about their work as a housing lawyer. They both had plenty to say about the new construction around the city. Vivian occasionally inter-jected. She might have been scrutinizing Isabel. Or maybe Isabel was imagining things.

She was starting to relax. Maybe she could just enjoy the company tonight.

"Mira," someone said across the table, and she and Mira both looked up. It was her friend Anjali a few seats away. "Seth and I have been meaning to ask you for wedding advice. Did your parents just have separate Jewish and Hindu ceremonies, or did they have a combined one? My parents said they could be fine with either, depending on the details, so it's kind of up to us."

"You're asking the wrong person," Mira said. "My parents got married at City Hall."

"Wait, seriously?" Anjali said. "And their parents were fine with that?"

Mira laughed. "No, of course not. At least my dad's parents weren't. He didn't even try to win them over about marrying my mom." There were winces all around the table. Isabel guessed that no one here was a stranger to parental disapproval of some kind. "My mom's parents were more okay with it. Both the elopement and her choice of spouse. I mean, yeah, he's not Jewish, but they got over it. Anyway, my dad isn't religious, and my mom wasn't as observant back then, and they're not sentimental people. Also, they were probably broke and couldn't afford a real wedding."

Isabel smiled. She'd heard the story from Mira already, in one of their long late-night conversations under the covers, and she'd seen Mira's photo of a framed photo in her parents' house: two serious, dorky twenty-somethings in front of Chicago's City Hall, Mira's mother in an eighties pantsuit and her father in a lumpy sweater, both with the same curly hair as Mira.

"Oh my god," Anjali said. "That's incredible. How did your parents even meet?"

"Well, my dad went to the UK for grad school and got involved in politics, and he was in a student group that would picket with the coal miners during the strike. And my mom was freelancing for some lefty newspaper on her first overseas assignment, and she wanted to know what was going on with the Indian guy out there." Mira shrugged. "My parents have always been like that."

"I didn't realize your parents were so cool," Noah said. The conversation flowed on. The topic of parental expectations wasn't exactly Isabel's favorite, but at least she was among people who understood.

She squeezed Mira's hand under the table, then passed her the egg tart from her own plate when she noticed Mira eyeing it. Mira smiled. "Thank you."

"You know, I can see why you turned out the way you did," Isabel said. She had been taking in every bit of information about Mira, trying to fit it all together. Of course

Mira had been raised by radical intellectual types. Very different from Isabel's own parents.

Mira grimaced. "I don't know. I think my parents contribute more to society than I do, for one thing. I'm just a grad student. My mom still works as a labor journalist, and my dad quit academia to be a public high school teacher."

"Do they want you to do something different?"

"Not exactly. They've always done their own thing, and I think they expect that of me. Not that my parents don't have opinions on my life. Recently they've been trying to give me advice on union organizing." Isabel snorted. "And when I came out to them, there was a lot of... *Oh, no, not like that. You know we'd still love you if you were gay, right?* As though I didn't think of that myself." Mira rolled her eyes. "Well, I guess I am. Not in the way they thought."

Isabel laughed and gave her a sympathetic wince. Mira continued, "It's fine now. They defended me to their families, which counts for a lot. My dad cut ties with some of his family over it. Although they already weren't happy with him about a lot of other things." Mira smiled ruefully. Isabel squeezed her hand. She knew what all this was like, or at least a version of it, and Mira clearly didn't want to dwell on it. "Not his whole family. I mentioned his sister who gave me that jewelry you like." Mira was wearing those dangly gold earrings now. "And some things for my wedding, supposedly, although I think those are going to sit in the box for a while."

Isabel's heart beat faster. "Too fancy for City Hall? Or you don't believe in getting married?" Her ex hadn't, which was fine. Commitment was commitment. But Isabel would be lying if she said she didn't care about marriage either way.

"It's not that. I don't have a problem with it in theory."

Mira paused. "I guess I've just never thought of it as a real possibility."

Isabel wasn't going to ask what that meant. She didn't want to give herself away. "Fair enough."

She relaxed into the atmosphere, talking with Mira's friends, making sure Mira was well-supplied with sweets, holding her hand under the table. At the end, Mira excused herself and went to the restroom, and they all began to stand up. Vivian walked toward her, followed by Frankie.

"It was nice to meet you today," Vivian said, smiling thinly. "Mira told us that you're living together for another year. Is that right?"

"That's right. Uh, nice to meet you too." Isabel's nervousness returned in full force.

"Frankie and I have known Mira for a long time," Vivian said. "We were worried about her when she was with her ex-boyfriend. I'm sure she told you about him."

Isabel nodded, fixed to the spot. No surprise that Vivian was a lawyer. Isabel was practically being cross-examined in court.

"She's had a hard year," Frankie said. "We're glad she's found a good place to land." Frankie was the friendlier of the two of them, but they were obviously on the same team when it came to grilling Isabel.

"We want her to be happy," Vivian added. She and Frankie shared a look that was indecipherable to Isabel. But the meaning of their words was loud and clear. They may as well have asked Isabel what her intentions were.

"Understood." Isabel gripped the chair next to her, trying to keep her composure. "I'm absolutely serious about Mira. And I'm going to work as hard as I can to be good to her."

The two of them shared another look. Had her answer been good enough? "I'm glad to hear that," Vivian said.

Frankie nodded. "That's sweet. She really likes you, too." That, too, was a warning. *Don't hurt her.*

"We'll look forward to seeing more of you," Vivian said.

Mira returned. "Some of my favorite people," she said. Isabel tried to not look as unsettled as she felt. If she ever hurt Mira, she'd never forgive herself.

Mira looked between the three of them. "What were you talking about?"

"Just telling Isabel it was nice to meet her," Vivian said. "It's good to see you again. Come over any time, okay? You too, Isabel."

Isabel did her best to smile. It was good that Mira had friends who were looking out for her. That ought to be reassuring. They said their goodbyes.

"Thank you for coming out with me," Mira said, on their way back to the subway. "It's wonderful to get to introduce you to my friends. This means so much to me."

"Me too." Isabel gripped Mira's hand, hoping she'd never have to let go.

26

Mira sighed as she read the email in her office. The union election was scheduled in less than two months—that had been the big news this week. Everything was coming to a head. But the university was going to fight them at every turn.

They were announcing pay raises for all the grad students. It might have been welcome news in some other context, but it was a transparent attempt at weakening support for the union. The increase wasn't nearly enough, and it wouldn't kick in until the next year. There was nothing about health insurance or parental leave or any of the other things they'd been fighting for. And, of course, it could be taken away at any time. Without a real seat at the table, they were entirely at the administration's mercy.

Mira put her elbows on her desk and her head in her hands. The winter break had been so idyllic. She'd spent nearly every waking moment of it with Isabel, mostly in bed, and the memories had warmed her as she'd headed to work in the freezing cold and slush all week. And Isabel was taking her on a date again tonight. Having that to look forward to was making the day a little more bearable.

But she was still fully back in the grind of work, whether she liked it or not. And the crushing fact bore down on her: If they didn't win the election to force the university to recognize the union, they'd lose everything they'd worked for.

The benevolent tone of the announcement was infuriating. Mira was still fuming when her office door opened and Shreya entered. "Do you have a second?" she asked. Mira nodded. "Come walk with me."

Mira got up. "Is this about the announcement?"

"Not just that."

They walked in the direction of the lounge. Shreya said, "You know that Leila has to step down as area captain for the Classics department soon." Mira nodded. Leila was headed to North Africa for her research. "So, we want you to replace her."

"What? Me?"

"Yes, I'm talking to you."

A sense of dread came over Mira. They were in really dire straits if Shreya was asking *her.* "Why not Ifeoma or David? Or anyone else, for that matter."

"Ifeoma's too busy trying to finish her dissertation. And I'm already asking David to fill in for me on the international students' working group."

"Really? You're not—"

"Yeah, I'm too busy with my visa issues, ironically." Shreya's problems with her student visa had plagued her on and off for years. She had reluctantly set up a crowdfunding link a few months ago for her thousands of dollars in legal expenses, and dozens of other grad students in the union who were equally broke had chipped in, but there was no end in sight. "I'll tell you about it later. Anyway, you've been part of the union for years and you've been canvassing regularly, and you know what's going on."

"Um," Mira said. "I don't know if I can do that."

"Is something preventing you, or you just think you're not capable?" Shreya had a way of getting to the point. She was a perfect VP, efficient and ruthless. Mira didn't have that in her.

"Both. I'm not sure if I can keep up with it, for one thing." She was under enough stress already. "What would I have to do? I know about leading trainings, but I don't even know all the things Leila was doing."

"It'll probably be about ten or fifteen hours of work a week until the election. You'd run trainings, and they'll become more frequent closer to the election when more people want to help get out the vote. You'd be updating the database and tracking down the people we haven't talked to or are still on the fence. Oh, and, obviously, you'd be on the executive committee, which will be fun for you." Shreya's tone implied the opposite. "We meet every Tuesday night in addition to the Thursday meetings."

Mira nodded to show she was listening. "There's something else, too," Shreya added. "We think what the administration is doing might be considered an unfair labor practice, which is illegal."

"Wait, really?"

"They're giving us a suspiciously timed pay raise, and claiming in their official communications that there's no money in the budget for anything else regardless of whether we unionize. Which isn't true, but it's going to hurt us in the election. We're talking to our lawyer about it. What it comes down to is that we might file a complaint to get the administration to stop their tactics, but it'll delay the election."

"For how long?"

"We don't know. It could be until next semester. Or even later."

"That doesn't sound good."

"Well, it's not going to be good if we go ahead with the election, and we lose because the administration convinces everyone that the union won't do anything to help them." That much was true. "Anyway, we're going to discuss it in the committee and make a decision. Just so you know what we're up against."

"Uh, I don't know." Mira sighed. "Okay, I could make time for this. But I've never done anything like this before. I don't know if I'm qualified."

"Maybe not, but you're the best person in the department who's currently available, according to Leila. You'll learn as you do it, which is what we all did." Mira remained silent. Shreya continued, "You know, there's no perfect candidate who's going to appear out of nowhere. Someone in the Classics department is going to have to do it. It might as well be you."

"Wow, thanks, Shreya. That's really encouraging."

"I'm not saying this to discourage you. You know the only way this is going to happen is if we put in the work ourselves."

Mira couldn't argue with that. *We are the union*, Isabel had once said, and Mira had learned over the last few months what this really meant. There was no one but them to do the work of organizing thousands of grad students and winning the election. If Mira didn't do her rounds every week, talking to people at every opportunity, the work wouldn't get done. Last semester, week by week, she'd helped add to the ever-increasing count of union cards. And now she had to do whatever it took to win.

Maybe she couldn't wait around for someone else to do it. But her life would be so much easier if she could. Talking to her coworkers was one thing, but being in charge was another. "What if someone else runs?"

"They're not going to if you decide you want to do it. We'll vote next week, and it'll be you."

Shreya's pragmatism was oddly reassuring. Mira wasn't being inflated beyond her actual abilities. If Shreya truly thought she couldn't do it, she wouldn't have asked. "Can you give me some time to think about it?"

"Let me know by Monday," Shreya said. "Look, you're not bad at listening and talking to people, and I know you care about this. Don't sell yourself short, okay?"

"I DON'T KNOW," Mira said, for what was probably the hundredth time tonight. "I know Shreya's right, that one of us is going to have to do it. I just don't want to let anyone down. It's frightening to have that kind of responsibility."

Isabel's thumbs dug into a particularly tense muscle between Mira's shoulder blades. She exhaled and relaxed into the touch. It had been a good night: an early movie, a leisurely dinner at their neighborhood Greek restaurant, a quiet walk home through gentle flurries of snow. The warm, shimmery pleasure of being taken on a good date. A break from thinking about the hard things for a few hours.

"What are you afraid of?" Isabel asked.

Nestled between Isabel's thighs on the couch as Isabel massaged her back, Mira was warm and safe. The harshness of the world outside, and all that she was up against, seemed far away. She could get some distance from her anxieties, at least for the time being. "I guess I'm afraid of being in situations where I won't know what to do and people are relying on me. Like if someone asks me questions during a training or runs into a difficult situation and needs help. I don't trust myself to know what I'm doing. I don't see why other people should trust me."

"How many grad students do you think you've talked to since the beginning of the year?"

"Um, several dozen? About a hundred, probably." It was hard to believe the number was that high. But Mira had met all the first-years in the Classics department that she'd been too jaded to talk to before, and she'd made connections with other grad students in biology and music and architecture that she never would have otherwise, and she'd even rebuilt a few friendships she'd let lapse since she started dating Dylan. It wasn't only the individual relationships, either. Mira was part of something bigger than herself.

But that didn't mean she was qualified to lead anyone. "There's a lot more to being the area captain than just talking to people, though. I have to make decisions about what to focus on and how to deal with problems, and I don't know if I can do that."

"Well, that's my point." Isabel's thumbs worked out another knot in Mira's back. It was painful and good. She really needed to fix her posture instead of hunching over her laptop all day. "You know all these people, and you know what they want. It means you can represent them and do what's in their best interests. That's what leadership means. It's mostly about listening, and you're good at that."

"Maybe you're right. Good enough, anyway. Well, I don't know if it's enough." Mira sighed. "Do you think I should do it?"

Isabel made a noncommittal sound. Her hands moved lower. Mira groaned, from Isabel's fingers digging into her tense muscles as much as from frustration. "Don't go all strong and silent on me now."

"I think you *can* do it. Whether you decide to do it is up to you."

"I knew you were going to say that."

"You still asked." Isabel kissed her on the crown of her head, then pushed her thumbs in hard. Mira whimpered. Taking some more stretch breaks wouldn't kill her. Isabel stroked her back, soothing her. "Too much?"

"No. Keep going."

It wasn't as easy as simply deciding to do it. But a sense of pride was swelling within her. Before this year, she'd rarely thought of herself as someone who could use her power to push back against the world, to act for herself and for others instead of merely surviving. It made a difference that hundreds of other people were working alongside her now, including people she didn't know.

Of course she was scared. But four months ago, she'd been afraid to have a conversation with a stranger. She had come a long way, and there was so much more to do, and she owed something not only to herself but to her coworkers, too. And if just one other trans girl at this institution could escape having to rely on a partner's whims for her housing and healthcare, it would have been worth it to Mira.

"You know, I'm going to tell Shreya yes before I lose my nerve," she said. "I was planning to think about it all day tomorrow. But there's no reason to overthink it."

"That's good." Isabel put her hands on Mira's shoulders and kissed the back of her neck. "Relax with me this weekend. And when you go to work on Monday, you can fight like hell."

"That's the other thing. It's going to take up a lot of time. And I'll have to figure out how to manage my time better." Shreya was probably underestimating how much time Mira's new responsibilities would take. Shreya was the most organized person Mira had ever known, and Mira's organizational skills were middling at best—if she were an old, tweedy male professor, people would call her absent-minded. "But I'll get a break after the election is over. And I'll keep part of my weekends free so I can spend them with you."

"Don't worry about me," Isabel said, as Mira got off the couch and grabbed her phone to text Shreya. "I'm proud of you."

Mira sent the text. "I did it." She took a deep breath. "Thanks, Isabel. That means a lot to me."

Isabel smiled. She seemed uncharacteristically shy. "That reminds me. I have a present for you."

She got up and returned with a bundle the size of a manila envelope, wrapped neatly in plain brown paper—clearly the work of her own hands. Mira unwrapped it carefully, and something pink and silky tumbled out.

Mira held it up. It was a lacy slip, in absolutely sumptuous pink silk the same color as her pajamas, cool and soft in her hands and nearly iridescent. She laughed in delight. Isabel knew what Mira liked, and she knew what she herself liked, too, when it came to what Mira wore. The slip was going to be luxurious to sleep in and to wear under her dresses. And, of course, Isabel had...first-hand knowledge of her proportions.

Mira rarely bought nice things for herself. But she knew a nice thing when she saw one, having endured two years of living with Dylan. This was *nice*. She didn't even want to imagine how much it must have cost.

But she didn't feel smothered by this gift. She felt...cherished. Isabel knew her tastes, and the slip was both sexy and practical. Mira wasn't just a dress-up doll to her. Isabel had been thankfully low-key about money so far, letting Mira split the check more often than not. Maybe it wasn't so bad to be spoiled every once in a while.

"It's more of a present for me," Isabel said. She was so flustered Mira could barely believe it. Isabel was hot when she was stoic, but she was so, so hot when she wasn't. "If you don't like it—"

"Isabel, I love it," Mira said. She was wildly turned on, and she could think of some other things to do that would feel luxurious. She was loosened up and warm from her back rub, and emboldened after she'd texted Shreya. Now she was ready to pounce. "It's not just a present for you. The things you're going to do to me while I'm wearing it are all for me."

Isabel's eyes widened. But she recovered quickly. "Like what?"

"Will you get your strap?"

Isabel's smile was impossibly suave, and her blush was adorable. "Be right back."

27

MIRA CLOSED the curtains in the living room, undressed, and pulled the slip on over her head, shivering as the fabric tumbled down over her body. The silk was as cool and soft as she'd imagined, clinging to her in all the right ways, caressing her and teasing her. Very unlike Isabel's sturdy hands, but it felt like Isabel touching her, all the same. The slip came halfway down her thighs, but the slit up the side was deep. Perfect.

Isabel returned—wearing her strap, with her jeans pulled back on and unzipped, which really had no right to be as hot as it was. She looked at Mira like she wanted to devour her. Mira giggled and twirled in place, sparks of anticipation rushing over her skin.

Isabel came behind her and pulled her close. She nipped at the side of Mira's neck and ran her hands hungrily over Mira's body over the slip. Her strap dug into Mira's back, thick and solid, sending a warm jolt to Mira's core. "How do you want me?" Isabel asked, her breath tickling Mira's ear.

Mira tried to think, which was difficult. Isabel's thumbs

slowly rolling over her nipples over the silk made it impossible. She moaned, buckling in Isabel's arms. Isabel said, "On the couch? On the armchair? You want it over the table again?"

"Couch," Mira gasped out.

They made their way over. After a moment, with Mira still standing, Isabel said, "Oh. That's what you want, huh?"

She sat on the couch and made a come-hither motion with her fingers. A dizzying wave of lust overcame Mira, and she dropped to her knees. Isabel handed her a pillow—considerate as always—and Mira put it underneath her, wrapped a hand around the satisfying heft of Isabel's strap, and took it in her mouth. The weight of it against her tongue made her pussy throb, the hot, heavy ache burning brighter. "Oh, sweetheart," Isabel said, her breaths ragged, already so gorgeously worked up. "Look at you."

Mira loved this—loved making eye contact with Isabel as she got the strap warm and wet, loved the way Isabel watched in disbelief and ecstasy, loved the way she stroked Mira's hair and shoulders like she couldn't get enough. Loved the way it teased both of them, and the way her own pussy clenched, waiting to be filled up. Loved being cherished and a little bit filthy at the same time.

She relaxed her throat and carefully took Isabel's strap all the way down until she was kissing the harness—quivering, overwhelmed, so *full*, savoring the way Isabel's breaths stuttered as though Mira's mouth were right up against her nerve endings. Mira ran her hands over Isabel's thighs through her jeans—such nice thighs—and Isabel let out a moan. "Baby, come up here and let me touch you," she said, gasping.

Mira eased off the strap, caught her breath, and stood up shakily. She took out the lube they stashed in the end table—very practical—and got Isabel ready. Then she pulled the slip up over her hips and swung a leg over to straddle Isabel, resting her thighs against Isabel's unzipped jeans and belt buckle. Isabel's eyes widened. This was going to be good.

Isabel liked to call Mira femme, and it was a thrill to be femme in moments like this: wrapping her manicured fingers around Isabel's strap, being pink and frilly against Isabel's flannel and denim and roughness. It was a refuge from the world telling her that she was too feminine in all the wrong ways or not feminine enough. With Isabel, she could let herself blossom.

Isabel couldn't come just from Mira riding her, but that didn't mean Mira couldn't make it good for them both. She grabbed Isabel's strap and rubbed the head of it against her clit, the pulse of pleasure making her gasp and her thighs tense. With her other hand, she pulled the straps of the slip off her shoulders until it fell down over her breasts. Isabel groaned. Took Mira's breasts in her hand gently at first, and then roughly when Mira arched her back for more.

Teasing Isabel—and herself—was fun, but it wasn't enough. She clutched Isabel's shoulder, angled the dildo toward herself, and let it ease her open. She was feverish as she lowered herself onto it, thighs trembling, Isabel plucking at her nipples and driving her crazy. Settling on the harness with Isabel deep inside her was sheer relief.

But she needed more. She lifted the lacy hem of the slip over the triangle of hair above her pussy, and started moving, swirling her hips at just the right angle, letting the stretch and friction and pressure light her up inside. Giving Isabel a show.

Isabel was panting, her eyes dazed. "Oh, god, Mira." Her gaze darted down to where Mira was fucking herself, then back up, like she didn't know where to look. "I can't believe..." For all of Isabel's confidence, she acted like every time they had sex was the most astonishing thing that had ever happened to her. Mira laughed breathily. Her thighs were already burning. But this wasn't going to take long for her.

"So gorgeous," Isabel said, her voice reverent. "You're incredible." Her hand wandered down over Mira's body, hot and voracious through the silk draped over her stomach, rough over her bare thigh. And then hard and insistent on her clit, jolting Mira so intensely she squealed, nearly losing her balance. "Careful," Isabel said. Mira let out a laugh, and they settled into a new rhythm with Isabel rubbing her clit, their bodies effortlessly attuned to each other.

Mira wasn't in a hurry, but she was close. Isabel's other hand was splayed over Mira's ribcage, her thumb teasing Mira's nipple, her hips thrusting up to give Mira a little more. "Love watching you ride me," Isabel murmured. "Love how good it feels for you. Love these sounds you make." Mira squirmed, pleasantly self-conscious, and Isabel clutched her tighter. "So fucking gorgeous with my strap in you. You're all mine—"

Mira came, just like that, crying out as she convulsed and gripped Isabel's shoulder, riding her harder—and Isabel tensed underneath her, too, with a throaty groan. That was new. It was so unexpected and hot that Mira couldn't help but grind down hard, giving herself one last intense after-shock, and giving one to Isabel too.

She collapsed on top of Isabel, panting. The strap was warm and wet against her stomach, making a mess of this expensive slip. Isabel ran a big, comforting hand over Mira's hair, her heartbeat thumping fast against Mira's ear as she caught her breath.

You're all mine. Mira hadn't thought she liked that kind of thing. It had been disorientingly hot, and so right in the moment, when she'd been bouncing and giggling and enjoying herself as Isabel's precious femme. She wanted to hear it again in bed. She didn't have to overthink this.

"I'm not sure I ever said thank you," Mira said, still aglow. "Thank you so much. I love it." A surge of raw emotion washed over her. Sex with Isabel had a way of doing that. "I'll wear it under my dresses. That way, I'll always have a way to have you with me. Touching me and holding me all day."

Isabel paused for a second too long. "You're very welcome, sweetheart."

Mira replayed what she'd said. She'd become less shy about using her words in bed; Isabel had been so patient with her over the last month, coaxing her desires out of her on her own terms. In the afterglow just now, she'd felt so good and uninhibited that the words had spilled out. But what she'd said hadn't been dirty talk. It had been something else.

The thing was, she'd meant it. She wanted a reminder that Isabel cared for her and believed in her. She wanted to feel precious and brave and a little bit sexy as she took on the world outside this apartment.

And it was not the kind of thing you said to someone you were trying to take things slow with, trying things out with, just going on dates with between hanging out and kissing and fucking in the apartment you happened to share.

Mira propped herself up, her limbs still wobbly. She gave Isabel a peck on the cheek. There were questions looming on the horizon, far away. But she was well-fucked and tired from a good night, and those questions could wait. "I'm going to wash up. And then we should go to bed."

"You're making me less jaded about union politics," Isabel said, pushing their grocery cart down the aisle. "I might run for an elected position one of these days." They reached the rice section, and Isabel stopped. "I think we're running low. What kind do you want?"

Mira pointed to one of the big bags on the bottom shelf, and Isabel picked it up and put it in their cart as though it were a feather pillow. Of course Mira could do it herself, in the same way that Mira could open her own doors, in the same way that Isabel could pack her own lunches, but she wasn't going to complain about Isabel making her life a little easier. Or the view of Isabel bending over. "When do you think that'll be?"

"Five years from now, maybe. Don't hold me to that when the time comes."

Five years from now. Maybe last night was still lingering in her mind, but Mira's train of thought got stuck on the implications, even if Isabel hadn't meant they'd be *together* then. Lesbians were supposedly good at being friends with their exes. There was no reason why they shouldn't be in touch after five years. "Why do you want to wait until then?"

"I need to put in the time first. Get to know more people. It's how these things work."

"That makes sense. And they'll vote for you if they know what's good for them."

Isabel shrugged skeptically. Mira smiled. Isabel had plenty of complaints, most of them well-founded, some more severe than others, in the way that only truly committed lifers did. "You know," Mira said, "I can't even imagine what it's like, knowing you'll have the same career for the rest of your life if you want it. It's amazing that you knew that's what you wanted when you were twenty."

"Or I was a dumb kid who got lucky. Didn't you know you wanted to become an academic at that age?"

Mira looked over the pasta section. "Well, I don't have the job security part," she said absentmindedly, picking up a few boxes. "If I'm fortunate enough to get an academic job after grad school, I'll almost certainly have to move. You're presumably staying in the city until you retire."

There it was again. They were silent as they continued down another aisle, and Mira was needled by the same uncertainty she'd felt last night. The same vague sense that there were decisions in her future—far away, but not infinitely far.

"You know, I don't need to stay in New York," Isabel said. "If I need to move, I can transfer to another local. They need electricians everywhere."

Mira's heart beat faster. They glanced at each other, and then turned back to the rows of cleaning products.

Maybe Isabel was thinking the same thing: This conversation was heading into out-of-bounds territory. Isabel liked her—that was so obvious and unchanging that Mira didn't have to question how much, exactly. And she liked Isabel, but she wasn't ready to figure out how much, either.

Maybe Isabel hadn't intended to go there. But now the implications were hanging between them. And it was entirely beside the point, but...Mira had never been with anyone who would have considered moving across the country for her. It simply wasn't the kind of situation she had to face, in the same way that she'd never had to buy a house or pick out a private jet.

Isabel hadn't offered that. Time to come to her senses. "That's true. It'd be nice if I could say they needed classicists everywhere."

Isabel smiled. "Okay, let's say there's a labor shortage of experts in lyric poetry, and you can live anywhere you want."

"Don't get me hot and bothered like this. We're at the grocery store."

Isabel snorted. "You think you'd want to stay here?"

"I think so." It was the truth. For all Mira had been through, she'd grown into herself in this city, and it was difficult to imagine living anywhere else. "If only it were that easy. Would you really ever leave New York? Your family is here."

They were getting into even messier territory now. This wasn't a conversation to be had in the grocery store. She should have changed the subject.

But part of her wanted to know.

Isabel shrugged too casually. "I don't know. I might want a change of scenery. It'd be hard. But I could visit. And once Grace gets married, I guess she won't need me." Isabel's hair was in a braid, but she tried to run her hand through it anyway and stopped short. "Maybe I could actually afford to buy a house somewhere else. And it'd be cheaper to raise— To do a lot of things."

Mira took a breath, trying to clear her head. She didn't believe for one second that Isabel would leave New York— the city she'd called home all her life, the city whose skyscrapers and subway stations she worked on with pride— simply for a change of scenery. They stopped in front of the toilet bowl cleaners, as though that were the big decision to make.

Of course Isabel wanted commitment. Maybe not from

Mira, but...from someone, eventually. She'd been in a relationship for six years before this. Isabel never talked about it, so Mira had barely thought about it until now. And, apparently, Isabel wanted kids.

Of course they weren't going to date casually forever.

They were having a good run so far. But sooner or later, they'd part amicably as responsible adults, and then Mira would hear all about Isabel's new life with her wife and kids. Isabel would be pushing a cart around a grocery store with someone else.

The idea was surprisingly painful. But that was reality. And Mira would always have these memories: the dates, the laughter, the astonishingly good sex, the cold winter nights where they'd kept each other warm. Isabel had raised the bar so high for her. Vivian would be proud.

Or...

No. She couldn't think about it.

With Isabel, it was too easy to forget why Mira had needed guardrails in the first place. Things were good. Not just the dates and the sex and the hours they spent talking, but everything else, too—learning to share space, working through the few tiny road bumps they'd hit, even cleaning the bathroom and going to the laundromat. Mira would never admit it aloud, but this was exactly what she'd once dreamed of, in her less cynical days, when she'd imagined moving in with someone.

She'd dreamed of more, too. Building a life with someone she loved. Being a wife, a mother. Those longings had been locked up tight, squeezed into the smallest, most hidden places in her heart. But she couldn't deny they were there, even if all her decisions might be easier if they weren't.

The truth was that dreams could become nightmares in

an instant. A strange anxiety set in: What if she wasn't being anxious enough?

She blinked. And picked out a toilet bowl cleaner and put it in the cart. "Yeah, you're right."

Isabel said nothing. Maybe she was also relieved to move on. Mira said, "I thought about what we could do next weekend. Assuming I'm not too busy with my new area captain responsibilities. Can I take you to see a play?"

A different shadow fell over Isabel's face. "I want to, but... Did I mention that next Friday is Chinese New Year's Eve? I'll be staying with my parents overnight."

Isabel had not mentioned that. Probably on purpose. Her casualness was clearly false. "You're going to see Grace?"

Isabel sighed. "I asked if we could talk on Saturday morning after we have dinner with our parents, and she said yes."

"Oh, that's great," Mira said, but Isabel didn't look relieved. "How are you feeling about it?"

"I don't know." Isabel was closing herself off, which made Mira nervous. "I'm going to apologize. I just don't know if I can do it in a way where she'll actually forgive me. I know it's bigger than just her fiancé. Kevin." She seemed reluctant to say his name. "Never mind. I can't do anything about it until I see her. Anyway, we could do something on Saturday night or Sunday."

Isabel wasn't getting off the hook that easily. "Do you want to talk more about seeing your family?" If Isabel didn't want to, Mira was at least going to make her say so.

"No." Isabel still didn't look at her. "Maybe later. Just not now."

"Well, I'll be here," Mira said. Isabel could be so sweet and open, and it was easy to forget how much pain she was hiding until Mira ran up against the jagged boundaries of what she refused to talk about.

There was more Mira didn't know about Isabel—and she realized, with unease, that she didn't know how vast and deep those unknown parts were. "You'll tell me what happens after you talk to her, right?"

"Of course." Isabel's mouth turned into a flat line.

"I'm proud of you," Mira said. Isabel scoffed, as though Mira couldn't possibly be serious. "I mean it." Maybe someday, Isabel would let this particular wall down, but all Mira could do was wait.

28

Isabel stood at the front door of her parents' house, decorated with red banners, and took a deep breath. She was their oldest child, and she had obligations. She could do this. She rang the doorbell.

Her mom opened the door, wearing a red sweater, and they exchanged New Year's greetings and hugged in the doorway. Isabel had been taller than her mom ever since her teenage growth spurt, but now her mom seemed older and smaller than ever. "You're not so skinny anymore," her mom said. "That's good. Your job is so hard on you. Do you still have to work on weekends?"

Isabel's parents had never understood why on earth she'd become an electrician. They thought that it was far too dangerous for a woman, that she was always one accident away from certain death. Her parents' parents had been garment workers, restaurant cooks, home attendants. Her po po had worked hard to send her daughter, Isabel's mom, to college. Isabel knew why her parents wanted her to sit at a desk doing a job she hated. But it was her life.

"No, not anymore," Isabel said. She had never

explained to them, either, that working overtime had been her choice. She took off her boots and put on the house slippers that her parents kept around for her in the entryway. "Here's the fish you asked for. Where's Dad?"

"He's upstairs with your po po. Grace and Kevin are arriving later for dinner. You can put that in the fridge for now." Apparently Grace wasn't excited to spend extra time with Isabel, which was both understandable and a relief. Her mom updated her on household news as they headed to the kitchen.

Here, Isabel could be useful. She filled dumplings while her mom rolled out wrappers, chopped and blanched the pork belly, and cut ginger into batons under her mom's instruction, trying to memorize every step. Her parents wouldn't be around forever.

More than that, she was realizing again that she had a future in front of her. Most of her life, if she was lucky. This wasn't the reckless optimism she'd had in her early twenties, when she'd thought she and everyone she loved were invincible. This was a cautious hope after her last two years of despair. She wanted to cook for her own family, if she ever got to have one.

She knew who she wanted to start a family with. But it was dangerous to think so far ahead.

She filled their big stockpot with water and brought it to the stove so her mom wouldn't have to wrestle with it. As they waited for the water to boil for the poached chicken, Isabel started washing dishes. Her mom said, "Grace says you two are going to talk tomorrow morning."

"That's right." Grace lived nearby, and she talked to their parents more often these days than Isabel did. That was another thing that Isabel felt guilty about, but it wasn't easy to move when her work was in the five boroughs. And her argument with Grace was hurting their parents, too. Yet another source of guilt. "I'll apologize to her."

"You know, you two are the only daughters I have left." It wasn't as though Isabel didn't think about that every day, but hearing it from her mom was excruciating. "I hope you two can get along for dinner. Your dad and your po po and I hate to see you like this."

"I know."

"Your dad and I know that Kevin isn't like James." James had been the platonic ideal of a son-in-law. He was working as a surgeon in Seattle now, but he kept in touch often with Isabel's parents. "But we've talked to Kevin, and he's very nice, and he makes Grace happy. You know your dad and I have let you all make your own choices."

That was true. Isabel had never shaken off the sense that she had asked too much of her parents in letting her live her life, as a butch lesbian and a construction worker. They had been slightly frosty to Reina at first, although they'd come to like her. They'd been disappointed when Isabel reported that it was over. But the fact remained that when Alexa had become a doctor and married a man she'd met in medical school, their parents' approval had never been in question.

There was nothing else to be said about Grace for now. And something was weighing on Isabel. "I wanted to tell you something. I'm seeing someone new."

Her mom smiled. Isabel had told herself it didn't matter, so her own relief surprised her. "Oh, is she Chinese?" her mom asked. "What's her name? How long has it been?"

"Uh, she's Indian. Her name is Mira, and she's a Ph.D. student." Isabel told her the prestigious university where Mira did her research, and then realized she was still seeking her mom's approval. "I met her a few months ago."

It might be too hard to explain that they already lived together.

"Oh, that's nice. So she's going to become a professor?"

"If she can get a job. She's really smart."

"That's good. You're taking good care of her?"

If Isabel were dating a man, her mom would have asked her if her boyfriend was taking good care of *her*, but Isabel didn't mind. "I hope so. I try."

"Good. Will you bring her to Grace's wedding?"

Isabel looked away. She wasn't going to scare Mira off by asking her to meet the family. And on the hypothetical occasion when she did meet them, Isabel would want her sister to not resent her presence, which might be too much to expect. "Maybe. It's a little early for that."

"If she's important to you, you know your dad and I would like to meet her." Isabel's mom put a hand on her shoulder. Her parents had never outright said *We accept you for being a lesbian*, but this was their way of saying essentially the same thing. "Your sister, too."

The water in the stockpot was boiling. Isabel dried her hands and put her arm around her mom. "I know. We add the ginger and scallion to the water now, right?"

They got on with poaching the chicken. Isabel's dad entered, munching on shrimp chips, and started washing the dishes in the sink. "Can I tell your dad?" Isabel's mom said. Without waiting for a response, she continued, "Isabel is dating someone new. A Ph.D. student. She's going to be a professor."

THE NEXT MORNING, waking up on the too-small pull-out bed—Grace and Kevin had taken the extra bedroom—Isabel's dread was cut with optimism.

Dinner had gone as well as she could have hoped. She'd asked Grace about wedding preparations, and Grace had replied stiffly, but at least they were talking again. The food had been delicious, and it had been good to see her relatives. Kevin had a full-time job now, working at a store that sold board games. It put Isabel's mind more at ease about her sister's future, even though she told herself it didn't matter what Kevin did for a living.

Everything would be fine. She and Grace would reconcile. And then she'd tell Grace about Mira, too. She had asked her parents not to last night, not wanting the best thing in her life to be tangled up in the mess she'd made with Grace. But she would fix things, and her family would be as whole as it could be. Maybe—and this was purely wishful thinking—she could even bring Mira as her date to the wedding.

She had leftovers with a big mug of tea, brought breakfast to her po po, and anxiously took a walk around the suburban block. She—and Alexa—had worked so hard to buy this house for their parents. That had to count for something.

When she returned, Grace and Kevin were eating at the kitchen table. The two of them stiffened when they saw Isabel. Fair enough. "Hey," Isabel said, feeling like the interloper she was. She nodded neutrally at Kevin, and turned to Grace. "You want to talk soon?"

"Sure." To Kevin, she said, "I'm going to talk to Isabel. Want to wait for me upstairs?"

They exchanged whispered words. Grace smiled. They pecked each other on the lips, and Kevin got up, taking both bowls with him.

Isabel was never going to get used to her baby sister being an engaged adult, let alone a married one. When

Alexa had gotten married, that had been different. But there was no point in thinking about that now. She sat down.

Grace stared at her silently. She wasn't going to make this easy for Isabel.

"I, uh, I'm sorry," Isabel said, working hard to look her sister in the eye. "I shouldn't have said what I said. That, uh —" It was humiliating to have to say it. "That I told you that Alexa wouldn't have wanted you to marry Kevin. That was really fucked up."

"Yeah." Grace's expression didn't soften.

The silence expanded. Isabel sighed. "And I'm sorry for saying what I said about Kevin. I might have...underestimated him in the past, and I'm sorry for that. It's good— I mean, I'm glad he has a job now. And, uh..." She tried to remember what her mom had said. "I can see he makes you happy. I think that's what I meant, that I know Alexa would have wanted you to be happy. I just didn't say it right."

"You're sorry for *underestimating* him?" Grace said.

Isabel winced. "I—"

"Do you really still think it's up to you to judge the quality of whoever I decide to marry? This is the apology you've been working up to?"

"I didn't mean it like that." Hot fear rose in Isabel's chest. What *had* she meant? "I didn't—"

"You know what? Forget it. This isn't about Kevin. If you don't like him, fine. That's your right. You don't have to condescend to me and pretend you didn't mean what you said. I'm marrying him whether you like it or not." For a moment, Grace's tone sounded uncannily like an echo of Isabel herself. "This isn't really about that. Ever since Alexa —" Grace's voice quavered. "You've been acting like you know what's best for me, and you've been trying to do everything for everyone, like if you do enough, it'll make up for Alexa being gone—"

"I don't think that." Isabel was shaken. She'd once thought of Grace as her other best friend. But now they were both using whatever closeness they'd had to twist the knife. "Nothing I could do would make up for that. I know nothing's going to bring her back. I don't know why you said that."

"I'm saying it because it's true, and you need to hear it. Who else is going to tell you?"

Isabel looked around. "Can you be quiet? You're going to disturb—"

"Can you stop being the perfect daughter for one fucking second?" In the ensuing silence, even Grace seemed stunned by what she'd said. "I get it, okay? You pay for our parents' house. You take care of them. And you want to be the perfect older sister, treating me like I'm still the same age I was when Alexa died, like I'm still barely out of college as opposed to being an adult with a job and a fiancé. And you thought you just wanted the best for me when you told me how much you looked down on my fiancé the day I told you about my engagement. The best thing that had happened to me since—" Grace wiped her eyes, but she looked defiant. "Did it ever occur to you that Kevin feels awkward around you because you treat him like he's an annoying toddler every time he comes over? Did you ever even put in any effort? Just because he wasn't doing what *you* did when you were twenty-four—"

"That's not what this is about. This has nothing to do with me," Isabel said, with dawning horror that Grace had landed a hit. "I don't care if Kevin is awkward. I care if he's pulling his weight." This wasn't the path she wanted to go down, rehashing their argument from months ago, but she didn't know how to stop. "I want him to be a good partner for you. I don't want you to be tied down to someone who isn't. That was what I meant."

"A good partner?" Grace laughed humorlessly. "You would know all about that, right?"

Isabel stiffened. Pain and shame seared her. She stood up and left the kitchen without a word.

THE DOOR to her bedroom opened and the light turned on. "Oh!" Mira said. "You scared me. I didn't know you were back. I was just looking for my reading glasses. Are you okay?"

Mira had a habit of falling asleep in bed while reading, at which point Isabel would gently take her reading glasses off her face, set them on the nightstand, and let her sleep. The tender memory only made Isabel more afraid. Maybe none of this would last.

She couldn't bring herself either to say no or to lie. She tucked her knees closer to her head and said nothing at all.

"Oh, no," Mira said. She sat down on the bed next to Isabel and put an arm around her.

But Mira might as well have been a mile away. What separated them was a growing chasm of fear. Isabel didn't deserve someone so good, and Mira deserved better, and eventually Mira would find that out for herself.

Mira's warmth seeped into her. Isabel was calming down, despite herself. "I'm so sorry, Isabel. Do you want to tell me about it?" Mira said, so unbearably good to her even now.

Isabel shook her head. "Not now," she managed to say.

"Take all the time you need," Mira said. Isabel's dread returned. How much time would she have?

29

"THE ADMINISTRATION HAS GIVEN us no choice," said Patrick, Mira's counterpart in the history department, more loudly than was necessary. Most of the rest of the executive committee murmured or nodded agreement.

The university had been stepping up its tactics. Every day there were new emails, fliers, and so-called information sessions. The pay raise was evidence that the administration cared about the grad students, so they claimed. Money was tight, and there was no room for health insurance or parental leave or housing in the budget, so there was nothing more the union could do for anyone. If the grad students tried to unionize, they'd waste their money on dues and get nowhere. That was the way of things, and the grad students ought to shut up and be grateful.

The worst part was that it was working. They were losing support and enthusiasm, and Mira couldn't blame anyone for it. The grad students were all exhausted, and the administration had money and time on their side and could spend endless resources campaigning against them.

"I agree that we don't have much of a choice," Shreya

said, at a normal volume, clearly chagrined to be agreeing with Patrick. "The closer we get to the scheduled election, the worse things look—"

"Right," Patrick said. "I've been saying, we can't even trust our data about who's committed to voting yes anymore. People have changed their minds. I—"

"—and we don't have time to talk to everyone and convince them that the university's lying to them," Shreya continued. "Let's get started on filing an unfair labor practice complaint as soon as possible, get the administration to stop, and then maybe we'll be on a more even playing field. That's better than taking the chance of losing the election entirely."

"But that's going to postpone the election indefinitely," someone else said.

"It'll probably be a few months," Patrick said. "If we have the election now and lose, it'll take years to try again."

They had been going in circles for the last two weeks, their meetings running over time even more than usual. Shreya sometimes complained to Mira that this was the biggest group project of their lives, with hundreds of flaky, difficult group members, and Mira saw her point.

Mira hadn't said anything so far. She was the newest committee member, and she'd mostly limited herself to giving updates in these meetings. Everyone else knew better than her—didn't they?

The room was leaning reluctantly toward postponing the election. Maybe they were right, no matter how much Mira hated the idea. Disagreeing with Shreya felt wrong. But the idea of delaying everything for months, maybe longer, was unbearable.

She had enough money to scrape by for now, but not enough to save anything. What if her prescriptions became much more expensive? What if she had an emergency? What if the university screwed up their payroll and took their sweet time fixing it, like they'd done in Mira's second year? And—she didn't like to think it—what was she going to do when she wasn't living in Isabel's apartment at a discount anymore?

Mira was so fortunate. She was going to be fortunate for as long as this lasted. The truth was, they weren't taking things slow. Their relationship, whatever it was, was somehow both exhilarating in its newness and comfortable like they'd been together for years. But a fling being this intense didn't mean it would last.

She wasn't about to make financial plans for the next several years of her life. No matter how good Isabel made her feel, no matter how tempted she was to fantasize about the future. When she left, she would need a place to go.

"I don't know about this," said Liz, on Mira's right. "We'll lose a lot of our momentum if we have to wait until next semester. We're going to have to get all the first-years on board. And the administration might try something worse in that time."

Mira had thought of that too. She had been too nervous to say it. Patrick looked like he was about to respond.

"I agree with that," Mira said. Everyone turned to look at her. "I think we can win next month if we focus on canvassing and stay on message—"

"We're already canvassing all the time," Patrick said.

Mira tensed up. She tried to regather her thoughts. Did Patrick ever interrupt the men on the committee? The worst thing was, she couldn't write him off entirely; he had a point. "When I've been talking to people recently, what seems to work is when I emphasize that it's not just about the money and benefits, because the real point of unionizing is having power. And it's not good enough for the administration to give us more money if we don't have a voice in the decision-making process."

She took a breath. Patrick cut in, saying, "That doesn't—"

"Let me finish." Mira trembled with frustration. This shouldn't be bothering her so much. But it was one thing to have strangers be rude to her, and another to have someone who was supposed to be her equal on the committee treating her this way. "I know we've won people over by emphasizing how little money and how few benefits we get, because that's what matters to people who are just trying to get by. But I think if we emphasize the difference between the administration deigning to give us something, versus us having the power to demand what we deserve, we'll win more people over."

She was gathering conviction, determined to just get her words out without interruption as much as anything else. "What this pay raise really means is that the administration is afraid of us. They're afraid of the power we have. And we should encourage people to see it that way. We can take the administration's attempt to weaken us and use it to our advantage."

The room was silent. Everyone's eyes bore into her. Maybe Mira didn't know what she was talking about. She'd only been on the committee for a few weeks, and if Patrick and Shreya agreed on something, they were probably right.

"We're already having trouble getting people to sign up for canvassing shifts," Shreya said. "How do you think we'd get this message out to everyone in the next four weeks?"

"I'll personally go door-knocking every weekend and make phone calls every day. I'll run more trainings," Mira said impulsively. She sounded more confident than she felt.

Maybe she was actually right, and they stood a chance. Or maybe she was trying to lead them down a path that would destroy everything they'd worked for in the last four years. "We can go all in on that, internally and externally. Tell people who have volunteered that if they've dropped off recently, they can come back. I'll do as much as I possibly can."

"I like that idea," Liz said. "Focusing on how the administration is afraid of us. If it were true that the union wasn't going to do anything anyway, there's no reason for them to give us a pay raise and go all out trying to defeat us."

Other people were nodding. That was more terrifying than reassuring. Patrick was silent for once.

Shreya said, "We need to decide today. Is this what we want?"

Around the room, people voiced their agreement, which mostly filled Mira with dread. She had said something, and the committee agreed with her, and she was going to be on the hook for this. She just had to hope she'd made the right call.

30

Mira was home early, sitting at her usual spot at the table, wrapped up in one of Isabel's flannel shirts. She got up and greeted Isabel with a kiss—not a chaste peck on the lips, but a real kiss, overwhelmingly hot and sweet after a hard week of work. And then another, and another, until Isabel had thawed from the cold.

"Sweetheart, let me take my coat and boots off," Isabel said after they broke apart, both panting. Coming home to Mira was a balm. Isabel had started at a new job site an hour and a half away in the Bronx, working twenty stories up in a building with no walls in the bitter wind. She'd been on her guard all week, making sure her crew knew better than to try anything with her. Nobody had, but it had been exhausting all the same.

She wanted to get lost in kissing Mira. They'd seen so little of each other since Mira had taken on her new responsibilities, and all week long, Grace's words had never stopped echoing in Isabel's head. But Mira was so clearly happy to see her, and they had the whole weekend to enjoy each other and be close again.

The fear was receding. Maybe she could even talk to Mira about it, leaving out the truly painful parts, if she worked up the resolve.

Isabel hung up her coat, slipped out of her thick sweatshirt, and took her boots off and kicked them aside. Mira immediately grabbed her by the belt loops and pulled her in, pressing those delicious curves close, and Isabel went hot and weak.

She tugged at the flannel shirt Mira was wearing, adorably oversized on her. "This is mine."

"Oh, is it? What are you going to do about it?"

Isabel slipped the shirt off Mira's shoulders and let it fall to the floor, finding a sleeveless blouse underneath. "Now I'm cold," Mira said. She batted her eyelashes.

Isabel laughed. She couldn't resist even if she wanted to. She loved this woman so much it hurt. She pulled Mira close again and kissed her, stroking Mira's bare arms and back as Mira happily squirmed against her. "Is that better?"

Mira replied with another kiss, making a contented sound into Isabel's mouth. Her fingers roamed over the back of Isabel's head and pulled out the bobby pins that kept her braid under her hard hat all day. Pins clattered to the floor as they kissed and kissed. Finally, Mira got the braid loose, unraveled it, and ran her fingers over Isabel's scalp through her hair.

Isabel moaned, a shudder rippling from her head through the rest of her body. Undoing her tightly fastened hair after work was always a relief for her poor scalp, and Mira doing it for her was heavenly. Then Mira reached for the top button of her flannel shirt. Isabel smiled. "I'm gross from work. Let me shower first."

"God forbid I enjoy my butch girlfriend when she gets home from her construction job." Mira buried her face in

Isabel's neck and inhaled. Isabel flushed, hopelessly pleased. She'd never heard Mira say *girlfriend* before. What she wouldn't give to keep hearing it. "Can I join you?" Mira asked. "You can say no."

The idea of Mira naked under the spray of water, moans bouncing off the tile, made Isabel shiver. They hadn't gotten around to fucking in the shower yet, and it was time to fix that. Truthfully, after the week she'd had, baring herself in the shower would feel like taking her armor off, which was nerve-wracking. But she could handle it. "Sure. You couldn't wait?"

"I didn't want to. Also, I'm freaking out a little. I could use a distraction."

"What's wrong?"

"Nothing bad. We decided today we're going to have the election as scheduled." Mira sighed. "I'll tell you more about it later."

They went to the bathroom. Mira shoved her against the narrow strip of wall and started kissing her again, hot and messy, with plenty of tongue. Isabel moaned as she kissed back, giving as good as she got, heat blazing in her core. She could use a distraction, too.

Mira made quick work of her flannel shirt. Then came her undershirt, and then her sweaty sports bra. Mira looked at her with such greedy desire that Isabel flushed all over, her skin prickling and her nipples hardening from Mira's gaze alone. She was already so fucking wet. She knew she looked good, but she would never, ever get tired of being looked at like this by the woman she loved.

Mira scooped up Isabel's breasts in big handfuls, bent her head and took a nipple in her mouth, and moaned like she'd been waiting all day. Isabel cried out as pleasure arced through her. After a day of being hard and closed off while using her body for work, it was shocking to be soft and sensitive again, gasping as Mira sucked her nipple with that gorgeous mouth and looked at Isabel through those long lashes.

"Sweetheart," Isabel said, her voice shaky. "We do have to shower."

They ended up under the hot spray, Mira with her hair in a messy bun on top of her head. Water streamed down her body as the shower fogged up. Isabel was going to exercise self-control—she really did need to wash her hair. After that, she'd back Mira up against the tile and trace her tongue over those rivulets of water. See how many times Mira could come before the water ran cold.

"Could you get my shampoo?" Isabel said. It was in a far corner. The shower had been taken over by Mira's curly hair products.

Mira handed it over. "Can I wash your hair?"

Isabel hesitated. She was suspicious of anything requiring her to relax and be patient. Even getting her hair washed before a haircut made her antsy. But Mira's fingers had felt so good against her scalp earlier...

It wouldn't kill her to enjoy this. And she wanted Mira to keep touching her—it reassured her that Mira wanted her. That Mira *still* wanted her. So simple, but it was everything.

"Sure," she said. "Sounds nice." She turned around, facing the showerhead, and let the water run over her body.

Behind her, Mira opened the bottle of shampoo, squeezed it into her hands, and massaged it into Isabel's hair. Mira was getting her nails done differently these days: short on the right hand, and even longer than before on the left. She was being careful to not scratch Isabel, but the contrast still made Isabel smile.

Slowly but surely, Mira loosened her up. It wasn't too hard to stay still and enjoy herself. She had leaned back into Mira's hands without noticing, and Mira was cradling her head and giving her just the right amount of tingly pressure.

"Your hair is so luscious," Mira said, her voice soothing against the backdrop of the shower spray. Isabel held on to every single one of her compliments, so sweet and sincere. "It's so dark and glossy and a pleasure to run my hands through. I could do this forever."

She let Isabel rinse out the shampoo, then worked in the conditioner and carefully loosened the tangles, as patient as she probably was with her own curls. Being taken care of like this wasn't so bad.

Then Mira gently pushed her against the wall. Isabel's back hit the cold tile, and she gasped and let out a laugh. "What are you doing?"

"Helping you shower." Mira squeezed body wash onto her hands, lathered it up, and ran her slippery hands down Isabel's sides. "Is that okay?"

Isabel nodded. Her arousal had been simmering before, but Mira was bringing it back to a full boil. Mira pressed their bodies close, her warm, lush curves sliding against Isabel's, and kissed Isabel's neck as her hands slid between them. She took Isabel's slick, soapy breasts in her hands again and rubbed Isabel's nipples with her thumbs.

The shock of pleasure made Isabel moan and her knees go weak. She grasped the soap holder behind her and gripped Mira's hip with her other hand. Waiting this long had made her needy. "You know, there are other parts of me, too."

Mira was still diligently soaping up her breasts. "I'm just being thorough. Can I tell you a secret?"

Isabel nodded. She would have said yes to anything.

Mira said, "Remember that night I ran into you in the living room? Literally."

Of course Isabel remembered, which had to be obvious from her reaction. Mira smiled slyly. "I didn't actually take a shower. I leaned against the sink and made myself come thinking about you."

At the thought of Mira sliding a hand into those little pajama shorts, eyes closed and head tossed back, fantasizing about *her*...Isabel shivered as she sucked in a breath, utterly helpless. Mira gave her nipples a light, teasing tug, with a taste of those long nails on one side, and Isabel whimpered, the sound echoing off the tile. "Oh, god, Mira," she gasped out. "Did you really—"

Another tug at her nipples, just as gentle, but the pressure was building. Isabel whimpered again and clutched Mira's hip, unable to help herself. Mira hadn't even touched her below the waist, and she was already desperate. She squeezed her thighs together, chasing relief, and Mira noticed and smiled. She was irresistible like this, shy but blazing with desire. "I did. I couldn't sleep after we put up those shelves." She looked down, both self-conscious and coy, before looking Isabel in the eye again. "I knew your hands would feel good on me. I just didn't know how good."

Isabel groaned. She was a mess. Hot, needy, roiling with the thought of Mira wanting her so much. Part of her wanted to flip Mira around, push her against the wall, remind her exactly how good Isabel's hands could feel. But another part of her...

"I made myself come thinking about you, too," she said. "Here in the shower. The day before we kissed." She hadn't wanted to tell Mira before. Hadn't wanted to recall those long months of yearning. But now...maybe it was Mira's hands working her up so much she couldn't think, or maybe it was Mira tenderly washing her hair, or maybe it was how emotionally raw she'd been. But the words had spilled out.

Maybe it was because Isabel wasn't done yearning. Mira wanted sex, and fun, and comfort, and the assurance that she could leave.

Mira's hands went still. Isabel realized she'd clenched her eyes shut, and opened them again. Mira's eyes were wide.

"Will you show me?" she asked.

Isabel inhaled sharply. She'd been naked all this time, but now she was exposed. She'd watched Mira make herself come at least a dozen times—flushed, writhing, tangled up in their sheets, so beautiful it hurt to look at her. But Isabel had never let herself be watched.

She could say no. But she wanted to keep going, to bare herself for Mira here and now, even if she couldn't do it anywhere else. She nodded.

She gripped the soap holder behind her, closed her eyes, and tipped her head back against the tile. Heart pounding, she slipped a hand between her legs. She found her clit, swollen and needy and more than slick enough even in the shower, and whimpered, more naked than she had ever been with Mira.

"Can I keep touching you?" Mira murmured.

Isabel nodded, her eyes still closed. Mira cradled her breasts so gently, rubbed her nipples so slowly, like she knew just how sensitive Isabel was—and even so, it was overwhelming. At every touch, Mira's and her own, bursts of light and heat spread through her body, building up the pressure until it was unbearable. She moaned and quivered, entirely at Mira's mercy.

"So gorgeous," Mira said, her voice thick with desire. "Can I go inside you? I want to feel you when you come."

Isabel opened her eyes. Mira's intent, scorching gaze made her burn even hotter. She nodded.

Mira rinsed the soap off her hands as Isabel made room between her thighs. Mira had been a fast learner these last few weeks, and she didn't waste time. She easily slid two fingers in, the ones with the short nails, and curled them just the way Isabel liked as she raked Isabel's scalp with her talons. Isabel gasped, trembled, squeezed around Mira's fingers involuntarily. She clutched at Mira's soft, slippery body.

"Oh, that's good," Mira said, voice full of wonder as she sped up.

It was too much, and Isabel needed more. She found her clit again, and her hand pressed up against Mira's as they both moved. The intimacy of it made Isabel shiver. "So gorgeous," Mira said again, her lips next to Isabel's ear. "Such strong muscles *there*, too." Isabel exhaled a laugh. She was so close to coming, so helpless, so in love.

She came with a quiet, high moan, clenching around Mira's fingers. As her legs shook, Mira held her up.

Isabel slumped against the wall afterward, oversensitive and raw. Mira sucked her fingers into her mouth and licked them clean with a satisfied hum, making eye contact, and Isabel was overcome by a surge of...everything. Too many emotions she couldn't name.

"I was going to let you have your turn first," she said, still getting herself under control.

"Oh, I have," Mira said. "And I will."

They finished up in the shower. Isabel let Mira lead her to her bedroom, and immediately ended up on her back with Mira straddling her. Mira pulled her scrunchie out of her hair and shook it loose, and it tumbled over her shoulders, wild and a little frizzy from the steam. She was irresistible.

Isabel reached up, squeezed Mira's small, lovely breasts, and swiped her thumbs over the hard brown nipples. Mira giggled. "Don't distract me."

"From what?" Isabel ran her hands down Mira's ribcage, down her stomach, over her soft thighs.

"I'm thinking about what I want from you."

"Why don't you sit on my face while you think about it?"

Mira's eyes widened, and she laughed. If only Isabel could have her like this forever—comfortable and happy in their bed. "Okay," Mira said. "If you insist."

"OH, I ALMOST FORGOT," Mira said. "You distracted me too well. I never told you about the committee meeting today."

After a late dinner where they'd split most of a bottle of wine, catching each other up after a long week of work, they were tangled in bed again. Isabel had forgotten. "What happened?"

Mira told her the news. "So, I'll be knocking on doors every weekend for the next month," she continued. "It's going to be a lot of work. But I think I have to. I can't ask people to do something I'm not willing to do." She rested her head on Isabel's shoulder. "I really, really need us to win."

"I know, sweetheart." Isabel kissed her on the forehead and stroked her hair. But Mira was still tense.

Truthfully, it would have been nice to have Mira relaxed and distracted for a little longer. But Mira was someone with obligations weighing on her, like Isabel was. They couldn't keep out the rest of the world forever.

Mira sighed. "It's also... To be honest, I don't want to be wrong. I don't want Patrick to say *I told you so.* I don't want Shreya to be disappointed in me." Mira was silent for a few seconds. "I know it's not all my responsibility. But I *am* responsible. That's the point of being on the committee in the first place."

Isabel kept stroking her hair. Mira liked to work out her thoughts in words, unlike Isabel, and sometimes she just needed space to do it. Mira continued, "I know you think I should trust myself. It's just so much easier said than done." She nestled closer. "I hate how this feels. I hate not knowing."

"I know." Isabel kissed her again.

"Do you think I was right?"

"If you think it's the right choice, it probably is. You made a lot of good points. You'd know better than me." Mira looked dissatisfied. "I mean that. You know that's true. You know your own coworkers and your own union better than I do. I'm proud of you for speaking up."

Mira had a hard time making up her mind. She was too used to being disregarded, and whenever her decisions mattered, it scared her—that much was clear. Isabel would keep being patient. These things took time. But there was one question where she knew she couldn't be patient forever.

And Isabel didn't have all the answers, even though Mira occasionally seemed to think she did. Sometimes it felt like a burden, and Isabel had so many burdens already. She couldn't protect Mira from the real risk that they'd lose the election after so many years of hard work.

The grueling uncertainty was the worst part, Isabel

knew from experience. But there wasn't much she could do to ease that for Mira. It was up to Mira and her coworkers now.

And Isabel didn't like the thought of Mira being constantly busy for the next several weeks. It was selfish, and she had no right to feel that way, but the sense of loss made her ache. "You're going to be out all day tomorrow?" she asked.

"And Sunday."

Isabel tried to not show any disappointment. They'd barely had any time together all week, but Isabel would just have to deal with it. "You're going to do great out there," she said, and held Mira a little tighter.

31

Time to be the bigger person. Isabel had to text Grace. She couldn't leave their argument hanging like that forever.

But she didn't know what to say. Every time she thought about it, the pain and shame washed over her again. How was she going to move on from this? She'd been afraid to ask Mira for help and hadn't had time to work up to it, and now Mira would be canvassing all day. Isabel was on her own. Sitting on the couch, dread gnawing at her, she took out her phone.

Huh. James, Alexa's widower, had texted her. She couldn't think of any obvious reason. They'd already caught up over text last week after they'd wished each other a happy New Year.

As it turned out, James was seeing someone new. It was getting serious, and he wanted Isabel to hear it from him. He would always treasure the years he'd had with Alexa...

Isabel put her phone down halfway through reading the text.

This was great for him. She was happy. She truly was. It

wasn't that she begrudged him this. But somehow, in the last two years, everyone seemed to have moved on faster than she had. She constantly had the sense she was still picking up the pieces, both her own and everyone else's. But Grace was getting married in a few months, and James had found someone new.

Maybe it was just Isabel. Alone and left behind. She looked out the window at nothing in particular. Bare branches, slush and salt on the street.

Texting Mira was out of the question. She was busy—and, anyway, Isabel was too lost to know what to think, what to feel, what to say. If Mira were here, and they had all the time in the world, she might help Isabel untangle it all. But she wasn't here.

Isabel picked up the phone to call Cat, who had probably known about her older brother's new girlfriend for some time. As soon as she pressed the button, she regretted it. What was she even going to say?

Cat answered, looking frazzled on their video call. She was in her bedroom with piles of laundry on her bed. Loud, rhythmic thumping came through Isabel's phone speaker. "Hey," Cat said. "Sorry, one sec." The music stopped. "What's up?"

"Is this a good time?"

"Yeah, it's good." Cat sounded distracted. "I have a big set tonight, and I got behind, so I'm a little stressed. But it's fine. Is this about James?"

"Kind of. If you're busy—"

"No, no, what's up?"

"I'm not upset or anything. I'm happy for him. I just..." Isabel shook her head. "Finish what you're working on. Let's talk later."

"You can feel however you need to about it." Somehow,

Cat's sympathy made Isabel feel even lonelier. "We can talk now. What's going on?"

"Let's talk when you're less busy. Good luck tonight."

"Uh, thanks. If you're sure. Okay, I think my work schedule is... Let's just do our usual time on Wednesday. Is that okay? If you want to talk sooner than that, I can—"

"That's fine. Talk to you then." Isabel hung up.

She made instant ramen with eggs, dumped in some frozen spinach for nutrition's sake, and ate it standing up at the counter. The apartment felt empty without Mira. It was almost like those endless months of last year when she'd been completely alone.

No, that was ridiculous. She needed to snap out of it. It wasn't as though Mira had never left the apartment before. Mira would be home in a few hours—at six or seven, she'd said. There was no reason to be so needy.

Isabel took a long walk in the cold, went grocery shopping, and texted Mira to ask exactly when she'd be home. She made dinner for them both. At seven, she checked her phone: nothing. No notifications from anyone.

Isabel's gut twisted in anxiety. Maybe Mira's phone had died. But any number of awful things could have happened to her on a cold, dark winter night. She would be with a partner while door-knocking, but what if something happened to both of them?

Had she been in an accident?

There was a pettier, uglier fear rising within her, too: that Mira was fine, and just hadn't thought it was worth texting Isabel or being home on time. It didn't make sense. This was the same Mira who sleepily clung to Isabel when she slipped out of bed at five, who snuck notes into her lunch box that made her grin and blush, who flung herself into Isabel's arms when Isabel got home. Mira wouldn't do that to her.

The idea shouldn't be rattling her this badly. But maybe Mira's priorities had changed. The thing about being alone in the apartment all day was that it was too easy to let poisonous thoughts fester. Isabel knew that too well, but the fears had dug their venomous hooks in.

She called Mira, and it went to voicemail.

Isabel made herself wait ten minutes, paralyzed by anxiety at the dining table. She called again. It went to voicemail.

MIRA HURRIED up the stairs to the apartment. She was still buzzing from a full day of canvassing, and her feet ached, and she was cold, but at least she was finally home.

They'd gone door-to-door around the grad student apartments near campus, asking their coworkers to vote for the union. As much of a slog as it had been, it seemed like their plan could be working. When she'd made her case—if just threatening to unionize could scare the university into giving them a raise, think of what they'd accomplish once they actually unionized—some people had cared enough to listen.

And others had slammed the door in her face. It was too early to tell.

They'd gathered at a bar afterward and shared stories and tactics over food. Mira had needed it. Surrounded by her coworkers talking and laughing, she'd felt a little warmer, a little more hopeful. She was where she was meant to be, and she was part of something important, and the future they'd all worked toward for years might finally arrive.

But everything depended on them winning.

She had no idea what time it was. She'd forgotten to charge her phone last night, in the delicious haze of sex in the shower and more sex in bed and two glasses of wine, and it had died in the middle of the day. She unlocked the apartment door and found Isabel sitting at the table.

Isabel stood up. "Where were you? I was worried about you. What happened?"

The clock in the kitchen read half past eight. Last night, Mira had said she'd probably be home at six or seven, or something along those lines. "Sorry. My phone died. It was a really long day. You weren't waiting up for me, were you?" Of course Isabel had. Mira regretted the words as soon as they left her mouth. "I'm sorry," Mira said again, walking over and putting her arms around Isabel. She'd been excited to share her victories and process her defeats, but now she was deflated. "I didn't mean to make you worry about me."

"It's fine." Isabel squeezed her too tightly for comfort. "Do you want to have dinner?"

Mira had already eaten. But Isabel clearly had something on the stove. "I ate a little because I got hungry. But I could use more food. Thank you."

Isabel went to reheat whatever she'd cooked. "How did it go today?"

Mira recounted her day. Her excitement was tempered by her guilt, though she wasn't sure she'd actually done anything wrong. Now that she was finally sitting down at home, the adrenaline was fading, and she was too tired to think.

Isabel put a bowl of kimchi tofu stew in front of her along with a bowl of rice. It smelled so delicious that Mira's guilt faded. She *was* hungry again. She'd done a lot of walking today.

"I'm glad you're making progress," Isabel said, sitting down at the table. She seemed distracted, not entirely in tune with what Mira had said.

"Thank you." Mira let her calf rub against Isabel's. It was good to be home regardless. She ate a spoonful of stew, and the warmth revitalized her. "What did you get up to today?"

"Not much." Isabel paused. "I got a text from James. Alexa's widower. He said he's seeing someone new."

"Oh!" Mira tried to figure out how to respond. Isabel's blank expression didn't give her any clues. "How are you feeling about that?"

"I'm happy for him." Isabel took a bite of rice.

Isabel had been quiet ever since her visit to her family. Her conversation with Grace had ended in disaster—that was all Mira knew, since Isabel had been vague on details. Maybe Mira couldn't help, and maybe it wasn't any of her business, but the silence still troubled her.

But Isabel was determined to clam up, and there was nothing more Mira could do. "I can't believe I'm about to do all this again tomorrow," she said, changing the subject. "Today was good overall, I think. Just exhausting."

"Come to bed with me early, then." Isabel gave her a hopeful smile.

"That would be wonderful." After a day in the cold, walking from building to building and talking to dozens of people, she longed to be in Isabel's arms under the covers. Last night had been wonderful, and she'd been so content as she drifted off to sleep. Maybe everything would be all right again once they got back in bed. "I just have to finish writing a letter of recommendation for my student from last semester. Lauren. I told you about her, I think. I'll be done in an hour or so."

"I'm starting to worry about you," Isabel said. Mira looked up, surprised. "Don't tire yourself out too much. You should rest."

Mira bristled. "I know. I can take care of myself." Of course she was sacrificing her rest for this work. She had thought Isabel understood why.

"It's easy to get burned out when you're organizing." There was something all-knowing about her tone that irked Mira. "I know what it's like. If you keep going like this, you're not going to last through the month."

Mira's indignation rose. "I know how tiring it is." She was proud of what she'd done today, even if it had exhausted her. It would be nice if Isabel acknowledged that a little more. "I'm asking everyone else in my department to do this all-out push before the election, and I need to be there with them as their area captain, like I've been telling you. It's worth it to me."

These days, Mira had a budding sense that she wasn't just someone who happened to be the Classics area captain, but someone who made decisions and faced the consequences for herself and others. She was someone whose choices mattered. The way she saw herself was changing, and she'd thought Isabel understood. Maybe Mira had been wrong.

Mira was rattled. She had always counted on Isabel to see her the way she wanted to be seen. Isabel had helped her see herself this way in the first place. But now the foundation of Isabel's trust in her felt shakier than it should.

"I know," Isabel said. "I'm just saying I'm worried about you."

Her words were the opposite of reassuring. "Are you just saying this because I didn't come home when you wanted me to?"

"It's not about that," Isabel said, too quickly. "You've been working late most nights. I barely ever see you anymore. It's not just about tonight." Isabel seemed like she wasn't finished. "But I don't think wanting to know where you are and wanting you to be home on time is too much to ask, either."

Mira put her face in her hands. How had it come to this? She was exhausted, and she still had work to do, and now a sickeningly familiar fear loomed over the conversation. These little arguments over where Mira had gone and whom she was with could easily build up to something worse, until she was trapped. "Like I said, I'm sorry for not texting you, but I never promised you I'd be back at a specific time, and I never asked you to wait up for me. It's my life. I don't tell you how to spend your time or what you can and can't do."

Isabel looked taken aback. "I didn't tell you that."

"I'm doing this so I'll never have to be exhausted and burned out from being overworked ever again," Mira continued, pressing on despite Isabel's hurt expression, desperately needing to make herself heard. "I need us to win this election, and I need us to win a fair contract as soon as we can, and I'll do anything to make sure it happens. If we lose, I'll be back to where I've been for the last five years."

"I'm sorry. I know how important this is to you. I really do."

"Do you?" Something previously unspoken between them was bubbling up. "It's the only way I can have a living wage and can afford to choose where I live. You understand that, right?"

Isabel's eyes widened. She put her hands on her lap and went very still.

Mira had never lost sight of that fact. Isabel would

blanch at the idea of ever treating her the way Dylan had, or having anything in common with him at all. But maybe Mira was fundamentally still in the same situation she'd been in with him. She could leave Isabel now, but where would she go?

She hadn't had any reason to worry about it since they'd started dating. Isabel had been wonderful to her. But with Isabel being this pushy about where she was and what she was doing, the fear was returning to lurk in the corners of her mind.

Isabel rubbed her face and sighed. "Yeah. I do." She was pulling the stoic, responsible mask back on, but Mira could see she wasn't calm at all. "I got worried about you and I overreacted. I didn't mean to tell you what to do."

Regardless of anything else, Isabel cared about her. That was a fundamental difference. Mira hoped it was enough. "I know."

"I don't want to get in the way of your organizing or anything else you do." Isabel looked miserable. "I know it's your life. I'm sorry."

Mira softened. They were both anxious and tired, and it was a terrible time to be having an argument. They should have just gone to bed and saved it for tomorrow. Except that Mira would be busy again tomorrow, and then it would be Monday, and Mira's evenings were now booked too...

Mira moved her chair closer to Isabel, leaned against her, and pressed their foreheads together. Isabel thawed and relaxed into her touch—only partially, but it was something. "Well, I'm sorry for snapping at you earlier. And I'm sorry for being careless and not texting you back. I'll bring my backup phone battery with me tomorrow. That would have saved us a lot of unnecessary anguish." They shared a small smile. "And I'll do a better job of warning you the next time

I'm out late. I can tell you it'll be the same thing tomorrow, and I don't want you to wait up."

"Thank you, sweetheart," Isabel said, still stiff. "I appreciate that. Don't worry about me."

Mira twined their hands together. "I do worry about you. And I wish I could spend more time with you. But it's just until the election, and then we can make up for lost time. Will you text me tomorrow and tell me how you're doing?"

Isabel hesitated. "I might go into work tomorrow. They're behind schedule and looking for some people to work overtime."

Are you sure? What about your knee? Why are you doing this? Mira bit back her questions. She didn't want to be a hypocrite, and she wasn't sure she had enough softness left in her for Isabel's hard silences tonight.

Maybe the good, easy days were over. Mira was chilled. She'd known those days had to end eventually. But she hadn't known how soon, and she hadn't expected it to hit her so hard.

She had been naive. They couldn't be a refuge for each other forever. They'd both been battered by the world, and the world would keep battering them.

She held Isabel tighter. "Promise me you'll take care of yourself?"

Isabel nodded. "I'll text you during my breaks." Maybe that was the most Mira could hope for.

Under the covers, with Isabel softly snoring, Mira's mind was still racing. She was so physically tired. But she couldn't sleep.

They'd had a fight and gotten through it. For now. Just like any couple. And they *were* a couple, as much as Mira had avoided thinking about the word. In those idyllic days when everything had been good and easy, their lives had become intertwined. If Mira had to leave, she'd have to rip out and leave a part of herself behind.

Maybe it had always been a mistake to think they could be casual with each other.

That night at the club, Mira had plunged into that wild, reckless, wonderful kiss while still half in denial about what she was doing. Now, once more, she'd gotten herself in too deep. And now she had to face what she'd done, just like on that cold night, walking alone by the river as Isabel waited for her.

They'd had a couples' fight, the kind of fight between people who mattered to each other, who had a shared past and present and maybe a future. It was the kind of fight that didn't end in a single night. Mira was in for more of this—if she stayed.

The more intertwined their lives were, the more it mattered whether she had a way to get out on her own. They needed to win this election. She didn't want to imagine what would happen if they didn't.

32

"Looks good," Isabel called down to her new apprentice Carla. "Nice work."

Isabel was worn down. Just four weekends of working overtime had made her knee pain return with a vengeance. There were good days and bad days, and today was a bad one. This late-winter cold snap was stiffening her joints and making her hobble, and she hadn't been able to walk it off.

It would be over soon. Mira's union election was in two days. Win or lose, she'd have more time for Isabel, but Isabel hoped as desperately as she'd ever hoped for anything that the union would win. Maybe Mira would feel safer, then. Maybe they could be close again, without this distance between them that kept growing by the day.

Asking anything of Mira seemed out of reach. Whenever Isabel considered asking for more time together, more promises, she was sickened by the fear that Mira might not feel free to say no. And she hated feeling like a burden, like someone who needed Mira more than Mira needed her.

Over the last two years, she'd pushed everyone away, and now she had nothing left but work. That had never been more painfully obvious. But work wasn't so bad. She could look at her installations with pride, and she could teach Carla something. She knew how to be useful at work.

Still lost in her thoughts, she took a step back down the ladder. The pain in her knee flared.

A stab of panic, a split-second of useless flailing, and then she was tumbling from six feet off the ground. Her foot smashed into the floor at the wrong angle, and the sharp, throbbing pain in her ankle took over. Even her work boots hadn't saved her.

Carla rushed over. "Oh, shit, are you okay?"

"I'm fine." Isabel tried to stand. A stab of pain forced her back down.

She was setting a bad example for Carla. "Maybe not," Isabel said, gritting her teeth. "I think there's something wrong with my ankle."

When Mira walked through the door, after a grueling day of teaching and phone-banking, Isabel was laid up on the couch with a foot brace. "Oh my god," Mira said, dropping her messenger bag. "What happened? Did you break your foot?"

"I sprained my ankle at work." Isabel looked more embarrassed than pained.

Mira rushed over. "And you didn't tell me?" Isabel hadn't so much as texted her.

Isabel flinched at her approach, which hurt to see. "I went to urgent care and they said I was fine to go home. I didn't want to make you worried. You've been busy."

"Obviously that doesn't mean you shouldn't tell me if you get hurt," Mira said, boggled. Was she missing something? She sat down next to Isabel. "What happened?"

Isabel grimaced. "I fell off a step ladder. Dumb mistake. It wasn't that high up."

Her glibness was worrying. "Is there anything I can do for you? Is it just the ankle?"

"It's just the ankle." Isabel's posture softened, her defenses lowering. "Thanks. I appreciate it. I'm just embarrassed."

"For being injured?"

Isabel looked sheepish. "I should have been more careful. Now I can't work for two weeks."

Mira winced. "Oh, Isabel. Please don't blame yourself for this. Will you be okay pay- and insurance-wise?"

"Yeah, that's not a problem. I have good benefits." Isabel let out a sigh, tormented by whatever was locked up in her head. "This is going to be the longest amount of time I've taken off work in years."

"Really?" It wasn't the most surprising news in the world, but it was disturbing. "Well, maybe you don't want to hear this. But it could be nice to rest for a while, like you're always telling me to do. And you need to, or else your ankle won't heal."

Isabel looked away and said nothing.

Mira's anxiety spiked. Of course Isabel, more than most people, would be upset by two weeks of mandatory downtime. For one thing, it meant two weeks of having to accept help. But when Mira had lived with Dylan, his bad moods had taken over the entire apartment they'd shared, like a dark cloud that had pushed her into the corners and made her so small she nearly disappeared.

She caught herself about to apologize, and bit it back. "I know you'd rather be working. I know it's hard. I can swap shifts with someone and do my phone-banking from home—"

"No," Isabel said, her impatience breaking through. Mira flinched. Isabel rubbed her face. "It's fine. Just do your election work."

"Are you sure?" This new side of Isabel—distant, imperious, patronizing—had emerged during their argument a few weeks ago, and it had never quite gone away. Mira had been walking on eggshells far too often at home. And Isabel's injury was bringing out this side of her more than ever.

Mira ached for her. But she couldn't relieve Isabel's pain, or her sense of powerlessness, or whatever else it was that Mira couldn't see. Obviously, Isabel hated being injured. But whatever was bothering her seemed far bigger than that.

The honeymoon was over. They couldn't go on like this. The questions looming on the horizon had always been closer than Mira had thought.

Isabel looked at her foot brace. "It's my fault. Don't worry about me."

AFTER A RESTLESS NIGHT, Isabel limped to the kitchen for coffee. A pot was waiting for her, still hot in the carafe, along with a note in Mira's elegant cursive: *Please take care of yourself.*

Isabel took the note and clutched it for a few seconds. She really didn't deserve Mira.

She poured herself a cup. Her ankle felt a little better. Or, at least, she would keep telling herself that.

Isabel was used to working ten-hour days in the blazing sun and freezing cold. It was ridiculous that something as minor as falling off a ladder could put her out of commission this badly. Two weeks away from work.

She sat at the table, the dull throbbing from her ankle intruding into her thoughts. Mira would have to cook and clean and run errands for them during her busiest week of the year, all while Isabel sat around uselessly because of a stupid mistake she'd made. She remembered the way she'd lost control of herself last night, letting her frustration with herself spill over into being curt with Mira, and how hurt Mira had looked.

What did she know about being a good partner?

Her phone buzzed. It was a text from Mira. *How are you doing? I just wanted to make sure you're okay.*

Isabel was falling apart. She hadn't been this powerless since the early days after Alexa's death. At least in those days, she could get lost in the endless rhythm of work. There had always been more conduit to run, miles and miles of it, until Isabel had been too exhausted to stand. Now even that was gone.

She texted back: *I'm fine.* She had said the same thing to Reina a million times until Reina finally left her.

Isabel was so restless that it was painful to sit still. For the first time in months, she opened up Instagram on her phone.

There was Grace at her bridal shower. Happy and surrounded by friends. Obviously, Grace hadn't invited her.

Isabel put her face in her hands and groaned, in this empty apartment where there was no one to hear her. She had to do *something*. She stood up, and her ankle complained, but she would just have to get used to that. She would have to figure out a way to become fine.

The grocery store was a block away. She could stay on her feet for an hour or two. That was enough to shop for groceries and cook a simple dinner, to apologize, to make amends, to put things right. She wanted to do so much more for Mira, but it was better than nothing at all.

Isabel plodded to the coat rack and put on her jacket. She puzzled over what shoes to wear, and settled for running shoes, unlaced on one side to fit over the brace. Her ankle nagged her on every step, but she pressed on.

She was going to be fine. She left the apartment, hobbled down the stairs, and walked into the falling snow.

33

MIRA WASN'T GOING to be happy about this. It was the only thought in Isabel's mind. The unrelenting white-hot pain in her wrist crowded out everything else.

She groaned incoherently as she lay on the sidewalk. A stranger above her was saying something she couldn't make sense of. An ambulance siren was getting louder.

The memory was unreal. Slipping on the patch of black ice, and the perfect, clear, heart-stopping moment of regret. *Not again.*

EMTs were emerging from the ambulance, carrying a stretcher. They said something to her and grabbed her. She flailed, panic rising, the pain turning her mind blank. Not the ER, she didn't want to go there—

"Isabel? Is that you?"

That was Mira. Isabel thrashed, trying to turn around and see her, relief momentarily overwhelming the pain. She was ashamed to let Mira see her like this. But she wouldn't have to go to the ER alone. "Oh my god," Mira shouted. "What happened? Why the hell are you outside?"

From her vantage point on the ground, this now seemed

like a very good question. *I'm fine*, Isabel tried to yell. It came out as a garbled cry.

There was jostling above her. The EMTs were trying to get Mira to back off. "Let me ride in the ambulance," Mira said.

More commotion. "Ma'am—"

"That's my wife." Mira's voice cut through everyone else's. Isabel let out a laugh despite everything. Pain shot up her wrist, and she winced and gritted her teeth. "I need to go with her," Mira said. Her tone was even, but she left no room for disagreement. "She needs me."

Somehow, Mira got past the EMTs, and then she was right above Isabel. Mira was an angel. But the wild anguish on her face was unbearable to see. An EMT said, "Is this woman—"

"Yeah," Isabel gasped out. She went limp and let the EMTs take her into the ambulance.

"If you're angry with me, you can tell me," Isabel said.

They were still in the hospital at midnight. Mira had stayed with her during the entire agonizing wait in the ER. They were waiting for the final sign-off from the doctor, and Isabel had enough painkillers in her that she could talk.

All night long, she'd sensed the walls closing in on her. If Mira hadn't been by her side, she didn't know how she would have made it.

"I am," Mira said. She looked exhausted, hunched over in the chair next to Isabel's hospital bed.

"I'm sorry." The guilt was killing Isabel. "I'm wasting so much of your time."

Mira sat up. "Oh, that's not why I'm angry." She sounded like her patience had finally run out. Maybe this was it, the moment Isabel had been fearing all these months. "I'm not angry because you're injured and you need help. I don't want to hear you apologize for that ever again. I'm angry because you did something reckless and endangered yourself, right after you got hurt at work yesterday and refused to tell me anything about it. And I'm angry because over the last few weeks, you've been upset about something and taking it out on me, and you won't admit it or tell me what's wrong. It makes me feel awful."

Isabel's stomach sank through the floor. Was that really how Mira saw it, that Isabel had been taking something out on her? "I don't know why you've been acting like this," Mira continued. "I wish I knew, and I wish I could help you. I don't know what else to do."

Even now, Mira's expression was full of concern. Isabel closed her eyes and shut out the terrible sterile room. Then she forced herself to look at Mira again, even as her shame overwhelmed her.

"You're right." She rubbed her face with her good hand. "I'm sorry. I don't even know where to start. It's been an awful last few weeks for me. It has nothing to do with you. There's a lot I probably should have told you."

"Like what?"

Mira wanted to know, and it hurt her to not know, and Isabel wasn't going to hold on to Mira by hiding things from her. It was humiliating how clear this was in retrospect, after Isabel had put herself in the hospital. "The fight I had with Grace was really bad. I didn't tell you all of it."

"From a month ago?"

Isabel nodded. "I told her that I was worried about Kevin being a good partner."

"I remember."

"That wasn't the end of it. I said that to her..." This was

excruciating. But she had to do it for Mira. "I said that to her, and she said to me, 'A good partner? You would know all about that, right?'" Isabel remembered each and every word. "And I walked out on her. I couldn't even say anything. It hurt so much. I've been really fucked up over it ever since. I'm not blaming her. Just me."

"Oh, Isabel," Mira said, sympathetic to a fault as ever. "That's a cruel thing to say. Whatever else you might have said, that's not fair to you."

A wave of anger washed over Isabel. Anger at herself, pulling her under. "It is fair."

Mira reached out and squeezed her good hand, and it was a lifeline as she was drowning. "It's not. You know you don't have to blame yourself for everything, right?"

Isabel took a shaky breath. If she let herself believe that, her entire world would fall apart. She had responsibilities, no matter how much she was failing to meet them.

"Was she talking about us?" Mira asked.

Isabel shook her head. "I didn't tell her about you. I think she was talking about Reina breaking up with me."

Mira was silent. Her expression shifted. Finally, she said, with quiet determination, "I know this is beside the point. And I know it's only been a few months. But I hope I'm not a secret you're keeping from your family."

"No," Isabel said, horrified. Once again, she wanted to track down and fight all of Mira's bad exes. But maybe she was about to become yet another one of them. "No. Oh, god, Mira, I promise you I'm not. I might have fucked up everything else, but I promise I'm not doing that. Being with you is the best thing that's ever happened to me. And I want everyone to know. I told my parents about how much you mean to me. I want my whole family to meet you." She sniffled. "It hurts so much that I'll never introduce you to Alexa and she'll never get to see how much I love you."

Mira wasn't supposed to know any of this. But Isabel was crumbling, and everything she'd tried to hold back was rushing out in a torrent. She took her hand out of Mira's grasp and wiped her face, not even bothering to hide her tears. "I didn't tell Grace because I wanted to save it for when we made up. And because being with you was the best part of my life, and I thought I could keep it separate from all my mistakes with Grace. I don't know what I was trying to do. Whatever it was, I didn't do it right."

She was used to thinking of herself as strong and capable. Now, lying in the hospital bed, she just felt painfully small.

Mira's eyes were wide, her mouth open. She said nothing.

"I'm so afraid," Isabel said, barreling on. It was a relief to admit it, even though it wasn't going to do her any good. "I've been afraid that you were going to leave me because I didn't deserve you. I wish I knew how to be good enough for you to stay."

"Oh, Isabel." Mira took Isabel's hand in hers again. It was a few nerve-wracking seconds before she spoke. "I didn't know you felt that way. You've been holding on to that for a while."

"It wasn't just because of what Grace said. I was scared before, too. I don't know if I should tell you this. But Vivian and Frankie warned me at the restaurant."

"What? What did they say?"

Isabel recounted the conversation. "Oh," Mira said. She smiled sadly. "They told me about that too. Although it sounds like you remember it differently. Vivian said she just wanted to say hi and get a sense of what you're like. And they're a little overprotective. But she told me she might have scared you, and I told her that it would take a lot more than that." Mira grimaced. "I'm sorry. If I'd known that it bothered you..."

"It's not your fault. It's my fault. I got too scared. I tried to do too much for you and protect you and hide everything from you. And I couldn't handle it when that didn't work." Isabel shuddered, almost sobbing. "I know what that must have looked like to you. Being a controlling asshole just like your ex."

"I never asked you to do any of that." Mira was so patient. "You just assumed that was what I wanted."

Isabel somehow felt even more wretched. Why hadn't she realized that on her own? "I see that now."

"That's not all. When I said I didn't know you'd been feeling that way, I meant... You're talking about staying for the long term. You don't just want more of the same thing. You want something serious with someone who's committed to you. That's what you've wanted all this time." Mira hesitated. "That's what you want from me, isn't it?"

Isabel nodded. There was no denying it now. At least Mira hadn't brought up Isabel saying she loved her in the worst circumstances imaginable.

Mira sighed. She took her hand away. "First of all, you've been really good to me. Please believe me when I say that, Isabel."

Isabel braced herself. Here it was. "But I don't want to be a thing that you either deserve or don't deserve," Mira continued. "Or a thing you're either good enough or not good enough for. It makes it sound like if you did enough, you'd earn the right to be with me. I'm not a prize for you to win or lose."

Isabel nodded again. Everything was so clear when

Mira laid it out. Her gentle honesty made Isabel's heart ache. Mira was braver than Isabel would ever be.

"Are you leaving me?" Isabel asked. She needed to get this over with. Mira had cracked her open and changed her from the inside out, and Isabel would always be grateful. She would find a way to survive.

"No," Mira said. She took Isabel's hand again, squeezed it, and smiled. "If I wanted to leave you, I would have already. I wouldn't let you down easy."

Isabel snorted. Something light and fizzy bubbled up in her chest. The fear that had crushed her these last days, months, and even years was easing up on her. She still had to get herself out of this mess. But—hospital bed and injured limbs aside—when Mira smiled at her, the sun shone through the clouds. "You would have left me on the sidewalk?"

"Absolutely. So don't try this again." Mira's smile widened, the corners of her eyes crinkling, and Isabel was warmed all the way through. Then Mira's face grew serious again. "If I actually wanted to leave you, I wouldn't bother trying to get through to you like this. You are the most obstinate person alive. You tried to go out with a sprained ankle in the snow because you couldn't deal with your feelings and sit at home for one day."

Isabel winced, but she was smiling, and Mira was, too. Mira's open exasperation was the most reassuring thing Isabel had heard in a while. Mira took her hand and ran a thumb over the calluses. "You're lucky you're so tall and gorgeous. And such a caring, considerate girlfriend when you're not being so frustrating." Mira looked around. "I mean, wife. Can't have them knowing I lied."

Isabel laughed, a sharp tug in her chest. "I think they would have let you come if you'd just said you were my girlfriend." She wasn't going to replay Mira saying *my wife*, wasn't going to imagine a ring on Mira's finger. She still had so much to make up for.

Mira grinned. "I had to think fast. But, sure, I'll remember that for next time. If I decide to not just leave you on the sidewalk." Then she sighed. "Isabel, I don't know if I can promise you everything you want. But I do want to listen to you and try to understand you. I don't want you to worry I'm going to leave you if you say something that's too much or too difficult. You already have enough on your mind."

This was more than Isabel deserved. But that was the wrong way to think about it. "I didn't tell you the truth before because I was a coward. I hope you know that now."

"You're not a coward." Mira was blazing now, alight with passion and anger, all of it aimed right at Isabel. This was the fierce union organizer and brilliant scholar Isabel loved. "I'm not accepting that excuse from you, of all people. If this is going to work, you know we have to be able to trust each other. If you keep secrets from me about how much you're hurting or grieving, I can't trust you enough to stay with you and share a life with you."

Isabel was chastened. "I know."

"Well, I'm glad to hear that. Because I need to ask some things of you."

"I'll do anything." Isabel truly would. Anything to make this better.

"You need to talk to me about your feelings instead of... all of this." Mira made a broad gesture. "Trying to run away from them. Or trying to control me because you can't deal with them. Or working until you hurt yourself."

Isabel nodded. She needed to step up. She was afraid,

but Mira was worth it. "I'll try. You might have to be patient with me."

Mira smiled. "And you know you need to talk to Grace again. That's for you, not me."

Isabel ran her hand over her face. The prospect of it scared her as much as everything else Mira wanted from her. "Grace might not forgive me."

"No, you can't make her." Mira gave her a pointed look. "That's not what I'm asking. I think you have more to say to her, and she probably has more to say to you."

Maybe Isabel did have more to say. Not just to apologize, not just to blame herself for all the pain in her family over the last two years, but to actually talk to her sister and lay herself open. "I know," Isabel said. "I know. I'm just scared."

Mira squeezed her hand. "Why don't you tell me what you're so afraid of? Since we're going to be here for a while."

34

THE ELECTION HAD STARTED. For months, Isabel had looked forward to doing whatever she could today to support Mira. Instead, she'd needed Mira's help to get dressed, and she was about to spend the rest of this momentous day sitting on the couch.

"Text me if you need anything," Mira had said sternly. "Seriously. Don't be a hero."

It was only nine in the morning. Isabel had to get through the whole day without going anywhere except the fridge, microwave, and bathroom, and then she had to endure at least several more days of the same. If she was well-behaved, she might be allowed outside next week. The cast wouldn't come off for another two months. And yesterday, she'd thought that two weeks was a long time. "Sitting and reading isn't doing nothing," Mira had said, mock-offended. But Isabel had felt too chastened to joke around.

Mira had asked a few basic things of her. If Isabel couldn't even do those, she might as well pack it up.

One thing at a time. She picked up her phone and laboriously texted Cat with one hand: *I need your advice on Grace. And some other things.*

Cat was in LA for her West Coast debut, so Isabel didn't expect a quick reply. But the dots popped up indicating Cat was typing back. *I'm free if you want to call now!*

Isabel started a video call. Cat picked up, still in a black mesh top she'd probably worn to the club. "Hey, what's up?" she said, very loudly.

Isabel winced. "Hey. Why are you still up?" She knew perfectly well that Cat hadn't woken up before six in the morning on this calendar day.

"I just got back after my set. It was great. Really good vibes. What's going on?"

Just the thought of all that gave Isabel a headache. "Shouldn't you be sleeping?"

"I always get really wired for, like, two or three hours after my set ends. I'm at my friends' place. They're still out. So why'd you call me? This is about Grace, right? Wait, what's that thing on your arm?"

"I broke my wrist. I'll tell you about it later. How much did you hear from her?"

"Uh...okay. I think I heard all of it." Cat's tone was unexpectedly serious. "You know, she told me she feels terrible about how your fight ended."

"It's fine," Isabel said, out of habit.

"Doesn't sound like it. Although, to be honest, you know she had a point."

"About what?"

"You do kind of treat her like a baby. I'm not saying she couldn't have done a better job of telling you. But Grace does have her own life now. She likes her job, and she and Kevin are doing well. You can see why she thinks you look down on her." Cat paused. "I knew what she was saying because you do it to me a little bit, too, honestly. I know you don't think I have a real job—"

"Come on. I don't think that."

"Yes, you do. It's fine. We can't all be big, tough blue-collar workers like you." This was a recurring topic for shit-talking. But it actually bothered Cat, and Isabel hadn't seen that before. "I do like what I do, even if I have to crash on my friends' couches and work shitty day jobs. I feel like sometimes you don't take me that seriously, or like I need to grow out of it, or something."

Isabel let her head thump against the back of the couch cushion. She hadn't been ready for this many wake-up calls in a twenty-four-hour period. "Sorry. I really—"

"It's okay. This isn't about me. I didn't mean to get into it."

"No, I'm glad you said it." There was something she needed to tell Cat, something she never would have thought to say a year ago. Isabel was going to make a mess of it, but she needed to try. "I need to say something."

"Yeah?"

"I want to say… Thanks for checking up on me all this time. These last two years. It's been hard. Sorry I spent all that time telling you I didn't want to talk or that I'm fine, brushing you off, all that bullshit." Isabel's face burned. She wasn't good at this. "I don't know what I would have done without you. Seriously. So, uh, thanks again for that."

Cat wasn't very much like James, her overachieving brother, but she was just as loyal and kind. And she knew a thing or two about living in her older sibling's shadow. Isabel had never tried to open up and talk about what they had in common. She'd wasted so much time.

Cat smiled. "Aww, Isabel. You're a big softie. I've always known that about you." At that, Isabel scoffed. But she couldn't help smiling, which probably looked ridiculous on Cat's phone screen. "Don't worry about it, okay? I'm happy to talk any time. I mean it. So, how'd you break your wrist?"

Isabel groaned in resignation. She recounted the events of the last several days. "What?" Cat said. "You went out and tried to shop for groceries with a sprained ankle? Just so you could make dinner for this girl? Because you wanted to, what, apologize to her?"

Isabel grimaced. "Pretty much."

"Oh my god, Isabel. Here's the thing. I know you think *my* relationships are messy, but I've never done anything like—"

"Okay, okay, I get it." She deserved that. Thank god Cat was here to make fun of her. She needed some of that mixed in with Mira's infinite compassion.

"You are ridiculous. You have no right to judge me for anything I tell you after this. You know, it sucks now, but this is going to be a good story for your wedding someday. I'm not going to forget."

There was a familiar tug in Isabel's chest, the one she always felt when she thought about making a future with Mira. "Who says I'd invite you?"

"Yeah, like you're going to get a different DJ? Come on."

Isabel grinned. The muscles of her face were unused to smiling so much. "Can I ask you something?"

"Go ahead."

"Do you really think Grace and Kevin are happy?"

"Oh, they definitely are. Okay, look, I'm going to be

honest with you. If I were in Grace's situation, and I grew up with two older sisters with, let's just say, extremely strong personalities—"

"Hey," Isabel said, mildly indignant. "I know I'm overbearing. But Alexa—" She stopped herself. If Grace had found Alexa overbearing at times, growing up, it wasn't actually any of Isabel's business.

Maybe Alexa hadn't been perfect. But she had been a good sister, and she had been so loved. And if that was true for Alexa...

Isabel shook her head. "Never mind." For once, she didn't need everything to be spelled out for her. "What were you saying?"

Cat rolled her eyes. "If I had two *wonderful* older sisters who were just a little bit overbearing—your word, not mine —I might want to marry a guy who's pretty chill and just loves her and does whatever she tells him to do. I'm just saying. Make of that what you want."

When Isabel hung up, she was still smiling. She wasn't going to talk herself out of what she had to do next. If she was stuck in the apartment, she could at least do this.

"Hi." Grace didn't sound happy about Isabel calling her.

"Hey. I want to say sorry for being a condescending asshole and not treating you like an adult who can make your own choices. I'll listen to whatever you want to say to me. I mean it this time."

Grace sighed. "Did Cat put you up to this?"

"We talked. She didn't tell me what to say. It was, uh, mostly my girlfriend."

"You have— All right. I don't want to talk to you about

this over the phone. Can you come here? Maybe next weekend?"

"I can't. I sprained my ankle and broke my wrist."

"Oh my god, really? At work?"

"No. The ankle is from work." Isabel explained everything a second time today. It wasn't any less humiliating.

"Wow. So you're dating your roommate." Grace paused. "I have a dress fitting in Manhattan today. I could come to your place afterward at around three. You're still in the same apartment, right?"

"Yeah." Isabel glanced out the window. A few flakes of snow were falling. "It's going to snow. Hope you're not driving."

She could practically hear Grace rolling her eyes. "I'm taking the LIRR. See you soon."

MIRA TOOK off her headset and reached for her coffee cup. It was empty. Hadn't it been full just a moment ago?

She rubbed her eyes. She had been making calls or tabling outside in the cold all day, in between training other grad students to do the same; if they were getting involved on the day of the election, well, better late than never. It was almost four o'clock, two hours before the polls closed, and she was tired. She'd collapsed in her own room at two in the morning after helping Isabel get to bed, and Isabel had clearly resented needing help even as she'd put on a brave face about it. Old habits died hard.

It had been a long night. When she'd found Isabel crumpled on the sidewalk surrounded by EMTs, the agony had pierced her heart through. Only her desperation had kept her calm. She'd been acting on pure instinct—needing to see for herself that Isabel was alive and conscious, needing to protect Isabel from having to face the ER alone.

Mira had been shaking during the entire ambulance ride. With the terror had come clarity. They would have to decide what they were to each other.

Mira couldn't keep either of them waiting forever. Soon, she'd have to make up her mind.

She hadn't made any promises last night, and Isabel hadn't pushed her. But even saying what she'd said had taken so much out of her. She wanted so badly to believe Isabel's apologies and promises. But maybe it was futile to ask Isabel to treat her differently, futile to ask for anything at all.

She knew what Isabel wanted from her. But Mira had reached the limits of her bravery—it didn't extend quite far enough to cover all her fear. Isabel would have to keep waiting a while longer, if she was still willing to wait.

Mira's thoughts were swirling into a morass of dread. The election. Their odds of winning. How she'd live with herself if they lost. Isabel by herself at home, and all the ways she could break yet another limb. Every discouraging phone call Mira had made today, portending their loss. Isabel's words to her: *She'll never get to see how much I love you.*

She needed more coffee. She left the phone-banking room and found Shreya outside. "How are you doing?" Shreya asked.

Mira shook her head. "Not great. I've been here since eight. And I'm supposed to stay and be a witness for the ballot-counting." She yawned. "Isabel broke her wrist last night, and I was up late helping her."

"Is she okay now? Is anyone helping her at home?"

Mira grimaced. "No. She told me to come in today.

She's really stubborn." If Isabel had been just a little less insistent, Mira would have stayed home. Although, truthfully, part of her was relieved to be here. She needed a distraction, in the form of one of the most consequential, nerve-wracking events of her life.

Shreya seemed skeptical. "If you need to go home and be with her, I'll take over your phone-banking shift and deal with the ballot-counting."

"Thanks, but I'll be fine." Mira poured herself more coffee from the carafe on the table. She reached for the milk, knocked her cup over, and sent coffee flying all over the table and floor. She cursed under her breath. She was more jittery and more tired than she'd thought.

Shreya helped her clean up the mess with the napkins nearby. "You sure you don't want to go home?"

"It's only a few more hours."

"Let me buy you some better coffee, at least."

"That's okay. I should go back."

"Well, as the vice president, I get to tell you to leave your shift and come to the coffee shop with me." Shreya started walking and motioned at Mira to follow.

So much for democratic leadership. They left the building. Snow was falling, whipped around by the icy wind. Mira was wearing the silk slip under her sweater dress—it had kept her warm through these bleak winter days as she'd knocked on doors and trudged home in the dark. Kept her warm even when Isabel herself hadn't always.

Shreya said, "You know we're not going to win or lose depending on whether you stick around tonight. No offense to your ballot-counting skills, which I'm sure are exceptional."

"I know." Mira knew that perfectly well. But if there was anything she could do in these final hours to improve their chances, she would do it. If she didn't, and they lost, she'd never forgive herself. She yawned again. "There's still time to make more calls, though. We might convince someone at the last minute."

Over the last few weeks, the need to prove herself had slowly consumed her. It went beyond her own prospects of better pay and beyond her obligations to other people. She wanted to be vindicated.

She wanted to prove that she'd made the right choice in pushing to keep the election date. That her department was right to trust her to lead. That she was worth listening to, that her experiences mattered, that she deserved power in her own life. No abusive ex-boyfriend could tell her otherwise, no dismissive man on the committee. Not Isabel, if it came down to it.

It was too much meaning to attach to one election. Too much weight, on top of the real consequences of victory and defeat, and Mira was staggering. But she couldn't get out from under it.

She followed Shreya into the cafe and let Shreya order lattes for them both. "With an extra shot for me, please," Mira added. Shreya glared at her but didn't object.

They sat down. The snow fell outside. "Look, Mira," Shreya said, "I'm going to be honest with you." As though Shreya ever did otherwise. "If we lose this election, it's not going to be your fault."

"I know."

"Do you? Because the union stands or falls based on the work we've all done for the last four years. That's all done. It's not about you." She gave Mira a pointed look. "Don't forget why you're doing this."

"Why am I doing this?" Mira asked blearily.

"We're doing this for each other." Of course Mira knew

that, but Shreya wasn't usually one for this kind of talk. Mira sat up and paid attention. "Look, you know how much I hate delegating things to other people. I would do everything myself if I could. The problem was that I did so much that I got elected VP, and now I'm forced to delegate everything."

Mira snorted. No part of that was untrue. "I didn't start out as a big-picture kind of person," Shreya continued. "You know I care about our rights as workers and all that. But I joined at first because I just didn't have any more time to fight the administration about my visa issues on my own. And now everyone in the union is helping me, and I'm helping all of them. Turns out having lots of people working together actually helps. Even if I'm sick of all these people by now." Shreya rolled her eyes. It was for show—she was fonder of her coworkers than she liked to admit. "I'm taking a half-day off tomorrow no matter what. Anyway, this is all to say, go home to your girlfriend and let me take care of it."

Mira sighed, strands of longing and fear and hope tangling in her chest. Being nestled against Isabel's softness and warmth right now would be wonderful. But everything was complicated at home. "Maybe. I don't know. I didn't exactly have a fight with her, but..."

Shreya frowned. "Is something wrong? I thought I liked her."

Mira smiled. Shreya had met Dylan once; she had told him that she'd never heard of his novel, but he must be very proud of himself. It was endearing that Shreya was still looking out for her, but it wasn't necessary—Mira was about to say so when the barista called out their drinks.

Mira drank half of hers in a few gulps, and the warmth and caffeine suffused her. She gingerly rolled her neck to stretch the muscles. She was so stiff. "That much espresso can't be good for you," Shreya said. "Okay, are you going to tell me what's going on?"

"Nothing to be concerned about. It's just complicated." Was she really about to tell Shreya, of all people, about her relationship problems? Her life had taken stranger turns. "I think Isabel wants some space. She has a hard time being taken care of."

"Oh," Shreya said. "Well, just go home and do it anyway. What's she going to do, stop you? Her wrist is broken."

Mira sputtered, then laughed. That was hard to argue with. Something clicked into place.

Mira was always bracing for the people around her to hurt her. She had good reason to. And Isabel had made mistakes—she'd tried to hold on to Mira in all the wrong ways, ways that reopened Mira's old wounds. But Isabel was just an imperfect, scared, vulnerable, brave person like Mira herself. She was human, no more and no less.

It was time to stop assuming that Isabel would always have something Mira didn't have. Time to stop taking for granted that Isabel would always have the upper hand. If this was going to work, they were going to have to truly be equals, to truly be partners.

Mira hadn't been ready to see it before. But seeing Isabel broken and despondent in the hospital bed had changed her. And seeing Isabel this morning, too, full of wounded pride and hope as she'd wished Mira good luck.

They would make mistakes and hurt each other. But they could forgive each other, too, and they could forgive themselves. Isabel would have to play her part, and Mira couldn't force her to do it. But Mira could wait, and see, and make room.

Maybe this was what freedom felt like. Months ago, at

the start, she'd thought that freedom meant being able to cut and run. It was what she'd needed at the time. But now, finally, she felt free enough to stay—free to choose Isabel, to be with her through the good and the bad, to throw herself into the pain and joy of loving someone even if she didn't know what was on the other side.

"Anyway," Shreya said, apparently considering the matter settled. "I'm not just telling you to get some rest out of the goodness of my heart. You know that if we win, we're going to start nominating people for the bargaining committee next week." Mira nodded. They needed to start bargaining for a new contract, and they couldn't waste any time. "I'm going to nominate you, and so will a lot of other people."

"Really?" Mira couldn't even think about life after the election right now.

"Yes, really. I want you to run."

The idea of it was overwhelming. The needs of thousands of grad students would be on her shoulders when they sat down to negotiate with the university. It would be the hardest, most important thing she'd ever done. And her coworkers trusted her to do it. Maybe she'd had to prove herself to them less than she'd thought.

Half a year ago, she couldn't even have imagined it. Fresh from her breakup, she'd been afraid of never finding stability or safety again. But she had, and so much more: She had found solidarity, and she had found love.

Isabel's care for her, day in and day out, had changed her life. Mira had grown into the person Isabel had seen in her from the beginning: someone who knew what she wanted and needed, someone who would fight for herself and the people she cared about, someone who listened and spoke out even when she was afraid.

Mira was suddenly desperate to see Isabel again. "I'll think about it. I'm going to go. Thanks for the coffee."

"Good." Shreya smiled like someone who had executed a plan perfectly. "Rest up. We'll really get started next week."

"I will." Isabel had reminded her to rest and take care of herself, and Mira had been stubborn about it. She didn't have to do that anymore. It was time to go home.

35

"This place looks different," Grace said. She set her purse on the coffee table and sat in the armchair. It was disorienting to see her in the apartment again after so much had changed. "I like the new shelves."

"Thanks. They're Mira's books." Isabel resisted the impulse to go on about how many languages Mira knew, her teaching award, how brilliant she was. Maybe there would be time later if she and Grace got through this. She imagined Mira's kindness and understanding wrapped around herself like a mantle, giving her strength, and hoped it would be enough.

"She seems smart." Grace hesitated. "Anyway, I'm sorry about what I said last time, about you being a good partner. I really am. I didn't know about your new girlfriend. But I shouldn't have said it, either way."

Isabel bit back the urge to say that it was fine, to pretend to be the perfect magnanimous older sister. Grace deserved her honesty. "Thanks. Yeah, that really fucking hurt. But I think that was mostly about me and not about you. I shouldn't have said what I said about Kevin either. That was also mostly about me."

Grace gave her a look urging her to go on. Isabel shrugged with one shoulder. "I realized I was worked up over my own issues. I never got to know Kevin, and it's none of my business anyway. Like you said." Isabel's pride had already taken so many hits that one more couldn't deflate it further. "I really do just want you to be happy."

Grace smiled. "Yeah, you were making it about yourself," she said, as though it had been obvious. "You know, Kevin helped me a lot after Alexa died. We hadn't even been dating for long, and he just listened to me and didn't try to say all the right things or make it better, which was what I needed. He knew there wasn't anything else he could do. It's not a bad thing to not be constantly trying to solve other people's problems."

Isabel's jealousy flared, and with it, a sense of loss. "You never talked to me about how you were doing back then. I thought you just didn't want to."

"You didn't make it easy. All you ever talked about is how we need to support our parents, funeral planning, all that stuff. I don't think you ever told me a single time that you missed her."

"Do you seriously need me to say that?"

"You don't *need* to say anything. You already have too many things you supposedly need to do." The self-possessed way Grace spoke was jarring. She sounded like Alexa, or their mother, or Isabel herself. Not like the little sister Isabel thought she knew. They were both getting older. "The point is, we used to actually be able to talk. And after Alexa died, you became the perfect oldest daughter who had a stiff upper lip all the time, and you treated me like a baby. You always did, a little, but it got much worse."

Isabel grimaced. There was no arguing with any of this. Grace continued, "I know you don't want to hear it, but sometimes it does seem like you're trying to replace her. I don't know how else to say it."

"I'm not. I know I can't replace her. Not to our parents or to anyone else." Isabel was stopped short by a lump in her throat. This was hitting her harder than she'd expected. "I know I'm not her, and I know I'm not bringing her back. I'm trying to keep living without her even though it hurts, just like you are."

Grace eyed her with a faint smile. "What?" Isabel said.

"I'm just relieved, honestly. This is the most I've heard you talk about your feelings about Alexa in a long time."

"I— All right. Fine. I could have done a better job."

Grace rolled her eyes. "I'm not asking you to do a good job or be a good *anything*. I'm just saying, you can't refuse to talk to me and then get mad when I don't want to talk, either. Cat used to cry with me on the phone for, like, an hour at a time, when James was still in the hospital. Did you know that?"

"No." Isabel was bewildered. Her sister was moving through grief in her own way, still in pain but getting stronger all the time, growing up. In comparison, Isabel was a mess.

She wished Alexa were here. But Grace actually *was* here for her, and in trying to be there for Grace, Isabel had completely lost sight of that.

She sighed. "Sorry. Again. I know that's not enough. You've been holding this against me for the last two years."

"Yeah." Grace pursed her lips. "Honestly, I could also have been a better sister to you. I didn't talk to you enough, either. I thought you didn't need me. I know you think you're not good enough compared to Alexa. But you know that's how I felt about both of you. After Alexa died, I didn't understand how you just kept going."

"Well, I didn't." Isabel had thought she could, but everything she'd been running from was catching up to her now. "I thought you were the one who kept going without me. When you told me you were engaged..."

She was reaching something she'd been almost too afraid to tell Mira last night. But Mira had held her hand, refusing to give up on her. Isabel wasn't going to give up now, either. "When I said all that, I think I was also afraid of losing you. Reina had just broken up with me. You're the only sister I have left, and you were going to get married and start your new life with someone else. I know that's ridiculous." She shook her head. The irony that she'd reacted by pushing Grace away wasn't lost on her. "I'm an idiot."

"Yeah, you are." Grace leaned back in the armchair. Isabel's boneheadedness seemed to amuse her. "You're not getting rid of me that easily."

Isabel smiled. Yet another weight was easing from her chest. It would take them a long time to untangle everything, but at least they were finally starting. "I also fucked up with Mira. Basically for the same reasons, I guess."

"What happened?"

Never in a million years did Isabel expect to talk to Grace about her relationship problems. But Grace clearly knew some things she didn't know. "She had just left her shitty ex-boyfriend, and she told me she didn't want commitment. I got into this thinking I was going to be the perfect girlfriend for her, provide for her, take care of her, everything. Win her over. To make up for how my older sister is dead, and my ex dumped me for being a mess, and my little sister is pissed off at me and doesn't want to talk to me anymore." At that, Grace scoffed. "I was hiding all this from her and getting upset when she was trying to help, and then it all blew up. And she told me that if I didn't trust her with my real problems, then she couldn't trust me, either. I get it."

Grace winced. "Yeah. So..."

"I asked her if she was breaking up with me and she said no. But I'm worried it's just a matter of time."

"Why?"

"Because I keep fucking up and losing people." Isabel's voice cracked. "I'd do anything to have her stay in my life. I'm trying to change. I just don't know if it'll be enough." Last night, she'd told Mira she loved her. The memory was excruciating. Mira hadn't said anything at all.

Grace stared at her for a few torturous seconds. "You know Mira's an adult, right?"

"I know."

"Like I said, she seems smart. Either she'll break up with you at some point, or she won't."

That wasn't comforting. The truth lay before her: There was so much suffering in the world, and Isabel couldn't single-handedly protect herself or anyone else from pain. "I know. I know I have to take her at her word and see. But she stayed with her shitty ex for too long. He already hurt her so much by the time she left."

"Well, either you respect her as an adult making choices, or you don't." Grace sighed. "If I sound snippy about this, it's because I've been dealing with my older sister telling me I don't know what's best for me, an adult woman, so cut me some slack."

"So I'm Kevin?"

"You're not as good as he is." Isabel snorted. Grace continued, "Can I give you some unsolicited advice?"

It was only fair. "Go ahead."

"When something good happens in your life, you know you can just let it happen, right? That's what I've been learning over the last two years. Life is hard enough already without you looking for more reasons."

Isabel looked out the window. The flurries were thickening. A memory drifted to her: Mira—soft, kind, strong, brave, wonderful Mira—kissing her goodbye this morning, her coconut-scented curls brushing Isabel's face as she lay on the couch.

Maybe she didn't have to desperately cling to Mira. She could just let herself be held. For now, even if it wasn't forever.

Her little sister was full of sage advice these days. "I get what you're saying," Isabel said. This kind of sincerity was not her strongest suit. "Anyway, I want to support you and Kevin. If there's anything I can do—"

"Don't you dare offer to help pay for my wedding. Kevin and I have money saved up, and his parents are pretty rich and are helping him out." Isabel was going to have to figure out something else to do with the thousands she'd saved up, then. "But since you asked, there is something you can do for me."

"What is it?"

"You can be my bridesmaid."

Isabel teared up. "Of course," she said, voice shaking, overflowing with relief and love. Grace came over, kneeled by the couch, and hugged her, and Isabel hugged her back as well as she could with one arm.

"I'm still a little mad at you," Grace said, squeezing her tight for emphasis.

"Fair enough."

Grace got up and plopped herself on the other end of the couch, making herself at home. "I'm telling all the bridesmaids to just wear whatever red dresses they want. You still have that navy suit, right? You can wear a red tie."

"I'm going to look like a politician. You want that at your wedding?"

Grace rolled her eyes. "You can wear an all-red suit if you want. I'm not stopping you."

Isabel snorted. It was unbelievably good to laugh with her sister again. They sat in an easy silence, watching the snow fall. Then Grace said, "I never thought I'd get married without her being there, you know?"

"I know what you mean." Isabel paused. "Well, I don't. But knowing I'll never introduce her to Mira has been hard for me."

Grace turned to her. "I'm glad you're going to be with me. Kevin is as supportive as he can be, and I've talked to Cat and to Mom about it, but I don't think anyone else really understands what it's like."

Isabel nodded. She had sensed the mutual under-standing return between them, too, like a lost piece of herself being put back into place. She had thought she was broken. Maybe she would never be entirely whole again, but she was closer to it than she had been in a long time.

"What you said about Kevin earlier reminded me...Mira did that for me," she said. "On the anniversary. She made dinner for me and let me talk about it." Isabel was getting choked up again. "She's really special. I don't think I'll ever forget that, no matter what happens."

Grace raised her eyebrows. "Wow."

"What?" Even this was a relief, that they were ribbing each other.

Grace's look was piercing. No one else could give Isabel that look. No one else, aside from Alexa, had known her this well for two decades and counting. "You're really serious about her, aren't you?"

WHEN MIRA ARRIVED at the front door to her building, a familiar-looking woman came out. The third sister in Isabel's photo. This was Grace.

"Oh, hi, are you Mira?" she asked. Mira nodded. "I'm Grace, Isabel's sister. Good to meet you." She extended her hand.

Grace was an entire head shorter than Isabel, with a full face of makeup, but she had the same immediately recognizable no-nonsense demeanor. Mira was startled. Isabel constantly referred to Grace as her little sister, but this woman was clearly an adult, slightly tired-looking, with an engagement ring on her finger.

Mira shook Grace's hand. "Nice to meet you too." Grace and Isabel must have talked, but Mira had no idea where they stood now. "Is Isabel okay?"

"She's still in pain, but she'll get through it. She's tough." Grace smiled. "We had a long talk. It was about time."

Mira smiled back. Hopefully that was good news. "Thanks for checking in on her. She's been having a hard time."

"Of course. She's my sister, even if she's a huge pain in the ass sometimes." Grace rolled her eyes good-naturedly. She was acting familiar with Mira already, which was unexpected but reassuring. "I heard she was giving you a hard time, too."

"I don't know if I would say that. I think she and I need to have a talk too."

Grace gave her a knowing look. "Well, she loves you a

lot. But don't let that stop you from doing whatever you need to do. It's fine if you're still mad at her. I still am, a little."

Mira was taken aback. *She loves you a lot.* "Well, thank you. It was nice to run into you. Congratulations on your engagement."

"Thanks." Grace glanced at her ring and smiled to herself. "I appreciate it. I'll be coming back to check up on Isabel, so I'll see you again soon."

36

Isabel was, mercifully, intact and lying lengthwise on the couch. When she saw Mira, a hesitant smile spread across her face. "I thought you'd be gone all day."

"I wanted to come back and be with you." Mira dropped her bag on the floor, rushed over and kneeled on the rug, and carefully took Isabel into her arms. "I missed you."

"I missed you too." Isabel rested her forehead against Mira's, her voice tight with emotion. "I talked to Grace today."

"I know. I ran into her as she was leaving." Mira stood up. "Will you tell me about it while I make tea?"

"Oh." Isabel seemed knocked off course. "What did she say?"

Mira filled the kettle with water and turned it on. "She said she was still a little angry, but that you had a good talk." She returned to Isabel's side.

"She told me that, too. I can accept that. But what I was going to say is this." Emotions warred on her solemn face. "I apologized and had a real conversation with her for the first time. Everything you said to me last night... I needed to hear that. I've been making the same mistakes over and over again. Trying to take care of other people when I was hurt. Trying to run away from my own problems instead of actually doing right by other people."

Isabel wiped her eyes with her sleeve. "I'm sorry that I saw us that way, that I needed you to depend on me. The truth is that I needed you." Her voice shook. But a smile broke through. "Also, Grace asked me to be her bridesmaid."

Mira held onto Isabel tighter, as tightly as she dared in Isabel's fragile state. "That's wonderful. Oh, Isabel, I'm so happy for you. Did she apologize to you for what she said?"

Isabel huffed a laugh. "Yeah, she did." She told Mira about their conversation. "It's going to take time for both of us. But I can accept that. I haven't been respecting her feelings enough."

"I'm proud of you." Mira stroked Isabel's back. "I know you didn't do it for me. But I'm so glad you did it. And I have something to say to you, too." The water in the kettle started boiling. "One moment."

Mira got up, took Isabel's glass teapot from the shelf, and set it on the coffee table on a coaster along with two mugs. She returned with the kettle and rummaged in her bag for what she'd picked up on her way home.

"What is that?" Isabel asked.

"Chrysanthemum tea. You can't be drinking a gallon of coffee every morning if you're trying to rest and relax all day." Isabel started to say something. "Don't argue with me. Anyway, Frankie used to make this for me when I was crashing in her apartment. I thought the flowers would be perfect for your teapot."

Isabel's face wobbled, and she looked down. "Is that okay?" Mira asked.

Isabel nodded. "Thank you," she said, very softly.

Mira tipped the dried flower buds into the teapot. She poured water over them, and the flowers blossomed, bobbing in the water in the clear glass. She kneeled by Isabel on the floor and took her hand.

"I haven't been fair to you, either," Mira said. "I put you on a pedestal for a long time because I thought you were so strong and brave. And you are. But I don't think I let myself see how scared you felt or how much you needed." She took a deep breath. This was it. "Isabel, I want to stay with you. I want to keep coming home to you, and I want to keep falling asleep next to you and waking up next to you. I want to build a life with you. Not the version of you that's tough all the time. The real you."

A sweet, cautious smile lit up Isabel's face. She made a hiccupy sobbing sound. Mira went on. "I want to keep taking care of you while you're healing for as long as it takes. I want to keep hearing about Alexa and the rest of your family. I want to know everything you want to tell me." This was what her heart had wanted all along, and she was finally brave enough to bring it into the light. "Even when it's hard, and you think I can't take it. I'm tougher than I look."

Isabel's face contorted—with joy, with tears. She didn't try to hide them. "Mira..."

Mira gently massaged the tendons of her hand and stroked the calluses of her palm. "I got this tea for you to remind you that I'll always be here to take care of you. And that if you tell me how you're feeling, I'm not going to run away. Just make yourself a cup if you ever get worried. I think you can manage that with one arm."

Isabel took a few shuddering breaths, tears falling down her cheeks. Mira stayed where she was. They were both too unaccustomed to good things, and Isabel was more stubborn than Mira, and she would need more time. "I will," Isabel said. "Thank you. I..."

Mira kissed Isabel's palm, and Isabel cupped her face tentatively, as though she were afraid Mira would vanish with the slightest touch. "There was something you said last night," Mira said. It was time to go all in. "You said you loved me."

Isabel stiffened. "I do." She relaxed when Mira kissed her hand again. "I've known since I woke up next to you in my bed the first time. It was a bad time to say it. I don't expect you to feel the same way about me. But I'm not going to pretend I didn't mean it. You're too smart for that." She smiled sadly. "I'm not good at taking things slow."

Perfect calm settled over Mira. "I love you too, Isabel."

Mira had once tried to convince herself that she didn't need to fall in love. Love was sentimental nonsense, and real relationships were founded on pragmatism and sacrifice. Her parents—supposedly a love match—had been together for decades, and Mira had never heard them say *I love you* to each other.

She had told herself all that when she'd been with Dylan. But the sacrifices in their relationship had always been hers to make, not his. This time, it was Isabel giving something up for Mira: the walls she'd put up, and her terrible reserves of pride and shame. This was real love, the kind that had carried Mira's parents—two very different, strong-willed people—through three decades of marriage. *That* was what Mira wanted for herself.

She wrapped Isabel in her arms again. "I'm still afraid," Isabel said.

"I know," Mira said. "I know."

"I'm still afraid I'm going to let you down." Isabel sniffled. "I loved Reina, too. But it wasn't enough. I've already opened up to you more than I ever did with her. But I'm afraid I'm going to fall apart again."

"You have a cast on your arm and a brace on your foot and can barely get off the couch by yourself," Mira said. Isabel made a sound somewhere between a sob and a laugh. Mira rubbed Isabel's shoulder. "It's a little too late for that. Here, let me sit with you."

She stood and helped Isabel sit up, and then squeezed in on the couch behind Isabel, letting Isabel rest against her body. Isabel was tense. "I don't want to crush you."

"You won't. Relax." Mira ran her hand through Isabel's loose hair. "Can I braid your hair for you?"

Isabel nodded. Mira knew perfectly well that it wasn't easy for Isabel to accept her help, and Isabel's trust in her suffused her with warmth. She gathered Isabel's hair at the nape of her neck and started braiding it, luxuriating in its thickness as it ran through her fingers. "Why didn't you want to talk to Reina about what you were going through?"

Isabel was silent for a while, and Mira waited for her. It took time to unearth so much buried pain. "I didn't know how. We were together for years, and I was always the steady one supporting her while she got her painting career off the ground. And I was the first woman she ever dated, and her parents made her choose between them and me. So I thought I had to be everything for her."

Mira's heart broke. "Oh, no. That's a terrible responsibility for you to carry."

"I felt like I couldn't burden her." Isabel's voice was tight. "I still had a family who loved me. I didn't want to make her hear about it when her family had abandoned her.

She didn't ask me to do any of this. I don't even know if I realized that's what I was doing."

"Did you have anyone you could talk to?"

"I saw a therapist for a few months. But I had an argument with her and stopped going. She always said, you know, *your feelings are valid*. She didn't get it. I always felt terrible after I saw her because I had to dwell on my feelings during the session. It was too much to deal with, on top of my parents and my grandmother and my sister depending on me." She paused. "I asked the therapist if she actually knew what it was like, taking care of a big immigrant family, and she said no, and I told her... Well, it didn't go well after that."

Mira smiled. "I can imagine. My mother tried to see a therapist after my aunt Miriam died and was so uncooperative that the therapist basically fired her. She found someone else eventually. But she hated people telling her what to do."

"I want to meet your parents someday," Isabel said. "I mean, if— I don't mean to—"

"I want them to meet you too. They'll love you. My mother might try to interview you. She can't help it." Mira finished braiding Isabel's hair and secured it with a purple scrunchie she'd left on the end table. A cute new look for Isabel. "I'm named after my aunt Miriam. Did I ever tell you that?" Isabel shook her head. "I spent a long time trying to decide on a new name, and then my mother suggested it. It's a little unusual for us, being named for someone I knew when she was alive, but I'm grateful for it. Oh, also, she was probably the first lesbian I ever met."

Isabel laughed. "Oh, that's great. I'm glad you told me."

Mira kissed the top of her head. Isabel had a few premature gray hairs. She was going to be so sexy as she grew older, and Mira wanted to be there for every single day and year and decade of it.

She slipped off the couch and poured them tea. "There's something else," Isabel said. "I wish it were easier for you to leave me and leave this apartment. If you don't win this election—"

"Don't you dare push me away again because you're worried for me. I told you that if I wanted to leave you, I would."

"But—"

"It was a lot harder for me to leave Dylan, and I still did it," Mira said. "I thought I was alone and powerless then, and now I know I'm not. If I needed money and a place to live, it's not only Vivian and Frankie who would help me. My coworkers in the union would help me, even if we lost the election this time around and had to rebuild. We've been helping Shreya with her legal fees just because she needs help, and I know they'd do that for me, too, because we do these things for each other no matter what. And, you know, choosing to love someone means you could get hurt. You're not protected from that, either. It's a risk for both of us, and I'm taking the risk."

Isabel's fear was still written on her face. "I'm choosing to trust you," Mira continued. "All you have to do is trust that I trust you. I'd survive on my own, but I want you to take care of me. And I want to take care of you."

It took a moment, but Isabel's expression softened. "I want that too. I guess it really is that simple, huh?"

"Don't overthink it." Mira handed Isabel a mug of tea, which she took with her uninjured arm.

"Thanks." Isabel took a sip, and Mira did, too. The earthy, gently floral tea soothed her. "My po po used to make this for us. All three of us. She said it would cure any number of things, and I don't know if she was just saying that about whatever was going on with us at the moment." She smiled wistfully. "Alexa would know, with her medical degree."

Mira sat at the foot of the couch. "It couldn't hurt. You need all the help you can get."

Isabel snorted. Then she went quiet. "I've been thinking about something else," she said, finally. "I don't know if I should say this. You can say no."

"Just tell me."

"I had some money saved up for Grace's wedding. She told me she didn't need it." Isabel hesitated again. "I know you don't need my charity. But if you don't win your election and don't get a pay raise, and it'd be easier for you if you had some savings... If you tell me, I'll transfer it to you and never mention it again. I'd be less worried if I knew things were easier for you. But I can deal with that. It's your life."

They'd come a long way since the tense conversation they'd had in the park. "That's considerate of you," Mira said. "You know what? I'll think about it. You don't have to be so nervous talking about it, either. About money or your family or anything else that's hard." She put a hand on Isabel's cast. "It's both our lives, together."

"I love you, Mira." Hearing it in Isabel's utterly straightforward tones, Mira knew it was real. "You made my apartment feel like home again. I thought you were too good to be true."

"I'm not," Mira said. "I'm right here."

Her phone buzzed. She reached in her pocket to silence it, but then it buzzed again.

She checked her messages. They were from the union group chat. "We won." It couldn't be real—but it was. "We got 59 percent of the vote. We won."

She kneeled next to Isabel, and Isabel pulled her into a crushing hug. The pressure and uncertainty of the last several months, the exhaustion and jadedness from all her years of grad school—everything lifted off her. They had done it.

Isabel let go. She was grinning, and Mira realized she was, too. "Go talk to your sisters and brothers in the union," Isabel said. "I'll be here."

Mira put her phone down and slid it across the coffee table. They would celebrate and then get to work again. But for now, the snow was falling, she was safe and warm at home, and she was about to have a quiet, restful night with the woman she loved.

"I wasn't done talking to you," Mira said. She pulled Isabel close. "You must have been so lonely before."

Isabel relaxed, letting herself be held. "I was. But I'm not anymore."

EPILOGUE

"MIRA'S HERE!" someone shouted as Mira entered the bar, holding Isabel's hand. A round of cheers and whoops rang out.

Mira smiled, letting her eyes adjust to the dim lighting. It was hot for the first week of June, and only five p.m. on a Thursday, but everyone had left their offices early to celebrate. For months, Mira and the rest of the bargaining committee had endured endless rounds of negotiations, holed up in conference rooms with the university's administrators and lawyers. She'd squeezed in her teaching and research, and a little sleep here and there when she could. And now they had a contract.

Isabel was finally out of her cast and on light duty at work. She was in very short jean shorts, a baseball cap, and a T-shirt for her union local with the sleeves cut off—truly a sight to behold. She hadn't lost much muscle at all. They'd be doing more than holding hands once they got home, that was for sure.

Shreya emerged from the crowd and greeted them both. "So, you did it. We're proud of you. How does it feel?"

Surrounded by her raucously celebrating coworkers, all of whose futures and livelihoods she cared about as though they were her own, Mira had never been so full of joy. "I think I need a vacation. Maybe I'll take one when our back pay comes in." She had enough back pay coming to her to cover her rent for months, and good health insurance, and almost everything else they'd fought for.

Shreya wasn't so fortunate. She'd finally had her visa renewed, but the university wasn't going to pay her legal expenses retroactively. She'd had to ask her coworkers for more help. Isabel had found out, sent her a few thousand dollars, and said, "It's nothing."

Maybe it *was* time to take a vacation. The last few months had been some of the hardest of Mira's life. She'd been stretched thin, doing her union work by day and caring for Isabel by night. But it had been worth every second, and the ways it had tested her relationship with Isabel had made it unbreakable.

She made the rounds. So many friends, so many colleagues, so many people whose lives and struggles she'd gotten to know. Even Patrick thanked her and shook her hand. It felt good to introduce Isabel to everyone—again—and show them exactly who Isabel was to her.

They filed out early with Shreya and a few other people; it was, after all, a work night. On their way to the subway, someone in the front started singing "Solidarity Forever."

Mira winced and laughed. Singing in public? Seriously? But Isabel, still holding hands with her, joined in with a surprisingly loud, clear voice. Soon, other people came in. Mira had never thought much of her own creaky singing voice, but after the second verse, she joined in on the chorus: "Solidarity forever, for the union makes us strong!"

. . .

WHEN THEY REACHED THE APARTMENT, still holding hands, Isabel was more content than she'd been in some time. She'd been antsy over the last few weeks, forced on light duty at work and forced by Mira to take it easy outside of work. It had been good to go out for once and see Mira's friends, some of whom were becoming her friends, too.

Mira was deservedly proud of herself, and Isabel was overflowing with pride for her. The contract negotiations had worn Mira down. More than once, she'd fallen asleep on the couch or sitting at the table, and Isabel had needed to gently wake her up. She would have preferred to just carry Mira to bed, but she was making peace with her injuries.

Isabel was healing in all kinds of ways. She was keeping up with physical therapy, and seeing a new therapist, too, one who didn't make Isabel want to rip her own hair out. She and Grace were closer than ever despite the chaos of the impending wedding. She'd cautiously invited old friends to visit her and to meet Mira.

And, most of all, she and Mira had endured months of Isabel staying at home and needing care. It hadn't been easy, learning how to be patient against her will. They hadn't been perfect to each other all the time. But they'd been so good to each other, and their relationship had only grown deeper, stronger, better.

Isabel would keep being patient. She had her whole life ahead of her, with Mira by her side.

Mira was thrumming with energy as they climbed the stairs. As soon as they stepped through the door, she flung her arms around Isabel's neck, pulled her down, and kissed her. Lately, Mira hadn't had energy for anything beyond snuggling in bed. But she clearly had something else in mind tonight.

They stumbled to the bedroom, and she backed Isabel against the dresser, exactly as careful with Isabel's healing wrist as she needed to be. Between messy, breathless kisses, she pulled Isabel's shirt over her head, tugged her shorts down, and unclasped her bra and yanked it off. Once Isabel was down to her boxers, Mira said, "Lie down."

Heat swept through Isabel. Mira's bossy side had been in full force these last few months. Maybe it had been worth breaking her wrist for. She did as she was told, getting on the bed and leaning against the headboard. Mira made a show of looking her over. "Good girl."

Isabel laughed. She flushed, too. She adored this woman so much. Mira was still in her work clothes, and she slipped her light cardigan off her shoulders and set it on the dresser. Then she slowly unbuttoned her summery blouse, not teasing Isabel so much as simply taking her time.

The nude cotton bra underneath gave Isabel a quiet thrill. She loved Mira's lacy lingerie sets, loved seeing Mira in them and out of them. But she also loved seeing Mira at ease, relaxing at home in leggings with her hair in a scrunchie and no makeup, comfortable and happy.

Once Mira took off her blouse, she unzipped her skirt and let it fall to the floor, revealing her practical black underwear. She wasn't trying to be sexy about undressing, and the everyday-ness was the best thing about it. Isabel had seen Mira do this dozens of times, and it never got old. She would gladly watch Mira do it every day for the rest of their lives.

Down to her bra and panties, Mira climbed on top of Isabel and straddled her hips. Isabel stroked Mira's inner thighs, reveling in their silky softness. "You have no idea how frustrating it's been to only touch you with one hand," she said. "I can't wait to get both my hands on you."

Mira laughed. "Who says you get to?" She gently pinned Isabel's hands at her sides. Isabel let out a noise of frustration. "You will," Mira said. "Just relax. Lie back and let me take care of you."

AFTERWARD, teeth brushed, back under the covers, Isabel let Mira roll her onto her side. Mira spooned her, her smaller body soft and radiating heat against Isabel's back. "You've been taking advantage of my broken wrist to make me the little spoon," Isabel said.

"First of all, you're hardly little." Mira squeezed a handful of Isabel's thigh. "Second of all, it was your fault. Third of all, you wouldn't keep letting me do it if you didn't like it."

"I can see why they put you on the bargaining committee." Thank god they could joke about it now. It hadn't been easy relying on Mira for her most basic needs—getting dressed, showering, having her hair braided. At times, it had triggered her worst fears: that she wouldn't be able to take care of Mira or her parents or Grace anymore, that she was broken. But Mira had listened, and she'd stuck around.

Throughout these months, as the winter thawed to spring, she'd made herself chrysanthemum tea from the dried buds Mira had brought home. As she'd watched the petals unfold, she'd thought of her po po and her mom and her sisters—all the women in her family who'd cared for her, and now Mira among them, too.

"I wanted to ask you something," Isabel said. "Do you

want to move in with me? I mean, to this room. I know you've been sleeping in your room because you didn't want to disturb me. But you can have more space for your things, and we could turn your room into an office. I'll renovate it however you want."

"You're very sweet, but no," Mira answered immediately. She kissed Isabel on the shoulder. "I like sleeping in my own bed and not getting woken up at five by your alarm. And I like having my own space. You know I love sleeping in your bed and waking up next to you, but I don't want to do it every night." Mira nipped gently at her shoulder. "And I want it to be a special treat when you fuck me in your bed."

Isabel shivered. She wiggled out from Mira's grasp and lay on her back. Mira got on top of her again, entwining their limbs together like an octopus. "Okay," Isabel said. She kissed Mira on the top of her head and inhaled the familiar coconut fragrance, and the warm, unmatched scent of her skin. The scent of home. "We can stay roommates."

"This is what you do with your roommates?"

"If they're as beautiful and brilliant and sexy as you are, then, yeah, I might."

"Oh, stop," Mira said, grinning. She rolled over and turned the light off. "Still working overtime. Take a break. You've already seduced me." A lazy kiss, with the promise of so many more ahead of them. "You know I'm already yours," Mira said, pressing their foreheads together. Isabel waited for the rest. "And you're already mine."

They'd fall asleep and wake up together. They'd keep waking up with each other, whether in the same bed or apart. They'd keep doing their life's work and coming home to each other, day after day, year after year. And all Isabel had to do was allow herself to be loved—the hardest and easiest thing in the world.

She relaxed against Mira's warmth, closed her eyes, and let herself rest.

BONUS EPILOGUE

Thanks for reading! Want a spicy bonus epilogue where Isabel proposes to Mira on vacation? Get it here:

darcyliao.com/make-room-bonus

ABOUT THE AUTHOR

Darcy Liao writes swoony, steamy, diverse sapphic romance —always with plenty of pining and a happily ever after. They love seeing trans and nonbinary characters on the page, both as a reader and an author.

When they're not writing, you can find them taking long walks around the city, catching screenings of old movies, or sitting in the park with a coffee and a good book.

Want to be the first to hear about new releases? Sign up for Darcy's newsletter at darcyliao.com.